Texas Cattleman's Club

RANCHERS & RIVALS

Texas Cattleman's Club

RANCHERS & RIVALS

JANICE MAYNARD

SOPHIA SINGH SASSON

CAT SCHIELD

MILLS & BOON

DID YOU PURCHASE THIS BOOK WITHOUT A COVER?
If you did, you should be aware it is **stolen property** as it was reported
'unsold and destroyed' by a retailer.
Neither the author nor the publisher has received any payment
for this book.

First Published 2022
Second Australian Paperback Edition 2023
ISBN 978 1 038 90567 3

TEXAS CATTLEMAN'S CLUB: RANCHERS AND RIVALS © 2023 by Harlequin Books S

The publisher acknowledges the copyright holders of the individual works as follows:
Janice Maynard is acknowledged as the author of this work
STAKING A CLAIM © 2022 by Harlequin Enterprises ULC
Sophia Singh Sasson is acknowledged as the author of this work
BOYFRIEND LESSONS © 2022 by Harlequin Enterprises ULC
Cat Schield is acknowledged as the author of this work
ON OPPOSITE SIDES © 2022 by Harlequin Enterprises ULC
Philippine Copyright 2022
Australian Copyright 2022
New Zealand Copyright 2022

® and ™ (apart from those relating to FSC®) are trademarks of Harlequin Enterprises
(Australia) Pty Limited or its corporate affiliates. Trademarks indicated with ® are
registered in Australia, New Zealand and in other countries.
Contact admin_legal@Harlequin.ca for details.

Except for use in any review, the reproduction or utilisation of this work in whole or in
part in any form by any electronic, mechanical or other means, now known or hereafter
invented, including xerography, photocopying and recording, or in any information
storage or retrieval system, is forbidden without the permission of the publisher,
Harlequin Mills & Boon.

This book is sold subject to the condition that it shall not, by way of trade or otherwise,
be lent, resold, hired out or otherwise circulated without the prior consent of the publisher
in any form or binding or cover other than that in which it is published and without a
similar condition including this condition being imposed on the subsequent purchaser.

All rights reserved including the right of reproduction in whole or in part in any form.
This edition is published in arrangement with Harlequin Books S.A..

This is a work of fiction. Names, characters, places, and incidents are either the
product of the author's imagination or are used fictitiously, and any resemblance to
actual persons, living or dead, business establishments, events, or locales is entirely
coincidental.

Published by
Harlequin Mills & Boon
An imprint of Harlequin Enterprises (Australia) Pty Limited
(ABN 47 001 180 918), a subsidiary of HarperCollins
Publishers Australia Pty Limited
(ABN 36 009 913 517)
Level 19, 201 Elizabeth Street
SYDNEY NSW 2000 AUSTRALIA

MIX
Paper | Supporting
responsible forestry
FSC® C001695
www.fsc.org

Printed and bound in Australia by McPherson's Printing Group

CONTENTS

Staking A Claim
Janice Maynard

USA TODAY bestselling author **Janice Maynard** loved books and writing even as a child. After multiple rejections, she finally sold her first manuscript! Since then, she has written more than sixty books and novellas. Janice lives in Tennessee with her husband, Charles. They love hiking, travelling and family time.

You can connect with Janice at
www.janicemaynard.com,
www.Twitter.com/janicemaynard,
www.Facebook.com/janicemaynardauthor,
www.Facebook.com/janicesmaynard and
www.Instagram.com/therealjanicemaynard.

Books by Janice Maynard

Harlequin Desire

Southern Secrets

Blame It On Christmas
A Contract Seduction
Bombshell for the Black Sheep

The Men of Stone River

After Hours Seduction
Upstairs Downstairs Temptation
Secrets of a Playboy

Texas Cattleman's Club: Ranchers and Rivals

Staking a Claim

Visit her Author Profile page at millsandboon.com.au,
or janicemaynard.com, for more titles.

You can also find Janice Maynard on Facebook,
along with other Harlequin Desire authors,
at Facebook.com/harlequindesireauthors!

Dear Reader,

It's always fun to go back to Royal, Texas, and see what new drama is looming on the horizon. This time, we are looking at family secrets.

Does your family have some? I suppose they can be good or bad. As an adult, I discovered that my great-aunt (my grandmother's sister) had a six-month marriage years ago that was either dissolved or ended in divorce. By the time I heard this secret, all the people who could have enlightened me were gone.

As a kid, I assumed that my aunt was a typical "old maid" who had never married. Isn't it awful that we used to hear that term all the time? Children rarely understand the complexities of adulthood. I hope my aunt had a good life despite what must have been a terribly difficult period.

The good thing about a fictional family is that we can enjoy their problems without stress. I hope you enjoy getting to know the Grandins. There are a bunch of them, and they each have their share of stubborn traits.

Thanks for loving and reading romance!

Fondly,

Janice Maynard

DEDICATION

For Anastasia, Ainsley, Allie, Levi and Hattie.
You are the best of all of us!
I hope you continue to stay as close
as you are now...

One

Layla Grandin hated funerals. It was bad enough to sit through somber affairs with friends who had lost family members. But today was worse. Today was personal.

Victor Grandin Sr., Layla's beloved grandfather, had been laid to rest.

It wasn't a tragedy in the truest sense of the word. Victor was ninety-three years old when he died. He lived an amazing, fulfilling life. And in the end, he was luckier than most. He literally died with his boots on after suffering a heart attack while on horseback.

There were worse ways to go. But that didn't make Layla's grief any less.

After the well-attended funeral in town, many of Royal's finest citizens had made the trek out to the Grandin ranch to pay their respects. Layla eyed the large gathering with a cynical gaze. The Grandin family was wealthy. Even folks with the best of intentions couldn't help sniffing around when money and inheritance were on the menu. That was the burden of financial privilege. You never knew if people really liked you or if they just wanted something they thought you could give them.

For that very reason, Layla had been lingering in the corner of the room, content to play voyeur. Her newly widowed grandmother Miriam looked frail and distraught, as was to be expected. Layla's father was relishing the role of genial host, embracing his chance to shine now that his larger-than-life parent was out of the picture.

Layla wished with all her heart that her own father cared for her as much as her gruff but loving grandfather had. Unfortunately, Victor Junior was not particularly interested in his female offspring. He was too focused on his only son, Victor the third, better known as Vic. Her father was grooming Vic to take over one day, despite the fact that Layla's older sister, Chelsea, was first in line, followed by Layla.

Chelsea crossed the room in Layla's direction, looking disgruntled. "I am so over this," she said. "I don't think anyone here really cares about Grandfather at all. Some of them probably haven't even met him."

Layla grimaced. "I know what you mean. But at least Vic and Morgan are genuinely upset. Grandy loved all his grandkids."

"You most of all," Chelsea said. "You were the only one who could get away with that nickname."

Layla flushed. She hadn't realized anyone else noticed. As the middle of three girls, and with Vic their father's clear favorite, Layla often felt lost in the crowd.

Suddenly, Layla realized her father was deep in conversation with a man she recognized. She lowered her voice and leaned toward Chelsea. "Why is Daddy cozied up to Bertram Banks? Oh, crap! Why are they looking at me?"

"Who knows? Let's go find out." Chelsea, always the proactive one, took Layla's elbow and steered her across the room. Layla would have much preferred hiding out in the kitchen, but the two men obviously saw them approaching.

When they were in earshot, Layla and Chelsea's dad gave them a big smile. For such a sober day, it might have been a bit too big, in Layla's estimation.

"Here are my two oldest," he said, giving Bertram a wink. "Take your pick."

Chelsea raised an eyebrow. "That sounds a little weird, Dad."

Bertram chuckled. "He didn't mean anything by it."

Layla distrusted the two men's good humor. Both of them were known to manipulate people when the occasion demanded it. Layla had known the Banks family forever. As a kid, she had been a tomboy, running wild and riding horses and dirt bikes with Bertram's twin sons, Jordan and Joshua.

Back then, she was lean and coltish, not at all interested in girly pursuits. She could take whatever the Banks boys dished out. As she grew older, though, she'd developed a terrible crush on Jordan. It was embarrassing to think about now.

"What's going on?" Layla asked.

For once, Chelsea was silent.

Bertram smiled at Layla. This time it seemed genuine. "I have tickets to see Parker Brett in concert tomorrow night."

It was Layla's turn to raise an eyebrow. "Congratulations. I've heard those were impossible to get."

Bertram puffed out his chest. "I know a guy," he said, chuckling. "But the thing is, I've had a conflict arise. Jordan has offered to take you, Layla, you know—to cheer you up. We all know how much you loved your grandfather."

Layla was aghast. Chelsea bit her lip, clearly trying hard not to laugh. She knew all about Layla's fruitless crush.

To be honest, Layla highly doubted that Jordan had volunteered to do anything of the sort. She wasn't even sure he liked country music. "That's sweet of you," she said. "But I don't think I'll feel like going out. This has been an emotional week."

Her father jumped in. "It will do you good, Layla. Everyone knows you've had a crush on Jordan forever."

A split second of stunned silence reverberated between the uncomfortable foursome. *Did he just say that? Oh, yes he did!* Layla felt her face get hot. *Recover, Layla. Quickly! Think!* "When I was a kid, Dad. I've moved on," Layla mumbled.

Chelsea tried to help. "Good grief, Daddy. Layla's had a million boyfriends since then. Even a fiancé." She stopped short, clearly appalled. "Sorry, sis."

Layla forced a smile. Her doomed engagement two years ago was a sore spot, more because it reeked of failure than anything else. "No worries." She faced the duo of late-fifties males. "I'm sure Jordan can find his own date for the concert."

Bertram's expression was bland, suspiciously innocent. "You're it, kiddo. He'll text you the details later tonight."

Layla glanced around the room. "He's not here?"

"He went to the funeral, but he had another commitment this afternoon."

Victor beamed. "So, it's settled. If you two ladies will excuse us, Bertram and I are going to mingle."

When the two men wandered away, Layla groaned. "You have to be kidding me. Why didn't you say something? I needed help."

Chelsea cocked her head, her sisterly smile teasing. "Well, he wasn't wrong. You *have* always had a thing for Jordan Banks. What could it hurt to get out of the house? With you swearing off men after your engagement ended and now Grandfather dying, I think it would do you good. It's just a concert."

Layla couldn't disagree with the logic. "Fine," she said. "But I hope this doesn't put Jordan in a weird spot. I'll have to make sure he knows I'm not pining for him."

"I'm sure he doesn't think that." Chelsea grinned.

Layla had been too tense and upset to eat lunch before the funeral. Now she was starving. Her mother had made arrangements for catered hors d'oeuvres to serve the dozens of guests who showed up for the reception. Judging by the crowd, it might ultimately prove to be two hundred or two fifty. But her mother, Bethany, was an experienced hostess. No one would run out of food.

"Let's get something to eat," Layla said to Chelsea. "Good idea."

The two sisters filled their plates and retreated to a sunny alcove just off the large living room. Some people might be taken aback by the luxurious, enormous house, but to Layla and Chelsea it was simply home.

From their comfortable seats, they enjoyed the sunshine and the food. Chelsea sighed. "I can't believe it's only four days till May. Summer will be here soon."

Layla's composure wobbled. "Grandy loved the long days and even the heat. Not to mention watermelon and fresh corn. It won't be the same this year." She scanned the crowd. "I guess we should have asked Morgan to join us." Chelsea was thirty-five, Layla thirty-two. Morgan, their baby sister, was still in her twenties.

"She's hanging out with Vic," Chelsea said, stabbing a fat shrimp with her fork. "Did I tell you she sided with Vic over me yesterday? Again."

Vic was third in line, but first in their father's heart and plans.

Chelsea continued, "Every damn time she takes Vic's side. Just once I'd like her to take mine. Still, it's not their fault Daddy thinks I can't handle the ranch eventually. It makes me so angry. I love this ranch as much as anybody. It ought to be me. Or you and me together."

"Well, it won't, so you might as well get used to the idea. Besides, if genetics are any clue, Daddy will live another thirty years. You and I might as well forget about this ranch and find something else to keep us busy."

"True," Chelsea said glumly.

"Look at Mr. Lattimore," Layla said. "He must be grieving terribly, but he's as dignified as ever." Augustus was ninety-six. His wife, Hazel, was at his side speaking to him in a low voice. As a Black family in Royal, Texas, the Lattimores hadn't always had it easy, but they were equally as influential as the Grandins. The only difference was, their patriarch, Augustus, had been forced to give up the reins several years ago because of his struggles with memory issues.

"He and Grandfather were so very close. I wonder

if he understands that Grandfather is gone. They've been friends for decades." Chelsea's comment was wistful.

"His memory comes in flashes, I think. You've seen people like that." The two families were so close the Lattimore kids probably felt sad about losing Grandpa Victor even if he wasn't their blood kin. It would be hard to see the oldest generation begin to pass on, especially since they adored their own grandfather.

Chelsea put her plate on a side table and grimaced. "I hate funerals," she said.

Layla burst out laughing.

Her sister gaped. "Did I say something funny?"

"Not particularly," Layla said, still chuckling. "But I've been thinking the same thing all day. When it's my time to go, just put me in the ground and plant a tree. I don't need people kicking the dirt and fighting over my estate."

"Always assuming you have one."

"Touché." Chelsea's joking comment gave Layla something to ponder. After college, she had spent the last decade pouring her energies into this place. She assisted her mother with frequent entertaining. She helped train horses. And though her father was sometimes dismissive of her expertise, she used her business degree to make sure the family enterprise was solid.

Her grandfather had been proud of her ideas and her knack for understanding the ranching business.

Unfortunately, he was too old-school to ever think a woman could be in charge of anything that didn't involve cooking, cleaning or changing diapers. A woman's place was in the home.

No matter that he had been affectionate and supportive of Layla's thoughts and dreams, he had been forged in the patriarchal environs of Maverick County, and he agreed with his son. The only grandson, Vic, should be next in line to run things when it was Victor Junior's time to hang up his spurs.

Layla was at a crossroads. Her personal life was nonexistent. If Vic was going to be heir to the Grandin ranch, she might as well make a plan for the future. Many of her friends were married and had kids by now. Layla didn't feel any rush.

Her ex-fiancé, Richard, hadn't been too excited about the prospect of starting a family. That should have been a red flag. But Layla had taken his words at face value. He'd said he was concentrating on his career.

Unfortunately, the thing he'd been concentrating on was screwing as many women as possible in the shortest amount of time. The only reason he'd given Layla a ring was that he saw the benefit in allying himself with the Grandin empire.

For Layla, the entire experience had shaken her confidence. How could she trust her own judgment when she had been so wrong about Richard?

Gradually, the crowd thinned. She and Chelsea split up to mingle, to thank people for coming and to say goodbyes. The food tables were demolished. The furniture was askew. By all accounts, the funeral reception was a success. Hazel and Augustus Lattimore were just now being escorted home. Layla's grandmother Miriam looked shaky and exhausted as she headed for her suite.

Fortunately for Layla, Bertram Banks had disappeared half an hour ago. She definitely didn't want to talk to him again. She was already planning how to ditch the concert arrangements.

She had nothing against country music. Jordan would be a fun companion. But she was emotionally wrung out. In some ways, she had never completely processed the trauma from two years ago, and now this, losing her grandfather.

As the room emptied, only the Grandins and Lattimores remained, parents and kids, though the term *kids* was a misnomer. Even Caitlyn, the youngest, was twenty-five. The reception had been advertised as a drop-in from two until five. Now it was almost six.

Layla was about to make her excuses and head to her bedroom when her mother went to answer the doorbell and came back flanked by a uniformed person holding a legal-size envelope.

Oddly, the room fell silent. The young courier looked nervous. "I have a delivery addressed to The Heirs of Victor Grandin Sr.," he said.

Layla's father stepped forward. "That's me. Where do I sign?"

Ben Lattimore, her father's best friend, joined him. "What's up? Kind of late in the day for any kind of official delivery."

Victor nodded absently, breaking the seal on the envelope and extracting the contents. After a moment, he paled. "Someone is pursuing the oil rights to both of our ranches."

"Somebody who?" Chelsea asked, trying to read over Victor's shoulder.

He scanned farther. "Heath Thurston."

Ben frowned. "Why didn't I get a copy?"

"Maybe you did at your house." Victor glared at the document. "It's in incredibly poor taste to deliver this today."

"The timing could be a coincidence." Ben Lattimore was visibly worried. "If this is legit, our properties are in trouble. We're cattle ranchers, damn it. Having somebody search for oil would destroy much of what we've built."

Vic stepped to his father's shoulder. "I thought we didn't have any oil, right? So this is probably all a hoax," he said. "Don't worry about it, Dad. At least not until we investigate."

"That's the ticket," Victor said. "I know a PI— Jonas Shaw." His gaze narrowed. "But I'll start with my mother first."

Layla shook her head. "No, Daddy. She's grief-stricken and so frail right now. We should only involve her if it's absolutely necessary." It was obvious that her father didn't like being opposed. But he nodded tersely.

"I suppose," he said grudgingly. "But *you*…" He pointed at his brother. "I'm going to need cooperation from you, Daniel."

"I'm flying back to Paris tomorrow."

"Not anymore. No one leaves Royal until we meet with our lawyer."

Layla could tell Daniel wanted to argue. But he settled for a muttered protest. "This whole thing smells fishy," he said.

Conversation swelled as the two families broke up into small groups and began to process the bizarre information. Layla was surprised that Heath Thurston would pursue something like this. From what she knew of him, he was an honorable man. But if he and his brother thought they were entitled to the oil rights, maybe they were taking the only logical step.

Still, it was very suspicious that Thurston was claiming oil rights under *both* ranches. What possible claim could he have?

Layla spotted Alexa Lattimore gathering up her purse and light jacket, preparing to leave. Layla had talked to her earlier in the day, but only briefly. "Don't rush off, Alexa. I miss you." The eldest Lattimore daughter hadn't lived in Royal since finishing college.

"I've missed you, too, Layla. I was sorry to hear about your engagement. I wish I could have come home to give you moral support, but things were crazy at work."

Layla sighed. "It's no fun being the subject of Royal's grapevine. I don't think Richard broke my heart, but he definitely dented my pride." She tugged her friend to a nearby sofa. "I wanted to ask you something."

Alexa sat down with a wary expression. "Oh?"

"I was hoping you might think about coming home for a longer visit. I think Caitlyn would love having you around, and besides, it looks like your lawyer skills may be in demand. For both our families."

Alexa chewed her lip, not quite meeting Layla's gaze. "I don't know, Layla. I wanted to pay my respects at your grandfather's funeral, but this was just a quick jaunt. Miami is home now. There's no real place for me in Royal."

"If I know you, Ms. Workaholic, you probably have a million vacation days banked. At least think about it."

"I will," Alexa said.

Even hearing the words, Layla wasn't sure Alexa was telling the truth. Alexa had kept her distance from Royal and didn't seem eager to get involved with an ongoing crisis.

At last, Layla was free to escape to her bedroom and recover from this long, painful day. She stripped off her funeral dress and took a quick shower. After that, she donned comfy black yoga pants and a chunky teal sweater.

When she curled up in her chaise lounge by the window, the tears flowed. She'd been holding them in check all day. Now she sobbed in earnest. She would never see Grandy again, never hear the comfortable rumble of his voice. She had loved him deeply, but perhaps she had never realized just how big a void he filled in her life.

With Grandy gone, she felt adrift.

In the end, she had to wash her face and reapply mascara. The family would be gathering for dinner at seven thirty. It was the Grandin way, and old traditions were hard to break.

Just before she went downstairs at a quarter after, she glanced at her phone. All her family and friends had been at the house today, so there was no real reason to think she might have a text.

But Bertram had said Jordan would text her tonight.

It was dumb to feel hurt and uncertain. She knew Bertram. He was probably, even now, pressuring his son to take Layla to the concert. It was so embarrassing. Bertram would like nothing more than to have one of his sons marry a Grandin daughter. He wasn't picky. He would keep trying if this didn't work out.

The concert was a day away. If Layla hadn't heard from Jordan in the next couple of hours, she was done with this shotgun-date situation. She might have a long-standing crush on Jordan, but honestly, it was more like the feelings she'd had for a rock star or a movie idol growing up.

Doodling her name and Jordan's in hearts and flowers had been something fun. A fantasy to entertain herself. By the time she was an engaged woman, she had known her feelings for Jordan were mostly superficial. Still, the idea of a night on the town wasn't *so* terrible.

Layla would be the envy of every single woman in Royal, Texas.

What could it hurt to enjoy herself? She had been far too serious for far too long. She had let her mistakes and missteps make her afraid to live life.

Jordan Banks wasn't her soul mate. But he was handsome and temporarily available. And from what she remembered of him, he knew how to have fun.

That was what Layla needed…fun. This one date might not be a long-term solution to her solitary state, but it was a start. She needed to open herself up to possibilities…to surprises. No telling what might happen.

Two

Joshua Banks felt more unsettled than at any point in his life. He'd come home to Royal hoping for a signpost pointing his feet to a next step. It was time for a change. He was determined to seize control of his destiny, no matter how grandiose that sounded. Now, after an afternoon of driving aimlessly around Maverick County, his life in Dallas seemed a million miles away. Surely he had made the right choice.

Time would tell. For now, he was checked into a hotel and about to have dinner with his twin brother. Jordan would likely press for Joshua to stay at the ranch. It was the home where both men had grown up, after all. But Joshua needed some personal space...some time to sort out his feelings about his divorce and the really good job he had abandoned amidst a surge of hope about starting over in his hometown.

Thirty minutes later, he pulled up in front of a familiar steakhouse. The ambience was laid-back, the drinks cold and the music not so loud that he and Jordan couldn't talk comfortably. When Joshua stepped out of his car, he saw his brother execute the same maneuver a few spaces away.

That was nothing new. As identical twins, they'd always had the internal radar thing between them. To be honest, though, the sibling connection had weakened during the years Joshua had lived in Dallas.

His brother hugged him. "Man, it's good to see you, Josh."

Joshua was caught off guard by a wave of emotion. "Same here."

Inside, the hostess found them a table in a corner, handed over menus and left them alone. To his dismay, Joshua realized that he felt awkward. Maybe that's what happened when you hid too many secrets.

After they ordered drinks and dinner, Jordan rocked his chair back on two legs. "Damn, bro. You look good. Why do I have the beginnings of a beer gut, but you don't?"

Joshua chuckled. "It's called being a workaholic. No time for goofing off."

"If you say so." Jordan snagged an onion ring from their appetizer sampler and popped it in his mouth. "You know I don't beat around the bush. Why is this dinner just you and me? Why wasn't Dad invited?"

Joshua winced and rubbed the back of his neck. "Actually," he said slowly, "I'll have plenty of time to catch up with Dad. I've left Dallas for good."

The chair hit the ground. Jordan stared. "No shit? What about your job?"

"I resigned." Joshua could barely say the words out loud. What kind of person gave up a high-six-figure job with cushy perks? Especially with no definite plan in sight?

Jordan frowned. "I thought you loved your job."

"I did. Mostly. But I've been missing Royal. Dumb, huh? I always wanted to head for the big city, and now I find myself envying you."

"Dad will take you back at the ranch in a hot second."

"You think?"

"He never wanted you to leave in the beginning."

Joshua sighed. "If I'm hoping to come back into the fold, I'll have to eat a lot of crow and listen to a few dozen *I told you so*'s. He never liked Becky in the first place."

Turns out, the old man had been right about a lot of things. Becky had, indeed, been more interested in the Banks family money than in Joshua, himself. When they settled in Dallas after the wedding, the cracks in the relationship began to show.

Joshua had unfortunately been blinded by great sex and a master manipulator. He was partly to blame. He had convinced himself he was in love with Becky. It was why he had married her.

He'd never been more wrong.

The server dropped off two steaming plates. Jordan cut into his steak. "So where do things stand between you and the former Mrs. Banks?"

"Luckily I haven't seen her. When the divorce was final in February, as you know, she got the house in the settlement. I moved into an apartment and never looked back."

He and Becky had separated two years ago. The marriage had been over at least a year before that. It was a sad, sucky situation and one that had taught him valuable lessons. He was glad Jordan had been there whenever Josh needed him.

Joshua stabbed a bite of perfectly cooked rib eye. "And now here I am. What have you been up to… besides working your ass off at the ranch?"

"Well, today, it was a funeral. Victor Grandin died."

"I didn't even know he was still around. He had to be older than dirt."

"Ninety-three. The grandkids were broken up about it. And his wife, of course. But I don't think Victor Junior was too upset. He's been wanting to run that ranch on his own terms for a long time. The old man never would give up the reins."

"Wow." Joshua shook his head slowly, remembering the good times he had spent there. "I guess there will be some changes on the way."

"No doubt." Jordan finished his beer and grinned. It was a sly smile, one Joshua recognized all too well. His brother was up to something. "I need a favor, Josh. And in exchange, I'll run interference with Dad for you. Soften him up. Hint that you'd like to be back in the thick of things full-time."

"That's an awfully generous gesture. What would I have to do in return?" Joshua was on his guard. Jordan was a great guy, but he was slippery.

"Hardly anything at all. Take a beautiful woman on a date to a country music concert. That's all. One brief evening. And if you want to get back on the horse, so to speak, maybe a little uncomplicated sex?"

Joshua scowled. "I may be divorced and unemployed at the moment, but I sure as hell don't need my twin brother pimping me out to some strange woman. That's a *hell no* from me."

"You didn't let me finish. You'd be doing me a favor, honestly."

"How so?"

"Do you remember Layla Grandin?"

"Of course. How could I forget? She tagged along with us when we were kids. A cute tomboy. And as I recall, she grew up to be a very nice woman, though I haven't seen her in seven or eight years."

"Exactly. The trouble is, Dad has been meddling. He went to the reception after the funeral and chatted with Layla. You know how he's always wanted the two families to hook up."

"I do know that," Joshua said slowly. "But I married Becky and you—"

"I like variety," Jordan said quickly. "The thing is, Dad spun Layla some story about how he had concert tickets he can't use, and that I wanted to take Layla instead. But it was a lie."

"So the tickets are bogus?"

"The tickets are real. But I didn't know anything about it."

"So *you* take her. What's the big deal? It's only one night."

"I have plans," Jordan said. "And on top of that, don't you remember how Layla always had a crush on me?"

Joshua grimaced. "That's old history. Besides, I thought she was engaged."

"She was. A long time ago. You need to be better at keeping up with town gossip. Anyway, I don't know who ended it, but I hear Layla hasn't dated much or at all in the meantime. Maybe some guy broke her heart."

That thought bothered Joshua, but not enough to be sucked into one of his brother's wild schemes. "I just got back into town. I've got things to do."

"Come on, Josh. You're gonna need me in your corner. Ask Layla to the concert, pretend to be me, nicely of course. And then don't call her afterward. I'll be in the clear with Dad. Layla will get the message that I'm not into her. And you'll be free to get back on your feet here in Royal. It will be fun, I swear."

"It's too complicated. What kind of arrangements have you made with her?"

Jordan's expression was triumphant. "That's the best part. None, yet. The concert is Sunday night. All you have to do is text her that you'll pick her up at six. Feed her dinner. Take her to the venue. Drop her off later. Unless the sex thing is a possibility."

"I'm not going to make Layla Grandin a one-night stand." Joshua bristled.

"Aw, hell, baby brother. You know I was kidding about the sex. Will you do it? Dad will kill me if I mess up his grand plan. He's already put the ticket stuff in my name. But I have a very special lady on the hook for tomorrow night, and I don't want to disappointment her."

Joshua felt the urge to say yes. He and Jordan used to pull this trick on Layla all the time, but she always saw through them. It might be fun to try one more twin swap for old times' sake.

"Fine," he said. "I'll do it. But what makes you think she won't catch on that it's me and not you?"

"Layla and I haven't run in the same circles in a long time. I was at the funeral today, but not the reception, so she didn't see me. Your hair is a tad shorter than mine, and you're not as tanned as me, but other than that, we could still fool ninety-five percent of the people on any given day."

"Layla was always smarter than either you *or* me," Joshua said. "I might crash and burn, but it will be fun trying."

* * *

Layla glanced at the text on her phone for what must have been the twentieth time.

Looking forward to the concert. I'll pick you up at six. Dinner first. J.B.

Jordan Banks. Her childhood crush. Clearly, the senior Mr. Banks had orchestrated all of this. Jordan had had plenty of opportunities to ask Layla out over the years if he had been interested, but he hadn't. He wouldn't have suddenly invited her to a concert out of the blue if his father hadn't pressured him.

But even knowing that, Layla didn't mind. She needed a distraction.

Deciding what to wear had taxed the limits of her wardrobe. She wasn't really into the country music scene, but everyone in the world knew who Parker Brett was. Tonight's crowd would be upscale, wealthy and dressed to the nines.

Ticket prices were astronomical. Some radio personalities criticized Brett for ignoring his blue-collar base, but Layla didn't know if that was true or not. Parker gave incredibly generous donations to a host of charitable organizations, so who was she to judge?

Not much in her closet seemed appropriate for a concert. It was May. In Texas. Concert venues were notoriously hot and crowded. After some digging, she found an item she had bought and never worn. The halter-necked, button-up lightweight denim dress ended several inches above her knees and had a deep V-neck. She added red espadrilles that laced up over her ankles and a tiny leather purse that swung from a very long strap.

When she glanced in the mirror, she looked like a woman intent on having fun.

The dress bared a lot of skin. But with her wavy blond hair down tonight, she wouldn't feel too self-conscious. She added enough shadow and mascara to emphasize her blue eyes, then topped off her makeup with a light cherry stain and lip gloss.

Jewelry wasn't hard. She loved the large diamond hoop earrings her parents had given her for college graduation. They provided the final touch of glam to her appearance. She even added a dainty gold chain with a tiny diamond star.

Once she was ready and headed downstairs, it was hard not to freak out. For one thing, this was a date. With a man. After a long dry spell. For another, it was Jordan. Her crush on him had always been a combo of childhood nostalgia and female appreciation for a guy who was tall and handsome and charismatic.

As kids, she and the Banks boys had often been mistaken for siblings by strangers. Jordan's dirty-blond hair and blue eyes were enough like hers to make that a possibility. In some ways, she *had* felt like the twins were brothers.

They tolerated her and hung out with her and taught her how to climb trees and throw a baseball. Her own brother, Vic, had been a year younger than she was. Layla had always preferred the company of Jordan and Joshua, maybe because they made her feel grown-up and like she *belonged*.

At home, Vic was the only boy. Chelsea was the oldest, and Morgan the baby. Layla had always felt a bit like the odd man out. Honestly, she still felt that way even now.

When the doorbell rang, she sucked in a sharp breath and opened it. Jordan Banks stood on the veranda looking sexy enough to give any woman heart palpitations. Dark dress jeans molded to his long, muscular legs. His white, button-down shirt with sleeves rolled to the elbow emphasized his golden skin, and his hair was just tousled enough to make him look as if he had recently climbed out of bed.

She was mortified to feel her cheeks flushing. "Hi, Jordan," she said brightly. Maybe too brightly, because she saw him react. A tiny flinch? She couldn't exactly pin it down.

At last, he returned the smile. "Hey, Layla. It's good to see you. And man, you look gorgeous."

His sincere compliment soothed a few of the butterflies in her stomach. "Thank you." She closed the door behind her. "I'm looking forward to the concert."

"Me, too," he said. This time, the words weren't entirely convincing.

As he helped her into the car, she grimaced. "Listen, Jordan. I know your dad put you up to this. We don't have to go if you don't want to."

He slid behind the wheel and gave her an unreadable glance. "Don't be silly. You're a good friend. We've known each other forever." He paused. "I'm really sorry about your grandfather. I remember how much you loved him."

Layla's jaw wobbled, taking her by surprise. "Thanks," she said huskily. "It's hit me harder than I expected. I guess I thought he was immortal."

Jordan leaned forward and caught a tear that had escaped and clung to her lower lashes. "He must have been so proud of you."

For a split second, the air inside the car was charged with *something*. Layla shivered inwardly. She had always crushed on Jordan, but this was different. His tenderness reached the grief deep inside her chest and made her feel a little less devastated.

She swallowed hard. "I'm not going to fall apart on you," she said. "I swear."

His smile was lopsided. His left arm rested across the top of the steering wheel. "It would be okay if you did."

In that moment, she *knew* why this felt so weird and different. In a good way.

This wasn't *Jordan*.

The man gazing at her with such empathy was *Joshua*.

She would almost bet her life on it. But why? What was the point of this kind of subterfuge?

Years ago, the twins had often fooled teachers and classmates. They had tried their twin switch on Layla, too—all the time. Pranks. Silly fun. Nothing like this. Why would one brother pretend to be the other on a date?

Could she possibly be wrong?

Yet the more she stared at the man in the driver's seat, the less he looked like Jordan. Physically, yes, of course. They were two sides of the same penny.

But where Jordan was an extrovert and the life of any party, Joshua was the quieter, more thoughtful brother. The strong silent type.

Because she wasn't a hundred percent sure, she felt vulnerable. If this was a joke, it wasn't funny. Not at all.

"Shouldn't we be going?" she asked stiffly.

Jordan seemed to emerge from some kind of haze. He even shook his head slightly. "Of course. I made a reservation at Sheen."

"Oh, good. I love it there." Sheen was the perfect choice for a nondate date. The ambience was upscale and comfortable, but the tables didn't have the kind of shadowy intimacy that would have made the evening awkward.

By the time they were seated, Layla had relaxed some. If she was wrong, and the man across the table from her was Jordan, she would simply enjoy the evening. If he was Joshua, surely he would come clean eventually. In the meantime, she was determined to chill and have fun.

While they waited for their server to bring salads, Layla folded her hands in her lap. "Your father told me you were at the funeral. Thanks for coming. I'm afraid I didn't see you. It was packed."

"I was happy to be there," he said. "I'm sorry a prior commitment kept me from attending the reception afterward."

"Don't worry about it. Though you did miss some very good food."

He grinned. "Your mother always did cater a great meal."

"How are things at *your* ranch?" she asked.

Once again, she saw a tiny flinch. A weird look in his eyes. "Same as usual, I guess. Dad is always trying new stuff."

"I remember that about him."

"I suppose Victor Junior will be free to try new things, too."

Layla wrinkled her nose. "Oh, yes. He was always so frustrated by what he called my grandfather's *old-fashioned ways*. No telling what he'll be up to in the next few months. New feed, new bulls. The sky's the limit."

By the time they started on their second course, Layla was delighted with her decision to get out of the house. She was almost certain the man across the table from her was Joshua. He was thoughtful and funny. Their discussion of politics and books and movies was wide-ranging. But the most surprising aspect of the evening was how she responded to her escort physically. His overt masculinity made her shiver. She felt sexually aware of him in a way she hadn't done with any man in a long, long time.

Jordan's company might have been equally enjoyable but in a different way. Jordan would have been telling jokes and bantering with the waitress. Jordan would have flirted more. Maybe that was the origin of Layla's preadolescent crush. It had felt good to have a boy recognize the fact that she was a female.

At the concert venue, Jordan (or Joshua) kept his arm around her waist, holding her close in the midst of the crush. They each had very official-looking credentials that gave them VIP access and seating. Her date's name badge clearly said Jordan Banks. But Layla wasn't convinced.

Backstage, Layla did her best not to act like a gushing fan, even when she was introduced to the A-list movie star who was currently dating Parker Brett. When the woman's handler offered to take a photo of Jordan and Layla with Parker's lady friend, Layla almost betrayed her total fangirl status.

But she held on to her composure with an act of will. She wouldn't embarrass her date by being incredibly gushy and unsophisticated. After the photo op, Jordan and Layla were invited to partake of the buffet spread out on tables.

Because they had already eaten dinner, they skipped the main course offerings and instead sampled the desserts.

Jordan/Joshua grinned when she indulged in

cream puffs. "You have whipped topping on your chin," he said.

Before she could react, he picked up his napkin and leaned in to remove the sticky, sweet mess.

They were so close for a moment she could stare into the depths of his Texas bluebonnet eyes. The shade was lighter at the edges of his irises and deeper as it moved toward his pupils. Very distinctive.

They were sitting on folding chairs in a corner. It was still noisy, but for the moment, a bubble of privacy surrounded them.

As much fun as she was having, Layla couldn't forget about the fact that her "date" might not be who he was supposed to be. The uncertainty threatened to dampen the evening. She felt some definite chemistry with the man at her side, but her crush used to be on Jordan. Was she now flirting with *Joshua*? Because she so badly wanted to know, she decided to grill Jordan/Joshua. Maybe he would crack.

"So tell me about your brother," she said lightly. "What is Joshua up to? Still living in Dallas?"

This time she wasn't imagining the subtle reaction. The tiniest flinch. A stricken look in his gaze.

"Well, um," he said. "He's doing okay. In fact, he just came back to Royal very recently."

"Oh, how nice. Was Joshua at the funeral, too?"

Now Jordan/Joshua's face and neck turned red. He gulped his wine. "He wanted to be. But he had an important appointment at the bank. I think he may buy a house."

"So this is permanent? What about his wife? Am I remembering that right? Didn't he get married? It's been so long since I've seen him."

Layla should have felt guilty. The poor guy looked hunted. But if the Banks men thought they could pull this old trick on her, they deserved what they got. Let the games begin!

Her date paled now. "Joshua is divorced," he said.

"Oh, I'm so sorry."

He shrugged. "Becky was interested in the Banks money. Once Josh took a job in Dallas and decided not to accept any financial support from the ranch, she showed her true colors. He tried. Nobody likes to fail at marriage. But Becky wasn't interested."

Layla found herself confused. If this really was Joshua, he was being remarkably open with her. The words about his marriage were raw. She could understand his pain. Although she hadn't made it to the altar, she had thought her engagement was the beginning of a bright future.

She glanced at her watch. It was almost time to take their seats for the concert.

Jordan/Joshua leaned forward with an expression of urgency. "How about you, Layla? Any men in your life at the moment? Present company excluded." His lopsided smile made her pulse beat faster.

"I was engaged," she said slowly.

"Was?"

"My fiancé had a wandering eye."

"Ouch."

"Unfortunately, his other body parts followed."

Her companion winced. "I'm sorry."

"Thanks, but honestly, I was lucky. Being lied to is no fun. At least I found out before it was too late."

Jordan/Joshua looked desperate now. "I need to tell you something, Layla..."

Suddenly, the lights dimmed, and a bell dinged. Backstage visitors began moving toward the concert hall. Again, Jordan kept her close, his big strong body shielding her from getting stepped on.

Their seats were the best in the house—a box above and adjacent to the stage. From this vantage point, Layla could see everything, even Parker Brett's white teeth and sexy smile when he strode out onto the stage.

There was no opening musical act. Parker took command of the venue and the evening and didn't let loose for a full two and a half hours. He played all his familiar favorites plus a half-dozen new numbers.

Layla loved it. There was something about the energy of a live performance that couldn't be replicated. It was sorcery. During a slow, romantic ballad near the end of the evening, Jordan/Joshua slid an arm behind her shoulders, resting it on the back of her seat. Not touching. Just close.

It didn't mean anything. Just because Parker was singing about the spark between a man and a woman and the magic of new love... Coincidence. That was all.

She half turned in her seat, searching his face for the truth. "Thank you for bringing me," she said. "This is incredible."

Three

Joshua was in hell. He'd spent the entire concert watching Layla's expressive face. Parker Brett was a damned fine entertainer, but Josh couldn't take his eyes off the woman at his side. When Layla laughed, Josh got a funny feeling in the pit of his stomach. It felt a lot like desperation and desire.

His divorce had sent his libido into hiding for a very long time. Now he felt himself stretching, waking up from a long, painful sleep.

As they walked to the car, Layla talked nonstop. He caught whiffs of her light perfume occasionally, but it was watching her hair dance in the breeze that really got to him. The dress she wore was not particularly outrageous. Still, the way it hugged her modest curves and bared her long, toned legs made his mouth dry.

She was wearing red sandal-y things that gave her three or four extra inches in height. He couldn't help thinking that he and Layla would be a perfect match in bed. Or standing. Or pressing their bodies together in any one of a dozen other positions he could imagine.

He was sweating by the time they made it to the car, but it had nothing to do with the muggy spring night. After he unlocked her door, he rounded the car and opened the driver's side.

Suddenly, the intimacy ratcheted up about a thousand percent. "I'll turn on the AC," he said. He had to tell her the truth. It was the right thing, the only thing to do. But he didn't want the night to end with her being pissed at him.

According to Jordan's dumb plan, Joshua was supposed to wrap up the evening by saying *I'll call you*. Then Jordan *wouldn't* call. Layla would think her date was a jerk. End of story.

Maybe that was the way to go. Let this fiction play itself out. Then in a few days, Joshua could make arrangements to bump into Layla as himself. The two of them could start with a clean slate.

The trouble was, he was terrible at this kind of subterfuge. He'd been known to ruin surprise parties without meaning to…he sucked at poker. Anything that required evasion or deception was not his strong suit.

He started the car. Soon, cool air blew on their faces. It didn't help Joshua at all.

Hang on, he told himself. *Work the plan*. Jordan's plan, damn it. Why had he ever let his brother talk him into this frustrating night? It was supposed to be lighthearted fun, not sexual torture.

As they made their way through the darkened streets of downtown Royal, Layla carried the conversation, for sure. He hoped he made sense when he responded. Actually, he didn't remember saying anything at all, but he must have.

When they finally made it beyond the town limits and out to the sprawling Grandin ranch, he pulled up in front of the beautiful main house, shut off the engine and took a deep breath. "We're here," he said.

Wow. Not smooth at all.

The ranch was quiet. There were lights on in the very back of the house and upstairs, but here in the driveway, the only illumination came from the moonlight filtering through the windshield.

Layla half turned in her seat. "Thanks for taking me to the concert, *Jordan*. I had a lot of fun."

His brain raced. Had Layla deliberately emphasized his brother's name? Did she know the truth? If so, Joshua needed to come clean now. She had been lied to before...by someone important in her life. Joshua didn't want to add to her pain or reinforce her opinion of loser guys who couldn't tell the truth, even if tonight's ruse was meant to be a nod to their childhood game of twin switch.

I'll call you. That was what he was supposed to say. Three little words.

He couldn't make his lips form the syllables. If he had never left Royal and moved to Dallas, maybe he would have eventually asked Layla to go out with him. It could have happened.

He reined in his imagination and focused on the present. He hadn't had sex in twenty months, two weeks and three days. His life was in ruins. Layla represented everything he wanted in a just-for-fun relationship.

But it wouldn't be fair to play around with her. Not at all.

Three words. That's all he had to say. *I'll call you.*

She was looking at him oddly. Had she asked *him* a question? Was she waiting for an answer?

He shifted in his seat, wanting to jump out of the car and howl at the moon. Why had he let Jordan talk him into this? The mischievous twin switch had turned into an evening of sexual hunger.

Layla's smile faded. Moments before, she had been animated and friendly. Now her expression was definitely wary. "Are you okay, Jordan?" she asked.

Her head cocked to one side. She eyed him like a science experiment she needed to study. To analyze.

When she called him Jordan he ground his teeth. He wasn't Jordan. Never had been. This was a heck of a time to remind himself that young Layla Grandin had once had a crush on *Jordan* Banks, not Joshua.

Truthfully, it was Jordan, not Joshua, who had always juggled two or three beautiful girls or women at one time. They flocked to him. He made them laugh. Made them feel special. Joshua wasn't jealous of his brother's charisma. His own hard-to-get personality had snagged him plenty of women. But right now, he wouldn't mind having a smidgen of his sibling's easy charm.

"Jordan?"

If Layla Grandin said that name one more time, he was liable to snap. His blood boiled in his veins. He was frustrated with the dumb twin switch and desperately attracted to the woman he had taken on a faux date this evening.

"Layla?" He said her name gruffly, wishing he could blurt out the truth. But his original plan was best. Let this "Jordan" relationship expire, and then Joshua could swoop in and play cleanup batter.

"Yes?" Her smile was tentative now. Perhaps the tone of his voice had spooked her. It was hard for a guy to play it cool when every cell in his body wanted the woman sitting two feet away.

"Will you have dinner with me tomorrow night?"

What the hell? Where did that come from? No way was he going to let "Jordan" go out with Layla again.

He sensed her ambivalence. His weird behavior was freaking out even him. "Say yes," he urged. Her silence wasn't a good sign.

Finally, she twisted a strand of hair between her fingers and sighed. "I honestly didn't think you enjoyed yourself this evening," she said quietly. "I know tonight's arrangement wasn't your idea. Why would you want to do it again?"

The vulnerability in her words squeezed his heart. "I had a great time," he said. "I don't know what you're talking about."

"Jordan, I—"

Hearing his brother's name on Layla's lips made him snap. Jordan had plenty of women. This one was off-limits. Besides, Jordan himself had passed her off on Joshua. What kind of way was that to treat a sweet, sexy woman like Layla?

"Please," he muttered. "We need to talk."

A tiny frown appeared between her brows. "You said that earlier. Right before the concert started."

Now he had boxed himself into a corner. How could he let "Jordan" ride off into the sunset if Joshua made a big deal about *talking*? Was he going to tell Layla the truth tomorrow night?

She touched his hand. Briefly. Placating him. "I'd like to, but I can't. Our family has a very important meeting at the lawyer's office Monday at seven. It was the only time we were all free to get together. There's a bit of trouble about the estate."

Joshua frowned. "Tuesday night, then?" Without overthinking it, he leaned in, slid his hand beneath her hair and kissed her soft, shiny pink lips.

He'd watched her reapply the gloss after dinner and again after the backstage buffet. It was a simple feminine action. Nothing overtly erotic. But it had made him hard.

Now he discovered the gloss tasted like peppermint.

The kiss deepened for a nanosecond before he pulled back. He didn't want to kiss her as Jordan, but he hadn't been able to wait another minute.

"Should I apologize for that?" he asked gruffly.

Layla touched her lips with the fingers of one hand. He wasn't sure she realized she had done it. "No apologies," she said. Her gaze was wide-eyed. Had he shocked her? Wouldn't *Jordan* have kissed a beautiful woman on a first date?

"So dinner?" He repeated the invitation.

Her silence lasted long enough to make him squirm. "Sure. Text me tomorrow night and I'll see if I'm free Tuesday. It should be fine."

Joshua's personal life had been in the pits for so long, it was shocking to realize he was actually looking forward to something. "Don't change your mind," he said.

She grinned. "I've known you a long time, Jordan. Do you ever remember me being flighty?"

This time he was almost sure she emphasized the word *Jordan*. Did she know which brother she was talking to? And if so, why hadn't she said anything?

Maybe for the same reasons he hadn't. Maybe they were both wary. A failed marriage. A broken engagement. Neither of them was batting a thousand in the relationship department. And they weren't getting any younger.

Layla gathered her purse and stepped out of the car. He hopped out, too, and eyed her over the top of the vehicle. In the moonlight, she looked younger.

"Good night, Layla," he said.

She blew him a kiss. "Good night."

He could have left. But he lingered to watch her ascend the broad set of stairs that led to the porch. When she opened the front door and disappeared inside, he sighed. This had been the best night he'd had in forever.

But he had screwed it up.

He was determined to set things straight as soon as possible. If he could exit this twin switch gracefully, maybe he had a shot at coaxing Layla into his bed. Even as a kid, he had always wanted to one-up his brother, just for bragging rights. Now the stakes were higher and far more personal.

Layla found Chelsea watching a movie in the den. "Where is everybody?" she asked, sinking into her favorite chair and taking off her shoes.

"You look super cute," Chelsea said. "Mom and Dad went upstairs an hour ago. Grandma, too. Vic and Morgan are out on a double date with some friends of theirs. How was the concert?"

"Actually, it was great." Layla could feel her cheeks burn, especially since her older sister eyed her with a grin.

"So being set up by two old men wasn't a bust?"

"Jordan was nice about it. Parker Brett's concert was amazing. I had a good time."

"Why do I hear a *but* in there somewhere?"

"You'll think I'm crazy."

"No more than usual." Chelsea laughed at her own joke. "What aren't you telling me? Did you do the nasty with Jordan Banks?"

"On the first date? Of course not."

"Lots of women do."

"Not me."

"Then what has you all riled up?"

Layla fiddled with the hem of her dress. "I'm almost positive the man I went out with tonight was *Joshua* Banks, not Jordan."

Chelsea sat up straighter and turned off the TV. "You can't be serious."

"I am. I realized it in the first hour we were together. I know those twins. They may look identical, but their personalities are completely different."

"Did you say something?"

"No. Because I wasn't a hundred percent sure. I haven't seen either of them in a very long time."

"But I thought Joshua lived in Dallas. And was married."

"He did. But he's back. Divorced, unfortunately."

Chelsea wrinkled her nose. "Sucks for him, but it sounds like you should be glad he's single again. I haven't seen you this flustered in ages."

"I'm not flustered," Layla lied.

"Riiiggghht..."

It was impossible to fool a sister who had known you forever.

Layla decided to change the subject. "How's everybody doing after the big bombshell?"

"Daddy's freaking out, of course. And he's mad as hell. Mom spends all her time trying to calm him down. Vic and Morgan don't seem to care. Uncle Daniel was supposed to fly back to Paris, but Daddy forbade him to leave until we sort this out."

"*Forbade?* Good grief, we're not the royal family."

Chelsea snorted. "Our male parental unit has let his new position as patriarch go to his head already."

"So Uncle Daniel stayed?"

"Only until Tuesday morning."

"I don't really want to go sit in a lawyer's office," Layla confessed. "They give me the heebie-jeebies."

"I don't want to go either, but it's a command performance."

Layla rubbed her temple where a headache was beginning to brew. "Do you think our family is weird?"

Chelsea rolled her eyes. "Can I plead the Fifth?"

"I'm serious. Is it strange that we all live under one roof?"

"This place is sixteen thousand square feet. With another five thousand in the guest house. We each practically have our own suites anyway."

"I guess. But what about Vic? He always has a woman in his life. Shouldn't he want more privacy?"

"Ewww." Chelsea shuddered. "I do *not* want to talk about our brother's sex life."

"But why does he stay here? Shouldn't an unattached male want his own place?"

Chelsea shook her head slowly. "Sometimes I forget how sweet and naive you are. Believe me, Layla. I'm pretty sure our dear brother has had an apartment in town somewhere for a long time."

"But why does he still make the pretense of living here?"

"You know he likes being the favored son and grandson. He wants control of the ranch to come to him someday. Squatter's rights dictate that he shouldn't stray too far from Daddy's sphere."

"I suppose."

"We all have plenty of our own money. Any of us could leave if we wanted to. Is that it, Lay-Lay? Are you feeling the need to spread your wings?"

For some reason, hearing the childhood nickname made Layla teary-eyed. "No," she said. "I don't want to leave. At least not right now. I'm like Vic, I guess. I keep hoping Daddy will eventually see that you and I have as much right to run the ranch as his precious son."

"I wouldn't bet on it. Apparently, having a penis is a prerequisite for being a real rancher in Texas."

The sarcasm made Layla smile. "Or at least here in Royal." Layla yawned. "I'm beat. I'm gonna take a shower and go to bed."

"My movie is almost over. I'll be up in a bit."

As Layla climbed the stairs, she pondered Chelsea's half-serious question. *Did* she want to get her own place? Sometimes it might be nice to avoid all the drama.

In the bathroom, she undressed and had to avoid looking at herself in the mirror. She kept remembering the feel of a warm male hand cupping the side of her neck ever so briefly. Try as she might, she couldn't convince herself that the man at her side tonight was Jordan Banks.

If he was *Joshua*, what did that mean? Why the switch? Bertram Banks had mentioned Layla's adolescent crush. So clearly, the older man had no clue his boys had something up their sleeves.

As she climbed into bed and turned out the light, she moved restlessly under the sheet. When she closed her eyes, all she could see were those beautiful blue irises, the spark of humor and desire. Was it really desire?

She'd been fooled once.

She couldn't afford to be so stupid a second time.

But even after giving herself a stern lecture, she had a feeling she was going to dream about the man who had kissed her tonight…

Four

Lawyer's offices were about as bad as funeral homes. Layla drove her own car to the meeting. She'd had drinks and dinner with a girlfriend earlier, so she had promised to meet the family here. When she walked in, the mood was glacial and uncomfortable.

Layla took a seat beside Chelsea and prepared for a long, boring hour. Hopefully not more than that. As she scanned the room, she saw that most everyone had showed up, including her grandmother. Uncle Trent and Aunt Lisa were noticeably absent. Maybe because they didn't have anything to gain or lose, they had chosen not to attend.

The lawyer was in his late sixties or early seventies. His silver hair and conventional clothing made him the epitome of upscale legal representation. He had worked for the Grandin family for decades.

"I'll get right to the point," he said. "I've contacted the attorney who prepared those papers you received on the day of the funeral. He has apologized for sending them at such a stressful moment for your entire family. Claims he didn't know."

Layla's father bristled. "And you believe him?"

"I have no reason not to." The lawyer addressed Layla's grandmother. "Mrs. Grandin. Did your husband ever mention anything about oil rights?"

Miriam straightened in her chair. She was a tough woman, and one who had remained in the shadow of her husband's forceful personality. "Never that I recall. But Victor kept his own counsel. If he took anyone into his confidence, it would have been Augustus Lattimore. Those two old men were thick as thieves."

Again, Layla's father was visibly upset. Layla felt sorry for him actually. It must have been hard to be shut out of all the decision-making. He was at an age where some men began to think about retiring in a few years. But Victor Junior was just now getting his chance to be in charge of the ranch.

Would *he* cling to control for three more decades? Like his father had?

Vic spoke up. "We don't really have anything to worry about, do we? Isn't this probably a scam? Anyone with a good digital printer can produce documents."

Chelsea nodded. "And according to the internet, if you wad up your paper and soak it in tea, you can make it look old."

Bethany Grandin glanced at her daughter. "Good grief, Chelsea. You're letting your imagination run away with you."

The lawyer must have sensed he was losing control of this session. He cleared his throat. "Let's stick to what we know. I asked Thurston's legal counsel for additional information about this situation." He directed his attention to Layla's uncle. "Mr. Grandin. Thurston claims you had an affair with his mother, Cynthia." The accusation was blunt.

Daniel shrugged, looking almost defiant. "Years ago. So what?"

The lawyer grimaced as if he had been hoping for a denial. "There was a baby. A girl. Ashley."

Daniel shook his head. "I did have a brief relationship with Cynthia—when I was in Royal for a couple of months. But there was no pregnancy." He ran a hand across the back of his neck, betraying his unease. He was solidly built though thinner than Layla remembered. His hair was going gray, but his dark brown eyes were the same. Layla wasn't close to her uncle, because he had lived in France for decades.

The lawyer continued. "So, you have no knowledge of this alleged child?"

Layla's uncle didn't look happy. "I do not," he said curtly. "I won't deny having a physical relationship with Cynthia Thurston many years ago. But I had no further contact with her after that."

"Is it possible she couldn't find you to tell you there was a baby on the way?"

Victor scowled. "My brother has lived in France for a long time. But he has never been off the grid. Any of us could have been in touch with him if this woman asked us to intervene. The timing of the whole claim is suspect."

Layla wondered privately if her uncle's lover would have been too embarrassed to contact a family as well-known and influential as the Grandins. Maybe she decided to handle things on her own.

Layla spoke up. "Daddy, I think you're forgetting something. Cynthia and Ashley were killed in a car crash a couple of years ago. Heath and Nolan may have just now stumbled onto these papers."

The lawyer nodded. "Anything is possible. However, Thurston is intimating that the oil rights were due Ashley, because she was a Grandin by birth. I'm still looking into why the Lattimore ranch was included. I have a call in to their lawyer. The burden of proof is on the other side. That buys you some time. I know you're thinking of hiring an investigator. Probably a good idea. We can all keep digging. Ms. Miriam, perhaps you could look through your husband's papers for any clues."

"I'd be happy to…"

After that, the meeting adjourned, and the room began to empty.

Layla realized her uncle was standing alone. She approached him and put a hand on his shoulder. "I'm so sorry," she said. "You must be in shock."

He nodded slowly. She could see the stunned bafflement in his gaze. "It's bad enough to find out I fathered a child and Cynthia didn't say a word. But it's killing me that it's too late. I can't do a damn thing about it. I can't ask Cynthia for an explanation, and I can't get to know Ashley. I would have been better off not knowing."

Moments later, Layla left him, sensing that he preferred to defer his emotions until he had privacy to think about the situation.

She said a word to Chelsea and then headed out to where her car was parked on the street. All evening she had wanted to glance at her texts, but she made herself resist. Now was the time. She slid into the driver's seat, shut the door and turned on the engine so the car would cool down.

Then she checked her phone. She sucked in a breath. There it was…

As promised. I'm checking in about dinner tomorrow night. J.B.

Layla couldn't help but smile. Even if this rendezvous resulted in an awkward moment of truth, she didn't want to miss it. First of all, she wanted to satisfy her curiosity about which of the Banks boys had taken her to the concert. And second—because she was almost positive it was Joshua—she wanted to see if the spark of attraction was more than a fluke.

She responded quickly...

I'm free! What time?

Are you up for a picnic? If so, I'll pick you up at 5, and we'll go for a drive...can you supply a quilt?

Layla was surprised, but she had no objections. A picnic would give them more privacy to clear the air.

Sounds good to me. See you then...

She tossed her phone in her purse so she wouldn't be tempted to continue the conversation. She probably should be mad. Mad at either or both of the Banks men. But maybe it was a harmless prank. She hoped so. She would give them the benefit of the doubt, mostly because she wanted to explore the tantalizing sparks she had experienced last night.

The following day, she was busy with a million and one things around the ranch. And she spared a couple of hours to help her grandmother. Miriam was intent on donating her husband's clothing as soon as possible. It was her way of coping with grief.

The two women sorted through hangers and checked pockets. The only things they found were old pieces of hard butterscotch candy, still in the wrappers.

Layla put her arms around her grandmother at one point and hugged her. "I'm so sorry about Grandy. Are you going to be okay?"

Miriam nodded, wiping her eyes. "Oh, yes. But he and I were together so long, it feels like I've lost a limb. We had good days and bad, Layla. Still, the two of us were rock solid. I hardly know what to do with myself now."

"I promise we'll all be here for you, Grammy. I know this must be so very hard."

Later that afternoon, Layla showered and changed into a new sundress she had bought recently. The material was a pale yellow gauzy cotton scattered with tiny teal flowers. The spaghetti-strap bodice was lined, so she skipped a bra.

A picnic sounded sedate enough. She settled on cream leather ballet flats. They were more cute than practical. Not the thing for tramping around the ranch, but perfect for a date with a handsome man.

When Jordan/Joshua arrived at five on the nose, she went out to the porch and down the steps to meet him, not waiting for him to come up and ring the doorbell. There were too many unanswered questions. The last thing she wanted was for her nosy family to grill whichever of the Banks brothers was picking her up.

Her date shielded his eyes from the sun. "Hey, there."

"Hey, yourself." She handed him the quilt. Again, her gut feeling told her she was being greeted by

Joshua. Jordan was louder and more gregarious. This man gave her a tight smile, tucked her into the front seat of a luxury sports car and got in without saying another word. It was a different car tonight. Had the other one been Jordan's?

To be honest, Layla didn't mind that the drive was mostly silent. It had been a long, stressful week. She was happy to lean back and take a deep breath.

The car was a dream. Top-of-the-line engineering and every possible creature comfort. It was also a stick shift. Outside town when they found a two-lane road that was straight and deserted, the man behind the wheel hit the gas.

Layla smiled. There was something about speed that helped wash away tension and stress. It was one reason she liked riding horses. But today was even more exciting. She could feel the powerful engine as it worked its way higher and higher.

Watching her companion out of the corner of her eye was entertaining in its own way. Though he might not even know it, the tiny smile that tipped up the corners of his masculine lips told Layla he was enjoying himself.

He was dressed beautifully, but casually. Well-worn jeans showcased long legs, a narrow waist and powerful thighs. His expensive tooled-leather cowboy boots were the real deal. The navy-and-yellow-plaid cotton shirt was soft, the sleeves rolled to his elbows.

He also smelled really, really good.

Layla didn't ask where they were headed. It was nice to sit back and let someone else steer the ship for a change. She was, unfortunately, a bit of a workaholic. It was a tendency made even worse in the wake of her broken engagement. She had buried herself in work and scarcely come up for air.

Now she felt her muscles going lax, her body nestling into the embrace of a butter-soft leather seat. Even her bones seemed willing to loosen and unkink. Drowsy contentment wrapped her in a cocoon of well-being.

Joshua didn't know whether to be insulted or amused when he realized his passenger was asleep. She had kicked off one shoe and tucked her leg beneath her. In that position, her dress rode up, revealing a tanned, toned thigh.

His hands tightened on the wheel. He had no idea how this picnic was going to play out, but he hoped Layla would give him a chance to explain. He wasn't looking forward to confessing the twin switch, but it had to be done.

When he stopped the car at last, they were parked atop a low rise miles from the nearest house. This property was for sale. He had toyed with the idea of buying it. But such a decision would mean staying in Royal, and he wasn't sure he was ready to commit to that.

He studied Layla as she slept, glad of the opportunity to catalog how the young tomboy had morphed into a capable, extremely feminine woman. Her hair was still the golden blond he remembered. From his close vantage point, it looked soft and silky.

His sex stirred, reminding him that a man his age shouldn't be sleeping alone. Layla was the first woman in forever to tempt him. Seriously tempt him.

The dress she wore wasn't meant to be provocative. But it bared her arms and shoulders. Her legs were bare, too. In fact, she was probably completely bare underneath except for whatever underwear she wore.

Since he could see the tiny outline of her nipples, maybe nothing but panties.

He gripped the steering wheel and told himself he had to keep a rein on his baser impulses. For one thing, Layla thought she was out on a date with Jordan. And for another, if he wanted Layla's forgiveness, he couldn't seduce her on this gorgeous spring afternoon, no matter how much he wanted to…

He said her name quietly, not wanting to startle her. "Layla. Wake up, Layla. We're here."

It took three tries, and on the last one he actually shook her shoulder. The feel of her delicate bones and soft skin seared itself into his fingertips.

Layla yawned and opened her eyes. He witnessed the exact moment she realized what had happened. Her whole face turned red.

"Oh, gosh," she whispered, scrubbing her hands over her cheeks and straightening her hair. "I'm so sorry. Did I fall asleep on you?"

"Not *on* me," he teased. "But beside me, yes."

When he realized she was genuinely mortified, he chuckled. "Don't sweat it, Layla. You've had several hard days. I'm glad you felt comfortable enough with me to relax. You must have needed the rest."

"I haven't been sleeping at night," she admitted. The embarrassed color faded, leaving her pale.

"How is your grandmother doing?" he asked.

"I helped her pack up Grandy's clothes today. She's hanging in there."

Joshua rubbed his chin. "Isn't that kind of quick?"

Layla's smile was wistful. "You'd have to know my grandmother. She's sort of the rip-off-the-bandage type."

"Everyone deals with grief differently, I suppose." He thought about his marriage—the separations, the long arguments…the realization that he couldn't save the relationship with Becky on his own. He had grieved.

Layla sat up and reached for her shoe, then slid her foot into it and adjusted the heel. "I seem to remember you promising me a picnic?"

He nodded. Layla was hurting, too, but she was very independent. "I did, indeed. The basket is in the trunk."

Both of them exited the car. Layla stretched and looked around.

They were parked amidst a small copse of cottonwood trees. Years ago, there might have been a small creek at the base of the rise, but it had long since dried up.

"This is nice," she said, giving him a smile that made him catch his breath.

He wanted Layla Grandin on several levels, but there was a hurdle he had to clear first. He wasn't sure what he was going to say, but sooner was better than later.

While he marshalled his thoughts, he spread out the beautiful thick quilt that had probably been handed down through the Grandin family. Though it was faded, the patina of age added charm. Unlike Layla, he and Jordan had no living grandparents. Nor a mother. Only their pushy, upwardly mobile father who had always aspired to be more than what he was.

Nothing wrong with that as long as a person understood acceptable boundaries. Bertram Banks was always pushing.

To be fair, Joshua couldn't blame his father for the current situation. Jordan could have said no to his father. Joshua could have said no to his brother. But he hadn't. Because a part of him had been intrigued.

When Layla sat down, her sundress settled around her like a patch of sunshine. She was graceful and unselfconscious. Joshua couldn't help thinking about the past. Some people might wonder why twin boys had allowed a younger playmate, a girl, to tag along on their adventures. As Joshua remembered it, the reasons were at least twofold.

Layla had kept up with them every step of the

way. And her presence—although she wasn't a girly girl back then—had been a way for the boys to show off, to continually try and best each other.

It was a pattern that had persisted over the years... though without their sidekick, of course.

Joshua opened the trunk and retrieved the large fancy picnic basket. "I ordered this from the Royal Diner. I hope I picked things you like. I did tell them no bananas in the fruit salad."

"I can't believe you remembered that I don't like bananas." Layla laughed, her eyes sparkling in the dappled shade. Though her irises were blue like his, the shade was different. Layla's were lighter with flecks of gold.

He toed off his boots and joined her on the blanket, crossing his sock-clad feet at the ankles. When he leaned back on his elbows, he sighed without meaning to. A weight he'd been carrying for months finally slipped away.

The past was the past. It was time for him to move on. He turned his head, looked at Layla. Took a deep breath. "I need to tell you something."

Her expression was both wistful and wry. "Is it that you're Joshua and not Jordan?"

Shock ran up and down his spine. He sat up, slinging an elbow over one knee. "You knew?"

She shrugged. "Not at first. But after half an hour, I was fairly certain. I haven't seen Jordan in a long time, nor you for that matter. So I had to question my gut feeling."

He frowned. "Not many people can tell us apart."

Layla gave him a look that questioned his intelligence. "I spent days and weeks and years running wild with you two when we were kids. I used to know you both very well."

"What gave me away?"

"Well, for starters, you're quieter than Jordan. Deeper maybe. He's a bit of a flirt."

Her comment stung, though Joshua was aware she hadn't meant it as a gibe. Becky had told him repeatedly that he was no fun. He'd heard it enough times that he eventually began to wonder if she was right.

"I'm sorry," he said, managing a grin. "Well, hell. If we're being honest, I'm not sorry at all. I had a great time with you at the concert."

"Me, too," she said. "But you still haven't explained why you and Jordan tried the twin switch with me."

"No big secret." He sighed. "Dad set all this in motion. But Jordan already had another date."

Her lips twitched. "Of course he did. I should have known."

"Otherwise, I'm sure he'd have been happy to take you to the concert."

"You don't know any such thing. I've seen the women your brother dates. I'm not exactly his type."

"Maybe." Joshua didn't want to wade into that one.

His confession hadn't extinguished the thread of heat between them. If anything, the *sizzle* intensified.

Layla tucked her hair behind her ear. "You want to start over?" she asked.

Joshua was struck by her response to the situation. She didn't sulk. She didn't hold a grudge. And she didn't punish him. Was this what normal, nice women were like? He had been ensnared with his ex-wife for so long, he had almost forgotten.

"I'd like that," he said.

"Let me help you set out the food."

They were both hungry. The conversation was lighthearted as they ate, but beneath the surface communication ran a vein of something else. Awareness.

He was in no place to jump back into anything serious. And he didn't know if Layla was the kind of woman to dabble in a short-term affair. But he was willing to find out.

She put him on the spot at one moment. "Was all that stuff you said to me the other night about your wife the truth? You know, when you were pretending to be your brother?"

He groaned. "You're not going to let me forget that, are you?"

Layla's grin was smug. "Probably not. At least for the moment."

"Yes," he said flatly. "It was true. My father warned me that Becky was after the family money. But I didn't listen."

"You were in love."

He shrugged. "I thought I was. I *wanted* to get married. I liked the idea of starting a family."

"But she never got pregnant?"

"Nope. In fact, she flatly refused to consider it. But that was the least of our problems. She loved Dallas, and the social life there. All she talked about was making the right connections, cultivating the right friends."

"And you?"

"I had a great job I loved—project manager for an energy company—but I had always assumed that one day we would go back to Royal and start a family. Unfortunately, I hadn't made those intentions clear *before* we got married. That was my mistake. I decided we should go to counseling and work on our problems. Becky agreed at first. We made it through three sessions, maybe four. But that was it. I discovered it's impossible for one person to save a marriage when the other partner doesn't care."

"I'm so sorry, Joshua." Her empathetic gaze made him feel marginally better. Rehashing his romantic past was not the way to impress a woman.

"It was for the best. We never really loved each other, I guess. We were separated for a little over two years. The divorce was final a few months ago."

Layla frowned. "But if you still loved your job, why are you here in Royal? Just for a visit?"

"Actually, I…"

"You what?" She prompted him when he couldn't get the words out.

"I quit my job. I told Jordan, but my father doesn't know."

"Wow. That's a big decision."

He gazed at her wryly. "After the divorce was final, I started feeling the pull of home, even more than I had before. I've missed the wide-open spaces. I think about the ranch a lot."

"What will your dad say?"

"Jordan thinks he'll take me back in a heartbeat."

"So, problem solved?"

"It's hard to tell. I don't want to step on Jordan's toes. I wonder if I should start over somewhere completely new."

Five

Layla was surprised by the sting of disappointment that settled in her stomach. She didn't even *know* the adult Joshua, not really. Yet maybe because of their childhood friendship, she felt a connection.

"If you don't mind a little amateur psychoanalysis on my part," she said, "I'll offer a theory."

He grimaced. "Feel free."

"I think you feel like a failure, and it has rattled your confidence."

Joshua blinked. His cheeks flushed. "You shoot straight, don't you?"

The rueful note in his words made her wonder if she had gone too far. "It's not a criticism," she said quickly. "But I've had some experience with the phenomenon. When I found out Richard was cheating on me, it shook me to the core. Here was a man I had chosen, a guy I was planning to spend my life with, and I had made a huge mistake."

"You and I are hardly the first or the last to misjudge other human beings."

"True. But up until then, I considered myself pretty smart and capable. Suddenly, everyone around me was giving me pitying glances. As if I was some poor, delicate creature. I hated it."

"I get that."

There was silence between them for a moment. Layla smoothed the skirt of her dress, not quite able to look at her companion. "I never thought this picnic was going to be a deep dive into our darkest emotions."

"Is that a bad thing? Maybe we've cleared the air."

"Maybe."

They finished their meal in companionable silence. Layla wondered if this was the last time she would see Joshua. She didn't often cross paths with the Banks family unless it was at some charity function or town event. If Joshua decided not to stay, this was it.

Something inside her wasn't willing to accept that. "You could do me a favor," she said. "If you're still around in a couple of weeks."

"What's that?"

"The Cattleman's Club is having their spring luncheon soon. I don't have a date, but I'd like to. You know how gossip in Royal is. I'm really tired of everyone discussing *poor little Layla*. They all know about Richard."

"I could do that," he said. "I'm still a member on paper. Though I haven't been inside that beautiful old building in years."

"You'll be surprised," she said. "We have an onsite day care now. And lots of other improvements. Change comes slowly, but it does eventually come."

"I take it your whole family belongs to the club?"

"We do."

"And how will things change at the ranch now that your grandfather is gone? You said your dad has been frustrated by your grandfather's old-fashioned ways."

"Ugh. Sore subject," she muttered.

"You don't have to discuss it if you don't want to."

"I don't mind. Dad is just as old-fashioned in his views, though he doesn't see it. It looks like I have a choice to make."

"Like how?"

"Chelsea and I are about to get sidelined, even though all either of us has ever wanted was to be an integral part of the ranch. She's furious about it. I'm more resigned to the inevitable, I guess. I train horses, and since my degree is in business, I keep an eye on the bottom line when no one is watching."

"Then what's the problem?"

"My father is fifty-nine years old, and he is just now getting a shot and running things his way. I don't know if my siblings and I are prepared to wait that long. It's frustrating when we have progressive new ideas, grounded in science, but Daddy won't listen. Grandy was the same in that regard, but at least he had the excuse of coming from a much older generation."

"Remind me how old your siblings are?"

"Chelsea is the eldest at thirty-five. I'm thirty-two, a year younger than you. Vic is thirty-one, and our baby sister, Morgan, is twenty-eight."

"Do all of them want to be significant parts of running the ranch?"

She grimaced. "Not Morgan. She owns a boutique in town. But it doesn't even matter. Vic has the edge in that sweepstakes."

"How so?"

"Grandy and my father were and are very patriarchal. Because Vic is the only boy, he's on deck to be the next lord of the manor."

"That doesn't seem fair at all." Joshua had reclined on his side. He looked sleepy and replete... but wickedly masculine. Layla realized she was both aroused by him and on her guard. Because Layla was lonely, and Josh was a huge part of her past, she might be tempted to wallow in sentimentality and sexual attraction and do something stupid.

"Enough about me," she said. "Maybe we should be getting back." The sun was sinking low in the sky, chasing the horizon.

"What's your hurry?" he asked with a teasing smile. That smile was deadly. It made all her secret vulnerable places tingle. As if a special kind of lightning was about to strike.

She cleared her throat. "No hurry. But I'm sure you have important things to do."

"Nothing more important than spending time with an interesting woman."

"Flatterer."

The smile disappeared. Now his gaze was warm, maybe even hot.

He played with the hem of her skirt, folding a tiny piece of fabric between his fingers. Layla was mesmerized, watching that big tanned hand so near her knee.

"Tell me something," he said, his voice deep and husky. "When I kissed you night before last, were you kissing Jordan?"

Yikes. Dangerous territory. She had a choice. Honesty or deflection. It was really no choice at all.

"No," she said. "I knew exactly who I was kissing. It was you, Josh."

The hot light in his eyes flared into male satisfaction. "Good." He leaned forward, curled a hand behind her neck and slanted his mouth over hers. No fumbling. Nothing tentative. Just a man intent on giving and receiving pleasure.

Somebody moaned. Probably her. Layla was too enmeshed in the magic of the moment to care. She trusted Joshua. She had always enjoyed his company. He was a decent, funny, kind man with a kick-ass body and worlds of experience.

Right now, he was everything she wanted.

Joshua deepened the kiss, his tongue stroking hers, his teeth nibbling her bottom lip. Eventually, he moved to her collarbone, pressing his lips to a particularly vulnerable spot. She caught her breath. Heat pooled in her sex. She wrapped her arms around his neck, trying to get closer.

She was ready to devour him, but her partner was being remarkably circumspect under the circumstances. Maybe he thought it was too soon.

"Do you have any condoms with you?" she asked.

When he froze, she felt humiliation engulf her in smothering waves. "Never mind," she muttered, pulling away abruptly. "That was the wine talking."

Joshua grasped her shoulders. His hands shook. His cheeks were flushed. "I do," he said. "But are you sure this is what you want?"

"Right now? Yes."

Her answer seemed to satisfy any doubts he had. Maybe this was reckless or even self-sabotaging, but Layla didn't care. She needed Joshua. She *wanted him*.

He eased her onto her back and leaned over her. One big masculine hand cupped her breast firmly. When her nipple peaked, he rubbed it, circling the taut point through the thin fabric of her dress.

Fire streaked through her, incinerating her doubts. She trembled, not because she was unsure, but because the magic of the moment left her breathless. If she was this strung out from a mere touch, how was she going to survive what happened next?

She had never considered herself a passive lover, but for the moment, she reveled in having Joshua take charge. He was sure of himself. Not arrogant. Simply intent on seizing what he wanted, what she had offered.

He peeled the small straps of her sundress down her shoulders and freed her arms. Now she was bare to the waist.

She saw the muscles in his throat ripple as he swallowed. "You're beautiful, Layla."

Suddenly, she was ravenous for him. "There's a zipper in the back," she whispered. "Hurry."

His smile was crooked. "What's your rush?"

"It's been a very long time since I've enjoyed… *this*."

The grin faded. "I'll bet I've got you beat. Almost two years. My ex slept around during our separation. I still felt married."

"And since February?"

He shrugged, his jawline rigid. "Nobody. I've been a mess, Layla. Are you sure you want to get involved with a guy who screwed up his life?"

She put her hands on his biceps, loving the feel of his muscles. "We're not getting involved," she said, finding the courage to stare into his eyes. "We're living in the moment. I can't say I have much experience with that way of thinking. I'm wound pretty tight. But for you, I'll make an exception."

Clearly, she had struck the right tone with her lighthearted teasing. Joshua's gorgeous smile returned, the wattage melting her body into a pool of feminine lust.

"I'm flattered," he muttered, bending to lick the tips of her breasts.

Holy hell. Layla arched her back, trying desperately to get closer. Somehow, he reached beneath her and dealt with the zipper. Soon he had her naked except for her tiny undies. Even though the sun was almost gone, she could feel its warmth on her skin.

Or maybe she was simply hyped up on the erotic way Joshua played with her body. He seemed fascinated with her flat belly, her navel, her thighs. When he touched her *there*, she bit her bottom lip to keep from begging.

For a man who professed to be celibate in recent days, he was remarkably patient.

When she said as much—muttering her disgruntlement—Joshua threw back his head and laughed uproariously.

"I wasn't trying to be funny. You're still dressed," she wailed, aggrieved.

Lightning flashed in his eyes, turning the placid blue to stormy skies. "I don't have much faith in my control once I get inside you, Layla. At least not the first time. I wanted the foreplay to be good for you, for me."

She dragged his head down. "We can always do the foreplay afterward."

Though she initiated the kiss, Joshua took control pretty damn fast. His tongue mated with hers. He sucked gently.

Heated need made her limbs heavy. Her sex throbbed with an insistent ache that begged to be assuaged. Layla felt a sudden dollop of unease. Why was she so susceptible to this man? Were nostalgia and hormones to blame?

And then the kiss deepened, eliminating any impulse on her part to think rationally.

There was no explanation for what was happening. None that made sense.

She wanted Joshua Banks more than she wanted her next breath.

He rolled away from her, panting. She watched as he extracted a square packet from his wallet and then unzipped his jeans. When he pulled his erect sex from his snug navy knit boxers, she sucked in a sharp breath.

Thankfully, Joshua didn't seem to notice. He positioned the condom and returned to her, settling between her legs. His gaze was hooded. "You ready?"

"Yes." The word was barely audible.

Joshua entered her with one powerful thrust. The clouds and treetops cartwheeled behind her eyelids as she squeezed her eyes shut and gave in to the sheer carnality of the moment. He was careful with her, tender even. But this was raw sex. No hearts and flowers. Just a man and a woman battling a powerful need.

They clung to each other on the sun-warmed quilt, struggling for more depth, more thrust, more everything.

She nipped his bottom lip with sharp teeth. "Don't hold back, Josh. I want it all."

The groan that ripped from somewhere deep inside him echoed the madness she felt. Desperation was a tangible cloud surrounding them. She inhaled his scent, felt the odd paradox of security and exhilaration.

He came first, but only seconds before she lost her mind. The orgasm was blissful, perfect, draining and energizing in equal measures.

In the aftermath, he kissed her forehead, then shifted slightly to give her room to breathe. But they were still connected. He was inside her, mostly still erect. Tantalizingly ready for round two.

At last, she found her voice. "Wow…"

He ran his thumb along her bottom lip. "Ditto…"

"Josh?" The shortened version of his name slipped out. It was what she had called him when they were kids.

"Yeah?"

"What was that we just did?"

"If you don't know, I must have done it wrong."

The humorous, self-deprecating words didn't match the solemn look in his eyes. It was hard to meet those eyes. They saw too much, perhaps. For the first time in her life, Layla had just indulged in the equivalent of a bar pickup. A one-night stand.

To a control freak, this total lapse of judgment on her part was terrifying.

"We're practically strangers," she whispered.

"Are we?" Joshua's face closed up. He rolled to his feet, straightened his clothing and turned his back so she could do the same.

When they were both dressed, she stood up, too. "I need help with my zipper," she muttered.

She presented her back to her lover and shivered when his warm fingers brushed her spine.

It took courage to turn around and face him. "I'm sorry," she said.

Now his scowl was fierce. He folded his arms across his chest. "For what?"

She shrugged, feeling small and uncertain and insecure. "I used you for sexual satisfaction."

Those blue eyes threatened to burn her. "I see. And you think I did the same?"

"Didn't you?" She wanted badly to hear him say otherwise, but the evidence was hard to discount.

In the time it took a breeze to ruffle the new leaves overhead, every emotion disappeared from his face. "I'll take you home."

"Wait," she said. "Don't be mad. I'm just trying to understand."

"It was sex," he said flatly. "Pretty incredible sex. But if it's spooked you this badly, it was clearly a mistake."

"I'm not spooked," she said quickly.

Finally, a giant sigh lifted his chest. One corner

of his mouth quirked in an almost smile. He unfolded his arms and slid his hands beneath her hair, cupping her neck. He bent his head to stare into her eyes. "Could have fooled me. Relax, Layla. We enjoyed each other. Is that so terrible?"

"I am *not* a sex maniac."

Now he chuckled. He brushed his lips over hers. "I wouldn't complain if you were. This was a hell of a way to break my fast."

"Why with me?" The words burst from her lips.

"Are you asking me to explain sexual attraction?"

She rested her cheek against his chest. "I've never had sex with someone just for the heck of it. It's always been part of a relationship."

"Are you proposing?" he asked, deadpan.

"Stop trying to make me feel dumb." She punched his shoulder.

He slid his fingers through her hair. "Can't we just enjoy ourselves? Does there have to be an answer for everything?"

She stared at him for the longest time, trying to read the mix of expressions on his face. If she didn't know better, she would think he was as surprised as she was by the connection between them.

"Why don't you kiss me again?" she said. "To see if it was a fluke."

"*It* what?" He moved closer, his big frame dwarfing hers.

Sharing the same air made it hard to breathe. "The spark," she croaked. "The fire."

That arrogant masculine grin was back. "I like the way you think." He held her head and tipped it the direction he needed, settling on the exact slant to cover her mouth with his and make them both groan with pleasure.

Layla wrapped one leg around his thigh. It was good. So good. Surely this was more than deprivation making her feel like she was melting into a puddle. She was ridiculously aroused. Clinging. Desperate.

She spared a half second to wonder who this woman was. She wasn't a version of Layla anyone would recognize.

Suddenly, Joshua scooped her into his arms and strode toward the vehicle. Layla was disappointed. She wasn't ready to go home.

But her companion had other ideas. He set her on the hood of the sports car. The metal was warm from the sun, but not uncomfortably hot.

The next round of kissing was more intense. Joshua moved between her legs, shimmying her skirt up her thighs. Getting close. And closer still.

His erection, covered in thick denim, felt good pressed against her center. When he rocked back and forth, Layla's fingernails dug into his forearms. "Please," she muttered. "Please tell me that wasn't your only condom."

Instead of answering, he growled low in his throat. His big hands cupped her butt and he lifted her into his thrusts. Like two teenagers fooling around, they tried to climb inside each other's skin.

Joshua's chest heaved with the force of his labored breathing. "Can't let go," he said.

"You have to. Right now. Please. I need you, but not without protection."

On the surface, she sounded logical and forth-right. Thank goodness he couldn't see inside her confused brain. If he had told her the first condom was the only one, she might have rolled the dice and taken her chances. *That* was how much she wanted him.

"Ten seconds," he promised. He left her and jerked open the car door. She watched through the windshield as he rummaged in the glove box. His jawline was granite. His hair was tousled, his cheek-bones flushed.

She rested her bare feet on the slick hood, trying not to slide off.

When he came back to her, he took care of business quickly and touched her undies. "Now?" he asked gruffly.

All she could do was nod.

Joshua didn't even bother removing her panties. He simply pushed them to one side and entered her with a raw, powerful surge that dried her throat and brought emotion to the fore. She didn't want that. All she wanted was sex.

But it was impossible not to feel things. Because she didn't know how to trust this madness, she shoved all those messy, warm responses away, concentrating on the carnal present.

Joshua Banks was good in bed. Or maybe not.

Who knew? But he was a heck of a lover in the great outdoors.

Now she linked her ankles at his back. She dragged his head closer so she could kiss him wildly. "Don't stop," she panted. "Don't ever stop."

His shoulders shook with laughter, but his eyes glittered with hunger. "I'd like to oblige, Layla, but you rev me up too damn fast."

His words were prophetic. Suddenly, he pounded into her feverishly. The hood of his car might never be the same. He moaned her name as he found his release. At the last instant, he shifted to one side and thumbed her center.

She shuddered and cried out his name as she hit the peak and tumbled over the other side.

Six

Joshua could hear his heart beating inside his ears. His knees were bruised from thumping against the side of the car. And somehow, despite their location beneath a broad, expansive Texas sky, he was starved of oxygen.

The woman in his arms stirred. "Sweet heaven."

There was no blasphemy in her awed whisper. He would have uttered words of agreement, but his tongue was thick in his mouth.

Truth be told, Joshua was as shaken as his partner. For months, he had found release with a hand job in the shower. His life had been in too much turmoil for anything else. And even after the divorce was final, he'd had a vague distaste for the idea of picking up a strange woman in a bar.

He might have done that a few times in his twenties, but he was older now. Wiser. Good Lord, he hoped he was wiser. Surely he should have something to show for a marriage that imploded. As it was, he had plenty of regrets.

The sex with Layla had been volcanic. Feelings and emotions he had ignored forever suddenly bubbled to the surface. Why had he never dated Layla? She was only a year younger than he was.

But when he still lived in Royal, she hadn't really been on his radar. She was just the funny, spunky kid who ran around with Jordan and him when they were all in middle school and early high school. Thinking of his brother brought up another sore point. What if Layla had been thinking of *Jordan* when she was having sex with Joshua?

His stomach curled. She might have done that without even realizing what she was doing. Joshua was damned if he would be a stand-in for his more gregarious sibling.

Only once had the twins fixated on the same girl. It had been eleventh grade. They both wanted to ask Tiffany Tarwater to the prom. Things had gotten ugly. After that, they made a pact. No fighting over females. Ever.

Suddenly, he realized Layla was stroking the back of his neck. His body tightened as another wave of arousal—one that had merely been simmering below the surface—seized him. His throat dried.

He had taken her like a savage. Never before in his life had he experienced more desperation, or more lust. Though he was shocked at himself, the woman in his arms wasn't trying to get away, so maybe all was not lost. Carefully, he lifted her into a seated position.

Her skin was warm and silky, her golden tresses a tangled mess. He buried his face against her bare shoulder, wanting to say something, but finding himself mute.

Layla combed through his hair with gentle fingers.

Separating their bodies was an actual physical pain. After he got rid of the condom and straightened his clothes, he turned around to find Layla looking at him.

What was that expression he saw in her beautiful eyes?

Try as he might, he couldn't come up with a single word.

Layla cocked her head, still staring into his soul… or so it seemed. "Your ex-wife is an idiot," she said calmly.

He felt his face flush. The implied compliment was reassuring, but still… "I don't want to talk about my ex," he said bluntly.

Layla grimaced. "Understandable."

"I suppose I should take you home," he said, try-ing—after the fact—to act like a gentleman.

His lover nodded slowly. "I suppose."

When he helped her stand, she wobbled. They both laughed.

Layla's smile was wistful, but at least it was a smile.

He retrieved the quilt along with the remnants of their picnic supper and followed her to the car. When he would have started the engine, Layla put her hand on his arm. "That was incredible," she said softly. "But I'm not sure where we go from here."

He sensed her need for clarification. But hell, he was befuddled. "What do you mean?" he asked, mostly to stall for time.

One slender shoulder lifted and fell in a feminine shrug. "You're having a personal crisis of identity. You have no idea if you're even going to stay in Royal. And my whole family is embroiled in a busi-ness emergency. Neither of us is in a healthy place to start a relationship."

Then she blushed. "Or maybe that wasn't what you had in mind."

He tried to frame a response. Honestly? He wasn't looking for a relationship at all. But his body appar-ently had a different agenda. The thought of leaving the lovely Layla free and unattached didn't sit well.

"All I know is that I want to see you again."

She blinked. Maybe the staccato, machine-gun words had shocked her.

"Ditto," she said. "But this week is packed."

"Can you find time for me? For us?"

Pink bloomed on her cheekbones. "I'll try."

"Fair enough."

This time when he started the engine, she didn't stop him.

The journey back to town was slower and almost as silent as the earlier trip when his passenger had been asleep beside him. He couldn't glean much from her expression. Her face was turned away from him as she stared out the side window, apparently fascinated by the fields of Indian paintbrush.

The bluebonnets were long gone. The winter had been mild, and they bloomed early. At the time, Joshua had still been in Dallas, closed up in his office by day and in his sterile apartment by night.

Why had he ever believed a corporate job was for him? He knew a hell of a lot about the oil industry, and he had been a damned good project manager, but the work hadn't satisfied an ache in his gut.

What had he been missing? Maybe everything.

At the Grandin ranch house, he parked in front of the steps and turned to face the woman who had bewitched him. He leaned forward and kissed her long and deep, though he kept his passion reined in for obvious reasons.

When he pulled back, Layla's pink lips were puffy. She touched his cheek. "It was a good picnic," she said solemnly. "I'm glad we cleared the air."

For a moment, he had forgotten all about the

Jordan/Joshua twin swap. Embarrassment cramped his stomach. "I'm really sorry about the bait and switch. I should have said no to my brother."

Layla got out and stared at him over the top of the car as he exited as well. "But think what we might have missed." Her mischievous smile brought his hunger roaring back.

He rounded the car and pulled her into the shadows, away from the illumination of the porch lights. "We'll figure this out," he promised.

"Maybe." She leaned her head against his shoulder. "Don't make promises you can't keep. We've both failed at important relationships. We're not sure what we want. Life is complicated."

The more negatives she threw at him, the stronger his impulse to convince her.

But now was not the time. "We've always been friends," he said, his tone mild. "We still are."

"True." She patted his chest with two hands. "I'll keep in touch. You, too. Maybe we can squeeze in dinner or a movie."

"I'd rather be alone with you."

Her eyes gleamed in the half dark. "Naughty, Mr. Banks."

"My brother isn't the only one who knows how to flirt."

"I'm sorry if my comparison was hurtful. I didn't mean it that way."

He made himself let her go. "You didn't hurt anything. At least not in a bad way. Some things hurt really, really *good*."

This time, she laughed. "And on that note, I'll say good-night."

"See you soon," he said. Was it a promise or a wish?

He watched as she climbed the stairs. On the top step, she turned and waved. "Good night, Josh."

Hearing her shorten his name gave him a funny feeling inside. Few people called him that anymore. But Layla had...once upon a time.

Back at the hotel, all he wanted to do was shower, flip channels for an hour or two and crash. But his brother was waiting for him in the hotel lobby.

Jordan jumped to his feet, his expression disgruntled. "Where in the heck have you been? You just got back into town. Surely your social life hasn't heated up that fast."

Joshua counted to ten. No point in taking his brother's taunting seriously. "As a matter of fact, I was out with Layla. I told her about our little stunt."

"Was she mad?"

"Actually, she was pretty cool about it."

"Ah..."

"What does that mean?"

"I'm guessing she was disappointed that it wasn't me."

"Sure didn't seem that way." Joshua glared at his twin. "Any crush Layla Grandin had on you is so far in the past nobody has the forwarding address."

"Very funny."

Joshua shoved his hands in his pockets. "Why are you here?"

"Dad wants you to come out to the ranch. So we can all talk."

"I see." Joshua couldn't decide if this overture was a plus or a minus. "Did you already tell him my divorce is finalized?"

"I had to. Otherwise, he might have thought she was here with you."

"Perish the thought."

"Indeed." Jordan ran a hand through his hair. "So you'll come?"

"Tell him I'll head out that way before lunch tomorrow. But I'm keeping the hotel room for now. I've got a lot to think about, and I need some space to decide my next move."

"Nothing to decide. You're back. End of story."

Actually, there was plenty more to the story, but Joshua wasn't keen to get into an argument now. "Thanks for coming, Jordan. I'll see you both in the morning."

They hugged, and with a jaunty wave, Jordan headed toward the exit.

Joshua made it to his room and crashed facedown on the bed. Unfortunately, he was far from being sleepy. He was hyped up on great sex and a million questions about his future. Coming home to Royal had been a gut-level impulse. Like an animal seeking shelter in its den, Joshua had wanted a place to hide out while he made plans.

But that was the trouble with hiding from reality. A man had only himself to blame when things went sideways.

The future was murky.

The morning after her picnic with Josh, Layla found herself energized and confused. Her family was still in disaster mode. Vic was still heir to the throne. But Layla was suddenly far more interested in her own personal life than anything about the ranch.

Maybe she was practicing avoidance. Or maybe Joshua Banks was impossible to ignore. The man was hot, sexy and too damn charming for his own good.

Her grandmother unwittingly offered a distraction. At lunchtime, she and Layla ended up in the kitchen together. While the housekeeper put together the sandwiches they had requested, Miriam leaned in and whispered, "Can we eat on the veranda out back? I need to ask you something. In private."

"Sure, Grammy." Layla was concerned. Her widowed grandmother didn't look good. She had deep shadows beneath her eyes as if she hadn't been sleeping well. But that was normal, right? The elderly woman had lost her husband. She was in mourning.

Once the two of them were settled on the wide screened-in porch overlooking the flower garden,

Miriam didn't start eating right away. Her hands twisted in her lap, plucking at the folds of her faded cotton *housecoat*. Although Miriam loved to dress up and had a closet full of fashionable clothing, here at the ranch house on a weekday she reverted to the relaxed workaday style of her mother and her mother's mother.

"What is it, Grammy?" Layla asked. "What's going on? And FYI, you really need to eat something. I don't want you getting sick."

Miriam smiled. "You're a peach, baby girl. Don't you worry about me. But here's the thing." She glanced around to make sure no one was close, and then she lowered her voice. "Will you drive me to the lawyer's office? I made an appointment for 1:30. But I don't want anyone else in the family to know."

"How are we supposed to pull that off?"

"Your father is out riding the range with his foreman. Bethany flew to Houston this morning with several friends for some fashion show. It's only Chelsea, Vic and Morgan we have to dodge."

"Only?"

"We can do it." Miriam didn't offer any further details. Instead, she bit into her sandwich and managed to finish half of it.

As they ate, Layla pondered the situation. Her grandmother was obviously being secretive. Although Layla's father was acting as if he had inherited the ranch outright, on paper he and Miriam were co-owners until his mother's death. So Miriam had as much right as anyone to meet with the family lawyers.

"I think this is the day that Vic and Morgan play doubles tennis at the Cattleman's Club," Layla said. "If I can make sure Chelsea isn't around, you and I should be able to get away with no one the wiser."

"And when we come home," her grandmother said, "we'll just say we went shopping." Her face lit up as if the small subterfuge tickled her.

"Sure," Layla said. "Whatever you want." Her grandmother meant the world to her. Layla would do anything to make Grammy happy, though it might be a very long time until Miriam Grandin regained her joie de vivre. Losing a spouse after so many years was a terrible blow.

As it turned out, Chelsea was spending the afternoon with a friend who had a new baby. So no one was around to see Layla and Miriam, both nicely dressed, walk down the front steps and get into Layla's Mini Cooper. Her father had poked fun at her for buying such a small, whimsical car, but Layla liked it.

At the lawyer's office, the two women had to wait only six or seven minutes in the lobby before they were ushered into the same room where the extended family had met to discuss the oil rights situation. Though Layla was prepared to step in if necessary, her grandmother handled herself with poise and determination.

She eyed the lawyer sternly. "I am here on a private matter. Do I have your word that what we discuss is confidential?"

The man's expression was affronted. "I assure you, Mrs. Grandin, I hold myself to a high ethical standard."

Miriam made a sound suspiciously like a snort. As she sat down in the chair closest to the man's broad cherry desk, she opened her 1960s' era handbag and pulled out a three-by-five leather-bound journal. The small book was maybe half an inch thick.

She paused, perhaps for dramatic effect. "I found one of my husband's diaries. More than one, actually, but this is the pertinent time period. I always knew he hid these, but I never bothered to look for them. My husband was one hundred percent faithful to our marriage. Other than that, his little secrets didn't really concern me."

She handed the tiny book to Layla, who had taken a seat as well. "I've marked the spot with a sticky note. Please read it aloud."

Layla eyed the lawyer and vice versa. Then she took a deep breath. The ink was faded. Grandy's spidery handwriting was immediately recognizable. This particular entry had been recorded more than three decades earlier.

She could almost hear his voice…

Augustus and I did what we had to do today. We signed over the oil rights on the adjoining ranches to protect Daniel. The boy is thriving in Paris. No need for him to come home and deal with a mess.

We put the rights in this Cynthia person's name and warned her not to claim anything until the baby was grown. I think she knows we have the money and the clout to make her life a misery if she tries any funny business.

Layla's nerveless fingers dropped the book in her lap. "My God, it's true."

Even the lawyer went pale.

Miriam straightened her spine. "Those two old men have caused untold damage with this stunt."

Layla stared at her grandmother. "We have to tell Daddy. And everyone else."

"No. We don't." Color stained the old woman's cheeks. "Cynthia and her daughter are dead. It's possible Heath Thurston fabricated a document based on rumors he'd heard from his mother. Who knows if Daniel was really Ashley's father? Victor has hired an investigator. For now, we let things run their course." She gave the poor lawyer a regal glare. "I wanted you to know the truth, so you can be prepared. We may be able to stonewall Thurston and buy ourselves some time."

The lawyer cleared his throat. "I can't be involved in anything illegal, Mrs. Grandin. Surely you know that."

Miriam stood, her chest heaving with rapid breaths. "I won't let my family's legacy be destroyed. That's all you need to know."

Layla saw the dampness on her grandmother's

brow and the way her pupils dilated. "We can meet here again if we need to, but, Grammy, I think I should take you home."

Suddenly, Miriam wobbled and collapsed to the floor.

Layla's heart jumped out of her chest. "Call 911," she yelled at the lawyer. She barely heard the man's words on the phone as she knelt beside her grandmother. The old woman's face was paper white.

For a few moments, Layla was terrified she had lost a second grandparent. But finally, she located a shallow pulse in her grandmother's wrist.

The next thirty minutes were a blur. Hearing sirens in the distance. Putting wet paper towels on her grandmother's forehead. Rubbing her frail arms.

As soon as the EMTs arrived, they took over with a minimum of fuss. They spent several minutes stabilizing Miriam and then lifted her carefully onto a stretcher. Fortunately, the law office was on the ground floor.

Layla felt her heart crack as she watched the stretcher being loaded in the back of the emergency vehicle. Grammy looked so frail and ill.

"I'd like to ride there with her," Layla said, preparing to climb in.

The young female medic shook her head, though there was sympathy in her eyes. "Sorry, Ms. Grandin. It's not allowed. The area is small, and we have to be able to work on your grandmother. You're welcome to meet us at the emergency room."

Seconds later, the truck sped off, sirens blazing.

Layla didn't know what to do. Her mother was out of town. Her father was riding on the far reaches of the ranch where cell service was spotty. And besides, Grammy had wanted this outing to be a secret.

Layla stood on the street corner, frozen.

Joshua was headed back to town after a not-so-successful visit to the ranch where he had grown up. As he made the turn toward his hotel, he saw Layla standing in front of a lawyer's office. She looked upset. Immediately, he pulled into a parking spot at the curb and jumped out.

"Layla. What's wrong? Are you hurt?"

She turned her head and stared at him blankly. Her face, even her lips, were pale. When he put his arms around her, she burst into tears.

It took him several minutes to drag the story from her. "I have to go to the emergency room," she said, looking frantic.

"You're in no shape to get behind the wheel. I'll take you."

He bundled her into the car and drove ten miles above the speed limit to Royal Memorial Hospital. Layla sat, huddled into herself, and closed her eyes. When they arrived, the state-of-the-art medical center was a hive of activity.

Layla tried to get him to drop her off at the door and leave, but Joshua wasn't about to do that. "They won't let you go back in Emergency. Not until they've fully evaluated her. I'll sit with you in the waiting room."

Joshua handed off his keys to the valet parking attendant, helped Layla out of the car and stuck with her.

No matter how upscale the hospital and how bright the paint and the floor coverings, all waiting rooms were essentially the same. Filled with antiseptic smells, the aura of fear and grief and an overwhelming sense of life and death.

Layla checked in at the desk only to be told that her grandmother hadn't been admitted yet. She looked up at Joshua, her brow creased with worry. "She's eighty-eight years old. Surely they won't send her home."

"They'll do whatever is best for her, I'm sure. Come sit down."

He tried to distract her with conversation, but to no avail.

At one point, Layla jumped to her feet and paced. "It's my fault."

"How?" He frowned, seeing her frantic state and unable to help her.

"Grammy wanted me to take her to the lawyer's office for a private meeting. She didn't want the rest of the family to know. So I said I would, but..."

"But what?"

Layla chewed her lip. "She collapsed while we were there."

"Do you want to tell me what was going on?"

"Maybe. But not now."

"Okay." He took her wrist as she made another circuit in his direction. "Sit, Layla. You're going to need to be strong to help your grandmother. Right now, you're wearing yourself out."

To his relief, Layla finally collapsed into the space beside him. It was a two-person love seat, no inconvenient metal bar in the middle. He slid an arm around her shoulders. "Breathe," he said. "Everything is going to be okay."

Layla half turned and glared at him. "You don't know that. People *die*."

Tears spilled from those blue eyes that made him weak in the knees. He pulled her closer. "Aw, hell, Layla. Don't do this. I can handle anything but you falling apart."

She had always been one of the strongest females he knew. To be honest, he and Jordan hadn't merely *tolerated* her presence when they were younger, they had *enjoyed* having her around.

Of course, being teenage boys, they never articulated those feelings.

Without warning, all the fire left her. She leaned into his embrace, not saying another word. But the slow tears didn't stop. Each one dug a little knife into his heart.

She looked even more beautiful than usual wearing a black pencil skirt, a sleeveless ivory silk blouse tucked in at the waist and low heels that matched the

skirt. Her hair was pulled back into a sleek, sophisticated ponytail.

He stroked the nape of her neck and waited with
her, wondering what he was doing with this woman
in this spot. He'd done a lot of soul searching after
he dropped her off last night. The negative column
was staggering.

First of all, there was the matter of her crush on
Jordan. Josh looked *exactly* like his twin. There was
a decent chance that Layla was unconsciously using
Joshua as a stand-in for the guy she really wanted. It
was a tough pill to swallow, but Josh had to at least
consider the possibility.

Second, Layla's family was in crisis mode. She
hadn't opened up to him yet about the specifics, but
it was something serious enough to involve the whole
clan. Which meant Layla needed to be there for her
parents, her siblings and, of course, her newly widowed grandmother.

Then there was the matter of Joshua himself.
It was hard to be confident about a new relationship when he had so badly botched his marriage. It
wouldn't be fair to any woman to get involved until
he knew what he wanted out of life.

Did he want to work with his father and Jordan?
Did he want to go somewhere else—create a new
life on his own terms? Houston was great. The mu-
seums, the art, the music. The sporting events. He
had buddies in Houston. It would be a perfect place
to relocate, and the job market was solid.

But then there was Royal. This quirky town with its history and its roots and its way of pulling a guy back home. Deep down, he felt like this was where he was supposed to be. But doing what? His father and Jordan didn't really *need* him. Joshua wanted to make his own mark in the world.

If he was smart, he would put the brakes on this thing with Layla.

Yet as good and sensible as his plan sounded, he couldn't work up any enthusiasm at all for any of the choices that didn't involve her.

She made him shudder…made him yearn. In ways that made him question why he had ever thought Becky was the one.

He wasn't stupid. He knew that sexual attraction could burn hot and bright and then ultimately flame out and turn to ash…or merely cool off gradually.

He'd had enough girlfriends over the years to realize that.

Was he kidding himself to think Layla was different? There was *something* between them, something almost irresistible. Lust? He'd known lust before. He was a guy, after all. And maybe the only difference with Layla was that they shared a past as adolescents.

But he couldn't convince himself that was it. Even now, in a setting entirely nonconducive to sexual thoughts, he knew he wanted her. He felt possessive and protective. Most of all, he trembled with the need to make love to her.

Was that normal? Was he having some kind of early midlife crisis?

She stirred in his embrace, sitting up straight and rubbing her face. "Talk to me," she said. "I can't stand this waiting. Tell me about your day. Or anything."

He nodded. "Well, I went out to the ranch to see my father this morning."

"Is this the first time since you've been back in Royal?"

"Yes. I needed a few days to get my thoughts settled."

"How did it go?"

He hesitated. "Not like I thought it would. Jordan says Dad will take me back in a heartbeat, but I don't think it's that simple."

"Oh? Why not?"

He shrugged. "Just a gut feeling. He wants me to admit he was right and I was wrong. He never liked Becky and didn't want me to marry her."

"So you think he wants you to eat crow?"

"Yeah…"

"And will you?" She looked at him curiously, not judging.

"I don't mind admitting I was wrong. But I'm not sure my being back at the ranch permanently is such a good idea. Dad and Jordan have things under control. I might feel like a third wheel."

"But don't you own a share of the property?"

"I do. I've been a silent partner since I moved to Dallas."

Layla opened her mouth to say something but was interrupted when a scrubs-clad doctor pushed through the swinging doors.

"Ms. Grandin? Ms. Layla Grandin?"

"Mrs. Grandin is stable. I've spoken with her at length. She
thinks she may have forgotten to take her medica-
tion this morning. Consequently, her blood pressure

Seven

Layla held Josh's hand in a death grip as she crossed
the room. His strong arm curled around her shoulders, and his warm fingers twined with hers. That
physical support was the only thing keeping her
grounded at the moment.

Desperately, she searched the doctor's face. Was
there some patient-care course in med school that
taught them how to keep all expression under wraps?

"How is she?" Layla asked, her throat tight with
fear.

The doc gave her an impersonal half smile. "Mrs.
Grandin is stable. I've spoken with her at length. She
thinks she may have forgotten to take her medica-
tion this morning. Consequently, her blood pressure

bottomed out. Stress is also a factor. In addition, she hasn't been eating and drinking properly since her husband died. We're going to keep her a couple of days for observation. I've expressed to her how vital it is to care for her body while her heart heals."

That last poetic turn of phrase made Layla re-think her opinion of the young doctor. "Thank you," she said.

"Does she have anyone to stay with her when she goes home?"

"Oh, yes. Plenty of us. Don't worry, Doctor. We'll wait on her hand and foot—I promise."

When the man returned the way he had come, Layla looked up at her rescuer. His hair was dishev-eled. He probably needed a haircut. But the thing that stood out most in this moment was Josh's absolute strength of character. She *knew* she could depend on him. Even before today—when he had dropped everything he was doing and stepped in to care for her—she understood that about his code of conduct. "Thanks," she said. "I was a wreck, but I'm okay now. You can go."

He frowned at her. "If I'm not mistaken, you'll need a ride back to your car. Or better yet, I'll take you straight home, and someone can pick up your car later. It's in the wrong direction."

Layla hated admitting he was right. Though she was grateful to him, she didn't want to feel obligated to anyone, much less Josh. Not after he had seen her naked. There were too many unanswered questions for her to be completely sanguine about his presence at the hospital.

"That would be helpful," she said grudgingly.

Josh kissed the tip of her nose. "That hurt, didn't it? Admitting you needed help?"

She scowled. "And your point?"

"Sometimes it's nice to let someone take care of you."

Layla felt herself leaning into him, drowning in blue eyes that promised all sorts of delicious delights. "I don't need a man to look after me." She whispered the words automatically, trying to ignore the warmth spreading in her chest. The warmth Josh had put there with his kindness.

Yet, *kind* wasn't the adjective she should have used. There was banked fire in his eyes, as if the sexual connection between them was on the back burner but ready to burst into flame. The intensity of that gaze made it hard to breathe for a moment.

Fortunately for her, a nurse approached them. "Mrs. Grandin is being admitted right now. She'll be in room 317. If you want to wait for her up there, it shouldn't be long."

"Thank you," Layla said. She turned to Joshua again. "Seriously. You don't have to stay. I'm going to text my siblings. They'll all be showing up soon. And my father, too. Somebody will take me back to get my car eventually."

A second ticked by. Then five more. Joshua sighed. "I'd like to stay. When someone else in your family takes a turn, you could go back to the hotel with me and relax. Then maybe dinner in the hotel dining room. Or even room service?"

Layla searched his face. "Is *relax* code for something?"

His grin was wry. "Only if you want it to be. My hotel is near the hospital. It saves you going out to the ranch. You could take a nap. Watch something on TV."

"Make love to my childhood friend?" Rarely was she so sexually direct, but Josh might not be sticking around Royal.

He blinked. "I'm at your disposal, Ms. Grandin."

The next hour passed quickly. When they went upstairs, Josh insisted on remaining in a nearby waiting room across the hall while Layla helped get her grandmother settled.

Not long after that, Chelsea, Vic and Morgan arrived. When a nurse came to check the patient's vitals, the siblings stepped out in the hall and sketched out a quick schedule of who would sit with Miriam.

Chelsea insisted on taking first shift. "You need some rest, Layla. You look terrible. Seeing Grammy collapse must have been scary as hell."

"It was," Layla sighed.

Vic and Morgan chimed in, too. "We've got this," Vic said. "And Dad will be on his way later. Take the rest of the day for yourself. Come back in the morning."

Layla allowed herself to be persuaded. All the

adrenaline had winnowed away, leaving her shaky and exhausted. After bidding her grandmother good-bye, she found Josh in the waiting room. "I'm ready," she said.

Despite the events of the day, she drew strength from his solid presence. But his hand on her elbow as they stood in the elevator made her thoughts go in a different direction. Her skin warmed and tingled where his fingers touched her.

Outside, as they waited for the valet, she decided to go for what she wanted. "Would you mind taking me to the ranch first? I can pack a bag, and then I'll probably book a room at the hotel, too. So I'll be on hand until Grammy is released."

Josh stared at her, eyes narrowed. "I like most of that plan. But there's no need for a second room. You're more than welcome to stay with me. In fact, I'll be pissed if you don't. I want to be with you, Layla."

His plain speaking touched something deep in a corner of her psyche that she seldom poked at. Her whole life she had felt invisible much of the time. Chelsea was the oldest. Morgan the youngest. Vic the beloved only boy.

Layla had gotten lost in the crowd.

Now here was Josh. Putting her first. Telling her how much he wanted her.

Was this more than physical attraction, or was she letting herself be blinded by lust dressed up as caring and connection?

On the drive to the ranch, they barely spoke.

"I'll stay in the car," Josh said as they pulled up in front.

It wouldn't have mattered. No one was home but the housekeeping staff. "Okay," she said. "It won't take me long to grab what I need." Less than twenty-four hours ago, Layla had been kissing Josh in the shadows of the front porch. Now Grammy was ill, Layla was going to spend the night in Josh's hotel room and Layla now knew for certain that Grandy and Augustus Lattimore had signed away the oil rights to both ranches.

The world didn't make sense anymore.

In her closet, she stood on her tiptoes and pulled down a medium-sized suitcase. She was an experienced traveler, so packing wasn't a problem. She would mostly need comfortable clothes for sitting in a hospital room.

Toiletries were next. A few personal items. The only thing that stumped her was what to wear in bed. It had been a long time since she had dressed up for a man at night. Though she enjoyed expensive lingerie, it felt naughty to deliberately pack things she knew Josh would enjoy. Maybe for that exact reason, she folded two beautiful gowns with matching silky robes and tucked them into her bag.

By the time she made it out to the porch and re-locked the front door, Josh surprised her by showing up to carry her bag down the stairs. "It's heavy," he said when she protested.

Her nerves grew as they got closer to the hotel. Josh reached over and patted her arm. "Quit panicking. We won't do anything you don't want to do."

"That's the trouble," she said morosely. "I want to do *everything* with you."

Josh's chuckle and smug smile told her he knew exactly what was on her mind.

She kept in touch with her family via a group text. Grammy was feeling much better. She was getting IV fluids and had eaten a small dinner.

Because Josh was already a guest at the hotel, there was no need to visit the front desk. Layla felt as if every set of eyes in the lobby followed them when they stepped into the elevator. She couldn't look at herself in the mirrored walls as the numbers lit up one by one.

What was she doing? To say she was choosing to spend the night in Josh's room because it was convenient and economical was a ridiculous stretch when it came to rationalization. She needed to be honest with herself. This was 99 percent about sex. Hot, sweaty, amazing sex.

She lost her nerve when Josh opened his door and stepped back for her to enter. Layla had been hoping he had a suite. But he didn't. Although the room was very large and luxurious—even with a comfy sitting area—there was no escaping the fact that the enormous king-size bed dominated the space.

Josh set her suitcase just outside the bathroom door and tossed his keys on the dresser. "So what will it be, Layla? Room service, or dinner out?" His cocky, sexy grin told her he knew she was not as confident as she appeared.

There was really no question. She needed some breathing space. "Dinner out would be nice," she said primly.

Joshua nodded. "There's a new French bistro just around the corner. The concierge recommended it to me."

She cocked her head and stared at him. "You don't really strike me as a French bistro kind of guy."

His grin broadened, making her tummy quiver. "Maybe you don't know me as well as you think. Or then again, I might be expanding my horizons."

Layla didn't take the bait. In this battle of wits, he would probably win out, simply because it had been a very long, stressful day for her.

The outfit she had worn to the lawyer's office was suitable for dinner, so all she had to do was freshen up in the bathroom.

When it was Josh's turn, he grabbed a clean shirt and dress pants and took a five-minute shower. Though Layla seated herself on the opposite side of the room, it was impossible not to hear the water running and imagine what he looked like, his fit, muscular body wet and steamy.

The lump in her throat grew.

She couldn't look at him when he finally exited the bathroom. His scent, something lime and woodsy, invaded her senses, though to be fair, it was extremely subtle.

His damp hair was a darker blond than usual. It struck her suddenly that Joshua Banks was an incredibly handsome man. A stupid thought, probably. After all, she had known him for many years.

But now, seeing him all grown up—masculine and self-assured—she perceived him differently. Not as a preteen boy, or even an older adolescent. He had filled out. Matured. This man might still be her friend. Time would tell.

But he was also the lover she wanted.

They walked to the restaurant. It was a pleasant evening. People filled the streets. Music spilled from a nearby sports bar.

The bistro was just fancy enough to be romantic, but not so uppity that it seemed out of place in Royal. Layla was startled to hear Josh order an expensive bottle of wine in flawless French. When the waiter departed, she raised an eyebrow at the man sitting across from her. "Since when do you speak French?"

He shrugged. "College. Turns out I have a knack for languages. I do fairly well in Spanish, too. It came in handy when I was working for the energy company in Dallas. I traveled to Europe a couple of times a year."

"I see." She wanted to ask if his ex-wife traveled with him, but she couldn't bring herself to do it. It wasn't really any of her business—unless Josh somehow harbored unresolved feelings in that direction.

Just because his ex-spouse had not been the woman he thought she was didn't mean he hadn't cared about her. Maybe still did at some level.

After Richard's many deceptions, Layla had learned not to take everything at face value. People told you what they wanted you to believe. She needed to guard her heart and her emotions with Josh.

Great sex didn't always equal honesty.

Despite her misgivings, dinner was delightful. The food was incredible. The wine even better. And since neither of them was driving, they lingered and enjoyed the burgundy.

Josh told her funny stories about his job. She shared a few anecdotes about college and how she and Richard had met some years later.

Josh leaned back in his chair. "So are you going to tell me what's going on with the Grandin ranch?"

She wrinkled her nose. "I can share some but not all. A few things are need-to-know."

He nodded. "Fair enough. What's the deal?"

"Basically, it seems my uncle had an affair years ago. There was a child he didn't know about. Or so we've been told. If it's true, this same source claims that my grandfather and Augustus Lattimore signed over oil rights on both ranches to this woman to hold in trust until the baby grew up. But years later, the woman and her grown daughter died in a car accident."

"That's bizarre." Josh frowned. "So the oil rights were never activated?"

"Apparently not."

"Then the story is a lie?"

"We're not sure," Layla said carefully, trying not to think about the small journal with the incriminating evidence.

"Who is it?"

"Heath Thurston."

"I don't know him."

"Our whole family is going nuts. Daddy has hired an investigator."

"Makes sense. The claim will have to be substantiated."

"I guess. And if it's true…" She trailed off, feeling sick.

Josh reached across the table and squeezed her hand. His smile was encouraging. "Maybe it's not," he said. "Otherwise, why wouldn't the girl have claimed her inheritance when she turned twenty-one?"

Layla hadn't thought of that. A tiny flicker of hope stirred in her chest, despite what she had seen in the lawyer's office.

"Let's talk about something happier," she said.

Joshua obliged. Soon they were deep into a conversation about sports and possible pennants in the fall.

They had started on the dessert course—a decadent sponge cake with fresh raspberry sauce—when someone appeared beside their table. Layla looked up, thinking it was the waiter. Instead, their unexpected guest was a man about Josh's age. He had full, dark brown hair, dark eyes and thick eyebrows. He was as handsome and striking as the Banks brothers, but in a different way. His faded jeans and well-worn cowboy boots looked out of place in the fancy bistro.

It was *Heath Thurston*, the source of all her troubles. She had googled him after the funeral to be sure she knew what he looked like.

Josh, clearly not recognizing the man, stared at him. "May we help you?"

Thurston ignored Josh, choosing instead to focus all his attention on Layla. "Ms. Grandin? Layla Grandin?"

Unease slithered in her veins. "Yes."

A smile added charm to his serious face. "I'm Nolan Thurston."

Nolan... Her brain scrambled to keep up.

When Layla was silent, he elaborated. "My brother is Heath Thurston."

Layla shook her head slowly. "What is it with this town and twins? I can't believe you have the nerve to speak to me, especially in public."

Josh rose to his feet, tossing his cloth napkin on the table. "Get lost, Thurston."

Again, the man ignored Josh. When he addressed Layla again, his expression was conciliatory, his words couched in pleasant tones. "I wondered if you and I might have lunch together soon. You know. To talk things out. It's possible we can find some common ground before all of this gets blown out of proportion. And you could bring your sister Chelsea. She's the oldest...right? I've been told the two of you are close."

Layla stood as well, now flanked by two imposing men. "You're out of your mind," she said tersely. "No lunch. No dinner. No nothing. And stay away from my sister. Your brother is trying to destroy my family's livelihood."

Nolan's smile faded. "*Destroy* is a harsh word. Heath only wants what's fair. The oil rights are ours. Surely you can understand that. Take a step back and look at the situation unemotionally. What would you do if the situations were reversed?"

Eight

Josh had seen enough. Layla looked as if she might punch the guy. He lowered his voice and infused it with an audible threat. "Go. Away. Or I'll call the cops."

Nolan Thurston was a cool customer. He didn't seem at all rattled by Josh's posturing. "I'm not trying to cause trouble," he said. "Besides, what's it to you? I fail to see your connection to the matter. Unless you're a fiancé? Or a boyfriend?"

Josh ground his teeth, wishing he could wipe the smug smile off Thurston's face. "My relationship to Layla is none of your business."

Nolan shifted his gaze back to Layla. "Lawyers are expensive. I think it would be much more civilized if you and I—or any other of your siblings—could arbitrate a fair outcome that will satisfy us all."

Layla's spine stiffened. It almost seemed as if she grew two inches, like an Amazon in training. "To be honest, Mr. Thurston, I don't give a rat's ass about what might satisfy you and your avaricious brother. Your mother is gone. Your sister, too. Even if such an agreement ever existed—and I doubt that it did—any obligation ceased with your sister's passing."

Nolan scowled. "You don't know that. Sounds more like wishful thinking on your part. Have lunch with me. Soon. It's in everyone's best interests."

Layla placed her hands on her hips and lifted a haughty eyebrow. "Don't presume to know what's best for me *or* my family, Mr. Thurston. Grandins have worked that ranch for generations. We don't intend to let you and your brother ruin a single blade of grass."

Josh moved toward the man, fully prepared to usher him out of the restaurant by force, if necessary.

Fortunately, Thurston got the hint. He tossed his business card on the table and sighed. "Think about what I've said. Let me know if you change your mind. I'll be in touch."

When Nolan Thurston turned on his heel and walked rapidly out of the dining room, Layla sank into her chair as if her legs had collapsed. She rested her elbows on the table and put her head in her hands. "This has been the week from hell."

Josh didn't say a word. But he sat down quietly.

Thirty seconds later, Layla lifted her head and gave him a sheepish smile. "Present company excepted, of course. You've made my soap opera of a life bearable."

Her pink lips curved in a self-deprecating smile that sent a shiver down his spine. Suddenly, he was calculating how quickly he might persuade her to go back to the room. "You've had a rough go of it," he agreed. "I'm sorry Thurston interrupted our meal."

Layla poked at her now-soggy cake. "It's still good. Go ahead. Finish yours. Or I will." She laughed at him with her eyes. Her mouth was full of syrupy dessert.

Damn. How did she do that? One minute he wanted to comfort her. The next he was ready to strip her naked and take her right here on the table. To be honest, his impulses when he was around Layla were beginning to freak him out.

He didn't have a shrink on retainer, but if he did, this would have been a good time for some intensive *what-in-the-hell-are-you-thinking* therapy.

But that was the problem. He wasn't thinking. At all. He was only reacting and lusting and generally acting like the poor little sphere in a pinball machine, getting whacked from one side of the game to the other with flippers. Everyone who played knew the outcome of pinball was hard to predict. All the bells and whistles served as a distraction. The ball could end up anywhere.

He suddenly had an epiphany. He didn't need to

find all the answers today. Or even tomorrow. The important point was not to lose sight of the prize. One thing he knew for certain. Layla Grandin had skin in this game, whether she knew it or not. They had both been burned by love. They had that in common. But so had lots of people. Knowing what relationships *didn't* work was easy.

Predicting the future was a lot more difficult.

Layla swallowed the last bite of her cake and chased it with a final sip of wine. Then she sighed. "I'm stuffed. Do you want to go for a walk?"

Hell, no! He swallowed, praying he hadn't said those two words out loud. "Sure," he said, hoping his smile looked more genuine than it felt.

After he paid the check and they made it back out onto the street, his mood mellowed. The sun was down. A light breeze fluttered new leaves on the trees. He took Layla's hand in his. "You choose the path, Layla. I'll follow your lead."

They walked for half an hour, barely speaking. Enjoying the spring evening. He wondered if Layla was worrying about the Thurston brothers, but he didn't want to bring up a sore subject.

Eventually, their circuitous route took them back to the hotel. In the elevator, he tucked a strand of silky blond hair behind her ear. They were alone. No one to see when his thumb caressed her cheek.

Layla blushed. She searched his face, her long-lashed eyes locked on his. "Thank you," she said softly. "It's been a very long time since I've had somebody looking out for me. I may not *need* it, but that doesn't mean I don't appreciate everything you've done for me today. I'm not sure what would have happened if you hadn't shown up when you did."

"You would have thought of something."

"Maybe. But then again, I might have gotten behind the wheel to drive myself to the hospital. I was in shock, I think."

"Yeah."

In the room, he could see Layla's nerves. "I need to make a phone call," he said. "Why don't I do that downstairs to give you some privacy while you get ready for bed?"

The relief on her face almost made him laugh, but he didn't.

"Sounds good," she said breezily.

Though her words were light, her body language and the wariness in her gaze told him she wasn't sure of herself...of the situation...of him.

He needed to earn her trust. A woman who had been lied to and cheated on would look for honesty in a man. Faithfulness.

The relationship was new. At the moment, it was fueled by a palpable sexual chemistry. He didn't know where this was headed. But for now, he would give Layla what she needed. He would keep her safe.

Layla took a hot, super-quick shower. She had washed her hair that morning, so all she had to do was tuck it into the hotel-provided shower cap and use the extra time to shave her legs.

The bathroom door was locked. By her. Was that weird? Now, when she turned off the water, she listened carefully. If Joshua had returned already, he wasn't making a sound.

Staring at herself in the mirror was a mistake. She looked more scared than aroused. But that wasn't true. She wasn't scared of Josh.

Her body ached for his touch.

Maybe she was so comfortable being sexually vulnerable with him because their relationship hadn't begun recently. Admittedly, a years-long gap meant she didn't know him as well as she once had.

But she was convinced the essence of the man was the same.

She dried off and slipped into one of the silky nightgowns she had packed. Lots of women preferred black when they wanted to look sexy for a partner. Layla fared better in lighter, brighter colors. This sapphire blue set flattered her pale skin and blond hair.

Finally, she knew she couldn't dally any longer. She brushed her teeth. Put everything back in her toiletry kit. Took a deep breath. Showtime...

When she entered the bedroom from the bathroom, she thought for a moment that Josh still wasn't back. But then he moved, and she saw him. He had been standing at the window, half hidden by the heavy navy drapes.

A streak of dark red colored his cheekbones. "You look amazing," he said gruffly.

"Thanks." She didn't know what to do with her hands. Suddenly, she felt awkward, really awkward. "Your turn in the bathroom," she chirped brightly.

Josh closed the distance between them, took her in his arms and kissed her hungrily. "Don't be nervous, angel. That's what you look like. The angel on top of a Christmas tree. Perfect in every way."

She shook her head. "I'm not perfect, Josh. Nobody is." His embrace made her melt. All her reservations vanished. "I'm just a woman who wants to enjoy a sexy, interesting man. All night long."

"Hell, yeah," he muttered.

She pushed at his shoulders. "Go. I'll be waiting."

When he vanished into the bathroom, she folded back the covers on the bed and tested the sheets with her hand. Smooth as a baby's bottom. Cool and pristine.

She tossed aside most of the decorative pillows and chose two of the best ones to prop against the headboard. For the first time since meeting Josh again, a thought flitted through her mind. What if Josh was her forever guy, her chance to start over, to have a *real*, lasting relationship?

After her engagement to Richard ended, she had been more dispirited than heartbroken. She had known for some time that he wasn't the man she thought she knew. It showed up in little things. The way he was careless with her feelings. The many times he broke simple silly promises. Or forgot plans they made together.

With the hindsight of two long years, she had come to believe that she *made* herself think Richard was her heart's desire, because she was hitting that dreaded "thirty" mark, and she had wanted what so many of her friends had. Love. Stability.

In retrospect, Richard wasn't entirely to blame. The signs had been there, but Layla ignored them.

The cheating, though, that had broken her. It made her feel cheap and used, as if all Richard wanted was an in with her family, and once he accomplished that, he no longer had to pretend. Honestly, she stayed with him longer than she should have, because she was embarrassed to admit to her family how badly she had messed up.

It had been Chelsea who first saw the problems, Chelsea who encouraged Layla to dump a toxic relationship. For that, Layla would always be grateful to her older sister.

When the bathroom door swung open, Layla lost all interest in the past. The tall, lanky man—naked except for the fluffy hotel towel wrapped around his narrow hips—stood framed in the doorway with a charming grin.

Layla pretended to fan her face. "Oh my," she said. "I'm feeling a little woozy. All that testosterone…"

Josh chuckled. "That's the Layla I remember. Smart and sarcastic." He dropped a handful of packets on the table, crawled in bed beside her and nuzzled his face against her belly. "You smell delightful," he said, the words muffled.

She combed her finger through his thick, damp hair. "It's the hotel shower gel. You do, too."

Josh lifted his head and frowned. "I remember you always did have trouble taking a compliment. Even as a kid."

"I guess I thought you and Jordan only tolerated me. So if you said something nice, I didn't know how to take it."

He sat up. "And now?"

His gaze was serious. Her fingers itched to explore all that smooth, tanned skin. But he expected an answer.

"Well," she said slowly. "I think men tell women what they want to hear."

His expression darkened. "I'm neither a liar nor a cheat. And I was faithful to my wedding vows, for what it's worth."

"I know that, but…" She wrinkled her nose. "I was expecting more crazy sex with you, not a heart-to-heart."

He leaned on one elbow now, his head propped on his hand. She didn't like the way he seemed able to see inside her brain.

Josh's sculpted lips twisted in self-derision. "So you're not really interested in us getting to know each other better? You'd rather me bang you on the hood of a car and call it a day?" His mood was surly.

"Don't be crude. Of course not."

"Sure sounds like what you said."

"I'm not great with feelings." The words slipped out, involuntarily released from the truth vault. The Grandin family wasn't mushy.

His expression softened. "Come here, sexy thing."

She allowed him to tug her down and ease her onto her back. Now he leaned over her, surrounding her with his warmth and his delicious masculinity. "I thought guys liked to get straight to the main event," she muttered, feeling incredibly vulnerable amidst a warm, sultry arousal.

Josh toyed with one narrow strap of her nightgown. His fingers felt hot against her skin. The airconditioning in the room worked very well. In fact, she *could* blame her tightly furled nipples on that very thing.

But again, she would be denying the truth. She ached to feel his hands on her bare body.

Her partner had more patience than she did. He traced her collarbone, then pulled both straps off her shoulders, trapping her upper arms. He kissed the sensitive skin below her ear. Nibbled her earlobe. Rubbed the curves of her breasts through thin silk.

"Josh…" She said his name raggedly. Pleading.

His smile was oddly sweet. "I'm glad my brother asked me to take his place on that date."

"Me, too," Layla said. "Very glad." She paused, wanting him to understand. "Everybody thinks I had a crush on Jordan when we were kids, and it's true, I did. But that's because he was easier than you. With Jordan, what you see is what you get."

"I'm not sure I understand." Josh's gaze was watchful, his expression wary.

"You're deeper. You have layers. That was true even back then. I was a little scared of you, I think, especially when we got to high school. You made me feel odd. I didn't know what to do with those emotions. They were the beginnings of sexual awareness. I realize that now. But for a girl of fifteen, those reactions were intimidating. It was simpler to field Jordan's dumb jokes than to talk to you."

"If I hadn't been a clueless adolescent boy, maybe I could have made it easier for both of us."

"Maybe." She ran her hand over the stubble on his chin, glad he hadn't felt the need to shave. "I sometimes envy those people who find their soul mate in high school. But broken engagements…broken marriages. They feel like failures, don't they?"

"Definitely. I guess most of us have to learn life's lessons the hard way."

She tugged his head down and kissed him, shivering when his tongue stroked hers possessively. When she could breathe, she rested her cheek against his chest. "I'm happy to continue this conversation later. But the gorgeous man in my bed needs attention."

Josh laughed. "*He* does, or you do?"

When she slipped her hand beneath the towel and wrapped her fingers around his erection, he groaned. It was Layla's turn to grin. "Both, I think."

Perhaps because things had moved so fast between them in the beginning, now they were able to momentarily harness the need, to bank the embers.

"I want to touch you all over," she complained. Her arms were still trapped at her sides.

Josh ignored her pleas. Slowly, ever so slowly, he dragged the bodice of her nightgown to her waist. As he tongued her nipples and bit them gently, Layla clenched her fingers in the sheet at her hips. The sensation was indescribable.

His voice, when he spoke, was low and raspy. "You were a cute kid…and an even cuter young teenager. But, Layla, you've grown into a stunning woman."

The raw sincerity in his words couldn't be feigned. The way he looked at her made Layla want to believe in fairy tales. The ones where the prince claimed his maiden.

Her body was on fire. "Get me out of this," she begged.

He finished removing her nightgown. Now she was naked. She tugged at his damp bath towel until she could pull it from under his hips and toss it on the floor.

Josh stared at her. "I want to devour you, and I'm not sure how I feel about that. You make me reckless. Desperate."

"It must be contagious." She ran her hands over his taut abdomen and up his broad chest to his pecs. Her fingernails dug into his shoulders. "Maybe foreplay is overrated. I need you now. I want you now."

The relief on his face told her they were on the same page. He grabbed protection, sheathed himself and moved between her legs. But he paused, the skin stretched tight over his cheekbones, his eyes glittering. "Maybe after the first fifty or sixty times, we'll want to slow down."

Layla wrapped her legs around his waist. "Don't bet on it, cowboy."

When he surged deep, she couldn't breathe for a moment. It wasn't his weight on top of her that was the problem. He had braced himself on his elbows.

The lack of oxygen was *forgetting* to breathe. As Josh buried himself inside her, bumping up against the deepest reaches of her sex, shock jumbled her synapses. All of her senses went on overload. She was hot and cold at the same time. Trembling with exhilaration and at the same moment teetering on the brink of despair.

Nothing this good could last. Nothing this good was real.

Were they both courting sexual oblivion to avoid their problems?

It felt as if she was flying without a net. Perilously close to crashing into oblivion.

His harsh breathing mingled with hers. The words he uttered were sexual and earthy. Praise and pleading. Her body raced to a climax that exploded in her pelvis and behind her eyelids in shards of blinding light.

She whimpered and lifted into his thrusts, desperate for every last ounce of completion.

When Josh cursed and went rigid, she knew he had found the same bliss.

They dozed afterward. She didn't know how long. When she tried to get up and go to the bathroom, Josh clasped her wrist. "Don't go," he said, slurring the words.

"I'll be right back." She kissed his hand and freed herself.

A few minutes later, she crawled back under the covers and burrowed into his embrace. His body was hot and hard and so wonderfully different from hers. She slipped one of her legs between his powerful thighs and stretched an arm across his chest.

For the first time in her life, she didn't question her future. It was enough to let things unfold one day at a time. She would live in the moment.

She yawned, replete and content, and let the waves of mental, physical and emotional exhaustion wash over her.

Nine

When Josh jerked awake in the middle of the night, he had no clue where he was. Gradually, his racing heart slowed. Had he been dreaming? A nightmare?

Then reason returned. And a grateful embrace of reality. Layla was in his arms. Soft, warm, deeply unconscious. She made the cutest little snuffling noises when she slept.

He cataloged his physical state. Sexually sated, but with a boner that could pound nails. Still unsure about the future except to know that at this very moment an anonymous hotel room with this very specific woman was exactly where he wanted to be.

They had fallen asleep early. Now he'd had

enough rest to be energized already. But it would be selfish to wake Layla.

Surreptitiously, he peered at his watch. One thirty in the morning. His stomach was growling, and he needed to visit the john. Carefully, he moved a feminine arm. Then a leg. Layla grumbled in her sleep, turned away from him, but didn't wake up.

While he took care of business and washed up, all he thought about was making love to her again. He was rusty about dating rules. Could a guy get in trouble for coaxing a drowsy woman into having sex?

When he rejoined her, she recoiled from his cold feet. He moved them, but drew her closer, spooning her and filling his hands with her breasts. The curves and valleys were delightful. He could almost be satisfied with this.

But his body urged him to take more.

He wanted more. In fact, he trembled with the need to be inside her.

"Layla." He whispered her name, willing her to wake up. "Layla, sweetheart. Can you open your eyes?"

It seemed like eons, but it was probably only a minute or two.

She rolled onto her back and shoved the hair out of her eyes. "What?"

That single grumpy syllable didn't bode well for his plans. "I was hoping you might want to…you know…" He stroked her center.

Layla made a noise that was halfway between a protest and a moan.

"Was that a *yes*?" he asked hopefully.

"Do you have something against sleep?" Her sarcastic question was clearly rhetorical.

He kissed her, sliding his tongue deep into her mouth. Then he nuzzled her nose with his. "How can I sleep when a gorgeous, naked woman is in my bed driving me insane with her incredible body?"

"Over the top, Banks. Over the top."

He rubbed his erection against her thigh. "I'm dead serious. So serious."

Because there was a light burning in the bathroom, and he had left the door cracked, he could see the grin that finally lifted the corners of her mouth, even though her eyes remained stubbornly closed. "Single-minded, aren't you?"

He played with her breasts one at a time, teasing the nipples. Plumping the curves. "I'm gonna need a clear affirmative from you, Ms. Grandin. Audible consent. Please."

Finally, her long lashes lifted. Her blue eyes looked darker in the dim light. "Yes, Mr. Banks. I agree to have sex with you. Under one condition."

He tensed. "What is it?"

"You've got to feed me afterward. I'm starving."

Twenty minutes later, Josh flopped onto his back, his chest heaving. "Damn, woman. What was that thing you did with your tongue?"

Layla giggled, a young, innocent sound that was more like the girl he had once known than the sophisticated, capable woman with whom he had recently reconnected.

She yawned and stretched. "If we're going to have sex this much, I may need to bring snacks and a cooler."

"Okay, okay," he said rolling out of bed to fetch the room service menu. "What do you want?"

With a naked Josh sitting four feet away in all his glory, Layla *knew* what she wanted. But at this point in the relationship, it seemed prudent not to give the man any more ammunition than necessary. "Nachos?" she said.

He winced. "Seriously?"

"Fine," she huffed. "You throw out a suggestion."

"No. I'll give you one more chance."

"We could split a burger."

His gaze narrowed. "Medium rare?"

"Is there any other way?"

"Cheese?" he asked.

"Swiss and cheddar both."

"I can see you like to live on the edge."

She stretched her arms over her head, enjoying the way his gaze settled on her breasts and glazed over. "You would know. And it's all your fault. I was practically a nun before you came back to town. I think you've corrupted me."

Josh tossed the menu aside and ran a hand up the inside of her thigh, his eyes flashing fire, his cheeks flushing. "Room service can wait," he groaned. When he buried his face between her legs, she shrieked.

It was three o'clock before they got any food.

Layla sighed. "That might be the best cheese-burger I've ever eaten."

They were tucked up in bed, shoulder to shoulder, devouring their meal. Layla had insisted on protect-ing the fancy comforter with a couple of bath towels.

Josh leaned toward her and licked her chin. "Ketchup," he explained solemnly.

She batted his hand away when he tried to tug at the sheet she used to protect her modesty. "Behave."

He shrugged. "If you insist." After snitching a handful of fries from her plate because his were all gone, he shot her a sideways glance. "I want to know more about the grown-up Layla. What is it you love about the ranch?"

She smiled. "That's easy. The horses. I tell them all my secrets. I love the way they move and the joy they feel when they gallop. The smell of hay in the barns. The way the mares whinny when they want the colts to settle for the night."

Josh was silent for so long, she felt self-conscious.

"What?" she demanded. "Was that more than you wanted to know?"

"That was beautiful," he said gruffly.

She ate another french fry, because it was some-thing to do. "Not everything at the ranch is so po-etic. I'm handy with the business part. I've got an

MBA that I put to good use when Grandy and Dad let me." She stopped, overwhelmed anew by the remembrance that her grandfather was gone.

Josh slid an arm around her shoulders, comforting her without words. He sighed. "They're lucky to have you."

"I don't know," she said honestly, ruefully. "I've been thinking it might be time for me to move on."

"Why?"

"Well, if Daddy goes by Grandy's example, he'll clutch the reins until he's old and gray. And even then, Vic will be the one to take over. I'm not sure there's any point in me staying in the long term. I've thought about finding something else to do with my life. Maybe after my grandmother is gone. I don't want to disappoint her."

"I can't imagine you being a disappointment to anyone."

"That's sweet," she said. But Josh didn't see the whole picture. Layla had disappointed her parents right out of the gate by not being a boy. Chelsea was bad enough. But now *two* girls? Only the advent of Vic had satisfied the familial expectations. And poor Morgan was likely supposed to be a boy, too, to even the scales.

Layla set her plate on the bedside table. "I should probably get some more sleep," she said. "I need to be at the hospital by nine."

"Of course."

They put the room service tray out in the hall and

locked the door. Josh turned out the light. It was silent for a moment as they got comfortable under the covers. He didn't allow any distance between them.

Layla's eyes were closed when he spoke.

"You can stay here as long as you want, if you can be away from the ranch."

She studied his words for hidden meanings. Was he simply being nice, or was that an ongoing booty call? "Thank you," she said. "I suppose it will depend on Grammy. When they release her, I'll need to be out there to help."

"Makes sense."

She rested her cheek on his shoulder. "Why are you staying in this hotel instead of with your dad and brother?"

Something in him reacted. He either flinched or froze or *something*. At last, he answered her. "My brother asked me the same thing. I've been gone for a long time. I've needed space to do some thinking about what comes next."

"I thought you wanted to come home."

"I did. I do. But sometimes life takes a turn we don't expect."

Layla pretended to fall asleep after that. What did he mean?

Soon, she heard him breathing deeply. He was out cold.

Unfortunately, Layla was awake far longer, wondering if she was making a huge mistake. She liked Josh a lot. They had a history of sorts. He was the kind of man she could fall in love with...could marry. Start a family with.

Was she weaving crazy dreams?

Maybe *she* needed some space, too. Her world had been turned upside down in the last month. She was emotionally vulnerable. Perhaps it was time to take a step back and protect herself.

Josh ordered breakfast from room service while Layla was in the shower. The sun was bright, too bright for his eyes, which were gritty from lack of sleep. But he wouldn't change a thing.

When Layla exited the bathroom, she was fully dressed. And in a hurry.

She grimaced when she saw the food. "I'm so sorry, Josh. I don't have time to linger. I'm trying to get to the hospital before the doctor comes by." She kissed his cheek on the way to the door. "I'll let you know how Grammy is doing. Bye."

The door closed with a gentle slam. And then Josh was alone.

He ate two thirds of the food and left the rest. When he was dressed and ready, he pulled out his phone and checked flight schedules. If he hurried, he could catch a midmorning hop to Dallas and be back before bedtime. He had a few loose ends to tie up.

It was a long day. Air travel was becoming more and more of an endurance test. He could have chartered a small jet. But it seemed like an unnecessary expense at this juncture. So he endured the packed plane and the inevitable delays.

By the time he made it back to Royal, retrieved his car and drove from the airport to the hotel, he was exhausted. Only the prospect of seeing Layla again kept him going.

It was an unpleasant shock to enter his room and find no sign of the woman who had kept him awake half the night.

Only a note on the pillow gave him a clue.

He read it with a sinking feeling.

"Hey, Josh—Grammy was doing so well the doctor released her right after dinner this evening. We've all headed back to the ranch. I stopped by to grab my suitcase as I'm sure you've noticed. Thanks again for rescuing me on the street and for such a fun night. Talk soon, Layla."

He crumpled the sheet Layla had torn from a hotel notepad. Tossing it in the nearest wastebasket gave him a moment's satisfaction. But then he reneged and rescued it, flattening the paper between his fingers.

The depth of his disappointment was significant. Instead of another night of hot, wonderful sex, he was going to sleep alone.

Without Layla.

How had she come to be so important to him so quickly?

He slept fitfully and awoke at dawn. Though he had put it off, he knew it was time for a serious talk with his father and brother.

Three cups of coffee later, he was headed out to the Bankses' ranch. Their property was prosperous and productive, but not on the scale of either the Grandins' or the Lattimores'. Those two families were Royal royalty. He grinned at his own joke.

When he came here recently, the three men had spent most of their time in the barn and on horses riding the property. Today, as Josh walked into the warm, cozy kitchen at the old farmhouse, it was almost as if nothing at all had changed in the last week or the last decade. His dad and his twin brother were seated at the scarred oak table eating pancakes.

Jordan looked up with a grin. "We saved you some," he said. "Pull up a chair."

While Josh ate, his father read the *New York Times*. Jordan stared at his phone.

They had never been the kind of family to wade into deep conversational waters. Which made what Josh was about to do all the more difficult.

Eventually, he finished his meal and screwed up his courage. "Hey, you two. I have a question to ask. And I need you to think about it before you answer."

Each man looked up with an identical expression of bewilderment.

Bertram waved a hand. "Well, don't keep us in suspense."

Josh swallowed hard. "Would the two of you consider buying out my share of the ranch?"

Jordan's mouth fell open.

Josh's dad paled. "Hell, son. We were just razzing you the other day…giving you a hard time. Of course we want you back. You have to know that."

Josh's brother nodded. "We're excited to have you home."

"I believe you—I do. But I'm not sure staying is the right choice for me. Clearly, I don't have a great track record with big life changes. Still, it seems to me that the two of you have things running smoothly here. I know I could help, but it would be the path of least resistance. I really want to try something new."

Bertram stood and refilled his coffee cup. "Like what?" His father had been perturbed to hear Josh had quit his job.

"I'm not sure. I don't have everything pinned down yet. But as soon as I land on a plan, you'll be the first to know, I swear."

Jordan shook his head slowly. "Cash flow is not a problem. We're doing better than we ever have. If you want us to buy you out, Dad and I can swing it. But you wouldn't be a third wheel here at the ranch. You're family. You're my brother, my twin."

Josh was taken aback when Jordan hugged him spontaneously. He returned the hug, realizing how much he had given up when he moved away. "Thanks," he said, his throat tight. "That means a lot. You know I love this ranch. It's home. But you two have made it what it is. I think I need to let this be your baby. I'm going to carve out something for myself—or I will if I'm lucky. Call it an early midlife crisis, I guess. The divorce rattled me. I don't want to screw up my life that badly ever again."

Layla hadn't seen Josh in ten days. It seemed impossible, but the hours flew by. Taking care of Grammy kept the family busy. Her medications had been worked out, of course, but she seemed frail after her collapse. Too much stress, perhaps.

The family had fallen into a schedule that was working for the moment. Chelsea, Layla and Morgan split up the waking hours. Layla's parents and brother took turns occupying the extra twin bed in Grammy's bedroom overnight. It was the one Victor Senior had slept in.

Miriam was grieving. They all were. But each day got a little easier.

One afternoon when Layla was off the clock, she went for a drive, needing to get out of the house and clear her head. Caring for her grandmother had turned out to be the perfect distraction to avoid thinking about Josh.

What was she going to do about him?

The two of them hadn't even talked on the phone. But they had texted now and then. She presumed he was busy, though he didn't give her any details, and she didn't ask. Miriam's health was the usual topic of conversation.

One night late, Layla got a short text.

I miss you...

Her heart did a funny little flip in her chest. She felt like a teenage girl crushing on a boy who smiled at her.

I miss you, too…

That was it. Just those two texts. And then nothing. But she wondered if Josh was just missing the sex, or did he really have feelings for her?

It was hard to read his mind. Not that she had been particularly forthcoming about her own feelings. Thinking about Josh made her ache. Though she had tried to downplay her emotions, even to herself, the truth was impossible to ignore. She was maybe/possibly falling for Joshua Banks.

He was likely being a gentleman, trying to respect the fact that Layla had a lot of responsibilities at the moment.

She drove aimlessly at first, leaving the town limits and seeking out the open road. Sunshine and blue skies were mood boosters, but it wasn't enough.

Eventually, she found herself headed toward the spot where Josh had made love to her for the first time. When she found the small hilltop, she parked her car and got out. If she closed her eyes, she could remember that afternoon in Technicolor detail.

There had been so much urgency, so much heat. The attraction wasn't one-sided. That much she knew. They had both been hungry, desperate to connect in the most intimate ways possible.

Thinking of those hours made her face hot with a blush that emanated from deep inside her. *Wanton* and *reckless* were not words she associated with herself.

But with Josh, she felt like a different person.

When she spent the night with him at the hotel, the magnetic lure had only strengthened. Pheromones on steroids.

Could that kind of sexual compatibility be only physical? Sex with Richard had been enjoyable. But not earth-shattering. Why were she and Josh combustible?

She didn't want to believe she had deep feelings for him. He was coming off a messy divorce. Admittedly, he and his wife hadn't been together in over two years before that. But still. The man might have a few *issues*.

Most friends she knew who had divorced weren't eager to jump back into any kind of serious relationship.

The Spring Luncheon at the Cattleman's Club was coming up very soon. Josh had agreed to be her date. Would that be the end of this fling or the beginning of a new chapter?

Truthfully, she was scared to make the next move. Josh had the power to hurt her, though he might not realize it. If he wasn't interested in anything more than sex, she would have to extricate herself gracefully.

She knew people who enjoyed physical affairs

without messy entanglements, but Layla wasn't made that way.

As the wind cooled her skin and sent her hair flying around her head, she knew this was a critical point in her life. She had never found validation in her family. Not really. To them, she was just Layla. Always around. Always available.

But surely there was more to life than being the middle child of four, as odd as that sounded. Who was she? What did she want? Was she willing to fight for Josh? Really, it was more than that. She could bring peace and purpose and challenge to her life with or without a man. Suddenly, one of the puzzle pieces fell into place.

Excitement buzzed in her veins. She spared one last wistful glance for the place where she had first felt the warmth of Josh's single-minded lovemaking, and then she drove quickly back into town.

One of her college classmates was a Realtor now. Layla burst into her office, out of breath and hopeful. Shana was a successful Black woman who possessed the kind of personality that made her a natural with customers.

After they exchanged pleasantries, Layla handed over her phone, where she had captured a screenshot of latitude and longitude. "I want to find out about this property," she said. "It looks like an old farm that hasn't been worked in years. I might want to buy it if the price is right."

Shana stared at the photo and then typed something into her computer. And then more. She frowned. "The owners were elderly. They died back in January, both of them. They had two heirs, a son and a daughter in their sixties. The property was definitely for sale, but now the listing says *not available*."

Layla's heart sank. "What does that mean? It doesn't say *sold*?"

"I'll get to the bottom of it," Shana promised. "And in the meantime, why don't I start looking for other properties? You can email me a list of what features you're interested in…acreage…etc. I know I can find something you'll like."

"Thanks," Layla said. "I appreciate it."

Ten

Back in the car, Layla blew her nose, trying to swallow the disappointment that made her eyes sting. She'd been on an impulsive errand anyway. In her head, she had already been building a cute house, right on the spot where Josh parked his car with a view of the surrounding countryside.

How silly and sad was that? Memorializing one amazing encounter with a man who was as mysterious as he was sexy.

Back at home, she found Chelsea on the back porch having coffee. "Where have *you* been?" her older sister asked.

"I went for a drive."

"To see Josh Banks?" Chelsea asked it with a teasing smile. Layla had shared only the G-rated details of her time with Josh.

"Nope. I don't think he's interested in anything serious. And besides, I've had far too much humiliation to go chasing after another man who doesn't know what the word *commitment* means."

"I can't imagine Joshua Banks cheating on a woman. He's always been a straight arrow, hasn't he?"

"He has. But I think that proves my point. It's been over a week. He hasn't asked me out again. I imagine he has other things on his mind besides me."

"I'm sorry, Layla. I could hear in your voice how much you liked him."

"It's not just that. I'm thinking about leaving the ranch. Dad is hung up on this Vic idea, and even if he ever relents, *you'll* be the logical choice to run things, not me. I've been the invisible Grandin my whole life. Is it selfish of me to want a guy to think I hung the moon? To give me his undying devotion?"

That last part was tongue-in-cheek. Chelsea heard the underlying plea and hugged her tightly. "You have to know that you're always welcome here, no matter who's in charge. And as for wanting more in the relationship department, well, don't give up on men."

"I'm not. But they sure make life complicated." She was ready to shift the subject to something less personal. "By the way, I forgot to tell you about one unpleasant experience I had."

"With Josh?" Chelsea seemed shocked.

"Not exactly. He and I were having dinner when this strange man showed up at our table. He introduced himself as Nolan Thurston, *Heath* Thurston's brother."

Now Chelsea's face reflected even more shock. "What did he do? What did he want? Did he threaten you?"

"Oh, no. Exactly the opposite. He asked if you and I might have lunch with him to *talk things out*. He thought we could come to some kind of understanding, I guess. But you know he was probably a spy for his brother...trying to find out what our family knows about the oil rights situation...what we're thinking."

"He hasn't contacted you again?" Chelsea asked.

"No. That's why I forgot about it until now. Why on earth do you care?"

"Well, it might not hurt for us to do the same. Get information from him. Strengthen our position."

"I don't want to have anything to do with either of the Thurstons." Layla still felt guilty about keeping her grandmother's secret.

"Oh, well. It may be a nonissue." Chelsea stood and collected her cup and saucer. "Will you sit with Grandmother for half an hour? I'm supposed to relieve Morgan, but I've got an important Zoom call. Won't take me long."

"Sure," Layla said.

When she reached Grammy's room, Morgan put

a finger to her lips. "Shh," she whispered. "She just fell asleep."

The two women stepped out into the hall. "How is she?" Layla asked.

Morgan smiled. "Really good overall. She's eating well. But I know she's grieving more than she wants us to see. You hear about people in long marriages dying of broken hearts when they lose a partner. It's selfish, I guess, but I hope she won't go too soon. I need Grammy. We all do."

"Definitely." Layla surveyed her baby sister's red hair and blue eyes and the shadows under those eyes. Morgan was the only one in the family who didn't work on the ranch. She owned a boutique in town called The Rancher's Daughter. It surely hadn't been easy to find the time to help out, but she had carried her share of the load.

Layla spoke impulsively. "Why don't you let me cover your hours tomorrow? You look beat."

Morgan's expression was wistful. "I'm tired, yes. And I appreciate the offer. But I feel so conscious now that our time with her is limited. I don't want to have any regrets."

"I understand. Still, if the shop and all this gets to be too much, let me know."

When Layla slipped quietly into the dimly lit bedroom, her grandmother opened her eyes, her expression mutinous. "I could hear the two of you whispering out in the hall. Talking about me, I'll bet. I'm not an invalid."

Layla sat down beside the bed. "Of course you're not. We were just being quiet because Morgan said you were asleep. Were you playing possum?"

That made Grammy smile. "I *was* asleep," she said. "But it was just a catnap." She sat up in the bed. "Will you take me to the back porch? I need some sun."

"Sure. It's a beautiful day."

Miriam Grandin wasn't about to accept help she didn't need. Though Layla held the wheelchair steady, her grandmother stood up and then seated herself. Layla tucked a fluffy afghan around her knees. "Here we go."

The old woman perked up even more when they got outside. When the housekeeper checked on them, Layla asked for cookies and cocoa. The calendar might say spring, but it was never out of season for Grammy's favorites.

With the wheelchair by the porch rail, Miriam could tip her face toward the sky. "This is nice," she said. "I'm damn tired of staying inside."

Layla smothered a snort of laughter. She loved her grandmother's indomitable spirit. Morgan probably didn't have a thing to worry about.

"Well," she said. "You're doing great. I don't see why you can't gradually get back to your normal schedule."

"The new normal, you mean."

The gentle rebuke reminded Layla that Victor

Grandin Sr. still cast a long shadow. "Yes, ma'am," she said meekly.

"So tell me what's going on with you and the Banks boy."

Layla flushed. "This family gossips more than the old biddies in town."

"You can't blame us. After the debacle with your Richard person, we just want to see you happy again."

"I'm happy," Layla muttered.

"Doesn't look like it at the moment. You should be out having fun. Now that I'm not at death's door anymore, I'll hire a nice girl to sit with me during the day. The rest of you need to get on with your lives."

"We love you, Grammy."

"I know that. But you've done enough."

Layla wouldn't win that argument, so she changed the subject. Her grandmother was strong enough now to have this discussion. "Grammy," she said. "Don't you think we need to tell the others about Grandy's journal? I feel bad keeping it from them."

Miriam shrugged. "No point in it. Without the paperwork, that journal doesn't mean a thing. It wouldn't hold up in court. Relax, girl. That fancy-ass investigator my son hired will follow the trail. Time enough to worry about things when his work is done."

"Okay..." Layla didn't want to go against her grandmother's wishes. And in this case, maybe she was right. The legalities were what mattered. No substantiated paperwork, no claim.

Three days later, Layla stood in front of the full-length mirror in her closet and surveyed her choice of outfit. Josh was picking her up for the noon event at the Texas Cattleman's Club in an hour. She had already changed three times.

First, she had picked out a tangerine Jackie O–style dress. It was sophisticated and springlike, but she didn't feel quite right in it. Next there was a trendy pantsuit, teal with a floral silk blouse to match. The cut of the jacket and pants flattered her figure, but again, she gave it a thumbs-down.

Now she wore a riskier choice. The dress she had chosen was blush-pink silk with a low neckline and spaghetti straps. The waist was fitted, then flared into a flirty skirt that stopped a few inches above her knees.

The layered skirt alternated between the lighter pink silk and a more vivid rosy shade of tulle that peeked out when she moved. Her shoes were three-inch heels in a nude color that didn't detract from the dress.

Jewelry had been a hard choice, but she settled on a single-diamond pendant that rode demurely on the slope of her breasts. Matching studs adorned her ears.

Last, but not least, she carried a pink-flamingo

clutch that perfectly completed the underlayers of her skirt.

On a normal day at the club, this outfit would definitely be over-the-top. But the Spring Luncheon was a notable social event. Layla wouldn't stand out for being overdressed. Though the men would be in dark suits, the female plumage would run the gamut.

Last year, one of Layla's old high school class-mates—renowned for making an entrance wherever she went—showed up in skintight silver lamé. The gossipmongers had a field day with that one. But not long after, the woman snagged husband number two, so as a strategy, it worked.

Layla's heart raced, and her cheeks matched her dress. The wardrobe choice wasn't the only thing giving her heartburn. It was the text she'd received earlier from Josh.

I'd like for you to spend the rest of the afternoon and evening with me. If you're interested, pack a bag...

On the one hand, she loved his direct communi-cation. It was clear and to the point. But why had he waited so long to coax her into his bed again? To be fair, she had disappeared from his hotel room after the first time and only left a note. But surely he un-derstood why.

Though she had a ton of reservations about get-ting in deeper with a sexual relationship that might never progress to anything else, she didn't have the will to say no.

She wanted Josh. It was risky. It made her vulnerable.

But she couldn't give up a man who made her feel both exhilarated and safe. It was a fascinating combination.

Though it seemed silly, she didn't put her suitcase on the bed. She kept it in the closet and packed it surreptitiously, not wanting Chelsea to wander in and ask uncomfortable questions.

A family friend was coming to sit with Grammy. No one had been hired yet. Only Grammy thought that was a good idea.

The remaining six Grandins were going together to the club. Except for Layla. She had invented an excuse about having to leave earlier. No one had questioned her. If she was lucky, she could go down the stairs that exited the side of the house. She had asked Josh not to ring the bell, but to text her when he arrived.

If he thought the request odd, he didn't let on.

Her phone dinged at exactly 11:13. Her ride was two minutes early. It wasn't a forty-five-minute drive to the club, but Layla wanted to disappear from the house before her parents and siblings congregated.

She tucked her purse under her arm, checked her reflection one last time and picked up the small suitcase. It wasn't heavy. A woman didn't need much when she was planning on being naked most of the time.

She choked back a laugh as she tiptoed down the stairs. When she rounded the corner of the house, Josh was standing beside his car. From the look on his face, she had to assume her outfit was on point.

He shook his head slowly as he looked her over from head to toe, his eyes flashing with male appreciation. "You look incredible, Layla. Are you sure we have to go to the Cattleman's Club luncheon?"

The question was clearly rhetorical. She hoped. "Thank you for the compliment, but I need to see and be seen," she said, smiling. "We're fighting this oil rights claim, so all the Grandins will be front and center today."

He reached out and took her suitcase. After placing it in the trunk of his car, he came around and opened the passenger side. "In you go." He tucked pieces of her flyaway skirt beneath her leg before carefully closing the door.

When he was behind the wheel with the engine started and the AC blowing cool air, he faced her. His expression was not so lighthearted now.

"What's wrong?" she asked, experiencing a fillip of alarm.

"I've missed you," he said gruffly. Carefully, he leaned forward and kissed her cheek. Then he followed it up with a second one just below her ear.

Everything inside her went on high alert. Wow. With only two chaste kisses, the man could make the cells in her body sizzle with wanting him.

When she would have pressed closer, he held her

at arm's length with a rueful smile. His hands were warm on her bare shoulders. "No more," he said. "If I start kissing you like I really want to, we'll never get to the club."

For half a second, she debated blowing off the big event and going back to Josh's hotel room. Unfortunately, she had always been the conscientious type.

Sometimes being a mature, responsible adult sucked.

Josh gripped the steering wheel with damp hands. His throat was dry. His chest was tight. Layla was everything he wanted in a woman. Smart. Funny. Sexy as hell. The faint scent of her perfume made the confines of the car a torture chamber for a man desperate to get laid ASAP. Seeing Layla appear with suitcase in hand moments ago had been a huge relief.

He hadn't been one hundred percent positive she wanted a do-over.

She looked different today, and it wasn't just the clothes, though that dress was tantalizing and provocative. Her body was curved in all the right places.

Maybe it was the way she wore her hair. This morning, it was twisted on top of her head in the kind of intricate style women seem to instinctively know how to do.

Unfortunately, the updo bared the provocative feminine real estate at the top of her spine. Which made Josh's hungry fascination about a thousand times more intense. All he could think about was nibbling the back of her neck while he reached around and cupped her bare breasts.

And they *would* be bare. No matter how gorgeous the dress, he planned to have her out of it as soon as possible.

Already, he was calculating how long they would have to stay at the club before he could spirit her away.

"You're awfully quiet today," he said as he threaded his way through the streets of Royal proper.

Layla sighed. "I've been looking forward to seeing you again, but I'm worried about the two of us."

"Why is that?"

"I'm in my thirties already. I should have my life together by now. But I've held men at a distance, because I felt so betrayed and rejected by Richard. I wish I could say I was in love with him, but I wasn't. And you've admitted you weren't in love with your wife. Not the kind of forever love we're supposed to want."

"Where are you going with this, Layla? No offense, but we're pulling up at the club in about six and a half minutes. Not exactly the time for a heart-to-heart."

"That's probably why I did it," she said. "I'm scared to get hurt again." She half turned in her seat. Now he sensed her staring at him, even though he kept his eyes on the road. "You're a great guy," she said. "But…"

"But what?" He felt his blood pressure rise, and not in a pleasant way.

Layla twisted a piece of her skirt restlessly. "Statistics for divorced people aren't good when it comes to future success with new partners."

"You sound like you've been reading encyclopedias," he grumbled, feeling his neck get hot. He *was* divorced. No way around it. If he could go back and undo all his mistakes, he would. But he was stuck with his checkered past. The missteps had taught him what was valuable and what was dross.

"I don't think encyclopedias exist anymore, do they?" she said.

"We're getting off track." He pulled into a parking space, slammed the car into Park and faced her, trying not to glower. "If you and I together is such a risky proposition, why did you bring a suitcase?"

Layla's bottom lip trembled. Her dewy cheeks were flushed—a shade of pink that almost matched her dress. Her blue eyes shimmered with something he couldn't quite decipher. It almost looked as if she might cry, but that made no sense.

They were together. On a day that was supposed to be fun.

"You didn't answer my question," he said quietly. "Why did you bring a suitcase if you're breaking things off?"

Her chin came up. "I never said that. Besides, there's nothing to break off. You and I are friends."

"With benefits." He wouldn't let her brush aside the incredible moments when they had been intimate—

first at the picnic and later in his hotel room. "I assumed you didn't have sex with me on a whim."

"I didn't," she whispered.

"But you've changed your mind? Because you think I'm on the rebound, and you've got sucky taste in men? Is that it in a nutshell?"

"You should have been a lawyer, Josh." Her eyes shot blue sparks. "And for the record, I don't like being interrogated."

Years ago, he had learned to keep his temper under control. Now it popped and sizzled, dangerously close to igniting. "Then what *do* you like, Layla? Tell me."

Even though they were early, he had deliberately chosen a parking space at the far reaches of the parking lot. It meant they would have to walk a fair distance to get to the club entrance, but for now, there were no cars anywhere close to them. Which was a good thing, because this argument didn't need witnesses.

Her continued silence pushed him closer to the edge. "What *do* you like, Layla? If we're such an unlikely pair, what *do* you like?"

Without warning, she put both hands on the sides of his neck and pulled him closer. Now he could see the layers of blue in her pupils, layers that threatened to submerge him and drown him.

"I thought it was obvious," she said, the words husky. "I like having sex with you."

When Layla pressed her mouth to his, he jerked,

shocked and stunned and crazy in lust with her. "Yes," he stuttered as her tongue and lips dueled with his.

He slid a hand inside the top of her dress and found bare skin beneath what appeared to be a lacy nothing of a bra. He squeezed reverently. "I've laid awake every night thinking about this. About you."

She groaned, wrapping her arms around his neck and teasing the whorl of his ear with her talented tongue. "Yes."

What was she saying yes to? Was she having the same sleepless nights?

He rubbed her nipple, feeling it peak beneath his fingertips. "It scares me how much I want you," he confessed. It was true. Layla brought him peace and agitation in equal measure. Her presence in his arms helped him reclaim the contentment of his child-hood when his biggest problem was how to keep his brother from eating the last ice-cream sandwich in the freezer. But touching her, making love to her, created the frenzied agitation of knowing he had no control when it came to Layla.

He was moments away from dragging her into the back seat and taking her wildly when some tiny voice inside his head whispered reason. Already, cars were lining up closer and closer in the parking lot. Today was a big deal, especially so for Layla and her family.

It took every ounce of determination he could muster to peel her arms from around his neck and ease her over into her seat. "Fix your lipstick," he muttered, already missing her warmth.

Her gaze was hazy and unfocused. There was a tiny red patch on her collarbone where he had nibbled her like the rarest of gourmet delights. She put a hand to her mouth. "What time is it?"

"A quarter till twelve."

"Oh my gosh." Frantically, she searched for her purse. The flamingo nested in the floor of the car. Layla grabbed it and found what she needed.

He pulled the visor down for her. "Don't worry. We didn't mess up much."

Not for the world would he mention that she had the look of a woman who had just experienced orgasmic pleasure. The dreamy expression in her eyes. Warm, glowing skin all over that made her seem young and lush. Lips puffy from his hungry kisses.

She was no ingenue, and yet she projected innocence and sweetness. The fact that she seemed unaware of her appeal made her all the sexier. When Layla was satisfied with her face and her hair, he shut off the engine. It was going to be a scorcher today.

He touched her arm. "Shall we make an appearance, Ms. Grandin?"

He saw Layla take a deep breath as she checked her reflection one last time. Then she curled her hand around his. "Thank you for bringing me today."

"Of course. And by the way, am I supposed to play the part of your adoring boyfriend, so the whole town will know Richard the ass is a distant memory?"

Her lips tilted up in a smile. "I like the way you think."

"The role isn't much of a stretch," he said, brushing the backs of his fingers across her soft cheek.

Big blue eyes searched his. Was she looking for assurance? The best way he could give her that was to keep showing up.

"Come on," he said. "Let's do this…"

Eleven

Layla had been coming to the Texas Cattleman's Club since she was a child. Sometimes her family enjoyed Sunday brunch on the terrace. On other occasions, she tagged along when her mother met friends for lunch. And then there were the holiday memories. The huge tree in the lobby entrance. The lavish parties. Cookies and stockings and other goodies. Adult laughter and conversation. Usually an appearance by Santa Claus.

As the daughter of a wealthy rancher, she had always been welcomed at the club. But even as a teenager, she had been aware of a rigid hierarchy that took some in and kept others out. Fortunately, in recent years as some of the old guard passed on and newer, more progressive ideas were incorporated, the membership had become more inclusive. Now she paid her dues like all the other members.

Josh had her arm tucked in his elbow. She liked how that felt. Honestly, she enjoyed the way other women in the room looked him over with interest. Though he'd told her he still maintained his TCC membership, it had probably been at least six or eight years since he had entered this historic building.

Appetizers were being served on small tables scattered around the main hallway. Fresh flowers hung from brass sconces. Someone had even whimsically decorated a stuffed moose head with a tiara of daisies.

Layla wasn't a particular fan of hunting trophies, but some of them remained, even after renovations and redecorating. A small brass plaque below each specimen recorded the hunter and the date. Taxidermists in Royal would always have a job.

She and Josh grabbed a couple of plates. The shrimp and cocktail sauce were legendary. Not to mention the tiny Angus beef sliders. "Pace yourself," she warned her companion. "You'll want to save room for lunch." She wiped her lips with a napkin. "Would you mind if I touch base with a few folks?"

He grinned. "With or without me?"

"Don't you know people?" she asked, cocking her head and staring at him to see if he was kidding.

"Go," he said. "It's been a while, but I still recognize half the folks in this room. I'll be fine."

She squeezed his hand and walked away, conscious of his gaze on her back. That little interlude in the car had left her with quivery knees and a marked lack of enthusiasm for socializing. Even so, she had work to do.

She found the Lattimores standing in two tight circles and greeted them a few at a time. Jonathan and Jayden. Alexa and Caitlyn. Their parents, Ben and Barbara.

Even though Alexa had flown in to attend the funeral of Layla's grandfather, she had returned for this event, probably at her parents' urging. Layla tugged her to a quiet corner. "How are things at your house?" she asked.

Alexa grimaced. Her long black curls and dark brown eyes made her stand out. The gorgeous Black woman sighed. "Like your family, everyone is worried about the oil rights business. And absolutely no one can understand why my grandfather would put *our* ranch at risk, when it was your uncle who fathered a child."

"I know I said it once, but you should really come home and help them. They need a lawyer they can trust. Surely your firm will give you a leave of absence... right? For a family crisis?"

"Poor naive Layla." Alexa grinned so Layla would know she was kidding. "My bosses are all about billable hours."

"But you'll try?"

"I don't know," Alexa said, looking torn. "It's not a good time for me."

"Emergencies never are."

Chelsea appeared at Layla's elbow, seeming out of breath. "Hey, Alexa," she said. "Glad to see you again. If you don't mind, I need to borrow my sister for a moment."

Alexa waved a hand. "She's all yours."

Before Layla could blink, Chelsea had backed her into a corner. Literally. Her older sister frowned. "I just peeked in the dining room. Your place card isn't at our table. Are you planning to skip the meal? Geez, Layla. You know this is an important day."

Layla shook her head slowly. "Calm down. Of course I know. Show of strength and all that."

"So why aren't you going to eat lunch?"

"Did it ever occur to you that my place card might be at another table?"

Chelsea's jaw dropped. "You're with someone?"

"Joshua Banks."

Chelsea's expression of bewilderment was comical. "But I thought you said that situation wasn't going anywhere. You told me you wanted someone with no emotional baggage, a man who would worship the ground you walk on."

"Now, you're editorializing." Layla laughed. "Relax. I'll be in the dining room the whole time. But Josh and I have a table for two."

"And *after* lunch?" Chelsea raised an eyebrow.

Layla felt her face get hot. "After lunch, we'll

see." She took her sister's arm. "Come on. Let's mingle for a few minutes. We need the support of the
town if this oil rights business gets ugly. Schmooz-
ing 'R' Us."

She and Chelsea worked the room for fifteen minutes. Then the president of the club announced that
lunch was ready to be served. En masse, the crowd
of people began moving toward the dining room.

Chelsea went up on her tiptoes. "So where *is*
Joshua Banks? Surely you didn't leave him alone in
this room of female piranhas."

Layla might have miscalculated. Josh was fresh
meat on the social scene. Why hadn't she thought
of that? "He'll be fine," she said, hoping her words
were true.

Suddenly, she spotted him, and her vision narrowed. *Wow.* Chelsea saw him at the same moment.
She whistled under her breath. "Your man looks
pretty darned gorgeous in that tailored suit. The
Joshua I remember didn't have a body like that. He
was skinny and quiet and barely looked at girls."

"He's changed," Layla muttered. Suddenly, she
wanted nothing more than to be at his side. But there
were several hundred people separating them.

She and Chelsea allowed themselves to be jostled
forward in the direction of lunch. Once they were
inside the dining room, guests milled about, finding
their spots. A few families, like the Grandins and the
Lattimores, had tables for six or eight.

There were multiple two-tops, including the one

where Heath Thurston sat alone at first. But the crowd parted when *Nolan* Thurston strode through the melee as if he owned the place. He shook his brother's hand and sat down.

Behind Layla's shoulder, she heard someone whisper. *I thought those two were estranged. Nolan hasn't lived here in years.*

Chelsea bristled and leaned in to whisper in Layla's ear. "There's our arch enemy Heath Thurston. Have you noticed that *he* hasn't spoken to us? At all? He's letting his lawyers do the dirty work."

"That makes sense," Layla said. "Keeps everything professional and clean. The other guy is the one I told you about who wants to have lunch with us. *Nolan* Thurston. The two Thurstons are twins in case you can't tell."

"Too many of those in this town," Chelsea muttered. "I guess we should sit down."

But Layla noticed that her sister's attention lingered on Nolan.

Layla was just about to cross the room to her table when someone came up behind her and put a hand on her shoulder. "Layla Grandin," the voice boomed. "Hot damn. If I'd known you grew up so beautiful, I'd never have let my brother take my place."

Before she could protest, Jordan Banks whirled her around, hugged her and kissed her square on the lips. Even for a childhood friend, his greeting was a bit much.

She freed herself as quickly as she could. "Hello,

Jordan. How are you?" He did look very much like his brother, but Layla could clearly see the differences.

Jordan shoved his hands in his pockets and rocked back on his heels. "I'm great. Texas-size great. Sorry I couldn't take you to the concert."

"No worries. I had a lovely time with Josh. I guess you and your dad are pretty happy to have him back at the ranch."

Jordan's expression changed visibly. In fact, he looked uncomfortable. That was so unlike him, Layla's stomach flipped. "What did I say?" she asked, trying to make a joke of it and failing miserably.

"I assumed he would have told you," Jordan said. "Joshua has decided he wants Dad and me to buy out his share."

Layla's chest tightened. "Well, he probably hasn't had a chance to say anything," she said, doing her best to pretend this was no big deal. "My grandmother has been ill, and I've been staying with her a lot. This is the first time Josh and I have seen each other in days. Two busy people. You know how it is."

Her scrambled explanation wiped the uncertainty off Jordan's face. Relief tinged his expression. "I'm sure he'll catch you up," he said. "I'd better get to my seat. Dad and I are together today."

"No date?" she asked, wondering if she could make him squirm. Jordan laughed and gave her a naughty grin. "She'll be waiting on me later," he said.

Layla made her way across the room, realizing as she approached her table that Josh had a frown on his face. "Sorry," she said. "Did you think I was never coming?"

"Nah." His smile didn't reach his eyes.

"Are you okay?" she asked, flipping out her napkin and spreading it in her lap.

"Sure," he said. "I see you and Jordan ran into each other."

Her mind raced. Was that pique in his voice? Surely he didn't think Layla had invited the over-the-top greeting or that she was at all interested, despite her old crush. "Your brother can be a bit much," she said. "But yes. We haven't seen each other in at least four years, I think."

The conversation was suspended when the emcee stood at the podium, made a few announcements and then handed out several awards for businesses that had grown substantially in the past year. Finally, the salad course came out.

Thankfully, Josh seemed to shake off his funk. He was funny and charming, and everything a woman could want in a date.

At one point, he grilled her. "You didn't tell your family that you and I were coming to this shindig together, did you? They've all been staring at us for half an hour."

She winced. "Sorry about that. They would have made a fuss. I thought it was easier this way."

"Do I embarrass you, Ms. Grandin?" he asked in a gentle voice.

"Of course not," she said, avoiding his perceptive gaze. "Don't be silly. But I didn't see the point in making a big deal about our date. It's not like we're official or anything."

"Official?" Some of the humor left his face.

"Don't be difficult," she said, lowering her voice. "You know we're just having fun. Who knows what the future will bring?"

"Indeed."

She never knew blue eyes could freeze ice cold. Josh's snarky response lit her temper. *He* was the one making plans to cut himself loose from the ranch where he owned a third of a share, the ranch where he had grown up, the ranch where he had spent many an hour raising hell with his brother and Layla.

The curl of hurt in her stomach grew tighter.

She pushed her uneaten salad away and then had to face the main course.

The pasta primavera was both beautiful and delicious. She poked at it, managing to eat enough bites not to draw attention to herself.

In the end, she focused her unhappiness on the Thurston brothers. "Look at them," she hissed in a low voice. "Sitting there in front of God and everybody as if they're pure as the driven snow."

Josh had been quiet throughout the meal, but unlike Layla, he had cleaned his plate. "They're not criminals. Just because they're claiming oil rights that they think belong to their family doesn't mean they're being vindictive."

"So you're taking their side?" She knew she was being unreasonable, but why wasn't he telling her about his decision not to work on the Bankses' ranch? That was news. Big news.

The dessert course was mostly silent.

Josh had no clue what was going on with Layla. She was upset. That much was clear. He didn't want to think her mood had anything to do with Jordan. Josh had felt sick to his stomach when his brother kissed Layla right on the mouth.

To be fair, Jordan's ebullience was nothing unusual. He was like that with most women. Heck, Josh had seen him hug men and lift them off their feet.

Abruptly, Josh stood. "If you'll excuse me, I need to go to the restroom." He exited the dining room and exhaled. Though the club was well air-conditioned, with that many people in one place, the temperature was rising.

When he came out of the men's room, he nearly bumped into Nolan Thurston. Both of them paused, feeling the awkward moment.

Josh stared at him. "Maybe you and your brother should rethink this oil rights business. The Grandins have a lot of clout in this town."

"Is that a threat, or are you pissed that we're upsetting your girlfriend?"

"If your mother or your sister was entitled to

something—and that's a big *if*—it doesn't follow that the two of you automatically have a claim. Why don't you let this go? Do you have a grudge against Layla's family? Is that it?"

Nolan's gaze narrowed. "What my brother and I are doing is up to us. You wouldn't begin to understand. So I think you should stay out of it. And a word of warning—if you're interested in anything serious with Layla Grandin, you'd better stake a claim. You aren't the only man in Royal to notice her. Things you care about can be taken away in a heartbeat. Be grateful for what you have."

Before Josh could craft a cutting response, Nolan disappeared down the hall.

The man's words lingered, though.

Oddly, Josh didn't think Nolan was a bad guy. But he couldn't figure him out.

Back in the dining room, the luncheon was winding down. People were beginning to leave. He saw Layla with the Lattimore crew.

When Josh joined them, Layla made a general introduction. "I don't know if you all remember Joshua Banks. He moved to Dallas a number of years ago. His dad is Bertram Banks, and Joshua's brother is Jordan."

After a round of handshakes, Layla filled in the gaps. "Jonathan and Jayden Lattimore. Next, their sister and my good friend Alexa, who now lives in Miami, and last, but not least, the baby of the family, Caitlyn."

Josh nodded. Caitlyn's smile was shy, but charming. "Nice to meet you all," he said.

Alexa raised an eyebrow. "I noticed the table for two. Are you the new man in Layla's life?"

Silence fell. Layla's cheeks turned pink. The four Lattimore siblings gave him measured glances as if to say he might not be good enough for their friend. Josh cleared his throat. "Well, I'm a man, and Layla is spending the day with me. As for the rest of it, I guess that remains to be seen."

Layla shot him a look of gratitude and took his arm. "It was great to be with you all today. I'm sure Josh has appreciated the third-degree, so he and I are going to scoot out of here. I'll see you soon."

In the parking lot, they strolled toward the car. He shot his quiet companion a sideways glance. "You up for a drive?"

"I'd love that," Layla said.

He still couldn't pin down her mood. But he was relying on sunshine and speed to smooth any rough edges. It was an impulse on his part to return to the spot where their physical relationship had begun so spectacularly.

When he parked on the exact same hilltop, they got out. Layla's shoes weren't suitable for the rough ground, so she took them off and tossed them in the car.

"Too bad we don't have a quilt," he joked.

Layla's expression was hard to read. "Can I tell you a secret?"

"Sure."

"I spoke with a Realtor this week about buying this property."

"You're kidding."

"Nope."

"But what about the Grandin ranch?"

She shrugged, her expression mutinous. "They don't really need me. Vic is going to take over one day, and if not him, then Chelsea. I've started thinking about…"

"About what?" Josh prompted. He took a strand of hair that had escaped the knot on top of her head and curled it around his finger.

"About having something that's my own. I'm tired of being second-best. Or third or fourth. I'm smart and organized. Nothing says a woman can't own a ranch."

"Of course not." He kissed her nose. "Especially a woman like you."

"So you don't think I'm crazy?"

He saw by her vulnerable expression that she really wanted to know his opinion. "You're a lot of things, Layla, but crazy isn't one of them. You're creative and hardworking. You have everyone's best interests at heart. You're a devoted granddaughter and daughter and sister. I'm damned grateful we reconnected."

Those eyes that kept him up at night darkened. "Me, too," she said softly.

Suddenly, his patience ran out. He cleared his

throat. "Are you still interested in going back to the hotel with me?"

Her gaze widened. "It's the middle of the afternoon."

He kissed her long and hard, pressing her body to his. Feeling the way her fluttery skirt tangled with his pants legs. When he could speak, he rested his forehead against hers. "Do you have a problem with that?"

"No." Her voice was barely a whisper. "Not at all."

Twelve

Layla had a decision to make, and she was running out of time. As Josh sent the car hurtling back toward Royal, she leaned against the headrest and closed her eyes.

She wasn't drowsy this time. Far from it. Her body hummed with sexual energy and anticipation.

Was she really going to sleep with a man—again—who was only interested in having a good time? The truth was brutal. She was halfway in love with Joshua Banks, but she was almost certain he was simply using her for sexual gratification.

Could she handle a physical relationship knowing they were both going to walk away when it was over?

Ever since her conversation with Jordan, she had

waited for Josh to tell her that his dad and brother were buying him out...that he planned to take the money and run.

The question was—run to where?

She knew he had no interest in going back to his ex-wife, but Dallas had been his home for a long time. Surely he would tell Layla if that was what he had in mind. Or maybe he was keeping her in the dark because his plans didn't involve her at all.

Maybe he was enjoying the sex. Maybe she was convenient.

It was all well and good to think about principles and self-respect and doing the right thing.

The truth was, Layla couldn't walk away. He had hypnotized her, enchanted her. That one slender connection—their childhood friendship—had lowered her defenses and let this complicated, devastatingly handsome man walk back into her life with impunity.

From the beginning, he had told her he wasn't sure he was going to stay in Royal. He had admitted that his life was in turmoil...that he needed and wanted to start over. Heck, the man had even confessed to being an emotional mess.

It was her own fault if she had been weaving fantasies about happily-ever-afters with Joshua Banks.

At the hotel, things got real. She knew if she stepped into the elevator with him, the rest of the day was a foregone conclusion. Still, her feet carried her on a path that led to infinite pleasure but an uncertain future.

Josh must have sensed her unease. He took her suitcase from the trunk of the car and handed his keys over to a dark-headed, bright-eyed young man who looked too young to shave, much less park expensive vehicles.

Layla stood on the curb, waiting. Josh joined her and cocked his head, his smile rueful. "This isn't an all-or-nothing deal, sweetheart. I can always take you home."

She searched his face, looking for a sign that she wasn't making a huge mistake. He was kind and sexy and had just enough bad boy in him to make a woman weak in the knees. "I don't want to go home."

It was true. She didn't. *Please don't break my heart, Josh Banks.*

He held her hand on the way upstairs. His palm was warm and slightly rough against hers. She gripped his fingers, telling herself this was light and fun.

But in her heart, she knew. This was Layla putting her heart on the line. Letting herself be vulnerable. Telling the Fates she was ready to try again.

Josh's hotel room was the same. Which meant she couldn't help staring at the bed and remembering the night she had spent here.

She kicked off her shoes and curled her toes in the thick, luxurious carpet. "Do you mind if I freshen up?"

"Help yourself. Then I'll take a turn." He opened the mini fridge and extracted a beer. "We're not in a rush." His teasing smile connected with something deep in her core, setting off a chain reaction of raw need and desperate longing.

Unlike before, it wasn't bedtime. In fact, it was a heck of a long time until lights out. How were they going to fill all those hours?

It was a hot day. At first, she thought about simply using a damp washcloth to remove her makeup and run over her arms and legs. But it seemed dumb to try that when she could simply strip down. She didn't want to get in bed and feel icky.

After the world's quickest shower, she dried off and debated her options. She had imagined Josh removing her fancy dress. But now she didn't want to put it on again. Instead, she grabbed one of the hotel robes on the back of the door, the one that had clearly not been worn.

It swallowed her. She belted it tightly and opened the bathroom door.

Josh looked up, his gaze hooded. Heat flared between them, invisible but undeniable. She thought he would say something. Instead, he brushed by her and entered the bathroom. Moments later, she heard the shower.

His was even shorter than hers. She was still dithering about whether or not to get in bed when he reappeared, wearing the second robe.

A man should look more relaxed, more approachable without his fancy suit. In this case, it was the opposite. Stripped of the traditional clothes he had worn to the luncheon, Josh was even more stunningly masculine.

His damp hair was tousled. Because the robe was belted loosely, a large portion of his beautiful, lightly hair-dusted chest was exposed. His shoulders were so broad, the hotel robe strained to fit them.

Layla found courage and went to him. In her bare feet, the difference in their heights was pronounced. She grabbed the robe's lapels and went up on her tiptoes. "Thank you for being my plus-one today," she said. "Every woman in the room was jealous of me." Then she kissed him.

She took her time, enjoying the taste of his mouth, feeling the intoxicating way their lips clung and parted and pressed close again.

Josh was breathing heavily, his chest rising and falling rapidly. Her own pulse was racketing along at about a thousand beats a minute. So far, he was passive beneath her kiss, mostly letting her take the lead.

She stroked his tongue with hers, growing bolder. He groaned low in his throat. The hair on her arms stood up at the guttural sound.

At last, he gripped her shoulders. "I've wanted you for days, Layla." Was that a note of desperation in his voice? He shed his robe and removed hers. Without warning, he scooped her into his arms and carried her to the bed.

Perhaps he meant to lay her carefully on the mattress, but when Layla bit his bottom lip, his knees buckled, and they tumbled onto the bed together.

Still feeling her power after that sensual, explorative kiss, Layla straddled his waist. "I'd like to be on top. Any objections?"

Josh stared up at her with a narrowed gaze. "Not a single damn one."

Now that she had assumed the position, she was left with a plethora of choices. There were plenty of condoms on the nearby table, but she wanted to play.

Carefully, she stretched out on top of him. She could feel his hard sex against her lower abdomen. Her breasts squished against his powerful chest. Now she could nestle her head on his shoulder and listen to him breathe.

"This is nice," she said primly.

Josh's laughter threatened to tumble her off her comfy perch. "*Nice* wasn't the adjective I had in mind," he said. He cupped her butt in his hands and squeezed. "Interesting. Stimulating. Tormenting. Any of those?"

She put her hands on his shoulders and pushed up so she could see his face. "Sure. I'll take them all. You looked very handsome today. I think I like a man in a suit."

He pinched her ass. "How about a cowboy in dirty boots?"

Awkwardly, she sat all the way up, straddling him. "Do I have to choose? Can't I have both?"

Josh touched her intimately. "If you'll give up this torture, you can have whatever you want."

Without meaning to, Layla closed her eyes. Seeing Josh's hands on her body was too much. Every light in the room was on. What was she doing? She'd never had an exhibitionist bone in her body.

"Josh," she whispered, not even knowing what she wanted to say.

He was a gifted lover. Soon, he had her at the edge of climax, her breath lodged in her throat.

Hazily, she remembered the condoms nearby. "I can't reach them," she said, waving a hand.

"Way ahead of you." The husky words were accompanied by action. He shoved her gently to one side and grabbed a single packet.

When he ripped it open, she stared at him. "Let me do it."

The stain of red on his cheekbones darkened. He handed over the protection. "I said it before. Whatever you want, Layla."

He reclined again and watched her. Her hands shook. This intimacy wasn't one she had initiated very often or at all. During the time she was engaged to Richard, she had been on the pill.

Now when she took Josh's erect shaft in one hand, he shuddered from head to toe. As if she really was torturing him.

His sex was fascinating, long and hard...covered with hot silky skin. She pressed a kiss to the head, eliciting a feral sound from her lover. He grabbed her wrist in one hand. But she ignored his unspoken command.

"Relax," she said softly. "I want to taste you." Taking him in her mouth, she sucked gently, feeling him flex and swell. Feeling the power she had over him was both exhilarating and humbling. But she didn't want power, not really. She wanted a lover who would be her mate, her equal, her partner.

In that instant, she recognized what she hadn't allowed herself to acknowledge. She was not *halfway* in love with Joshua Banks. She had fallen into the deep end—the water over her head. Offering her heart to him madly, passionately, extravagantly.

And yes, he was an enigma. He probably didn't feel the same. Even so, she was helpless to fight the emotion that stung her eyes or to ward off the wave of love and longing that tightened her chest.

"Enough," he said, the word barely audible. "Now, Layla."

She smoothed the condom into place and rose over him, then took him into her body like a silent pledge. This was what she had waited her whole life to find. A man who was worthy of her love.

Soon, she was no longer able to think rationally. Josh filled her completely. Even in the less dominant position, he took control. His hands on her hips might leave bruises. Layla didn't care. His firm hold was the only anchor in her universe.

His gaze locked on hers. "Are you taking what you want, my love?"

She nodded, mute. His beautiful sapphire eyes seemed to be telegraphing a message that was apparently coded in another language, because she couldn't read it. And when he said *my love*, that was just sex talk—right? He couldn't really be as besotted with her as she was with him.

Without warning, he rolled over, taking her with him, never breaking their connection. "Nice trick," she panted.

His low, amused laughter made her blush.

"I don't think I'll let you leave this room," he said, lazily stroking deep.

Layla wrapped her legs around his waist. "We can't screw 24/7."

"Wanna bet?"

She clung to him, feeling the cataclysm build. Josh seemed to know her better than she knew herself. Physically, he met her every need.

When he lost it and pounded hard, head thrown back, cheekbones tight with strain, Layla hit the peak and cried out. It was even better than the last time. Higher. Hotter. More out of control.

Josh came, too, his large frame vibrating. He moaned her name and slumped on top of her. She held him close. Feeling his strength. Memorizing this moment against the day when it might be nothing but a faint recollection.

Like every woman insecure in a budding relationship, she wanted to find the courage to ask where this was leading. But she was afraid of the answers.

Maybe the really brave thing was not to ask at all, but to take what Josh had to give and offer him her heart in return.

He would never know how she felt, perhaps. But a gift was only a gift if it was freely given.

They both dozed for a few minutes.

When Josh finally roused, he yawned. "Wow. You turn me inside out." He was rumpled and heavy eyed and so beautifully male it hurt to look at him.

"Same." She laughed, her heart squeezing.

"We have the rest of the day," he said. "What would you like to do?"

She wrinkled her nose, unwilling to state the obvious.

Josh nuzzled her cheek, kissed the sensitive spot below her ear. "Besides that, naughty woman," he said.

"I'm feeling mellow. You choose."

In the end, it turned out to be a perfect afternoon. They watched a movie in bed with room service snacks. Before dinner, they changed into running gear and did a quick five miles around downtown.

The shared shower afterward turned into something more. Josh took her up against the wall, face-to-face, her arms locked around his neck. It was the most intimately personal thing she had ever done with a partner.

She could swear she saw love and tenderness in his gaze, but the stubborn man never said a word about his ranch share or anything else that mattered.

After dinner in the hotel dining room, they danced to the romantic music of a small orchestra. Layla had packed a full-length red jersey dress that didn't wrinkle. With Josh's warm hand splayed on her bare back, she could have nestled in his arms for hours. But eventually, they went upstairs again.

Josh stared at her when she kicked off her shoes. "Are you happy, Layla?" he asked.

She tensed. "What do you mean?" He might be talking about this day in particular or life in general.

He shrugged. "It's a simple question."

Perhaps this was the opening she had been looking for. Maybe he was waiting for a sign from her. She looked him straight in the eye and smiled wistfully. "Meeting you again has been the happiest thing in my life for a long time, Josh. I have no regrets." That last was to let him off the hook if he was thinking about leaving.

He owed her nothing. No promises had been exchanged, no vows made.

Instead of continuing the conversation, he kicked off his socks and shoes. Then he removed his jacket and shirt and tie. While she watched, he took her wrist and reeled her in, pulling her tightly against his body so they were touching from shoulder to hip. He found the zip at the back of her dress, lowered it and shimmied her dress to the floor.

Now Josh was bare from the waist up, and Layla wore nothing but a strapless black bra and matching panties. "Are *you* happy, Josh?" she asked, her heart in her throat.

He held her tightly, his face buried in the curve of her neck. "You're a very special woman," he said gruffly. "And yes, I'm happy."

She winced. It wasn't exactly the answer she was looking for. When they made love this time, it was markedly different. Less urgency, more tenderness. Was this what goodbye sex felt like?

The question haunted her. She thought for a few moments that she wouldn't be able to have an orgasm, but Josh was endlessly patient. He touched her as if she was infinitely breakable, yet he coaxed fire to the surface. When she finally came, the pleasure was blinding, but tears clogged her throat.

Afterward, they slept, wrapped together in each other's arms. As dawn was breaking, Layla got up to go to the bathroom. When she returned, she climbed back into bed, determined to wring the last drops of pleasure from this interlude.

By the time Josh took her home today, they would have spent the last twenty-four hours together. It felt like forever, but it was far too short, especially since she was no closer than ever to understanding him.

When Josh's alarm went off, they got up and dressed. They both wore jeans and casual shirts. He talked. She answered. But the words were meaningless, utilitarian.

Josh took her suitcase as they made their way downstairs. He kissed the top of her head right before they stepped off the elevator and into the lobby. "This was great," he said. "Thanks for sneaking away a few hours."

"It was fun for me, too," she said. "But I do need to get home and check on Grammy."

Josh stopped suddenly when he saw a trio of men standing on the sidewalk just outside the portico. "I've been trying to get in touch with one of those guys for two weeks." He handed her his wallet. "Would you mind asking for the car? The claim ticket is in there. And give the kid a fifty. He's heading off to college in a couple of months."

Layla nodded. "Of course."

Josh set her suitcase at her feet and jogged over to join the group.

When Layla opened the billfold, she found the claim ticket immediately and passed it to the man at the podium. Then she looked for a fifty-dollar bill.

The money was easy to spot, but as she extracted it, a folded slip of white paper fell out. When she picked it up, her stomach clenched. It was a boarding pass for a flight from Royal to Dallas. Dated the day after Layla first spent the night in Josh's hotel room.

She stared at it blankly, trying to process what she was seeing. Most people had boarding passes on their smartphones now. But in the case of a seat-assignment change or an upgrade, a gate agent might print out a paper boarding pass.

Unfortunately, this was only one leg of the trip. She had no idea when Josh returned.

Why had he gone to Dallas? Why hadn't he mentioned it?

Was this the reason she hadn't heard from him in a string of days while Grammy was recovering at home?

Heartsick and confused, she stood frozen, praying the car would show up soon. The same bright-eyed young man from yesterday handed over the keys. Layla offered the tip. "This is from Mr. Banks," she said, managing a smile.

The boy's eyes widened. "Wow. Thanks."

Layla put her suitcase in the trunk and sat down in the passenger seat. She was numb. Hurt. Stunned.

She must have greeted Josh when he slid behind the wheel. Obviously, they chatted on the way out to the ranch. But she would have been hard-pressed to remember a word.

When Josh pulled up in front of the ranch house, it was all she could do not to bolt up the steps. Instead, she waited while he retrieved her bag. He insisted on carrying it to the front door.

"I'll call you," he said.

"Sure..."

When he bent to kiss her lips, she turned her head at the last minute, making it look casual. Josh's kiss landed on her cheek, not her mouth.

"I'd better get inside," she said, not quite able to meet his searching gaze. "Thanks for going to the luncheon with me."

He frowned, perhaps for the first time realizing

something might be wrong. "I'm glad you asked me. Will you let me know if there is any news about the oil rights?"

"Okay."

"Now that the Thurston twins showed up at the luncheon, I doubt they are going to ride off into the sunset."

She grimaced. "Probably not."

He kissed her again. This one landed smack on her lips—the same traitorous lips that returned the kiss in spite of everything.

Josh pulled back, his expression lighter. "Goodbye, Layla. We'll talk soon."

Thirteen

We'll talk soon. That stupid throwaway phrase rattled around in her head for the remainder of the day. The time to talk was over.

Clearly, Josh's agenda and Layla's were vastly different.

One upside of having a big family living under the same roof was that there were always plenty of distractions. She visited Grammy in her room and was happy to see her looking perky and healthy, even for a woman her age.

After that, she spent a couple of hours in the barn doing her own personal brand of equine therapy. Even though the horses couldn't talk back, Layla told them a few of her secrets. Their soft whinnies and the way they bumped her with their heads eased some of the pain in her heart.

Unfortunately, there was no family dinner that evening. Everybody was either on the run, or like Grammy, eating in their room.

Layla wasn't hungry. She made herself a smoothie with protein powder and forced herself to drink it. At nine thirty, she knew she couldn't procrastinate any longer. Though it was cowardly, she couldn't face Josh. This breakup was happening via text.

Josh...

She typed the single word and stopped, not sure how to say what she wanted to say. He didn't need to know she was in love with him. That would be the ultimate humiliation. Doggedly, she continued.

I know you and I have enjoyed reconnecting after so many years, but my family is in the midst of a crisis, as you've heard. Plus, by your own admission, much of your life is up in the air. I think it would be best all the way around if we don't see each other anymore. I wish you every happiness...

Layla

Well, that was it. Short, sweet and to the point. She felt sick. Deliberately torpedoing a relationship that had given her so much joy seemed self-defeating.

But she had no choice. She had too much self-respect to let another man keep her in the dark.

When she hit Send, the tears started. She didn't try to stop them. It was natural to grieve. Joshua Banks was a wonderful man, but he wasn't for her. Clearly, his needs had been sexual, first and foremost.

She hadn't expected a grand gesture. But *something…* Even a generic *I care about you* would have been nice.

Five minutes after she sent the text, her phone rang. If a ringtone could sound angry, she fancied this one did. Of course the caller ID said Josh Banks.

Just this one more conversation and she would be done.

She wiped her face with the back of her hand and answered.

"Hello?"

Josh's voice reverberated with confused rage and maybe even a hint of desperation. "What the hell, Layla? What's going on?"

She swallowed hard. "I think the text was self-explanatory. I've said all I have to say. Goodbye, Josh."

"Wait," he said urgently. "Don't hang up. Did something upset you? Is it your grandmother? Or the Thurston brothers? Let me be there for you."

"It's none of that, Josh. Just what I said in the text. Besides, I don't think you and I have much in common. Please let this go."

Dead silence gripped the phone connection for long seconds.

"You didn't seem to mind our differences when I was giving you multiple orgasms," he said tersely. "Talk to me, Layla. Please."

He was breaking her heart into tiny little pieces. She almost capitulated. But then she reminded herself that Josh Banks was only interested in sex. He had kept Layla on the periphery of his life. She needed to make a clean break.

"Goodbye, Josh."

Heartbreak was a funny thing. Layla was able to function almost normally during the daytime. But the nights were long. And painful.

After spending hours in Josh's bed, it was impossible to pretend that her own lonely room was where she wanted to be. She had done the right thing. No question about it. But oh, how it hurt.

In fact, her intense suffering told her more clearly than ever that Richard had damaged her pride and her self-respect, but he had never really possessed her heart. How had she believed she was in love with him?

It was possible Chelsea sensed something was wrong, but she gave Layla her space. That was a good thing, because Layla was holding herself together by sheer will. Sympathy from her sister would have pushed her over the edge.

In the midst of her grief, she struggled with her

grandmother's secret. And she finally decided that she had to tell her family at least the bare bones of it.

Three evenings after her exchange with Josh, the whole clan was in residence for the noon meal. Grammy had been picked up by a friend whose granddaughter was taking both women to lunch in town.

When the housekeeper had served the main course out on the back veranda, Layla set down her fork. "I have news," she said, keeping her voice low. "Grammy didn't want me to tell any of you, and I promised, but you deserve to hear at least bits of it."

Her father scowled. "My own mother conspiring behind my back?"

Chelsea thumped the table. "Oh, for heaven's sake, Daddy. Don't be so dramatic. Let Layla finish."

Five sets of eyes stared at her with varying degrees of suspicion. Only Morgan smiled. "Go ahead, Layla."

"Because of Grammy's wishes, I can't tell you all the details, but suffice it to say that she came across some of Grandy's scribbles. I've seen them. Unfortunately, it does seem as if Grandy and Augustus Lattimore offered the oil rights to Heath Thurston's mother."

Three beats of silence passed. "Hell," her father said. "I didn't want to hear that."

Vic stood and paced. "What are we going to do?"

Layla exhaled. "I thought we might be morally bound to produce this *thing* Grammy found.

Grammy says not. It's not anything close to being a legal document. Simply a passing reference. The burden of proof is on the Thurston brothers."

Chelsea stood as well, running her hands through her hair. "Good Lord. Are we really going to let them dig up this ranch?"

"We may not have a choice," Layla said. "Still, that photocopy we got from the lawyer has to be substantiated before things go any further."

The housekeeper returned, and all serious conversation was abandoned. But Layla could see from the expressions on everyone's faces that they were all concerned.

She was, too. Of course she was. But her breakup with Josh loomed larger at the moment. Maybe that made her a bad daughter. She didn't want to see her family's ranch ruined. Truly she didn't.

Despite that, Heath Thurston and the contested oil rights were the least of her problems.

When ten days had passed after the spring luncheon at the TCC, her nerves reached a breaking point. No one needed her at the moment. She had to get out of the house, off the ranch.

When she was in her car and driving, one particular spot called to her. She tried not to go. It was pointless to make herself miserable for no reason. But by the time she had traversed all the back roads of Maverick County, she discovered she couldn't return home until she made one final pilgrimage.

The Realtor had never called Layla back. Maybe

she was too busy selling actual houses and ranches to deal with a tract of land out in the middle of nowhere.

Layla made her way to the very same hilltop where she and Josh had first made love. Was that why she wanted to buy the land? Was she trying to preserve that day forever in her memory?

She got out of the car and leaned against the tree. A light breeze made the afternoon heat bearable. Overhead, a buzzard flew in ever-widening circles. Maybe he sensed the death of Layla's love life and was waiting to pick at the bones.

Even in her pain, she had to laugh at her own joke. She wasn't the first woman to want a man she couldn't have. And she wouldn't be the last.

It was just that the moments with Josh had seemed so very *real*. So perfectly intimate. So natural. So right.

The truth was, her romantic judgment still sucked.

She felt the tree bark against her back. Bits of sunlight made their way through the leaves and branches overhead. Time passed. Layla wasn't wearing a watch, and she didn't care. Maybe she had a bit of Irish in her. Perhaps she was holding a wake for the death of her dreams.

Loss was hard any way you looked at it...

Eventually, heavy clouds began to build, and the humidity increased. Texas weather was capricious. A storm was on the way...

She honestly didn't know how long she had been

standing there when she heard an alien noise. Not a bird. Not the wind. Not even an animal.

Instead, as the sound grew closer, it became clear that she had a visitor. When she glanced behind her where the road wound down the low rise, she clenched her fists. How could he possibly have known she was here?

When Joshua parked beside her car and got out, she schooled her face to show indifference, despite the fact that her heart was bouncing all around her rib cage.

"Are you psychic?" she asked with an edge in her voice.

"No. I went out to the ranch. Your sister told me you had gone for a drive. I took a shot." His voice was flat.

Layla didn't move. But she managed to gaze at him without flinching. He looked terrible, frankly. His beautiful hair hadn't been combed. His mouth was set in a grim line.

She went on the attack, hoping he would leave. "What do you want, Josh?"

He leaned against his car, arms folded across his chest. "I think I deserve an answer. Something other than the bullshit you gave me in a text and over the phone. One moment I had a warm woman in my bed, the next she was colder than a witch's tit in December."

"Charming," Layla drawled. "Is that the way men talk to women back in Dallas?"

"Cut the crap, Layla," he said sharply. "Why did you bail on us?"

Temper was better than despair. The hot rush of anger and indignation felt good. "There was no *us*," she said. "*Us* implies a relationship. You saw me as a fuck-buddy."

"Don't be crude," he snapped. "It doesn't suit you."

She infused her voice with ice. "Your opinions are irrelevant."

Suddenly, the aggression in his stance disappeared. For a split second she witnessed uncertainty. And pain? Surely not.

He stared at the ground and then back at her. "I thought we had something special, Layla. I could swear you felt it, too. What happened?"

She'd had enough. The Band-Aids she had slapped over her emotional wounds were being ripped away by this postmortem. "I'll tell you what happened, Joshua Banks. You lied to me, just like my ex-fiancé. You and Richard are cut from the same cloth."

Fury flared in those blue eyes she saw in her dreams. "I *never* lied to you," he shouted. "Never."

Could she jump in her car and drive away? Would he stop her? She honestly didn't know. And if he touched her—at all—she feared she would let him lie to her again.

She took a deep breath, wanting to destroy him with the force of her disappointment. But rational, cooler thoughts prevailed. "Lying by omission is still lying. I get that you weren't sleeping with other women when you were with me. But the end result was the same. I told you I had trust issues with men. You knew my weakness, and you exploited it."

Bewilderment brushed his features. "I honestly don't know what the hell you're talking about. I thought we were getting closer every day."

Either the man was a very good actor, or he thought what he had done wasn't wrong. Probably the latter.

It angered her that she had to spell it out. Because it made her humiliation complete.

"Okay, Josh," she said. "Here it is. You asked your father and brother to buy out your share of the ranch, but you never thought to mention it to me. You flew to Dallas for some unknown reason, and again, I didn't merit even the briefest of explanations." She swallowed, her heart aching. "Those are not the actions of a man involved in a relationship. You're a loner. Or maybe you just don't see me as having any lasting effect on your daily life. Either way, I don't want or need that. I don't want or need you."

Whew. That last sentence was a huge lie. And with the clouds churning overhead, the possibility of a lightning strike was not merely theoretical.

During her big speech, Josh went white. In fact, his pallor was disturbing. Grief and shock turned his eyes dark. "Oh, God, Layla. I—"

Just as he started to speak, a powerful bolt of lightning split a small tree less than three hundred yards away. The thunder was simultaneous.

His face changed. "We've got to get out of here."

Huge drops of rain began to fall. "Goodbye," she said, tears filling her eyes.

Josh took her shoulders in his hands. "I need twenty minutes," he said, his eyes as wild as the sky. "Swear to me you'll listen for twenty minutes."

A second beautiful but deadly lightning strike sizzled the air a little farther away. "Why? It's pointless."

He had to raise his voice to be heard over the wind. "Come to my room at the hotel. We need a quiet place to talk."

"Oh, no," she said, horrified at that idea.

"Please, Layla. You can sit by the door if it will make you feel better. Twenty minutes. That's all I ask."

It began to rain harder. Soon, they would be soaked. "Fine," she said, swallowing the pain of being near him again. Surely she could endure twenty minutes. Then this would all be over.

"We'll go in my car," he said. "I'll send someone for yours later."

"Absolutely not. I'll follow you."

They faced off, Layla resolute, Josh increasingly frustrated. A third lightning strike settled the matter. She dove for her car and locked herself inside. Josh stared at her grimly, got into his own vehicle and then began carefully turning around.

When he started down the hill, she followed him. They had made their decision in the nick of time.

The clouds opened up, and the rain let loose in huge driving sheets. The noise inside the car was deafening. Even with her wipers on high, she could barely see out the front windshield.

It didn't help that the rough lane they had come up was little more than two ruts in the ground. The entire hilltop was turning to mud.

She breathed a sigh of relief when they made it out to the paved road. For a few moments she considered eluding Josh and driving home. Unfortunately, she knew him well enough to assume he would simply follow her.

There was no way in heck she wanted to handle this volatile situation with her family looking on. She wouldn't put it past Josh to enlist their help.

The drive back to town shouldn't have taken more than twenty-five minutes. Today, it was almost twice that. Josh was forced to creep along at fifteen miles an hour. In some places, flash flooding was a definite risk.

Her hands were clenched so tightly on the steering wheel that her neck muscles gave her a headache.

It seemed like an eternity.

Finally, they pulled up beneath the hotel's portico and got out. Though she hadn't gotten drenched, she was wet enough to know she looked bedraggled. She grabbed her purse and joined Josh.

Neither of them spoke in the elevator.

Layla stared at the floor. No matter what he said,

she wouldn't be manipulated. His behavior was clear. He only wanted Layla in bed.

At last, Josh unlocked his hotel room door and stepped aside for her to enter. Immediately, Layla grabbed a desk chair and dragged it to a position right beside the door. Josh's lips tightened, but he didn't respond to her deliberate provocation.

Instead, he went to the bathroom, grabbed two towels and returned, handing one to Layla. She pulled a tiny mirror from her purse and checked her reflection. Not one-hundred-percent drowned rat, but close enough. She ran the towel over her damp hair and then combed it out.

When she was done, Josh sat down on the side of the bed. He looked so defeated and miserable that she almost relented.

She glanced at her watch pointedly. "The clock is ticking."

His spine straightened. He looked at her, an intense gaze that seemed to see inside her soul. "I love you, Layla."

Shock reverberated through her body. And stunned joy. Though it took all she had, she kept her expression impassive. What kind of ploy was this?

"I suppose you forgot to mention that, too?" she said.

He flinched visibly. Perhaps her sarcasm had been over the top, but for him to pretend now made her angry. She wanted so badly to believe him, but she couldn't trust that his words were real.

"I am *so* sorry," he said.

She shrugged. "For what? Things are what they are."

He rested his elbows on his knees, staring at her, coaxing her by the sheer force of his personality to look at him. "This isn't a game. I love you. I suspected it the first time we made love, but I knew it the night you spent in this very room."

Inside, she began to shake. "No."

He stared at her. "Yes. I've lived through what love isn't...which is why I knew so quickly when the real thing hit me hard."

"You don't have to do this, Josh." Her throat hurt from holding back tears of emotion. Everything he was saying delighted her. But was it sincere?

"Layla..." He looked frustrated now. "I know I messed up, but not for the reasons you think."

"What are you trying to say, then?"

Josh shrugged. Unbelievably, his face flushed as if he was embarrassed or bashful or both. What was going on?

He rubbed his jaw. "I was trying to make a grand gesture. All the planning and juggling was falling into place. I was almost ready."

"For what?"

"To make my pitch. To propose."

The joy tried to return, but Layla kept a lid on it. She shook her head slowly, wondering for a moment if this was an odd dream. "You were going to propose to me when you hadn't even said *I love you*?"

He muttered a word she had never heard him use. "I screwed up, okay? I was so busy trying to surprise you that I made you feel shut out and unimportant. That was never my intention."

Now he was definitely embarrassed. She didn't know what to say. Did she believe him? Could she?

When she didn't say anything, Josh doggedly plunged on with his explanations. "The reason your Realtor couldn't find any information about that piece of land you wanted to buy is because my sale was already in progress. I thought you and I could start a ranch of our own. Partners. Lovers."

She was dumbfounded. "You bought a ranch. For us. But you didn't think to include me?"

He stood now and paced. "I was all into this big surprise idea."

"I *hate* surprises," she said.

"Well, I know that now." He went to the mini fridge and grabbed two bottles of water, then tossed her one of them. "Drink something. You're kind of pale."

Layla caught the plastic container automatically. When she opened the lid and took a sip, she realized how thirsty she was. The whole encounter had made her dizzy and uncertain. This wasn't how romance unfolded in rom-coms. She was so tied up in knots, she didn't know *how* to feel.

When she finished two-thirds of the bottle, she sighed. "Go ahead. Finish your story. Tell me about your secretive trip."

He clearly didn't like the adjective, but he didn't quibble. "I went to Dallas twice actually...for a couple of reasons. I met with my ex-boss and pitched him the idea of me working remotely. It's not really a stretch, and I was pretty sure they needed me."

"And did they?"

"Apparently so. He gave me my job back with a raise. I figured if I was going to have a wife and a brand-new business venture, I was probably going to need some income flowing in until the ranch was up and running."

"A wife?" Her stomach quivered. Maybe dreams really did come true.

"A wife," he said firmly.

Layla was giddy, but she wanted the whole story. "You said *two* reasons. What was the other one?"

He stopped by her chair and rubbed the back of his hand over her cheek. His gaze narrowed, those beautiful blue eyes dark with intensity. "Do you love me, Layla?"

She hesitated. She couldn't help it. Trust was hard. She saw that her reaction hurt him.

When she didn't say a word, he crouched beside her. "Don't be afraid of me, Layla. I can't bear it. Don't be afraid of us."

He was so close. So very close. All she wanted was to launch herself into his arms, but this was crazy. Wasn't it?

"We barely know each other," she whispered. She waved a hand. "Give me some space, please." What she wanted him to do was ignore her demand, but then he wouldn't be the honorable guy she loved.

A frown line appeared between his brows, but he went back to his seat on the bed. "We've known each other for years," he said, the words flat. "Lots of people are still close to friends they met in grade school. Our connection may have weakened with time and distance, but once we were together again, I *knew* you."

"But love?"

His jaw was tight. "Men and women come from different planets, right? We look at the world differently."

"What's your point?"

"When you and I were intimate, our bodies connected in more than a superficial way. We saw each other's weaknesses. Our failures. Our hopes for the future. That kind of sex is rare, Layla. Tell me you realize that."

"I haven't had a lot of sex," she admitted. "Except with Richard the rat."

"And was that sex good?"

Fourteen

The room was so quiet, a person could have heard the proverbial pin drop. She thought about it for a moment. "It wasn't *not* good," she said. "Besides, my mother always warned Chelsea, Morgan and me not to ever confuse sex and lust with love. She told us it was a common female mistake."

"Was that what happened with Richard?"

That one stumped her. "Not exactly. I thought he was something I was *supposed* to want. Love and marriage and kids."

"And how did you feel the first time you and I were intimate?"

She thought back to that day. The quilt. The sunshine. The remarkable way she was at ease with Josh and yet so intensely aroused. "I felt like I was flying," she admitted.

At last, a tiny smile of relief tipped up the corners of his mouth, that mouth and those lips she wanted to devour. He watched her closely, so very closely. She didn't know whether to be flattered or worried. And he seemed to be waiting for something more. So she kept talking. "I don't think you know me as well as you think. I'm pretty boring—an introvert for the most part. And I'm not very adventurous. I like tending to the animals at the ranch. It grounds me, makes me feel safe."

He stood again. This time, he took her hands and pulled her to her feet. "And what about me, sweet Layla. Do I make you feel safe?"

It was an odd question, perhaps. And not very sexy according to the rom-com script. But he was so close and so very dear to her.

She took one step and rested her cheek over his heart. "You do," she said. And it was true. No matter how bizarre his behavior, now that he had explained, all her feelings for him came rushing back. She wasn't mad or angry or uncertain.

All she felt at this exact moment was *safe*. And relieved. And if she allowed herself to relax—so very, very happy.

Suddenly, one last question bumped up against her burgeoning peace. She was afraid to ask it. With Josh's big warm body pressed against hers, all she wanted was to bask in the incredulous glow of this man's confession of love.

But the tiniest doubt remained that perhaps he had unresolved issues with his ex.

She swallowed the lump in her throat. "I still haven't heard that second reason you went to Dallas."

Deep in his chest, a groan rumbled. He pulled back, looked in her face and bent his head to kiss her. Tenderly at first, but then with that wild passion that always washed over them and birthed insanity.

"Don't move," Josh said.

She put her fingers to her lips. They tingled. As she watched, Josh rifled in what looked like a piece of carry-on luggage and extracted a turquoise box. When he turned around, his expression was a mix of sheepish defiance.

"A buddy of mine manages the Tiffany store near University Park," he said. "I picked out a ring two days ago and made him swear I could return it if you wanted something else."

Before she could react, he knelt in front of her, tossed aside the outer package and white ribbon and flipped open the real box. "Marry me, Layla," he said, his voice husky. "I adore you. I want to spend the next fifty years making you happy."

He pulled the ring out of its nest and slipped it on the third finger on her left hand.

Somewhere along the way, Layla forgot to breathe. It seemed to be a common problem when Josh was around.

The ring was stunning. A single, flawless, round diamond. At least two carats, maybe more. The platinum setting included a duo of blue baguettes flanking the solitaire.

Josh rubbed his thumb over her knuckles. "Two sapphires," he said. "One for your eyes and one for the wide Texas skies where I found my soul mate."

She tugged him to his feet and searched his face. "Are you sure?"

His gaze was clear and heated. "Absolutely. But you still haven't answered my question. Do you love me, Layla Grandin?"

She sighed happily, holding up her hand to make the ring sparkle. "I definitely do."

Her honesty was rewarded with a world-class kiss. He held her tightly. Enough that she felt the evidence of how much he had missed her pressed against her.

His voice rumbled in her ear. "Will you marry me, Layla? Will you be my wife and my lover and my best friend? Will you build a ranch and a home and a family with me?"

For the first time in her adult life, she was absolutely sure she knew the right answer to a very grown-up question. She pulled back and smiled at him, her eyes brimming with happy tears. "I will, Josh. I will."

Epilogue

Five days later...
Las Vegas, Nevada

Josh held Layla's hand as they stood outside the wedding chapel. Even with dark sunglasses on, he had to squint against the blinding sun. He bent his head so he could see her face. "It's not too late to change your mind, sweetheart. You're a Grandin, the first in your crew to get married. You should be wearing a ten-thousand-dollar dress and having the entire population of Maverick County come out to see society's latest bride in all her finery walk down the aisle."

He worried that she would regret what they were about to do.

Layla removed her own sunglasses and gave him a sweet but naughty smile. She was wearing white, a sexy sundress that bared a lot of skin and showcased her body. "I don't want that," she said firmly. "In fact, it sounds dreadful. We can always have a fancy reception later. Besides, with this oil rights controversy dragging on, I don't think the timing is right for a big splashy wedding."

It was also why they weren't taking a honeymoon right now, other than two nights in Vegas. Josh kissed her forehead, not wanting to muss her makeup before they tied the knot. "If you're sure. I don't want to upset your family."

She laughed. "I guess that's one benefit of being the forgotten child. No one cares what I do."

He had a hunch she was dead wrong about that one, but he was getting his beautiful bride, so he was willing to be convinced. "Come on, darlin'. Let's do this."

Hours later, Layla couldn't remember a word of the vows she had spoken. Nor the officiant's face, or even the flowers she carried.

But what stood out was Josh's steady gaze and the unmistakable love in his eyes. When he looked at her like that, she knew she had won the jackpot.

At the moment, he was downstairs procuring some kind of surprise. When he told her that a few minutes ago, she had gaped at him and then rolled her eyes.

Josh swore this was one surprise she would be happy to receive.

When a knock sounded at the bedroom door, she checked the peephole and let him in. "That was quick."

Josh grinned. "All I had to do was check at the front desk." He handed her a large white envelope. "Happy wedding day, Ms. Banks."

Layla, definitely puzzled, opened the flap. She'd halfway been expecting another box with jewelry inside. Even when she extracted the sheaf of papers, it took her a second to understand what she was looking at. And then it sank in.

Her heart raced. "I thought we couldn't close until next week." They had added her name to the pending sale several days ago.

Josh kissed her forehead on his way to open the bottle of champagne that was chilling in a bucket on the dresser. "The sellers were eager to be finished. All the paperwork is final. You and I will sign on the dotted line day after tomorrow when we get back to Royal, but the deal is done." He lifted his glass and handed her one. "We own a ranch, Layla. Just the two of us."

Her heart fluttered in her chest. "Do you really think we can do this?"

"Of course we can. It's going to be the best damn ranch in Texas."

She drained her champagne and put her arms around his neck, pressing close, hearing him inhale a sharp breath. "I adore you, Joshua Banks."

He nuzzled her nose. "The feeling is mutual." His

big warm hands settled on her ass. "I like this wedding dress. A lot. But you'll be more comfortable if you take it off."

"Josh…" She ran a fingertip over his lips. "You're so thoughtful."

He shrugged, feigning modesty. "I'll do anything for my sexy bride."

"Anything?" She unbuttoned his shirt.

His face flushed. She had a feeling it *wasn't* the alcohol.

"Anything," he muttered. He picked her up and carried her to the bed. They had both laughed about the candy-apple-red bedspread with the embroidered cupids. Josh flipped back the covers and set her on her feet. Then he undressed her in record time. He took a deep breath and exhaled slowly. "I wish we hadn't wasted so many years."

Layla shook her head slowly. "Not a waste, Josh. Not entirely. We've grown. Pain and heartache do that to a person. But now I *know* what I want. I want you. For better or for worse. I love you."

She kissed him, trying to tell him without words how much joy he had brought to her life. Josh trembled as he held her tightly. Layla trembled, too. They were so lucky to have found each other.

He rested his forehead against hers. "Vegas is all about gambling, but what we did today isn't a risk. Not to me. I've never been surer of anything in my life. You're my one and only, Layla. I love you."

His words healed the scars on her heart.

They scrambled into the bed, and Layla helped with the rest of his clothes. When they were both naked and panting, he went up on one elbow and stroked her hair. "How do you feel about having twins?"

Layla gaped at him. Her heart raced in fear and delirious joy. "Oh my gosh. I never even thought about that."

Josh rolled to his back and laughed so hard tears filled his eyes. "If you could see your face," he gasped.

Happiness filled the room, swirling in the air. Fizzing like the champagne.

Layla stroked his chest, enjoying the buzz of sexual anticipation. She had no doubts. Not a one. This man would be by her side until they were old and gray.

"We did all this so fast I didn't have a chance to get *you* a wedding present," she said, feeling guilty.

Josh pulled her close. Kissed her hard. Settled between her legs, ready to go. His hot gaze stole her breath. "I have everything I could possibly want right here, my love. Now, close your eyes and let's see if we both remember how to fly…"

* * * * *

Boyfriend Lessons
Sophia Singh Sasson

Sophia Singh Sasson puts her childhood habit of daydreaming to good use by writing stories she wishes will give you hope, make you laugh, cry and possibly snort tea from your nose. She was born in Bombay, India, has lived in Canada and currently resides in Washington, DC. She loves to read, travel, bake, scuba dive, make candles and hear from readers. Visit her at www.sophiasasson.com.

Books by Sophia Singh Sasson

Harlequin Desire

Texas Cattleman's Club: Ranchers and Rivals

Boyfriend Lessons

Nights at the Mahal

Marriage by Arrangement
Running Away with the Bride

Harlequin Heartwarming

State of the Union

The Senator's Daughter
Mending the Doctor's Heart

Welcome to Bellhaven

First Comes Marriage

Visit her Author Profile page at millsandboon.com.au, or sophiasasson.com, for more titles.

You can also find Sophia on Facebook, along with other Harlequin Desire authors, at Facebook.com/harlequindesireauthors!

Dear Reader,

Thank you for taking the time to read my book. It is such an honor for me to write one of the Texas Cattleman's Club stories; even more so because I get to share a small piece of my culture with you. Dev and Caitlyn captured my heart and I hope they will make room in yours, too.

While Dev was born in the US, he struggles with some of the same things that I do as a first-generation immigrant. How do you integrate the Indian side of you with the American side? Why do you even feel like there are two sides of you? Reconciling his feelings for Caitlyn with his family expectations is a struggle I'm well familiar with. Caitlyn is someone for whom the emotional connection is even more important than the physical one, but it's hard to make that connection when you're not ready to open yourself up. I'm excited to share Dev and Caitlyn's journey with you.

Hearing from readers makes my day, so please email me at Sophia@SophiaSasson.com, tag me on Twitter (@sophiasasson), Instagram (@sophia_singh_sasson) or Facebook (/authorsophiasasson), or find me on Goodreads, BookBub (@sophiasinghsasson) or my website, www.sophiasasson.com.

Love,

Sophia

DEDICATION

This book is dedicated to all those who've ever
wondered—what's wrong with me?
The answer is absolutely nothing.
You are perfect as you are, and I hope you find
that special someone who thinks so, too.

ACKNOWLEDGMENTS

Thank you to the awesome Harlequin Desire editorial team, in
particular Stacy Boyd and Charles Griemsman, who have always
given me a chance, and my agent, Barbara Rosenberg,
for always looking out for me.

It's lonely being an author, but the amazing community of
South Asian romance writers always keeps me going.

Last and most important, I wouldn't be an author without
the love and support of my husband. Love you, Tom!

One

"So you just left?" Caitlyn Lattimore said incredulously. She was used to Alice's crazy dating experiences, but this one made her sit up in the pool lounger.

Alice slid her oversize sunglasses on top of her wavy blond hair, refilled her chardonnay glass and topped off Caitlyn, who had barely touched her first glass.

"The man ordered two appetizers, lobster for dinner and a bottle of wine from the reserve list. Then he pulls 'the left my wallet at home' crap. No, thank you. I told him I was going to the bathroom and then asked the waitress if I could escape through the kitchen door because he was a creep."

Her dating stories get scarier by the day.

Alice grabbed the bottle of suntan lotion and rubbed her arms. "I need to find a better dating site."

Caitlyn reached for the sunblock. It was early June, and the sun was strong. One touch of UV and her skin would turn shades browner. She had a number of Lattimore events to attend in the next month, and her makeup artist had just spent days perfecting the right shade of foundation for her. Alice called them rich girl problems, and Caitlyn agreed. She'd won the lottery when the Lattimores adopted her twenty-four years ago. Even now, they were sitting by the sparkling blue pool of the Lattimore ranch, their wine bottle perfectly chilled and a staff member readily available should they need anything else. Alice called it the Ritz Lattimore, but it was home for Caitlyn, one she loved not because of the luxuries, but because her family lived here.

"I wish I had your chutzpah. If that had happened to me, I'd have paid the bill and spent the night seething." Caitlyn said.

"Darlin', for that to happen to you, you'd need to actually go out on a date. To leave this gilded cage and venture into the smog and filth we mortals call the real world."

"You sound just like Alexa."

Alexa had left Royal for New York City, and then Miami, when she went to college and never looked back. She'd been home recently, though, for Victor Grandin's funeral.

Alice raised a brow. "I was sorry to hear about

Layla's grandfather dying. Victor Grandin was such a pillar in this community."

"He was. Alexa came home for the funeral and I suspect Layla would like Alexa to stay permanently, because her cutthroat lawyering skills will help our two families."

"Is this about that letter that came at the funeral? You never told me the full story."

Caitlyn's stomach roiled. "Turns out Heath Thurston is making a claim against the oil rights to the land beneath the Grandin and Lattimore ranches." It wasn't the claim that worried Caitlyn but the effect it was having on her family.

Alice leaned forward. "See, this is what happens when we don't see each other for a month—I miss all the juicy gossip."

"It's more than gossip. Those oil rights include the land that the Lattimore mansion is built on. Heath claims Daniel Grandin fathered Heath's late half-sister, Ashley, and that Daniel's dad gave Heath's mother Cynthia the oil rights. He says he found some of his mother's papers supporting the claim."

Alice's mouth hung open. Even she was speechless after that. The thought of what losing their family home would do to her siblings had consumed Caitlyn every second for the last month, since Victor Grandin's funeral.

"How did Ashley die?"

"In a car crash that also included her mother, Cynthia."

"Why did Victor Grandin Sr. give Cynthia the oil rights and not Ashley?"

"We don't know. And my grandfather signed the document, too, so he knew about it. Now he doesn't remember a thing, so Victor Grandin Jr. hired a private investigator for the two families to look into why they might have signed over the oil rights for our lands, and whether Daniel really fathered Cynthia's child."

Alice sat back, speechless once again. "Have you ever met Heath or his twin brother, Nolan?"

Caitlyn shook her head.

"I went to high school with them. They are hot. I'm talking freshly seared steak hot. I'd forgotten about Nolan, he left Royal but if he's back, that changes the dating scene." She wiggled her eyebrows at Caitlyn. "They're both single."

Caitlyn smiled. "There's enough drama in my family without me trying to date the men trying to destroy our ranch."

Caitlyn chewed on her lip. Alice was right about one thing—she needed to get a life; she was tired of her image as the quiet, shy woman who startled when a man sneezed next to her. Even though the last part was right. "Maybe I should sign up for one of these dating sites. Not all of yours have been that bad. What happened to the guy who sent you flowers and took you to meet his family?"

"He was fine, a bit boring in the sex department but I was willing to deal with that until he took a call with his mother while he was on top of me."

Caitlyn had just taken a sip of her wine, and it went flying out of her mouth, spraying all over the pool lounger. She covered her mouth in embarrassment.

Alice smiled and handed her one of the rolled hand towels from a basket on the table. Caitlyn wiped her mouth and the pool lounger. "You know not to do that to me when I'm drinking," Caitlyn said, laughing.

"Sorry, I forgot about that endearing habit of yours."

"The guy actually talked to his mom while you were in the middle of having sex?"

Alice nodded. "What's worse is he talked to her for a good two minutes, and wanted to continue on like it didn't make a difference."

"How could you not tell me about this?"

"That happened on the day of the Grandin funeral. I was so embarrassed I couldn't even think about it." Alice shook her head. "You and I need to meet men in real life. It's hard to suss out the creep factor online. It's singles' night at the Lone Star nightclub. How about we get all dressed up and go?"

I'd rather face down a pack of hungry wolves.

"You know that's not my scene. There aren't enough cocktails in the world to get me comfortable enough to talk to a strange man. It seems safer to start out with online chatting."

Alice shook her head. "Dating sites are not for you, darlin'. You need someone who's vetted, get some practice in before you go out into the world of vultures and mamas' boys."

Caitlyn nearly spit out her drink again. "I'll skip the mama's boy, but I could use someone who has the backbone to withstand the Lattimore siblings. The last time I went out on a date, Jonathan asked if he could have the guy's Social Security number to run a background check. The time before that, Jayden followed me to the restaurant where I was meeting a blind date. He didn't like the look of the guy, so he stayed parked on the street the entire time I was at dinner and followed us home."

Alice put her hand to her heart. "Your brothers are super sweet."

"No, they're overprotective. They don't pull that stuff with Alexa."

"Because she moved away." Alice took a sip of her wine. "I do have a nice, decent guy with whom you can practice your flirting skills." Alice smiled cheekily, and Caitlyn narrowed her eyes.

"There has to be something wrong with him or you would've dated him."

Alice laughed. "That would be really weird. I'm talking about Russ."

Caitlyn raised a brow. "Your brother, Russ? I thought you said he wasn't into serious dating."

Alice shifted on the lounger. "He's not, which is why he'd be the perfect person to practice your conversational skills. You two really haven't hung out, so he's like a strange man."

Caitlyn bit her lip. She didn't want to offend Alice,

but she'd never felt a spark with her brother, Russ. He was a nice enough guy, but he was just so *white*. Not that she had a problem dating white men. Her biological mother was white, but in the last couple of years she'd struggled with her identity, along with most of the country. Despite her closeness with Alice, her best friend didn't understand Caitlyn's struggle with being a woman of color. Alice had never been asked where she was from, as if her brown skin automatically meant that she was exotic or foreign. Caitlyn had struggled with that over the last two years, debating her own identity. Was she Black, white, both or neither? Whenever a form asked what her race or ethnicity was, she left it blank, because none of the categories fit her. That was the one thing she and Jax had in common. Her ex-boyfriend was also biracial, and he'd understood some of the things she'd struggled with. Yet it hadn't worked out with him, either. Maybe she really was a lost cause.

"Caitlyn, what's the harm? It's just Russ, and you could use the practice."

"I don't know.... Have you asked Russ?"

Alice shook her head reluctantly. "Look, he's coming home after months of travel. I was going to have dinner with him on Friday. Why don't you come? It'll just be the three of us. Low-key. No pressure. I'll be there to back you up and fill in if you stammer over your words or spit out your wine."

Caitlyn threw her dirty hand towel playfully at Alice. *What do I have to lose?* She was bored by the endless conversations about the fate of the Grandin and Lattimore ranches in her house and of making excuses about why she didn't date more. Ever since Layla Grandin and Josh Banks had gotten together, her family had been even more determined to see Caitlyn out and dating. She was tired of being pitied by her siblings. It was time to get over what had happened with Jax. It had been a year since they'd broken up. She'd been on a few dates since then—all failures, thanks to the scars Jax had left. She knew intellectually that Jax was just a bad dating experience, but it clung to her, haunted her thoughts at the most inappropriate times. It was time to replace those memories, even if it was with something meaningless.

"Come on, Caitlyn, what's the worst that can happen?"

She sighed. *That I'll hate Russ but you'll fall in love with the idea of me and Russ and it'll affect our friendship.*

"I'll order Italian from your favorite place," Alice said coaxingly.

"I'll come to dinner. As a friend. I'm not dating Russ."

Alice beamed. "Who said anything about dating? Think of it as a practice session."

"You've got to be kidding me." Alice glared at her phone.

"Trouble?" Caitlyn asked as she arranged the cutlery on Alice's table. Alice lived in a charming row house in the center of Royal. She had decorated it in a comfortable cottage style with soft pastel colors and wood furniture. Caitlyn had come early to help Alice with dinner preparations. She enjoyed the easy way she could make a salad in Alice's kitchen. At her house, the staff took it as an affront if she prepared her own food, feeling that they weren't meeting her standards.

"Russ is late, and he's bringing a friend to dinner."

Caitlyn smiled. While Russ was supposed to be her practice date tonight, it would serve Alice right if he brought another woman home with him. Caitlyn had suspected, but she now knew, that Alice hadn't told Russ she was setting them up.

"I'll set another place at the table," Caitlyn volunteered, her voice sugary sweet. "Don't worry, you have enough food to feed the entire block." If Russ was bringing a woman, Caitlyn could sit back and watch the two of them interact and take notes. The churning in her stomach slowed, and she opened a bottle of wine and poured two glasses. She didn't like to drink when she was anxious, but the evening was looking up.

"How dare Russ bring a woman." Alice seethed.

"Did you tell him he was here to give me boyfriend lessons?" Even as she said the words, Caitlyn realized how ridiculous the idea had been all along. There was no such thing as practicing dating skills. Was there?

She took a large sip from her glass, picturing herself taking notes as she watched Russ and his date converse during dinner as if she were sitting in a classroom. The idea made her giggle.

A half hour later, when the doorbell rang, both Alice and Caitlyn had polished off equal parts of an entire bottle of Bordeaux, and Caitlyn was looking forward to the evening.

Alice opened the door and greeted her brother. Caitlyn waited patiently on the gray leather couch, not wanting to interrupt the inevitable whispered shouting of Alice berating Russ for spoiling the date setup that he didn't know he was participating in. She felt bad for Russ and even worse for his poor date, who would have no idea what she had done to incur Alice's passive-aggressive wrath.

"I can't believe it's you!" Alice's squeals made Caitlyn sit up.

Before she could react, they all walked in, and Caitlyn nearly choked on her drink as she caught sight of the most beautiful man that she'd ever seen.

Two

Dev Mallik knew the moment he walked into Alice's apartment that Russ was going to hate him by the end of the night. He and Russ had been quite the pair in college, Dev with his dark hair, brooding green eyes and generally standoffish nature and Russ with his baby blues, dirty blond hair and the kind of aw-shucks face that made women stalk him after their relationship ended. Russ always got the girl and Dev was stuck entertaining the friend.

But their arrangement suited him just fine. He had enough drama with his family—he didn't need relationship issues to compound them. He preferred women who were vivacious, confident and ready to forget him after one night. Which was why Russ had convinced him to come to dinner at his sister's.

Apparently, Alice was prone to setting Russ up, and the last time he'd dated one of Alice's Royal friends, he'd ended up not being able to come home for six months in order to avoid running into the woman at the doorstep to his condo building. So, he'd brought Dev along tonight to distract the friend from Russ's irresistible charms.

Except, one look at Alice's friend as she put a hand to her delicate mouth and Dev's knees buckled. Before him was the most stunning woman he'd ever seen. She met his gaze and her deep brown eyes, brimming with innocence and laughter widened.

She stood slowly, and he noticed the wineglass in her hand tip forward, so he stepped toward her and placed his hand on her elbow to steady her arm.

Impossibly, her eyes widened some more, and he found himself mesmerized. Her lips parted and though he knew he was being rude, he couldn't help staring at how perfectly pink they were against her tanned skin. What would it be like to run his fingertips across their lusciousness?

Someone cleared their throat—Dev couldn't be sure whether it was Alice or Russ—but it seemed to jar the beautiful woman. She stepped away from him.

"Dev, this is my friend Caitlyn."

Caitlyn. He rolled the name on his tongue. The beautiful name suited her.

He smiled. "Nice to meet you." He extended his hand. She set the wineglass on a side table and took his hand. Her skin was silky soft and warm. It was the kind of hand he wanted to feel on his naked skin, and he held on to it a little too long.

Alice said something he didn't hear, and Caitlyn took her hand back.

"Russ, you remember Caitlyn," Alice introduced them.

Russ stepped forward. "Hey, Caitie, nice to see you again." Caitlyn winced at the nickname. Russ stepped toward her and enveloped her in a hug, and a twinge of jealousy pricked at Dev. Had Russ dated her before? Or was she one of the ones that Russ crudely categorized as *too good to screw with*?

"When did you get to town, Dev?" Alice asked.

"Today. I called Russ, and he spent the afternoon moving me from the Royal Grand Hotel to his condo."

"Well, of course!" Alice turned to Caitlyn. "These two were inseparable in college. It's been years since I've seen you, Dev. What gives?"

Dev smiled warmly at Alice. He'd always liked Russ's sparky little sister. "Right after college, Dad sucked me into the family business. After that it's been one thing after another. Thought I'd come to Royal to take a break from family drama." That was another thing he liked about Alice and Russ—while they may have their sibling spats, they were genuinely close and affectionate with each other. Their parents lived in Arizona and generally stayed out of their lives, but they supported Alice and Russ in whatever the duo wanted to do. Dev couldn't imagine his parents being so hands-off. As much as he loved his heritage, he envied the freedom Russ had to chart his own course.

His Indian parents interfered in everything, from what he ate for breakfast to what he wanted to do with his life. He'd just had a nuclear-level war with his family to come to Royal. He was looking forward to focusing on himself while he was here. It was time for him to pursue his own goals.

"He wants to open a restaurant here," Russ chimed in. "I'm going to help him."

"What type of restaurant?" It was the first time Caitlyn had spoken, and unlike Russ and Alice's Texas twang, she had the clean-cut accent of a finishing school graduate and a voice that was as sweet as a glass of perfectly chilled iced tea on a hot day.

It took him a second to remember what the question was. Russ slapped him on the back and jumped in. "Some hoity-toity fusion Indian cuisine. You should talk to Caitlyn—she's Royal upper crust."

Caitlyn narrowed her eyes, clearly not happy with the description. "We could use a nice Indian restaurant in this town." She gave him a warm smile, and a zing went through his body.

Alice handed the men a glass of wine each. "So, what're your plans?"

"I'm here for a month to scope out potential locations and do some market research. I understand there are already a lot of fine dining establishments here so I'll have to get to know the town to see whether there's room for another restaurant." His comment was for Alice, but he couldn't seem to take his eyes off Caitlyn. "Maybe a Royal native can give me a hand?" *Why waste an opportunity to mix business with pleasure?*

"Alice and I can take you around," Russ said affably, and Dev gave him an irritated look. Hadn't he brought Dev to entertain the friend? Then why was he butting in?

"Why don't we get dinner on the table? You guys were late, so the food is getting cold." Alice grabbed Russ's arm and took him to the kitchen.

A small smiled played on Caitlyn's lips, as if she was enjoying a private joke.

"What's so funny?" Dev whispered as he and Caitlyn stepped toward the dinner table. He needed to know what could bring such a beautiful smile to her kissable lips. Alice had pulled Russ into the kitchen, and they could hear furious whispering but not what was being said.

Caitlyn looked at him with mischief in her eyes, and heat licked deep in his belly. She lowered her voice. "If I had to guess, Alice is telling Russ right now that he needs to tell you to focus your attentions away from me. I'm supposed to be Russ's date tonight, although he doesn't know it."

Dev bit his lip so he didn't laugh out loud and catch Russ's attention. Caitlyn was staring at him, her eyes locked on his, and dancing with amusement. He bent his head and whispered in her ear, "Russ figured Alice would try to set him up, so he brought me here to entertain the friend." He caught a whiff of her fragrance, a muted vanilla and lavender. It was sweet and sexy and kicked up a fire deep in his belly.

He noticed a slight blush on her neck and ears and smiled.

"Ah, so you're his wingman." She took a tiny step away from him and sipped her wine.

"More like the distraction." He stood almost a foot taller than she, so he bent toward her to whisper, "Though I suspect that Russ has been trying to set me up with Alice for a bit now."

Caitlyn's smile dropped. "Would you like to go out with her?" Her voice was measured, but he heard the disappointment loud and clear.

"I've always seen Alice as Russ's little sister and therefore my little sister. I can't imagine dating her."

Her smile reappeared. "I agree completely. I've known Russ as Alice's brother, so it's hard to think of him romantically."

"So why did you come here tonight?"

Caitlyn sighed. "I need practice talking to men."

"Tell me you're kidding."

She shook her head. "I'm not good at making small talk and playing the dating game. Since Russ is exceptionally good at it, Alice thought it would be nice for me to practice with him."

He stepped closer, to see if she really was as skittish as she made herself sound, but she looked up at him, her eyes flirtatious, even challenging. *If this is what she calls shy, why isn't every man in Royal lining up to take her out?*

"So you were hoping to practice what, exactly, with him?"

Her neck and cheeks turned that delectable shade of pink, and he resisted the urge to place a hand on his heart.

"Just conversation. You know, flirting and small talk."

"Well, you don't seem to have any problems talking to me. Dare I say we're even flirting a little?"

She raised a brow. "Are you saying you're enjoying talking to me?"

He leaned in so his lips were almost touching her earlobe. She didn't back away, but he heard the sharp intake of her breath. "I'd like to do a lot more if you'd let me."

The pink in her cheeks deepened. "I mean talking, of course," he said cheekily. Though that was far from the truth. While he did want to talk to Caitlyn, what he really wanted was her alone to see exactly how pink her cheeks could get.

She took a long sip of her wine and gazed at him from under her lashes. Alice and Russ sounded like they were making their way back to the dining room with dinner. "You know what, you're right. I don't have trouble talking with you." She chewed on her lip and glanced toward the kitchen then back at him. "Can I ask you for a favor?"

Whatever you want, Caitlyn, you'll find me more than willing.

"I'm intrigued."

"Will you give me boyfriend lessons?"

Three

Caitlyn couldn't believe what had slipped out of her mouth. *Did I just ask a complete stranger to give me boyfriend lessons?* What was wrong with her? Had she had too much to drink? She looked down into her wineglass as if it would tell her how much she'd had. She calculated that she'd probably drunk a little more than two glasses. Not enough to blame her rash decision on alcohol.

It had been so easy to flirt with Dev, even for a short time. She'd never felt at ease with a date like that. With Dev, there was none of the paralyzing nervousness she felt when she met new men. She and Alice had just been talking about dating lessons, and then in walked a man she had no problem talking to, despite the fact that she was insanely attracted to him. If she could get comfortable with him, then she wouldn't have problems with other men. As a bonus, he was only in Royal for a month, so there was no chance that there would be awkwardness any time they saw each other in town. Nor would she have to avoid him like she'd had to avoid Jax over the past year.

Alice had arranged them around her rectangular dinner table so that Caitlyn was sitting across from Russ and next to Dev with Alice across from Dev. Alice had ordered a beef ragù ravioli in rosé sauce, steamed vegetables and garlic bread from the local Italian restaurant Caitlyn loved. It was a family favorite because of it's good food and unpretentious interior. Caitlyn had prepared a Caesar salad.

"This sauce is excellent," Dev said.

Russ scrunched up his nose. "I personally prefer the one from Primi Piatti. This one is too creamy."

"The creaminess comes from good-quality cheese. Most places just use cheap mozzarella." Dev scooped some sauce on his fork and licked it.

Caitlyn didn't want to stare, but she couldn't take her eyes off the way his tongue flicked out and licked the edge of the fork. A warmth pooled deep in her core, a feeling totally unexpected sitting at dinner. It usually took more than staring at a handsome stranger to get her going. A lot more!

"They also use Grana Padano in this sauce. That's what gives it the depth of flavor," Dev continued, and Caitlyn had to force herself to focus on what he was saying.

"You know your food," she said admiringly.

"In a different life, I would've been a chef."

"Why not in this one?"

Their eyes were locked together, and Russ and Alice faded from her consciousness.

He shrugged. "It's complicated. But that's why I'm opening a restaurant. I want to start a chain of high-end Indian fusion restaurants."

So he's Indian. Caitlyn had thought as much from his name. He was slightly darker skinned than she, but those green eyes—*oof.* His hair was thick and wavy and she wondered whether he'd like it if she ran her fingers through it.

"Why choose Royal for the first one?" Alice's voice broke through, and Caitlyn looked at her guiltily. She'd been completely focused on Dev beside her and had been ignoring Russ. Not that it mattered, because he seemed to be busy staring at his phone.

"Because Royal is far enough away from my family that they can't drop in on me. And from what Russ tells me, this town has the deep pockets and foodies to support a new restaurant. In a place like Vegas or LA, where new restaurants open every day, there won't be any buzz. I'd have to work ten times as hard to get attention. A town like Royal is full of wealthy—" While Caitlyn was studiously cutting a piece of ravioli into perfect square bites, she could feel his eyes on her. "—discerning individuals who appreciate fine dining."

Caitlyn looked up to see that he was indeed staring at her, a sparkle in his green eyes that sent her nerves tingling.

"Plus, the start-up costs in Royal are relatively low," Russ chimed in. "There are a number of places that went out of business in the heart of town, and their space is dirt cheap. I'm friends with the local Realtor. I'll set it up for you."

"Those businesses were lifelong Royal residents," Caitlyn said, irritated. "Mrs. Lowrey owned the little tea shop. It was passed down to her by her mother, who started it when she first moved to Royal in the 1920s. There's a hundred years of history that just got erased when they foreclosed."

"Russ didn't mean to sound so insensitive," Alice quickly jumped in. "Caitlyn tried to help those businesses get loans—even hosted charity events and got the wealthy ranchers to open their tight purse strings to help."

"What happened?" Dev asked, sounding genuinely interested.

Caitlyn shrugged. "We were able to keep several of the Main Street small businesses open, but a number of the older residents just didn't have it in them to keep going under the circumstances."

Dev smiled kindly. "You cared enough to do something about it. That counts for a lot."

"So, Russ, tell us, how is work going for you?" Alice said loudly, trying to get Russ's attention away from his phone.

Russ launched into a monologue of how he'd scored a major win. He worked as an investment banker, and while he was New York–based most of the time, he was back to take some "chillax" time.

Caitlyn found herself thinking about how she'd brazenly asked Dev to be her practice boyfriend, embarrassment mixing with anxiety and fear as the night went on. What must he think of her? She'd known him all of two minutes and had asked him to give her boyfriend lessons, like they were middle school children. Now that she had time to think, she wondered how best to extricate herself from the situation. Perhaps not mention it? Tell him she was joking? How could she even bring it up again?

When dinner finished, they all helped Alice pack up what was left of the food. Caitlyn was acutely aware of Dev moving around her in the dining room and kitchen. Alice took Russ to the kitchen to help her put away dinner—and probably to yell at him.

Caitlyn sat down in Alice's seat at the table so she was across from Dev. She didn't want to sit close to him again. All through dinner, she couldn't help glancing in his direction, and she hadn't missed Alice's glare every time she'd done it.

She took a sip of her wine, wondering where to start the conversation.

"So, how do I get in touch with my practice girlfriend?"

She clapped a hand on her mouth, but it was too late. The wine spluttered out of her mouth, across the table and onto his hand. She grabbed the napkin on the table and began mopping his hand and the table all at the same time, too mortified to even look at him. "Oh my God, I'm sorry. I'm so sorry."

He placed a hand on hers, stilling her frantic movements. She looked at him. There was a wide grin on his face, his eyes dazzlingly green. A warmth spread from her chest to her face. "I'm so sorry," she repeated in a small voice.

His hand was still on hers, and he stood and leaned over the table so his face was close to hers. Her entire body pulsed. His aftershave smelled like heaven, the scruffy five o'clock shadow on his jaw inviting her to rub her hands on it. "When we go out on our first date tomorrow, can you do that again? It's the sexiest thing I've ever seen."

She looked at him in horror. "I'm so sorry, it's a terrible habit."

He lifted his hand from hers and placed a finger on her lips as if to shush her. The feel of his finger made her lips tremble. He shook his head. "Don't ever be sorry for doing that again."

Alice cleared her throat, and both of them jumped back, as if they were teenagers caught by their parents.

"Dare I ask what's going on here?" Her voice was a little too high, and Caitlyn knew she was pissed.

"I did that thing I do when I get caught off guard while drinking wine," she said sheepishly, hoping to soothe the irritation etched on Alice's face. "Dev was helping me clean up."

Russ set down a stack of plates. "Uh-oh, you got the Caitie shower," he said. "We've all been victims."

Caitlyn wanted to crawl under the table and hide. Alice shot Russ a look. "Well, I have tiramisu for dessert, and Russ brought home a lovely ice wine that we opened."

Caitlyn wasn't hungry for dessert and wasn't sure she could stay much longer in Dev's company without incinerating and asking him to teach her more than just conversation. "I'm sorry, I have to leave. Since I knew I'd be drinking, I asked my brother to give me a ride, and he'll be heading home soon."

"Oh, stay. You can take an Uber later," Alice insisted, but Caitlyn shook her head. She was already planning to take an Uber—she'd used her brother as an excuse to make her escape.

Once Caitlyn had left, Russ decided it was time to play one of their old college games that involved a lot of drinking and a rehash of the most embarrassing/frustrating moments of their lives. Alice wasn't too keen and neither was Dev, but Russ's exuberance was hard to ignore. After a while Alice held up her hands. "I think we're out of alcohol."

Russ booed her. "Guess it's time to call it a night."

"Before you do…" Alice turned to Russ. "What did you think of Caitlyn?"

Russ cocked his head. "Caitie? What's there to think about?"

Dev tried not to laugh. "Well, I thought she was fantastic."

Alice glared at him. "Caitlyn was supposed to be Russ's date."

Both men laughed, much to Alice's chagrin.

"Sis, you really should let me in on these plans of yours. Though I will admit Caitlyn isn't the shy little creature I remember. She's really come into her own."

Dev caught the note of interest in Russ's voice, and his heart seized. Was Russ interested in Caitlyn after all? If they'd been at a bar and interested in the same girl, they'd flip a coin. But this was different. Russ knew Caitlyn, and if he was interested in her, Dev couldn't stand in his way. Even though Caitlyn had seized his interest in a way he'd never experienced before. It wasn't just her stunning body or looks. Normally he couldn't stop thinking about what it would be like to take the woman to bed, but with Caitlyn, he'd been genuinely interested in getting to know her. There was something about her—perhaps it was the genuine innocence—that tugged at his heart strings. She seemed sincere and authentic, like she said what she meant and every sentence wasn't a calculated step toward some hidden goal. Russ wasn't the right man for her—he was a ruthless investment banker with a golden tongue when it came to lying to women to get what he wanted. Dev hated to think of Caitlyn, with her charmingly naive request for boyfriend practice, in Russ's hands. He shuddered. The man wouldn't think twice about taking advantage of her.

"So you interested in her?" he asked Russ more insistently than he'd intended.

"Dev, your tongue was hanging so far out of your

mouth, I'm surprised you weren't licking the plate instead of your lips," Russ said.

Dev punched him playfully but thought hard about his words. "Yeah, I think I like her—that's if you're not interested in her."

His heart stopped as he waited for Russ's reply, but Alice jumped in. "He is absolutely interested."

"Excuse me?" Russ glared at his sister, and Dev sat back. Even if Russ was interested in Caitlyn, there was no way he was going after her now and letting Alice win. Dev knew his friend well enough to know that Russ hated the way Alice interfered in his love life and how judgmental she was about the women he dated. Dev understood. His own family was constantly presenting the "biodata" of eligible Indian women from around the globe with the expectation that one of them would catch his attention. None had. Not like Caitlyn. At the thought of his family, a shiver went down his spine. They would never approve of Caitlyn. He shook the thought away. He wasn't marrying her. There was no reason to ever bring his family into their potential relationship.

Relationship? He'd just met the woman tonight. They hadn't even had sex and Dev was already contemplating a relationship? *One step at a time, Mallik*, he told himself.

The first step was getting Caitlyn's number from Alice.

"Alice, Russ isn't going to date Caitlyn because you're setting him up with her."

Alice glared at Dev, and Russ sat back in the

couch. "I'm goin' to let m' man Dev here have her," he said insolently, his Texas accent a little slurred.

"Neither one of you deserves her," she said icily. "I don't know what I was thinking, bringing her into this vipers' pit. That girl is way too good for either one of you. I'd hoped you—" she used her finger to stab Russ in the chest "—had grown up some."

Dev sat up and struck a more serious tone. "Seriously, Alice, I do really like her. She seems like a nice person, and I promise you I'll treat her well. Plus, she asked me to be her practice boyfriend, so I feel like I should at least text her to let her know I'm interested."

Alice's jaw dropped. Literally dropped. "She did what now? What else did she say?"

"Nothing. We didn't really get a chance to talk, what with you trying to insert Russ into the conversation. I don't even have her number to follow up and ask her out on a practice date. Any chance you'd share it?"

Alice narrowed her eyes, and he cringed at the ice-blue glare. "Not a chance. If I have anything to do with it, you aren't getting anywhere near Caitlyn."

Four

Caitlyn awoke the next morning to a text message from an unknown number on her phone. She threw back her comforter, groaning at how bright it was in her room.

When she returned home from Alice's house the night before, she'd found her family, minus Alexa, who was back in Miami, and the Grandins gathered in their living room. They were meeting to discuss their favorite topic: Heath Thurston's claim. They'd rehashed everything they knew, which wasn't much. The private eye had confirmed that Daniel was very likely Ashley's biological father, because the timing fit. But they still didn't know why Victor Grandin had given the oil rights to Cynthia and not to Ashley if it was supposed to be her birthright. Even more

puzzling was why Augustus Lattimore had signed
the papers. Jonas Shaw, the PI, was also working on
finding out if the documents Heath Thurston had
shared were legitimate.

Layla and Josh had been there as well, and Caitlyn had spent the entire night studying them surreptitiously, wondering if she'd share something like
that with someone. Dev kept coming to mind, but
she pushed the thought away.

After the Grandins left, her parents went to bed,
but Jonathan, Jayden and Caitlyn stayed up talking.
For once it was not about Caitlyn's dating life. None
of them liked the idea of sitting around doing nothing
while the PI did his work. Jonathan suggested they
go through every single piece of paper that related
to the property. Augustus, Ben's father and Caitlyn's
grandfather, was so forgetful, even their father, Ben,
couldn't be sure that he hadn't hidden something in
the attic and forgotten about it.

Jonathan had hauled the boxes down from the
attic. They'd already been through all the files in the
study and Lattimore offices. It was time to unearth
what had been hidden away. They had started going
through the dusty, cobwebbed boxes. They found
some interesting historical pictures, a lot of dead
spiders and even a dead mouse in between some old
books. They'd given up at the first light of dawn and
Caitlyn had taken a quick shower to get the dust off,
then crawled into bed.

She had several text messages from Alice but

ignored those. She needed to give Alice time to calm down.

Then she saw the text from an unknown number.

How's tonight for a practice date? Dev.

Dev? Had she given him her number? She rubbed her eyes and reread the text. His number wasn't saved in her contacts, so they hadn't exchanged numbers last night. Then she saw the texts from Alice.

Russ got your contact info from my phone and gave it to Dev.
Has he texted you?
DO NOT go out with him.
Call me when you see this.

She turned her attention back to Dev's text. What did he mean about a practice date? Her brain was a little foggy from the whiskey she'd shared with her siblings. It took a minute for last night's memory to make her sit up in bed, wide-awake. She'd asked a complete stranger for boyfriend lessons. *What have I done?*

She stared at the text message and her heart jumped. It had been so easy to talk to him, the usual feelings of dread and anxiety hadn't overtaken her. Then there was the image of Dev's green eyes, his tall frame, the way he'd licked that sauce off the fork. Warmth stirred deep in her core. She'd be crazy to go

out with him. Surely there were better ways to practice her dating skills? She took a breath and typed
out her response.

"So what exactly is a practice boyfriend?" Dev
asked.

Caitlyn stopped before taking a sip of her water.
How could she explain it to him when she hadn't
been able to come up with an answer herself, despite
having thought about it all day.

"Are you ready to order?" Caitlyn was grateful
for the too-attentive waiter of the RCW Steakhouse,
one of the fine dining restaurants in Royal. Dev had
suggested it, and now he sat back in a collared shirt
with the top button open and khakis. He looked ef-
fortlessly perfect—not too dressy, but not too casual.

Meanwhile, she'd shown up in her standard ladies'
luncheon outfit—a knee-length pale pink sheath
dress with a boat neck. She'd tried on every outfit
in her closet. To ease the incessant fluttering that
had taken hold in her belly ever since she'd texted
Dev to accept his invitation, she'd chosen a familiar
outfit. One that boosted her confidence and made
her feel in charge.

"Tell me about the menu and specials." Dev asked
the waiter with a healthy dose of amusement in his
voice. The waiter launched into a description of each
steak on the menu, finally ending with the special of
the day, which was brisket.

"What do you recommend?" Dev turned to her.

"The steak," she quipped.

They both ordered French onion soup for an appetizer and prime rib for dinner, and then Dev let out a laugh. "Maybe I've been in New York too long, but steak houses there don't just serve steak. This is a really nice place but their menu could use some variety."

Caitlyn smiled. "This is a ranchin' town and RCW is a local favorite. I come here at least once a week."

"Does this town really need another fine dining restaurant?"

"It could." Caitlyn said quickly. "A lot of meetings and business gets conducted in restaurants. For example, the hospital board likes to come here for lunch. The women all order salads, minus the steak. They really come here for the whiskey. On that front, this place is the best in town, and if you want to attract the old ranchers, you need to make sure you offer premium alcohol at your restaurant."

He smiled and pretended to take notes. "Looks like you might be the one giving me lessons...on how to succeed in Royal."

Her cheeks warmed. What had come over her last night at Alice's? Maybe it was the wine, maybe it was the fact that she'd been unbelievably attracted to Dev. Or just some plain old crazy had come over her.

She went on to talk about wine, whiskey and bourbon, the drinks of the town. She wasn't usually this talkative, but she didn't want to go back to talking about what practice dating meant. The conversation flowed through dinner. Somehow, she didn't feel the tension that usually tightened her muscles on these dates. Dev's easy smile put her at ease.

"So what do you do?"

The dreaded question. There was no avoiding it. *Time for the spiel about all the important work I do to make it sound like I have a real job.*

She met his gaze and regretted doing so. His face was so open, his eyes warm and inviting. She remembered how he'd reacted when she'd spit her wine out at him. When that had happened with Jax, he'd made fun of her, repulsed like she'd thrown up on his good shoes. That's the way all men reacted. But not Dev.

She sighed. "I'm basically a socialite. As you gathered last night, my family is wealthy. After college, it was hard to focus on a job or career because my parents needed so much from me. Serving on the various boards that we get invited to, planning charity events, hosting events, etc. I'd be lying to you if I said that I was saving the world. I've just been untethered. I came back home after college and my family needed me, so I put my plans aside."

Every time a man found out that she didn't have a regular nine-to-five job, there were two types of responses—the guy either assumed that she wanted to live off her family money or that she was husband hunting. She couldn't decide which was more offensive. She searched Dev's face for which category he would fall into.

He reached out and put a hand on hers. The weight felt good on her hand, comforting. "Being there for your family is something to be proud of. Big families are complicated, and it takes an inordinate amount of work to keep people and business contacts on your side. Don't ever be apologetic for that."

Tears stung her eyes, and she blinked. "Do you also have a big family?" she managed to choke out.

He smiled. "I have big personalities in my family. I have one brother and one sister, both married with children. And parents who have a rather large business that they want me to take over, much to the discontent of my siblings."

She raised an eyebrow. She couldn't imagine fighting with her siblings for the family business. Part of the reason she took on so much of the family social work was because no one else wanted it, but it was an important part of keeping their standing in Royal and making sure that their ranching business got what it needed.

"Your siblings want the family business, but you don't want to give it to them?"

His lips tugged into a smirk as if the very idea was funny. He shook his head. "Ma and Dad grew up in India, where the eldest son takes over the family empire and takes care of the family. That's me. But I don't want to just inherit my father's wealth. I want to do something on my own, if only to prove that I can successfully run a business. That's why I'm in Royal. My siblings are more than happy to take over the family business, but they have a tendency to live lavish lives, and Dad is worried they'll run the business into the ground. He doesn't trust them, so I'm left playing the peacemaker between my father and siblings."

"Wow. So, what happens to your family business if you successfully launch your restaurant chain?"

"That is a question I refuse to think about. I'm hoping that me being out of New York for a month or so will give my sibs a chance to show Dad that they can step up. I love my father, but he's hard on all of us. Maybe if I'm not there, he'll see my sister's accomplishments. She really has a head for business, but my dad has refused to appreciate that."

Is this guy for real? Most men saw her attachment to her family and her constant focus on them as a sign of immaturity. But here was a guy who truly understood what it meant to love, care and sacrifice for his family.

"Are you going to miss your family while you're here?"

He shook his head and laughed. "I'm so done with family drama. Don't get me wrong, I would stand in front of a bullet for my family, but I need a mental break. That's why I chose Texas for my first restaurant. We have no businesses here, no reason for my family to appear. I need a break from family crises."

Caitlyn's heart fisted. She'd been about to share her own family's dilemma with him, but it was hardly fair.

"So, if you're done stalling with small talk, want to tell my why you need boyfriend lessons?"

No, I want to talk about anything but that.

He was looking at her with such a sparkle in his

eyes that her heart jumped and she lost the few words she'd formulated since the start of dinner. *Who asks such a gorgeous guy to be a practice boyfriend?*

"I find it hard to date." She swallowed, trying to get the words out of her dry mouth. "When I'm with a man, I get stiff and quiet. I need some practice dating, getting comfortable with small talk and flirting. You're the first one I've met who I didn't get all tongue-tied with. I didn't mean to spring it on you like that. I'd had a little too much to drink."

"Well, you haven't touched your wine tonight, and I don't see you having any trouble talking to me."

A fact that hadn't gotten unnoticed by her.

"Which is why you're the perfect guy to be a practice boyfriend. I'm comfortable with you and..." *Can tolerate the experience.* She stopped herself from saying the last part out loud. How could she explain to Dev the fear she felt every time she got close to a man? She couldn't even explain it to herself. *Cold fish.* Those were Jax's words but others had said a variation of them to her. The therapist she'd seen had called it a fear of intimacy. A fear that had come from what had happened with Jax.

The sex was fine, but it hadn't cured her inability to connect on an emotional level. She'd seen what Layla and Josh had, how they understood each other and the way they supported one another. Josh knew what Layla needed, and she intuitively took care of him. Was it too much to want the same thing?

He leaned forward. "So am I just meant for conversation or do we get to practice other things, too?"

A smile twitched on his lips, and while she tried to maintain eye contact, her heart skipped erratically. Her eyes involuntary dropped to his lips. They were so firm and lush. What would it be like to feel them pressing on the sensitive parts of her? Heat gushed deep in her core, and as she lifted her gaze and watched his eyes darken. She knew without a doubt that he could see what she was thinking.

We can practice anything you want. Wait, what? She broke eye contact and took a sip of her wine to do something other than think about him and her naked. She wanted to go out on dates, practice her conversational skills, learn how to get to know someone so she could connect with them emotionally. If she had sex with Dev, then their physical relationship would overshadow everything. She couldn't deny the attraction she felt to Dev, but what if she let things get physical and he also found her lacking? *No, that won't do. I have to make it clear to him that this is a platonic relationship.*

"Well, I was thinking I can keep you company as you do your research on the restaurants in town. I can show you around, introduce you to the movers and shakers, and in return you can teach me how to…"

"How to…?"

"Dessert?" Dev shot the waiter a dark look, but he didn't get the message, handing them the dessert menus. Caitlyn quickly declined dessert, and Dev followed suit. She didn't fully trust herself with him yet, it was best to end the date on a high note.

* * *

As Dev pulled out his wallet, Caitlyn waved to the waiter, pulling out her own credit card. "I should pay."

He shook his head. "Absolutely not. I invited you to dinner." When Alice had refused to give him Caitlyn's number, Dev had called in a favor with Russ to get her information. He hadn't been able stop thinking about her since last night. She was even more beautiful than he remembered from the night before. *Why would someone like her need a practice boyfriend?* Men should be falling over themselves to get a date with her. He'd just spent the last hour and a half enjoying talking about Royal, the history of Texas and foods from around the world. She was intelligent, witty and grounded. Not at all like the socialites he'd met in New York whose main focus was making sure they outdid each other, whether it was fashion, jewelry or Manhattan parties. She was the first woman he'd met in a long time whom he wanted to get to know, not just take back to his bed. Although *that* was something he also wanted to do. Eventually. As long as she was okay with the idea that their relationship was temporary. He had enough going on with his life that he wasn't interested in any type of long-term commitment. But while he hadn't planned on an affair in Royal, it would make his time here a lot more interesting.

"Yes, but you only invited me because I asked you to be a...practice boyfriend." She tripped over the last words, and he smiled.

As their server made his way over, Dev held out his card to the waiter, who plucked it out of his hand. "I asked you to dinner. Because I wanted to see you. Practice or not. Besides, this is a business expense, I'm here to check out the competition."

Caitlyn smiled widely, and he found himself smiling back, completely taken in by the sweetness in her eyes. "This place is a Royal institution. They'll be on of your main competitors."

"Russ has been telling me for years that there's no place like Royal to open a restaurant. Lots of deep pockets and a real appreciation for good food."

"He's right."

The waiter returned with the credit card receipt a little too efficiently. Dev was hoping to get some more time with Caitlyn. "Do you know a place where we can get coffee?"

She paused, and he was sure she was about to refuse him, but then she nodded.

As they walked out of the restaurant, he placed his hand at the small of her back. A gesture he hadn't even thought about until she stiffened. He removed his hand. *Did I do something wrong?*

They walked down the main street. The daytime heat had dissipated, so the night was warm but the slight breeze made it comfortable. The sun had set, but the last rays clung to the sky in hues of dark orange and purple. Old-timey streetlamps threw seductive shadows on the bricked sidewalk. It was the quintessential main street of old-town America. He longed to take her hand or tuck her arm in his, but he resisted. As they walked, she pointed out the various local businesses, most of which had closed for the day. He marveled at how she knew the names of each of the owners and their life stories.

She stopped in front of a red brick building with an old-fashioned sign that read General Store.

"Now if you are serious about opening a restaurant here, you need to make friends with Ol'Fred. Don't call him Fred. He likes to be called Ol'Fred."

"With the Texas twang?"

She smiled. "Yes. His family has been in Royal since the town was founded, and he not only knows all the landowners in town, anything you need to get things done, he's the man. He knows all the building contractors, the city inspectors and the permit architects at the county. And if you need a certain brand of tonic water for some spoiled brat cousin that even Amazon doesn't carry, he can get it for you."

They were standing underneath a streetlight, which emitted a soft golden glow on her face. He turned to face her, unable to take being so close to her and not touching her.

"Caitlyn, cards on the table. I like you. I want to spend more time with you, and not just because you can give me a crash course on all things Royal. What exactly do you want from me?"

She swallowed but didn't avert her gaze. "I don't want to be pitied because I usually can't get past a few dates. I want to learn how to open up to a man and have meaningful conversations, not just small talk. To connect on an emotional level."

He stepped closer to her. She stiffened but didn't step back.

"Is that all you want? To connect emotionally? What about physically, Caitlyn? Do you need practice with that?" His voice was low and thick, and he couldn't help it. She looked so devastatingly sexy and vulnerable that he wanted to—no, he *needed* to touch her, to let her know that she didn't need any help connecting with him, or anyone, for that matter. If she was having problems, the fault was clearly with the guy for not seeing the intelligent, caring person she was.

"I... I...don't know," she said helplessly. Her eyes darkened, and she dropped her gaze to his lips and her face tipped upward slightly.

"Then let me help you make up your mind."

He stepped closer and ran his hands down her bare arms, enjoying the soft, silky feel of her skin. He watched her face. She closed her eyes, and her lips parted slightly. Goose bumps sprang up on her arm, despite the hot night, and he knew she was feeling the same electric connection he was. He gently took her hand.

"Open your eyes."

She did.

"I'm going to kiss you now."

Her eyes widened. He bent his head and kissed her softly, just barely touching her lips, savoring the feel of her. He felt the slight pressure of her lips as she kissed him back and opened her mouth to him. He wanted more than anything to deepen the kiss, but he didn't want to scare her off. He put his arm around her waist to steady them. She felt so right pressed against him, and he couldn't help but pull her closer so he could feel the crush of her breasts against his chest.

That's when it happened. For the first time in his life, a woman pushed him away from her like she couldn't stand his touch.

Five

What have I done?

She hadn't meant to push him away so rudely.
What she'd wanted to do was kiss him hard then
untuck that stiff shirt and run her hands all over his
chest. She'd pressed herself against him and felt the
same heat that pulsed between her legs in his pants.
And that scared the hell out of her. She didn't want
to risk being rejected by him. *A cold fish.*

He stepped back from her and held his hands up.
The streetlamp lit his eyes, which were filled with
horror. "I'm sorry I misread things, Caitlyn. I didn't
mean to kiss you if you didn't want it."

Didn't want it? That's not the problem. She
wanted it *too much*, with a fire and intensity that

didn't make any sense. It was just a kiss. He was just a guy.

She shook her head. "No, I'm sorry. I didn't mean to do that."

"Kiss me or push me away?"

Both.

"Push you away. I don't know what came over me. I've never done anything like that before."

"Am I so bad a kisser?" he said lightly, placing a hand on his chest where she'd pushed him. He looked so devastatingly, boyishly handsome, her heart fisted. She'd expected him to get angry, to yell at her, utter some expletives. She had wanted the kiss. He had warned her that he was about to kiss her. She wanted to lie to him and tell him that she'd changed her mind about him being a practice boyfriend. That she didn't want to see him anymore. This non-relationship was already too intense.

But isn't that exactly what I want?

"It's the opposite problem, actually. It was just so… good."

"Now, that's a more interesting answer." He stepped closer to her. "What do you mean?"

"Do you mind if we walk?" It was too disconcerting, having him looking at her. As irrational as it was, she couldn't help feeling he could read her thoughts. She didn't want him to know how out of control he made her feel.

"Lead the way."

As they walked down the main town street, she resumed her informational session on Royal businesses. She was avoiding the conversation. She knew it, and Dev knew it, but he let her go on, asking her questions about Royal and about her family. Familiar, comfortable topics. When they reached the tack shop, she stopped.

"This is where everyone in town buys their fancy equestrian items for the horses they ride in shows."

"Do you ride?"

She nodded and looked wistfully at the shop. Dev was in town pursuing his dream, and yet hers was stalled.

"What is it?"

She turned to him in surprise. "Nothing."

He rolled his eyes. "I have a sister and a mother, so I know when a woman says 'nothing' it really means 'everything.'"

Now it was her turn to roll her eyes. "Oh, please, don't mansplain me. Sometimes it also means I don't want to talk about it, or more importantly, I don't want to talk about it with *you*."

He smiled. "C'mon, I'm your practice boyfriend. If you can't tell me, then who?"

The laughter in his voice was infectious, and it made her smile at her own ridiculousness. "Fine, if you must know. I have this plan—more of a dream, actually—of starting a horse-riding program for foster children on the Lattimore ranch. I've been around horses all my life, and it's been an amazing experience for me and a teaching tool in how to care for an animal, how to feel one with another living being."

She pointed to a belt buckle in the shop. It was

a big silver buckle studded with rhinestones. "That buckle costs what most foster families make in a month. They can't afford to send kids to horse riding camps. We have all these horses that we hire staff to ride because no one has the time to groom and ride them. Seems like such a waste."

"So what's stopping you?"

"I can't just open up the Lattimore ranch and ask kids to come on over and ride horses. I have to get permits, inspections—it's a whole process."

He raised an eyebrow. "I get it. You pissed off Ol'Fred and he's standing in your way."

She smiled. "Ol'Fred has been offering to adopt me since I was a little girl. He'd do anything to help me."

"So then?"

"It's just life. I have all these obligations and board commitments. It's hard to find the time."

"Sounds like excuses to me."

"What?" *How dare he?* He didn't have any idea what her life was like.

He turned to face her. The light from the tack shop threw shadows across his face. He raised his hands like he was going to touch her, then crossed them. "You seem like the type of woman who knows how to get things done in this town. If you want to open this camp, I bet you could make it happen with a snap of your fingers. So, what are you waiting for? What's stopping you? The real reason, not the one you're telling yourself and everyone else."

She wanted to give him an angry response, but

the warm look in his eyes and the crease on his forehead melted her heart. She was looking for genuine connection. What had her therapist said? That she put up blocks, hid behind her conversation talking points. Normally her dates didn't care to probe past what she said. They were too focused on how the night would end and whether she'd accept an invitation to their bed. But Dev wanted to know more. He wanted to talk about things she hadn't prepared for.

She swallowed, then looked into the tack shop window to avoid his gaze. "I'm the youngest in the family. I have two brothers and a sister. They've looked out for me my whole life. Made sure I'm successful in whatever I do."

"You've never done anything on your own."

She shook her head. "It's not that. I've planned many charitable events and social programs. You're right. I can do this in my sleep. But I've never done anything this important. Since the pandemic, the foster program has been overwhelmed. And it's not just the stories you expect—kids who are abandoned, abused or neglected. It's kids whose parents love them but lost their jobs and couldn't make ends meet. The state forcibly took the kids because they were living in cars and homeless shelters. Neither the parents nor the kids want to be apart, but the state has to put the kids in a stable home. Then there are cutbacks to the state program so the families who foster get little support and are overwhelmed themselves. These kids are moved from one family to another. And even when the kids find a good family, they feel they have to be loyal to their birth parents and don't know how to process the emotions they feel toward their foster parents."

Tears sprang to her eyes as she thought about the kids she'd met. She volunteered at the child protection services office, babysitting kids who were waiting for placement. Playing with them and giving them the attention that the social workers who were busy finding them families didn't have the bandwidth for.

"I want to give them something that's stable. A place where they feel safe and can connect with a living being without the complications of a label like 'foster dad' and 'real mom.'"

"Is that how you feel about horses?"

She startled. "What?"

"A horse only needs water, food, shelter and grooming. No complicated human emotions with horses."

A bitter taste swirled in the back of her throat. Was that why she'd always gotten along with horses? Because they didn't expect any real feelings from her? No, that couldn't be true. She loved her horses, talked to them, bonded with them. They sensed when she was sad or angry. But they didn't expect as much from her as a man, that much was true. Yet she wasn't about to admit that to Dev. They'd already gotten a little too close for comfort.

She sighed. "Horses sense feelings and emotions. They need love, which is why a riding program for kids is so perfect. They have so much love to give, and they just don't know where to direct it sometimes."

He bent his knees so he was face-to-face with her, forcing her to look at him. His eyes were soft, even a little shiny. "You are a wonderful person, Caitlyn. I hope you know that. To care about something other than yourself is something very few people know how to do."

Then why am I such a cold fish? she almost blurted out. She tried to smile at him, but tears threatened to spill out of her eyes, so she turned her gaze back to the tack shop window. "I was ready to start my program, but there's an issue with my ranch. I don't want to start the program and have to take it away."

"What do you mean?"

Could she tell him? "It's exactly the type of family drama you don't want to get involved in."

He laughed now. "As long as it's not *my* family drama, I don't care. C'mon, spill it."

She told him about Heath Thurston's claim.

"Let me get this straight. Ashley might be the blood relative, but Cynthia is Ashley's mother, and the oil rights were given to her."

"Correct, which actually makes the claim stronger, because Heath and Nolan are Cynthia's sons, so they directly inherit from their mother. But there are still some things that don't make sense, so we've hired a PI to find out."

"I'm sorry, I'm not a rancher. Why does Victor Grandin, is it?" She nodded, so he went on. "Why does he get to give the oil rights to your land to cover up his son's sins?"

"That's the baffling part. My grandfather signed the papers so the rights beneath our land are included."

"Didn't you say you live with your grandfather? Why not ask him?"

"Augustus is ninety-six years old and has memory issues. We've tried asking him, and each time we get a different story. We're trying to find out whether the signature is even genuine."

"So how does this affect your horse camp?"

"If the claim is real, and Heath and Nolan Thurston decide to exercise their rights, they'd be digging wells right where the stables are. We'd lose the stables and horses. I can't do that to those kids. While all this could take some time, I can't let them fall in love with something that then gets yanked away from them."

"Is that what happened to you?"

"What?"

"Is there something that got taken away from you?" he asked softly.

Her heart beat wildly in her chest, and her palms felt greasy. She was the most privileged child she knew. A biracial baby adopted by a wealthy, loving family who doted on her. There was absolutely nothing that she could have asked for in her life that hadn't been handed to her. The only thing she'd ever lost was Jax, her high school best friend and perhaps the love of her life.

She shook her head. "I'm the story every foster kid dreams of. My parents adopted me when I was a baby. My family, including my siblings, love me like crazy. I couldn't ask for anything in my life."

"Does that make you feel guilty?"

"What?"

"That you were given a chance with your family that the foster kids don't have? Is that why you want to open the horse ranch?"

She took a shuddering breath. *How did he know?*

"It's okay to feel guilty, for having it all, you know. To even feel resentful for it. You didn't ask for it."

This time she didn't stop the tears that squeezed out of her eyes. All her life, she'd been told how lucky she was, to be grateful for the gift she'd been given. That's why she'd returned home after college to take over the Lattimores' charitable and community work. To give back a little bit of what she'd gotten. Yet all she felt was guilty. For having it all. For not giving back enough. For not saving all the other kids, the majority of them Black, from the fate the Lattimores had saved her from.

Dev lightly placed a hand on her arm then extended his other arm, inviting her to step into his embrace. She couldn't resist. Stepping close, she placed her cheek against his chest and immediately felt his warmth strengthen her.

You know Royal has a ghetto? It's where people like me live. Where your butler, gardener, cook and Ol'Fred live. Jax had said those words to her when he'd gone off to college. It was his way of telling her there was a whole world she needed to see. The real world. He hadn't said it with malice, but it still hurt.

Dev was almost a foot taller than she was, even with her heels. Yet she fit perfectly against him. She focused on the beating of his heart, which seemed to be racing as wildly as hers. Closing her eyes against the rise and fall of his chest, she took deep breaths to push Jax out of her mind. Here was a man who wasn't obliged to be with her. He was here because he wanted to be. No one was forcing him.

"How about we make a deal?"

Caitlyn stepped back from Dev, blinking away the remaining tears in her eyes.

His green eyes sparkled. "How about I agree to be your practice boyfriend and help you figure out how to make your horse camp happen, and you introduce me around town and help me set up my restaurant?"

She smiled. "What exactly does being a practice girlfriend entail?"

He grinned. "I like how you turned this around on me."

While she'd pulled back from his embrace, his hands were still loosely on her arms, and she liked them there, liked the weight of his touch, the slight smell of soap and aftershave. Maybe it wouldn't be that bad an idea for him to be a full boyfriend. What if she slept with him? What's the worst that could happen? Their relationship would end the same way her others had? So what? Dev was only going to be in Royal for a month. He'd told her at dinner that he planned to open the restaurant, then return to New York to his family business before continuing to establish a chain of restaurants. He wasn't planning on living in Royal. He wasn't going to be a long-term anything, and she planned to be a lifelong Royal. If along the way he could help her get more comfortable with men, that's all she needed. Wasn't that the point of boyfriend lessons anyway?

"Here's what I can offer you as a practice boyfriend," Dev said, and Caitlyn followed the smooth, thick sound of his voice, letting herself get pulled in. He was a man—he would ask for the thing all men wanted. And she was ready to say yes.

"We can spend time together, go out on dates and get all the conversation time you want."

She nodded, waiting for the next part. Because suddenly, that's the part she really wanted.

"I'm not going to touch you without your permission. And I'm not going to sleep with you."

"Wait, what?" She hadn't meant to say that out loud. It had been in her head but had come out most unexpectedly.

He smiled. "I've never had to entice a woman into my bed, and I'm not going to start now. We'll keep it a platonic relationship, unless…"

Her throat closed. "Unless?"

He leaned over, his lips oh so close to hers but not quite touching. "There's a lot more that I can teach you other than conversational skills." She sucked in a breath, wanting desperately to move an inch forward and press her lips on his. But he seemed to be moving away.

"But if you want more, you're the one who's going to have to seduce me."

Six

She sat up, hot and sweating, in her own room with its pastel-blue ceiling and soft gray walls. She'd been dreaming about Dev giving her lessons in bed. The kind of lessons that made her breathing heavy, her body sweaty, and matted her hair to her head. Caitlyn rarely dreamed, but when she did, they were vivid and visceral. But this dream was crazy. It didn't take a genius to figure out what it all meant.

As if he could sense her thinking about him, her phone buzzed with a text from him.

Going to check out a restaurant on Colton Street at 9 am. Are you free to come with me? Practice brunch date afterward?

It had been less than twelve hours since she'd seen him, but the idea of going out with him filled her with excitement. She texted him back then sprang out of bed. With only forty-five minutes to get dressed, she wouldn't have time to wash her hair, which was a bit of a production. She did a quick conditioner wash to get the sweat out, then pulled it back into a ponytail, forgoing perfectly straight hair that she usually re-curled into perfect waves. Her hair was naturally curly, but not the tight curls or long locks Alexa had. She often envied her sister's perfect hair.

She chose a sundress, one of her favorites that she usually wore around the house, a peacock-blue dress that wrapped around her with a deep V-neck and a hemline that ended right before her knees. Her smart watch told her the day would be hot, so she knew better than to wear makeup. It would just melt and make her face look splotchy. Plus, she didn't have much time, so she settled for a swipe of lip gloss and threw on strappy but flat sandals in case there was a lot of walking to do.

She took one last look in the ornate full-length mirror in her walk-in closet and had to admit that she liked this new look. If she didn't know better, she'd say she looked like one of those flirty girls on the cover of a fashion magazine. She normally dressed so businesslike. Her hair was always perfectly pressed and styled, never in natural curls, as it was now with nothing but a scrunchie. Caitlyn wasn't vain, but she knew that she was generally a beautiful woman, having been blessed with big eyes, a small, straight nose and lips that fit her face perfectly. Her skin color ranged from a beige to a golden brown, depending on her summer tan. Looking at the bottles of different-colored foundations on her dresser, she quickly took an extra minute to put on sunblock. She had a series of Royal events on her calendar where it would definitely not be suitable to show up without makeup or with wild hair. But the morning belonged to Dev.

Dev had offered to pick her up, but she chose to drive into town. Against her father's wishes, she'd opted for a Tesla Model 3. It was dwarfed on the road and in her driveway by the bigger cars, but she liked the electric car among the gas guzzlers in town. It was Sunday, so she didn't have any meetings, but she did want to stop by the child protection services office to see if they needed her help later in the day. They'd been short-staffed lately, and she often found the social workers there on Sundays. She helped them with filing or photocopying so they didn't spend their entire Sunday working.

She arrived five minutes late. Dev had asked her to meet him inside the restaurant, but he was waiting by the door for her. She pulled to the curb. He had been leaning against the brick wall of the building, one leg bent, his eyes on his phone. He wore a V-neck T-shirt and jeans. His hair looked perfectly mussed, with soft waves that kissed his brow. He looked up when she arrived.

"That's not a legal spot. There's a parking lot in

the back." He gestured to the little driveway a few feet away.

"I know. But don't worry, I won't get ticketed. Sorry I'm late."

He came around the front of the car as she collected her purse and opened the door. Or tried to. It was locked. He grinned, and she unlocked it. When it clicked, he tugged again.

"These car manufacturers make it really hard to be chivalrous."

"That's because chivalry is dead. Instead, those gentlemen of yesteryear are replaced by creeps that try to carjack and assault women, which is why car doors automatically lock."

He shook his head as he extended his hand to help her out of the car. She didn't need help but liked it. It gave her an excuse to touch him.

As she brushed past him, he whispered, "You look amazing, by the way." She warmed, not at the compliment but by the thickness in his voice as he said it.

He let go of her hand, then held his out. She looked at him, confused.

"Am I supposed to give you something?"

He smiled. "Your car keys, so I can park it in the lot."

She laughed. "Actually, this car has no keys. It runs off the app on my phone. Is that what women in New York do? Hand you their keys and say 'park the car'?"

"Not exactly, but they are used to a certain amount of male chivalry."

She shook her head. "My car is fine here. I know the cops on the parking beat—they never ticket my car."

His eyebrows rose. "Well, don't you have the town of Royal wrapped around your little finger."

"It's amazing how much appreciation a few charity events, and bagel and coffee at the precinct buys you."

He did a mini bow. "You are truly the princess of Royal."

The door opened, and a man in a suit stepped out of the restaurant. He was tall, lanky, with sandy blond hair and blue eyes. He smiled widely as he saw her. "Miss Caitlyn, I had no idea you were the friend Mr. Mallik said we were waiting for."

"Greg, it's so nice to see you," Caitlyn said genuinely. "It has to have been over a year since you were last at the ranch. Your dad told me you'd gone into commercial real estate."

He nodded proudly. "And doin' real well, thanks to Mr. Lattimore's recommendations, miss."

"Greg, we're the same age, please call me Caitlyn."

Dev looked at Caitlyn. "How do you two know each other?"

"We live in the same town—a lot of us know each other."

Greg piped up, "She's bein' too kind. My daddy works as a ranch hand on the Lattimore estate. I grew up workin' every summer at Miss Caitlyn's."

"Greg, please call me Caitlyn."

He turned slightly red at her second request, seeming unsure whether it would be more offensive to heed her request or undo his very traditional father's strict request to call everyone up at the mansion by Mr. or Miss or Mrs.

"Let me show you the place. It used to be…"

"…the old Stevens brewery," Caitlyn finished.

Greg nodded. "Miss…sorry, Caitlyn here knows more about Royal history than anyone. Well, except Ol'Fred."

Caitlyn realized that she was interfering with Greg's carefully planned spiel, so she deferred to him to tell the rest as Greg showed them the space. The brewery had been closed for almost a decade. The Stevenses had been an old couple who ran it for nearly thirty years. When they died, they left the brewery to a nephew who lived in Los Angeles, and he put it up for sale. It had changed hands a couple of times—a local rancher tried to open up a steak house, which competed with the RCW Steakhouse and it became a town feud. The rancher gave up on it and sold the property to a chain restaurant. It didn't do very well. The leftovers of the red icon still hung over the old wood bar. The place was in rough shape, having been on the market for several years with little maintenance. Someone had swept up recently, but the old wooden floors were caked with mud and dirt, and the stale smell of old water, dead mice and long-ago yeast still hung in the air.

Dev asked Greg several questions about the sale terms and the condition of the kitchen equipment.

Greg had done his homework, and Caitlyn made a note to tell his dad just how well he was doing. She knew Mr. Hodges was always tough with him. Caitlyn hadn't really known Greg when they were growing up, even though she visited the stables daily. *You never socialize with those who aren't in your stratosphere.* Jax had said that to her when he had first returned home from college. At the time he'd said it with a laugh but she later learned that he'd meant those words.

"How about I leave you two to discuss it? I'll just be two doors down at the café when you're done. Let me know and I'll lock up," Greg said, smiling.

Dev turned to Caitlyn once Greg had left. "If I didn't know better, I'd say the lad was crushing on you."

Caitlyn frowned. "What? No! Greg's just…he's Greg."

"Greg is an all-American male, and he has a crush on young Miss Caitlyn." Dev added Greg's accent when he said her name, and she laughed.

"So what you do think of the place?"

They stood in the center of what was supposed to be the dining room. Caitlyn had never been in this place before, but she'd heard about it from the locals when it was the brewery.

Dev was deep in thought. "It's nice. It certainly has good bones and old-world charm, but it's just so…"

"Just so…"

Dev clicked his fingers as if trying to find the words.

"... Texas," Caitlyn supplied.

He grinned. "Yes. Exactly. Like the RCW Steakhouse."

"It's the kind of place old men would come to eat bloody steak and smoke cigars."

They both laughed at that. "I need my place to feel like you're coming to eat at a relative's house. It's different, it's not everyday, but it's homey."

"And you're looking for that in Royal?"

"Would you eat in a place like that?"

She nodded, acknowledging the trap. "I think the younger generation of Royal is not quite as big on stuffy and formal restaurants. They are well traveled and appreciate new and refined cuisine."

Dev nodded. "Well, this is the first of three places Russ had prioritized for me to see. Let's hope the other ones are better."

"You'll find something," Caitlyn said reassuringly.

They looked at each other for a moment. "I really like this look on you," he said.

"What look is that?"

His lips twitched. "This natural look, like you don't have a care in the world."

"This Caitlyn usually doesn't step out of the house."

"Why not?"

Why not indeed? She shrugged. "I just feel like it's an expectation, you know. I'm a Lattimore, and

I need to represent the family." Even as she said the words, she knew they weren't true. Her parents had never put any pressure or expectations on her, and her siblings certainly didn't act that way.

"Are you sure it's not body armor?"

"What would I need body armor for? I have everything I could possibly ask for." She didn't like the pitch of her voice when she said those words, even though they were true.

"Well, I like all your looks, Caitlyn, but this is definitely my favorite." He stepped closer to her, and she felt a slight tug as he wrapped one of her curls around his finger.

"I like your hair natural."

He was close to her, and she breathed in the spicy scent of his aftershave. It was seductively woodsy. Why did she want a platonic relationship again? He was nearly a foot taller than her, so she was looking up and noticed a tiny shaving cut on the side of this jaw. She touched her finger to the cut, and he froze, then stepped back from her.

"Wait, you got to touch mine, but I don't get to touch yours?" she said playfully, marveling at the seduction that had naturally crept into her voice. It was as if she was someone else entirely. His green eyes darkened, and her insides melted.

She lifted her fingers and touched his hair. He sucked in a breath, and she smiled, feeling a surge of excitement. His hair was soft, not textured like hers, but thick and naturally wavy. He didn't use a lot of hair product. She liked that. What would it be like to run all her fingers into his hair and tug? Would he like it?

He cleared his throat. "Are you done fondling my hair?"

She retreated her hand and stepped back several paces suddenly embarrassed at the naked lust that she was sure was written all over her face.

He closed the distance between them. "Caitlyn, don't get me wrong. I want you to touch my hair. I want you to touch a lot more than my hair." His voice was low and thick and his eyes dark pools of molten heat. Her own skin was enticingly warm and tingly. "I'm doing my best to be a gentleman here, but know this…" He bent a little closer so his lips were mere inches from hers. His breath was so close to her mouth that she wanted to suck it in. "…anytime, anyplace you want me, you can have me. No questions asked."

She did suck in that breath, unsure of what to say or how to react. Deep inside, a voice screamed, *Take me now, put me against the bar, lift up my skirt and show me just how much you want me.* But that voice stuck in her throat. He waited for what seemed like an eternity, then straightened and stepped back from her. The silence stretched between them until he broke it. "I guess Greg is waiting for us. Let's give him the keys and I'll take you to brunch."

She nodded and followed him out, knowing the moment was lost and wondering if she was falling into the same old patterns again.

Seven

"This could be the set for a horror movie," Caitlyn said.

They were sitting in Dev's rental car waiting for Greg to show up. It was early in the morning, but the place they were visiting was clearly deserted. They had unbuckled their safety belts but felt it best to wait for Greg before they went exploring. The structure before them looked like it had been a diner once. The large neon sign had stopped working, but the letters were visible. The windows were large, and beyond the coat of dust and grime, they could barely make out gingham curtains. The parking lot was spacious, with no spaces for handicapped parking, indicating the place had been closed a very long time.

"I think Russ is purposely setting me up with

these terrible properties to punish me for moving out to the hotel."

"Was he mad?" Caitlyn asked.

Dev nodded. "He took it as a personal affront to his hospitality. Never mind that the guy's idea of breakfast is still Froot Loops, 'cowboy style,' as he calls it, meaning dry, because it's too much to keep fresh milk in the fridge."

"You should do something to make nice with him."

Dev nodded. "I promised him we'd go out one night. Apparently, there's some Lone Ranger night-club that he's dying to take me to."

Caitlyn felt an irrational bubble of anger. "The Lone *Star* is a meat market. It's where singles go to hook up."

Dev looked at her, his green eyes mischievous. "Would it bother you for me to go there?"

Caitlyn looked toward the diner so he wouldn't see her eyes. He had an uncanny way of reading her. It had been two weeks since the first night they'd met and she had seen Dev almost every day, either to look at a property with him when her time allowed, or at dinner. They were almost in a routine. He texted her each morning asking what her day looked like then suggested a way for them to see each other. Yesterday she'd been tied up all day, so they'd met for coffee in between her afternoon meeting and her dinner charity event at the Texas Cattleman's Club. Caitlyn had wrangled with whether to invite Dev as her date rather than showing up alone yet again, but she had ultimately decided against it. There would be too many questions—ones she wasn't ready to answer yet. She didn't need any more gossip among the Royal residents. They still asked her about what happened with Jax and they'd broken up a year ago.

Jax. The other reason she hadn't invited Dev to the gala last night. She hadn't known if Jax would be there. On the off chance he would, she wanted to face him alone. They hadn't seen each other since *that* night, but she knew it was time for them to talk. They'd spent too long avoiding each other. In an odd way, spending time with Dev made her less nervous about the difficult conversation that lay ahead with Jax.

Despite the sexual tension that simmered between them, it was easy to talk to Dev. Maybe it was that he didn't let her get away with canned answers. He always pried and probed until she felt coaxed into talking. She'd shared more of herself with Dev in two weeks than she had with any other man. Even Jax. She knew Dev was only here temporarily, but she didn't want to share him with someone else, even for one night.

"What would you do if I said I don't want you to go?"

He didn't answer, so she looked at him. He was staring at her. Since the day in the old Stevens brewery, their time together had been physically distant. While she enjoyed spending time with him, she was reminded of her physical attraction to him and could no longer ignore the sexual frustration she felt.

"Why don't you want me to go, Caitlyn?"

The ball was in her court. She understood that. But she couldn't help fearing what would happen if she took the next step. She'd never had such an easy rapport with any man. They flirted, laughed, shared deeply personal thoughts, and she finally understood what her therapist meant about her needing to open up. She didn't want to lose that. What if they slept together and it didn't work out? As it is, there were a scant two weeks before he left Royal. Maybe friendship was all she should take from him.

"I don't want us to practice anymore. I want to be with you, physically." The words tumbled out of her before she could stop them. His darkening eyes mesmerized her and she leaned forward. He didn't hesitate, and closed the distance between them. His hand cupped her cheek, and he pressed his lips firmly to hers. His tongue flicked across her bottom lip, and she lost all rational thought. Her entire body quivered, her core hot and desperate for his touch. This time she didn't hold back. She let her tongue tangle with his. When the kiss wasn't enough, she twisted her body and tucked a knee underneath her so she could get even closer to him.

The kiss broke and she moaned in protest, but Dev pulled back and cleared his throat. "Greg is here."

She noticed him adjusting his pants, and she looked down to see that her wraparound dress was twisted so her ample cleavage was on full display. She didn't miss Dev's appreciative glance but sat back in the seat and quickly adjusted her dress.

Greg tapped on the window, and Dev and Caitlyn looked at each other and smiled.

The diner was in such rough shape that they couldn't really go inside. When Greg unlocked the door with a set of old-fashioned keys, the lock was so rusted that he had to force the handle, which in turn led to the door splintering on its hinges. The wooden flooring inside had significant cracks, and none of them felt like testing whether it could hold their weight.

Greg smiled apologetically. "As I said, the property is in rough shape, but there are really no more options on the west side of Royal. This is at the very edge. I know this building would have to be a tear-down, but this property comes with fifty acres of land and a barn that's in usable shape."

Dev's eyebrows shot up. "Fifty as in five zero."

Greg nodded, and Caitlyn had the urge to giggle at Dev's wide eyes.

"This is Texas, darlin'. That kind of land is not uncommon." She smirked.

"Yeah, I'm used to New York properties, where we talk in inches, not acres."

"It's a pretty nice parcel of land—flat, clear lot. I know the ladies' auxiliary has been rentin' it regularly for their clothing drives."

"That barn has an entrance through *Piedmont Road* right?" Caitlyn confirmed.

Greg nodded. "But you see that little footpath there?" He pointed to the other side of the parking lot. "That'll lead you right through the trees and to the barn. You might want to go see it since you're already here."

Caitlyn turned to Dev. "I've been in that barn once. It's actually pretty nice. Maybe the restaurant can be situated there."

Dev raised his brow. "Really?"

"No harm in checking it out," Caitlyn said.

"Well, you folks go ahead. I'm gonna have to do some callin' around, see who I can get to come board up that door," Greg said. "It won't be right to leave it like that." He handed them a set of keys. "These will open the side entrance. Drop them off in town at the real estate office when you're done. Now you be careful walkin' around."

Dev still looked skeptical, but Caitlyn grabbed his hand. "C'mon."

She took him out back. Thick shrubbery overwhelmed the narrow footpath. "Are you sure about this?" He looked pointedly towards her bare legs and sandaled feet.

She nodded. An idea had come to her when Greg mentioned the barn, but she wasn't sure Dev would understand it until he saw the space.

She led him through the thicket of trees, and they emerged in a field that had long ago browned and dried up. A large red barn stood about two football fields away.

"Wow, that looks like it could be on the cover of *Farm and Country*."

Caitlyn was pleased that the barn was the one she remembered. From the outside, it looked like a quintessential farm barn—tall with a sloping gray roof and white cross-hatched windows. The once-red paint was now a dull maroon, and as they got closer, they could see that the wood siding on the barn was cracked and peeling in several places. They walked around to the side, past the big front doors, as Greg had instructed, and to a side entrance. They unlocked the padlock, and the door opened easily.

Inside, the cavernous space smelled like earth and pine cones. It must have been recently used, because rubber pavers had been added to the floor, and several six-foot tables were set up in the center of the room. There were a number of cardboard boxes here and there but overall, the space was neat. The artificial pine cone smell came from several tree-shaped air fresheners that had been hung across the wooden slats delineating the hayloft. Caitlyn smiled. Only the ladies' auxiliary would try to freshen up a barn. She walked over to the double front doors and deftly unlocked them from the inside, throwing them open and bathing the barn in sunshine and fresh air.

"So, I have a crazy idea."

Dev smiled, "I can't wait to hear it." There was no snark in his voice, just pure interest, and she tried not to notice how alluring his emerald green eyes shone in the sunlit barn. There was no doubt in her mind that he was more interested in picking up where they left off in the car. Not that she wasn't. The barn was deserted, after all, and oddly romantic.

"This town has plenty of upscale restaurants. What if you opened a family Indian fusion restaurant? Imagine dining tables inside where parents can sit and enjoy a nice meal. And outside, you set up a playground where the kids can run around, get some fresh air. You can even have an indoor-outdoor kitchen. Build a tandoori oven outside where your chef can bake fresh naan."

"Someone's been doing their homework on Indian cuisine."

She smiled shyly. She had been doing a lot of research, but she wasn't about to admit just how much time she'd spent trying to learn a little more about his culture. She'd learned that *chai* meant tea, so saying "chai tea" was redundant. Just like *naan* meant bread, so saying "naan bread" was the same thing. She'd realized that he spent so much time asking about her that she hadn't learned much about his heritage from him.

"I like the concept, but to renovate this space will require a lot of resources. I was banking on creating a luxury brand. I don't see the clientele from RCW Steakhouse, or a lot of the ranchers in this town, sitting down to eat in a barn. In New York, yes, people would drive hours to have this type of experience, but not here. They'd feel like they were in their own backyard. I think upscale is the way to go."

He wasn't wrong on that front, and her heart deflated.

"Hey, what's wrong?" He stepped toward her and bent down so he could look her straight in the eyes. How was Dev such a mind reader? She shook her head, not trusting herself to speak.

"It's written all over your face." He placed his hands on her bare shoulders, and his touch heated her insides.

"I guess I want you to find a space here in Royal so you don't leave."

He smiled. "You're enjoying my company that much, huh?"

She lifted her face so she could meet his gaze. She ran her fingers along his jawbone, then across his bottom lip. His lips parted, and she grabbed his chin and pulled him toward her. Their lips crashed, and every single second she'd spent holding herself back from being with him destroyed the last threads of inhibition still holding her together.

She wrapped her arms around his neck and pulled him closer, pressing her body to his. With her flat sandals, she had to go on tiptoes even with his head bent. She fit perfectly into him, and just as she felt the hot heat between her legs, his erection pressed hard into her belly. His hands went around her waist. She thrust her hips forward, unable to control the maddening need for him.

He moved his hands to her butt and bent down and lifted her. She wrapped her legs around him, enjoying him hot and hard between her legs. She'd never wanted anything as much as she wanted him inside her. Her panties were wet with need, and her core throbbed painfully. He carried her to one of the folding tables, then set her on it. He hadn't broken the kiss, and she searched wildly for his hand, but he was ahead of her.

As she plundered his mouth, he put his hand on her knee and ran it up her thigh. She moaned, arching her hips instinctively to encourage him. Her hands were still around his neck, and she ran them down to his chest. He put his palm between her legs, pressing against the silk of her panties, and she moaned. The warmth of his hand provided temporary relief. She pulsed against his hand, then broke the kiss. "More, Dev, I need more."

He didn't hesitate. He slipped the fabric of her panties aside and put his thumb on her core. The rush of heat that flew through her belly was so intense that she sucked in her breath. His lips moved from her mouth to her neck as his thumb circled her clit. "More," she said hoarsely. She needed him inside her, filling her, pumping into her, releasing her.

He slipped a finger inside her but kept his thumb on her core. She gasped and grabbed a fistful of his shirt, unsure if she could keep her balance on the table. Her entire body throbbed with pleasure. "I need you," she begged, so close to the edge, she couldn't stand it. She thrust her chest forward. His mouth moved down her chest. He pushed down the v-neckline of her dress and she reached down and undid the knot holding the wraparound dress in place. The front of the dress opened and he pushed the lace bra aside. His mouth gripped her nipple just as he slid another finger inside her, and she lost her mind.

When the last waves of ecstasy finally subsided, she dropped her head on his chest, feeling satiated yet wanting more. He extracted his fingers from her, and a moaning sound of protest escaped her lips.

"I'm sorry I didn't wait for you," she said, somewhat embarrassed. She'd been so caught up in her own pleasure that she really hadn't considered his. She hadn't been prepared to orgasm so quickly. It almost never happened to her.

He kissed her ear, and another ripple of pleasure tore through her. She extended her arm and touched him through his pants. He was still hard, and she started to unbuckle his belt. Maybe her unlucky streak with men was over. If she could keep Dev hard this long, after she'd already orgasmed, maybe there was hope for them. Maybe she wasn't a cold fish after all.

Her hands trembled as she tugged on the belt. Dev put a hand on hers.

"Caitlyn, no."

She froze. He didn't want her. He'd pleased her because she'd asked—no, begged, no, *accosted*—him for it, but he didn't want her back.

She pulled away from him, adjusted her bra, pulled her underwear back in place, and re-tied her dress. Her breaths were coming faster than they should but she couldn't slow down the beating of her heart. It was happening again. Why had she forgotten that this was what happened every time? Why did she think things would work with Dev? *Because things have been different with him.*

"Hey, are you okay? Did we go too far?"

She couldn't meet his gaze. There was no way she was letting him see the tears brimming in her eyes.

She shook her head, unable to speak. She hopped off the table, nearly tripping as her feet landed unsteadily. He caught her and lifted her chin so she was forced to look at him.

"Hey, what did I do wrong?"

The traitorous tears wouldn't stay put, and his face crumpled. "Oh my God, did I hurt you? What did I do? Please say something."

Somehow, she was making things worse. *Why can't I get hold of myself?* The one thing she could always do was put on her armor and extract herself with dignity.

She took a breath. "If you didn't want to be with me, you just had to say so."

"What? You think I don't want you?" He pulled her into his embrace and held her tight, pressing his body against her. "Does it feel like I don't want you?"

It sure doesn't.

"Then what is it?"

He kissed her forehead tenderly, then trailed kisses down her cheek. Despite the doubt flooding her thoughts, her body responded immediately, wanting, needing him. She pressed against him, her body seeking reassurance that she did indeed turn him on.

"I don't want our first time to be in a barn. Call me a hopeless romantic, but I want it to be special." He kissed her neck. "I want to take my time, treat you the way you should be treated." He nibbled on her earlobe, his breath warm, and her entire body molded itself to him. She moaned sinfully. *I don't want to wait. I want you right now.* "I want to see you naked. I want your hands all over my body. I want us to have the whole night to enjoy each other, not just this stolen moment."

How could she argue with an offer like that?

"Tonight," he promised.

Eight

"No, Ma! I haven't seen her biodata, and I'm not interested," Dev said, his face reflecting the frustration he felt. His mother was on a video call with him, so he couldn't even fake that he was in the middle of a meeting. Ma had caught on to that trick and insisted on scheduled video calls.

"Dev, your younger siblings are married. I talked to *Pandit-ji* and he said the stars are aligned for you to marry."

"I'm only twenty-eight, Ma. It's the time to build my business, not get saddled with family obligations."

"Your father was married when he was twenty. Do you think he built his empire by himself? Why do you think a wife is a liability?"

Because I've seen how my siblings' spouses have drained them, financially and emotionally. He loved his brother and sister, but he'd witnessed them slowly giving up their goals in favor of what their spouses wanted. His brother hadn't wanted children, yet his wife convinced him to have two. She was pregnant with her second when the first was barely two. His sister, the cutthroat businesswoman, had agreed to quit her job and stay home to help her husband with his elder-care duties. He didn't want to be forced to make the same choices. He had a specific plan for his business. First the restaurant in Royal, then a chain across the United States. He needed to be a free agent, not saddled with a wife.

So what're you doing with Caitlyn? He pushed that thought aside. He'd been honest with Caitlyn from the beginning about how he planned to leave.

"It doesn't matter anyway. I'm dating someone." He knew it was a dangerous thing to admit to his mother, but it would temporarily get her off his back. At least buy him some time until he was back in New York and could avoid her in person.

"Very nice, very nice. Can I see her picture?"

He rolled his eyes. "How about asking me what type of person she is, Ma? Why is it straight to the looks for you."

"*Aaare*, you think I haven't learned your type by now? You want the impossible in a woman. She has to be intelligent, she has to be kind and caring, she has to be this, she has to be that. All the goddesses in the Vedas combined couldn't meet your requirements for a woman. If you selected a girl for yourself, then she must be something. So, I want to see her picture."

He knew why his mother wanted to see Caitlyn's picture. First to make sure she was real and he wasn't just making an excuse. Second, so she could see what attracted him. He knew it was a bad idea, but maybe complying would get his mother off the phone faster.

He'd already texted Caitlyn to see if she wanted to come with him to check out a restaurant location, and she'd just texted him back asking what time. He wanted it to be as soon as possible. He was eager to spend more time with her. But first things first.

He pulled up her picture on his laptop. She was on several local committees and boards, and many of them had a picture of her on their website. His favorite was a standard yearbook-style picture where she had only the slightest smile on her face. It was meant to be serious, but he loved that photo. She looked so innocent and sexy, wearing a strand of pearls around her long, elegant neck, her makeup minimal and her wavy hair down around her shoulders. It had only been a few hours since he'd seen her, but he was already anxious to see her again. He had the whole night planned out.

She'd sparked an idea this morning, and he'd called Greg, who had found a promising place. Dev had already been to see it and was going to take Caitlyn there in the evening. Then they'd pick up Italian from her favorite restaurant and bring it back to his hotel room, where he hoped to have her to himself all night and all day tomorrow.

He shared his screen with his mother, who gasped.

"*Wah!* You have good taste. She is beautiful."

He didn't know why, but his mother's approval sat well with him, even though he hated that fact. He was trying to become an independent man, but somewhere inside was still a child who sought his parent's approval.

"Is she Indian?"

He flinched. He'd hoped the conversation wouldn't come to that. He knew how his parents felt. They expected him to marry someone whose ethnic background was from India. Even though he and his siblings had been born and raised in the US and lived like Americans, his parents firmly believed that someone who wasn't Indian couldn't understand the closeness of their family and their values. Dev had disagreed even before he met Caitlyn but even more so after getting to know her. She knew exactly what it meant to put her family's needs before her own. She'd been doing it all her life. In many ways, she lived her family values far better than he did.

"No, she is not."

"She's definitely not white. Then what is she? Mexican?"

He winced. Typical of her generation, social standing and general lack of tact, his mother did not feel the need to filter her bluntness.

"No."

"Dev," his mother said warningly, and he knew her patience was wearing thin.

He sighed. "She's biracial, Mom, half white, half African American."

His mother was silent. When she finally spoke, it was worse than he'd braced himself for. "Are you trying to punish me?"

He stayed silent. It was a rhetorical question. He studied his mother's pinched face. She was only forty-eight, having married when she was eighteen and had him when she was twenty. Yet she looked like she was in her thirties, her face unmarred by wrinkles and perfectly made up with eyeliner and dark red lipstick. She wore diamond solitaires in her ears, and her hair was dyed perfectly in shades of black and reddish brown where the gray would have been. Dev got his green eyes from her, but when they stared at him from his mother's face, he felt a chill down his spine.

"Do you know what it will do to our social standing if you marry a Black woman?"

He didn't bother correcting her as to Caitlyn's race. In truth, he didn't know how she identified. For all he knew, his mother might be right. He'd only just realized that he hadn't bothered to ask.

"You are the most eligible bachelor in our community. You can have any desi girl you want from around the globe. I get no less than three offers a day for you. For good girls, educated girls, beautiful girls. Girls who know our language, our culture, and can teach it to your children. I've given you a lot of slack thinking you just need some time to go do some *maasti*, and if that's what this is, I'm fine with it. But I will tell you in no uncertain terms that you will not marry a girl who is not Indian."

"Ma!" he said, exasperated. "Who is talking marriage? I'm just dating her." It was the coward's way out of the conversation, but he was in no mood to have it right now. He knew how his parents felt, and there was no point in battling with them unless there was a reason to do so. He was nowhere close to marrying anyone, and Caitlyn was far from a contender. It was clear from their conversations that she was tied to Royal. She had no interest in traveling or leaving her comfort zone.

Appeased, his mother gave him a small smile. "Have whatever fun you want. You know I'm very modern thinking that way. As long as you know what we expect of you."

How could I not?

He managed to get his mother off his back by scheduling their next video chat and with a promise that he would read the biodata she'd sent of the latest wife prospective. The biodata was a résumé-like dating profile with a picture, their likes, dislikes, education, etc. He'd wait a day to pretend as if he'd studied it, then send an email to his mother saying he didn't like it. Since the next video call was a few days from now, that would give her enough time to calm down.

His phone pinged, reminding him that Caitlyn was

waiting for an answer from him. He quickly made plans to see her in a few hours.

"Who are you texting with?" Alice asked suspiciously.

Caitlyn guiltily clicked a button on her phone to darken the screen as Alice leaned over. They were in Caitlyn's bedroom, which remained largely unchanged from when her mother had redecorated it during her teenage years. A queen bed with a gray upholstered headboard stood in the middle, decorated with an elegant silver-and-gray comforter and pillow set. A small couch stood underneath a bay window with end tables on either side and two chairs across for a cozy sitting room. But the two women were sitting cross-legged on the bed like they had when they were in college. Alice and Caitlyn hadn't gone to the same high school, as Caitlyn had been in private school and Alice had gone to the public school. Yet they'd met in college and instantly bonded over their Royal roots. More than once, Caitlyn wished she'd become friends with Alice instead of Jax.

"How many have we gotten done?" Caitlyn asked, changing the subject.

Alice rolled her eyes. "What does it matter, we have like a million more to do. I can't believe I let you talk me into this."

"It's for a good cause." They were making brown bags for the foster kids. The snacks fed the kids on the weekends when there was no school breakfast or lunch. Normally, the high school kids packed the bags, but it was prom weekend, so they'd been short on volunteers and Caitlyn had agreed to pick up the slack. One of the Lattimore charities she oversaw funded the snack bags. She knew Alice wasn't really complaining—she had offered to help.

"I still think you need to give Russ a chance."

"Alice, he's not interested in me."

"Listen, I know Dev. Russ always brought him home for Thanksgiving because his own family didn't celebrate the holiday. He's a nice guy, he really is, but he's never going to be serious about anyone until his business is established. He's pretty much said so to me and Russ."

"Who said we're getting serious? I just asked him to help me practice my conversational skills and get comfortable around men. Didn't you tell me that's what I need to do?"

"Hardly! I told you to date a nice guy. Like Russ."

"The guy who personifies the love-'em-and-leave-'em motto?" Caitlyn said with a tinge of annoyance in her voice. Alice sometimes forgot how much time she spent lamenting Russ's dating exploits.

"He's changed, and he's ready to settle down."

"No, *you're* ready for him to change and settle down. There's a difference."

Alice glared at her, and Caitlyn softened her tone, well aware that she'd be just as defensive if someone tried to tell her that she was wrong about her brothers. "Listen, Russ is a great guy, no doubt. But it's a little hard to think of him as anyone other than your brother.

There's no spark, you understand?" Alice didn't look convinced.

"I don't want this to affect our friendship, Alice. How would you feel if I tried to set you up with one of my brothers and you didn't like him? Could you please let this go?"

Alice sighed. "Okay, I'll lay off Russ. Will you tell me whether the mystery man you're texting is Dev?"

Caitlyn sighed. "Yes."

"I knew it!" Alice screamed.

"A mystery man, huh."

Caitlyn groaned as she turned to see Alexa in the doorway. Her long black curls were loose, and she was wearing a gray T-shirt and bike shorts, her standard gym uniform. The last thing Caitlyn needed was for Alexa to get involved with the conversation regarding Dev. It was so rare for Alexa to be home, she didn't want their time together to be about her dating life.

Alexa homed in on Alice, knowing she was the weaker link. "Nice to see you, Alice." She sat on the bed and picked up one of the bags to fill, so Caitlyn could hardly object. "So, you have a mystery man. Looks like a picked a good weekend to make a trip home. Spill."

Alexa had always intimidated Alice a little. It was the lawyer in her—she had a way looking at you like she could read your mind. Alice shifted on the bed. "That's what I've been trying to get out of Caitlyn, but it's a secret mystery man. Maybe you can get more out of her."

Devious. Caitlyn glared at her best friend as Alexa turned to her. Caitlyn knew it was fruitless—Alexa would hound her until she gave in. "As Alice well knows, the not-so-secret and utterly unmysterious man is Dev Mallik, Russ's best friend. I met him at dinner at Alice's house."

"So dish some more. What's he like?" Alexa pressed.

"He's nice. He's in Royal to open a restaurant, and I agreed to show him around town. We've gone out to dinner five or six times and talked on the phone a few times. No biggie."

Alexa and Alice exchanged glances, which irritated Caitlyn. They were both supposed to be on her side. "What is it?" Caitlyn asked.

"You met him two weeks ago and you've already been out with him five or six times," Alexa didn't bother to hide the surprise in her voice.

She had actually seen Dev more than that, but Caitlyn wasn't going to add fuel to the fire. Each date had been more frustratingly platonic than the last. Dev had stayed true to his word. While there was the inadvertent hand or shoulder brush, until this morning there hadn't been anything sexual. They'd sampled all the Royal restaurants like a pair of food critics and decided that Dev had his work cut out for him. If he wanted to compete in the Royal restaurant business, he'd have to offer something extraordinary. Dev had talked about the chef he'd lined up for his restaurant and the dishes they were working on together, and Caitlyn was impressed and genuinely looking forward to the new place in Royal. The only hiccup had been that Dev hadn't liked the places Russ had lined up for him as potential locations, and he'd gone through Greg's list too.

Then this morning happened. She didn't know whether it was the knowledge that he might leave earlier than he was planning, or the sexual tension that had been simmering between them, but she'd been ready to take things to the next level with him. She needed to see whether her practice relationship could turn into a real one. Tonight would be the test.

"Earth to Caitlyn." Alexa snapped her fingers.

Caitlyn turned back to the conversation. "So what if I've been out with him a few times? I'm helping him get to know Royal, and he's helping me with my conversational skills. It's not like we're headed down the aisle. It's a temporary friendship."

"For you, darlin', that many dates is a serious relationship," Alice chimed in.

Caitlyn shot Alice and Alexa an irritated look.

"I'm just worried that you're getting involved with someone who's going to be leaving town in a couple of weeks," Alice said.

I'm worried about the same thing. "He's planning to stay a little longer." She didn't know if that was true, but she hoped she could convince him to stay longer if things went well tonight.

"For how long? Once he finds a location, he's going to leave and go back to New York," Alice said.

"And he'll be back occasionally to check on his

restaurant," Caitlyn said, hating how defensive she sounded. "We can see each other then."

"I thought you said this was temporary," Alexa said softly, and Caitlyn cursed under her breath. Trust the lawyer to find the flaw in her argument.

She knew it was the norm in her family to baby Caitlyn, but she was a grown woman now. She knew how to handle her affairs. *Just like you handled Jax*, a condescending inner voice jibed at her.

"Look, I know you guys mean well, but trust me to make my choices. I know full well Dev is not from around here, and that he's going to leave. I know whatever I have with him is short term. I don't need you guys to explain it to me like I'm a teenager with a crush."

Alice cleared her throat. "There's something else you should know about Dev."

She shifted on the bed, and Caitlyn lost her cool. "Out with it, Alice."

Both Alice and Alexa raised their brows but wisely didn't comment on Caitlyn's tone.

"Russ wanted to set me up with Dev, because he's a nice guy and Russ knows I want to settle down and get on the marriage train. Dev confided in him that he can't marry someone who isn't Indian. Apparently, his family is quite traditional."

Her heart fisted. She and Dev had never talked about marriage, but somewhere in the back of her mind, she realized they'd actively avoided the topic. He talked about his family and all the expectations they weighed down on him but never what it meant for his romantic future, just his professional one.

"Wow, let's just hit pause here a second, guys. Everyone's been harassing me to get out more. I go out on a few dates and here you are evaluating whether he's marriage material and questioning whether we have a future together. Haven't we fast-forwarded a bit too much?"

Both Alice and Alexa had the grace to look sheepish. "Sorry, darlin', I just don't want to see you hurt, and aside from Jax, I've never seen you spend so much time with one guy," Alice said. "Russ said all Dev can talk about is you. I'm seeing things moving too fast and just want to make sure you don't get hurt."

Alexa nodded. "I'm glad you're out and dating. It's time you moved on from Jax."

"How many times do I need to tell you that I'm over Jax?" Caitlyn tried to keep her voice level. She knew she'd fallen apart after Jax, but could anyone really blame her, given their history?

Alexa leaned forward and took Caitlyn's hand in hers. "When you were six years old, you loved this old horse called Shooting Star."

Caitlyn nodded. She remembered that horse clearly—he was an Appaloosa, a beautiful white horse with brown dots and a sandy blond mane.

"You loved that horse so much you rode him every day, rain or shine. But he ended up with colic that wasn't treatable, and the vet recommended we put him down. You were devastated. No matter how hard we tried, you refused to believe that Shooting Star couldn't be cured."

"I was ten," Caitlyn said defensively. "And as I remember, he was eventually put down."

Alexa squeezed her hand. "Do you remember that you spent two days and two nights sitting by his stall, refusing to let the vet take him? You were adamant that he would heal on his own, that your sheer force of will could cure him. Daddy didn't want to forcibly remove you, so we took turns staying with you until you fell asleep out of sheer exhaustion. That's when we were finally able to take Shooting Star."

"I don't know what all this has to do with Dev." Caitlyn shifted on the bed. She wanted this conversation to be over with.

"It has to do with you, Caitlyn," Alexa said gently. "You have so much love in your heart, and you give it all to the people you care about. Sometimes you give too much. Even though I wasn't here, I could tell that things were moving too fast with Jax, but I didn't say anything, and I wish I had."

Caitlyn softened her voice and looked directly at Alexa. "I'm not a fragile baby. I know I'm loved and that I have an amazing support system…" she blew a kiss to Alice and squeezed Alexa's hand "…but you guys need to trust that I can take care of myself. I'm doing exactly what I set out to—I'm going out with someone where I know there's no chance of a future, so I can relax and get some flirting practice." She injected just the right amount of casualness in her voice, but her stomach churned painfully.

Had she really thought through where things were going with Dev? She'd been so focused on how easy it was with him, convinced that it would end at any second, that she hadn't really considered the opposite possibility—*what if it went well?*

Nine

"Little thing like you should not be carryin' those big boxes," Ol'Fred bellowed. Caitlyn set down the boxes containing the snack bags they'd packed.

Ol'Fred stood where he always did, behind a wood checkout counter. His place looked more like a gas station pit stop than the fancy places that surrounded him, but Ol'Fred's shop had been here since the day Royal was founded, and no one told Ol'Fred how to run his general store. He carried basic groceries, knickknacks, tools—anything that someone doing real work in Royal might need on an urgent basis. He also carried specialty drinks, high-end whiskeys and wines that forced the elite of Royal to trudge to his store. It was the only place in town where every resident of Royal could shop.

"I'm not as fragile as I look. Can I leave these here? Yolanda said she'd pick them up in the morning."

"You don't have to ask. Y'know I'd do anything for the kids." He called out to one of his store hands to take the boxes.

Ol'Fred pulled out a can of Fanta and handed it to her. Caitlyn smiled and popped the tab, careful not let the fizz spill over. It was their tradition since she was a little girl. Her mother never let her have the orange drink because it was full of sugar, so Ol'Fred would sneak it to her.

"You just missed Jax."

Caitlyn looked around the store. "Don't worry, he's gone." She didn't know whether she was relieved or disappointed. They'd done the avoidance dance for a year—she needed to get it over with.

"You never did tell me what happened with you and Jax." Ol'Fred's tone was fatherly.

Caitlyn leaned over and kissed Ol'Fred on the cheek. "What do you always say, one day a rooster, the next day a feather duster? That was mine and Jax's relationship."

"Guess I'm gonna have to leave it with you."

She thanked him for the Fanta and walked out of the store. Just as she opened the door, she bumped into someone, dropping the almost-full can of Fanta. She murmured an apology and bent down to pick up the can before it made more of a mess.

"I see Ol'Fred is still taking care of you."

She froze. A knot formed and twisted in her stomach. She took a breath then stood. "Jax."

He smiled at her, but she couldn't bring herself to do the same. He was wearing his standard-issue basketball shorts and a T-shirt. His hair was freshly close-cropped.

They stood for a moment, staring, each unsure what to say to the other. Jax spoke first. "Listen, I think we should talk. We've avoided each other long enough. We can't leave things like this."

She nodded. Wordlessly, they walked to the park, to their bench. It was the place where they used to meet to do their homework; it was the place where he'd told her that her father had paid for his tuition to her exclusive private school so she'd have a friend; it was the place where they'd met when he first came back from college; it was the place where they'd first kissed. It was only fitting that it be the bench where they finally closed their relationship.

Her throat was tight. She didn't know how to begin, what to say. He didn't seem to have that problem.

"Look, Caitlyn, I'm sorry about the last time we were together. I shouldn't have left like that, and I shouldn't have said the things I did. I hope you didn't dwell on it."

She'd played that night in her mind for months after their breakup.

"Did you mean it? What you said?" She hated the high-pitched tone of her voice, but she needed to know whether they were words of anger or whether he'd truly meant them.

He was silent. "We've been friends for a long time, Jax. I need you to be honest with me."

He sighed. "Look, your father might have paid for my tuition and asked me to be your friend, but he didn't make you my best friend. You did. You were the only one who was nice to me at that high-brow place. I felt intimidated by that crowd, being one of the few Black kids, being the only kid who didn't summer in Europe and on and on. But you gave me confidence—you treated me like I belonged there. That's why we became best friends. It had nothing to do with your father paying my way"

She gave him a small smile. "You were the only kid in school I liked. It was easy to be your friend."

"The only reason I told you about your father paying my tuition is because I didn't want you to find out from someone other than me. What I didn't tell you is that you weren't just my best friend. You were also my childhood crush. But my ma worked for your family. If things didn't go well between us, it would've meant ruin for my family. I had no choice. I could only be your best friend."

"That's what brought us back together when you returned home after college"

"But that's just it. Four years had passed. I was a different person than I was in high school. And I hoped you had changed, too."

"What exactly does that mean?"

"Remember Declan Grayson?"

Her cheeks warmed. "That was high school, Jax."

"It was junior year. You were so in love with him. You did anything he asked of you but then, just like that, you dumped him. I tried talking to you about it, but you wouldn't tell me a thing."

"It that what this is about? Some old high school secret..."

He shook his head, but before he could say anything, she jumped in. "You want to know what happened with Declan? He was a high school crush. I went out with him, and he wanted to go further physically than I cared to. I told him I wanted to wait and he didn't, so I dumped him. Pardon me if I didn't feel comfortable talking to my male best friend about how I hated some other guy's groping."

The knot in her stomach twisted painfully. Perhaps this had all been a bad idea. What had she hoped to gain from this conversation? She knew what the issue was, had experienced it ever since high school.

"I knew all about it, Caitlyn. Declan told the whole school you were a prude and some other not-so-nice words. That's not why I bring him up." He sighed. "You put your heart and soul into everything you do. Including relationships. You went all in for Declan. You hardly knew him, and yet you were making little hearts in your notebook and writing *Mrs. Caitlyn Grayson*."

Heat rose up her neck and to her cheeks. She should have known Jax would've noticed her schoolgirl notes. "I was sixteen, Jax. Give me a break."

She wished she had the Fanta can that she'd just thrown away to clear the nasty taste in her mouth.

Jax rubbed his neck, a gesture she knew well. "What are you trying to say, Jax? Just spit it out."

"When I came back to town, I wanted to give us a chance. I didn't want to go through life wondering what might have been with you. But you wanted to pick up as if no time had passed. It was like we went from catching up over coffee to being engaged in one day. You didn't even bother to get to know me."

"I do know you, Jax. We spent four years together."

"When we were kids."

He gave her a small smile. "I'm not that person anymore. Do you know, for example, that I led a Black Lives Matter protest in DC? Or that I took the LSATs to see if I can get into law school to become a civil rights lawyer?"

That stung. Caitlyn narrowed her eyes. "You'd only just gotten into town—we hardly had time to talk."

"That's my point exactly. You didn't bother to get to know me fully before jumping into our relationship. We'd barely begun, and you were already showing me off at every Cattleman's Club event, dragging me here and there every single weekend. You were even making wedding plans."

Caitlyn shook her head. "That's not true, Jax. I was enthusiastic about our relationship because of our past. Just like you, I'd thought about us on and off through high school, but I didn't want to ruin our friendship. We weren't strangers."

"But we were, Caitlyn. We were old friends who should have taken the time to get to know each other, but we jumped right into a serious relationship without going through the dating part first. I'm not saying it was all you. I did it, too. I came back and found you grown into a beautiful woman and couldn't help falling into the fantasy you painted for us. After six months it just all came crashing down, the reality of what we'd been doing."

"So it's my fault. I put too much pressure on our relationship."

"That's not what I'm saying. I think it was both our faults. We let things move too quickly."

She shook her head and stood. "Are you done with what you had to say?"

He hung his head, then nodded slowly. "I'm not handling this right, but I want you to know that I care about you very much."

Just not enough. That's the part he didn't want to say, but she understood. She wanted to tell him that she'd trusted him, as a former friend, as her boyfriend, and that he'd broken her heart. But she couldn't bring herself to do that. The all-too-familiar knot in her stomach had grown and risen up to her throat, choking her. At least he didn't refer to her as a cold fish again.

"Thanks for the talk. Have a nice life," she managed to cough out, then walked away as quickly as she could without breaking into a run.

One thing was for certain—she wouldn't make the same mistakes with Dev. She wasn't getting into anything serious with him.

Ten

It was the first time he'd picked Caitlyn up from the Lattimore ranch, and Dev couldn't help be impressed. The ranch seemed to be an endless sprawl of perfectly landscaped lawn and picturesque barns. No peeling paint and rusted doors here. The one-mile drive from the front gate to the mansion was lined with perfectly trimmed hedges. Russ hadn't been kidding when he'd pitched the idea of Dev opening a restaurant in Royal—the kind of wealth here put the fancy Manhattan penthouse circle to shame.

The property he'd seen today had the potential to make not only his dreams come true, but also Caitlyn's. He couldn't wait to show it to her. He'd already spoken to the chef and restaurant manager he'd lined up and walked them through the space on video.

They agreed with his plans. All he needed was for Caitlyn to get on board.

They'd only known each other a short time, but he'd connected with her on an intellectual and emotional level. She understood the two parts of him, the one that belonged to his family and the one that longed to be an independent man. Getting into business was the perfect way to keep her in his life. It would give him time to sort out their romantic relationship.

She was waiting for him under the portico of a circular driveway. She looked stunning in a strappy ice-blue dress with a crisscross design that gave him a peekaboo view of her lovely back. The dress ended midthigh, showing off her shapely legs. It was the kind of sexy dress he'd never seen her in before. Her hair was left loose around her face, not straight and pressed as it normally was, but curly and wild, just the way he liked it. She was wearing flat shoes, and he was glad she had thought practically.

Before the car fully stopped, she tapped on the window. He unlocked the car, intending to get out and open the passenger side for her, but she yanked open the door, got in and smiled. "Let's go."

"In a hurry to get out?"

"Yes!" she breathed. "If my siblings find out you're picking me up, trust me, they'll be all over us and will monopolize the entire evening. You can forget any plans you may have."

Is that the only reason you don't want me meeting your family?

He punched the accelerator, eager to get to their destination. "Listen, your idea this morning gave me one of my own. So, I asked Greg to look, and he found the perfect place."

"That's great."

"But I need you to say yes to make the place work."

"Why me?" He caught the tentative fear in her voice but pushed it aside. He was being mysterious, after all.

He reached over and patted her hand. "You'll see."

Greg had given him the keys to the small ranch. Dev wanted privacy to explain his idea to Caitlyn. He had no idea how she'd react. He hadn't let himself fully consider what he would do if she said no. Because in that case, he was out of options in Royal and would have to move on. Already he'd spent more time here than he should have. Although he'd given himself a month, he'd seen most of the properties that would have been suitable for his restaurant in the first few days, but he'd kept looking. Not because he didn't have other places to go, but because he wanted to see where things went with Caitlyn.

He'd come to that realization after talking with his mother. He rarely shared information about who he was dating, and he knew his mother would have an issue with Caitlyn not being Indian, but he'd told her anyway. He'd told her so that his mother could start getting used to the idea of Caitlyn. He'd told her because he'd never met a woman he felt as comfortable with as Caitlyn. The fact that he hadn't even slept with her and was thinking these thoughts made it all the harder to ignore his feelings for her. She understood him, really listened to what he wanted without trying to impose what she wanted. Tonight was the ultimate test to see if she felt as strongly for him as he did for her. Would she go along with his plans? Would she be willing to share and mold her dream with his?

"We're going to the east side of Royal?"

He nodded. "Yes, we've exhausted everything on the west side, so I asked Greg to expand the search to all of Royal. Why? Is that a problem?"

She stayed quiet for a few minutes, as if formulating her thoughts. He snuck a look at her and saw frown lines on her forehead. "East Royal doesn't have the social demographics you're looking for to support the luxury restaurant you're envisioning."

He smiled. "You mean it's the poor part of town."

"Yes," she said quietly. "And I don't mean it disparagingly, I just mean that's where the working-class families live. They can't pay the type of prices you're considering. The wealthy ranchers on the west side aren't really going to drive to a high-end restaurant on this side of town."

"I have an idea for that," he said.

"Now I'm really intrigued. You know, Ol'Fred's shop is the only one on Main Street that's for regular people and not there to cater to the hoity-toity of Royal. It would be nice to have another place like that in Royal."

"Aren't you one of those hoity-toitys?" he asked playfully.

She nodded. "I absolutely am. Which is why I really want to do that horse camp. I know my family participates in boards and charities, but that stuff barely scratches the surface. Half the time I'm not even sure where all the money goes. I want to do something where I can see the results in front of me, not on a piece of paper."

He smiled. "Any news on the oil rights claim on your ranch?"

She shook her head. "We're still waiting for the private eye to find whether the deed Heath Thurston has is valid. We looked through our own family papers but haven't found anything."

She sighed. "I just want this to be over with so I can start working on my camp. I thought by now we'd have some resolution."

"Maybe it's for the best?"

"What do you mean?"

"I could fund my restaurant from my trust fund. Or by simply selling one of the cars my father has gifted me that mostly sits in a New York garage at a rent that constitutes most people's annual salary. But I didn't touch any of that money. Do you know why?"

"Because you want to be your own man."

"That's part of it, but it's a lot more than that. Everything in my family is intertwined—our home, our finances, our social lives, you name it, and it's all one big happy family. The problem with that is there's no room for real disagreements. If I want to

go against my family, I can't. This is my way of en-
suring I have an escape chute if I need it."

He pulled into the driveway of the small ranch
Greg had found for him. He parked the car and
looked at Caitlyn.

"You really think you're going to need an escape
from your family?"

"I'd rather not find out."

She shifted in her seat. "I can't imagine a scenario
where I'd need to flee from my family."

"There are a lot of expectations in my family that
may not exist in yours."

"Like who you marry?"

His heart slammed into his chest. He didn't want
to talk about this now. He wanted this evening to
be about them and their relationship. He needed to
know whether she felt the same connection he did.
Whether her heart was going in the same direction
as his. It was too soon to contemplate the future
with a woman he'd only known for two weeks. He
knew that intellectually, but his gut and his heart said
something different. What he and Caitlyn had was
special. Unique. Wasn't it? Sitting here with her, it
certainly felt that way, but the conversation with his
mother had unsettled him. He'd found himself anxious to make sure that Caitlyn shared his feelings
about their relationship, that she was also seeing a
future for them.

She was waiting for a response.

"I will marry whom I want," he said firmly.

"Your parents don't get a say?"

"Does your family get a say in who you marry?"

She paused then shook her head. "They'd never stand in the way of my happiness. They do have strong opinions about who I date, and I'm sure any man I bring home will have to stand up to a CIA-level interrogation, but ultimately they'll support my decision."

He wished he could say the same thing about his family.

"Let's go see this place."

It was nice sized property, nestled on a relatively flat area of land bordered by trees. They drove up to the ranch house, which was a charming, sprawling one-level.

"I don't know this property. Who lived here?"

"From what Greg told me, it belonged to a Mr. and Mrs. Fredrick. They left the property to their son, and he's recently decided to sell."

He opened the front door and they stepped into a large foyer with hardwood floors.

"You want to convert the house into a restaurant?"

He nodded and pointed out the various rooms. "It's already got a large kitchen. I'd only have to put in commercial appliances. The rest of the house can be easily converted into a dining room. The smaller rooms can be for small private groups."

She peeked into the formal dining room. It was a cozy space with a rectangular dining table that sat ten people. "I can see my family eating in this room. And the house has so many windows, it feels bigger than it is."

He nodded.

"I like the feel of this place. I can totally see seating on the porch and the back deck, and a beautiful dining room on this main level with the current bedrooms as private meeting areas for business dinners. But the Royal elite still aren't going to drive all the way over here."

"I have a plan for that," he said. But the plan hinged on her. His stomach flipped. The next few minutes would tell him how she felt about him. In a way, the next moments would decide whether or not he stayed in Royal.

"Looks like the old owners took really good care of the house. The floors are polished, the baseboards are clean…and they're mostly moved out. Why hasn't it sold yet? The real estate market in Royal is pretty strong."

"Well, there's a rather big catch that's in the property covenant."

She raised a brow, and he led her to the back door and opened it. She gasped. The twenty-acre backyard held two riding rings and two large barns. There were a couple of horses turned out into the rings, a black horse and a white one with black spots.

Caitlyn gasped. "I was not expecting this. Those horses are beautiful." She pointed to the black one. "That's actually a mustang—a pretty well-bred one, from what I can tell. And the other is an appaloosa." Her voice caught.

He placed a hand on the small of her back. She stiffened slightly. "What's wrong, Caitlyn?"

She shook her head. "Nothing. I used to have an appaloosa when I was a little girl. He died."

He placed an arm around her shoulders. "I'm sorry."

"It just brings up a painful memory."

He took a breath, wondering if now was the time to bring up his plans. *What the hell!* "Well, maybe it's a sign."

"Of what?"

"That this horse is meant to be yours."

She looked up at him, frowning. "I don't understand."

"The catch with this place is that it comes with those two stables that can take a total of twenty-some horses and those two beauties there. The owners want someone who will agree to take the horses and keep them together. Apparently they're bonded—whatever that means."

"It means they're attached to each other. Horses that bond together are hard to separate. They get sick if you do."

She was staring at the horses. "Let's go see them."

He pointed to the stairs leading down from the deck. As they approached the ring where the horses were roaming around, the appaloosa stopped and considered them. When they were within a few feet of the ring, the black mustang snorted, whinnied and reared.

Dev put a hand on her shoulder to hold her back. "Careful, Caitlyn, I don't know anything about these horses."

She smiled back at him, and his knees went weak. The setting sun backlit her in soft orange and yellow hues. *How can one woman be so stunningly, perfectly beautiful?* Despite his busy afternoon, there wasn't a moment that had gone by without him thinking about their morning together. Had that just been this morning? It seemed like a lifetime ago that she'd pulsed against his fingers and thrown her head back in such abandon that he'd nearly lost it. He'd been with enough women to know how to control himself. That he'd almost lost it with her told him there was something special about Caitlyn. Something so special that, for the first time in his life, he was intimidated by the thought of a night with her. What if he couldn't control himself? What if he couldn't live up to her expectations? What if he couldn't give her what she deserved?

He pushed the last thought out of his head. He didn't even know if she felt the same way about him. Before he started making plans, he needed to know that they were on the same page.

"Trust me," she said. "Stay back a little."

There was no way he was going to let her walk so dangerously close to the horses. He walked right behind her, ready to leap if the horses decided to jump the fence.

She began talking softly to the horses. "Good boy. That's right, you're a good boy." The appaloosa snorted and scuffed the earth with his hind leg. The mustang hung back.

Caitlyn bent down and tore some of the grass from

the earth. He did the same. "Not the grass—get the clover that's growing." She un-fisted her hand and showed him the green plant. She approached the horse slowly. When she got to the fence, she extended her arm. The appaloosa sniffed, then clopped over to her. He buried his nose in her hand, then ate the offered clover.

She petted his head and then rubbed behind his ear. The mustang whinnied, then joined his friend. Dev offered the clover he had picked to Caitlyn, and she fed the mustang. *Maybe this will go better than I thought.*

"Who is taking care of these horses if the owners moved out?"

He smiled. Trust her to be worried about the animals. "Greg said there's a ranch hand that comes by to feed, water and turn them out."

She rubbed the mustang's back. The horse was practically rubbing up against the fence begging for Caitlyn's touch. Dev knew the feeling.

"Well, he's not doing a great job. The horses need grooming. Looks like they haven't been brushed in ages. I'll call Greg and ask to talk with the ranch hand."

"You can do one better."

She turned to look at him, and the appaloosa buried his nose in her neck. She automatically smiled and started rubbing the side of his face. Insanely, he felt jealous of the horse.

He cleared his throat. "Here's my idea. What if this was your horse camp?"

Her eyes widened. "What?"

"What if my restaurant wasn't just a restaurant but a riding club? We board horses for the rich and famous, and when they aren't riding those horses, you run your camp. This property is cheap enough that instead of renting like I had planned, I can buy it. This place can be ours. We can run it together. You run the stables, and I'll run the restaurant. I'm thinking I'll even create a café portion where I can serve up more family-priced dishes. Upscale restaurants in New York do that all the time—they have food trucks with better-priced dishes." He stopped. He'd been so busy pitching his idea that he hadn't stopped to look at her face.

She stepped away from the horses, and they began galloping around the ring.

"Caitlyn?"

She was turned away from him, so he placed a hand on her shoulder. "What is it?"

"Don't you think we're moving a bit fast?" Her voice was small.

"It's a business partnership," he said carefully. "Your idea this morning really resonated with me. I want to put my restaurant in this part of town. I want to create a place where everyone is welcome and can afford to eat. If we board some expensive horses, it'll attract the rich, and there's plenty of space here for you to run your camp without worrying about the claim on the Lattimore land."

"What exactly do you mean by a business relationship?"

Why was her voice so cagey? *Did I move too soon? Am I reading our relationship all wrong?*

"It's whatever you're comfortable with, Caitlyn. We can co-own the land. I can run the restaurant and you run the stables. This is just an idea, one I hoped we could work on together."

"What happens when our personal relationship ends?"

She said when*, not* if. He moved around so he was facing her. The sun had set quickly, and it was getting dark pretty fast. She refused to meet his eyes, and her body was so straight and stiff, it was as if one touch would send her fleeing. He put his hands behind him so he wouldn't be tempted to touch her. He could sense her fear. He'd felt it himself after realizing why he'd shown his mother her picture. He was falling in love with Caitlyn. For the first time in his life, he was thinking about a future that included more than just his business and family.

"You tell me. How far do you think our personal relationship can go?"

She still wouldn't look at him, intently studying the horses. "We hardly know each other, Dev."

He moved so he was in her line of sight. "Ask me anything you want to know. Go on—what is it that you want to know about me?"

"Is your family expecting you to marry someone Indian?"

He sucked in a breath then nodded. "Yes, but what they're expecting and what they'll get are two different things. I told you, I know I'll have disagreements with my family. They want me to marry someone they approve of, and the whole reason I want to be financially independent is that I don't want to be hostage to their standards. I want to marry the person I love."

"And how does this hypothetical love of yours fit into your plans to jet around the country building your empire?"

Her words were a knife in his gut. This was not at all how he'd hoped the conversation would go, but now that it had started, he had to finish it.

"Caitlyn, let's not talk in circles." He placed his hands gently on her shoulders, the lightest of touches. She stiffened but didn't move away from him. "Please look at me." She lifted her face, and his heart clenched painfully. Her brown eyes were shining, her nose and face flushed.

Had his words caused her grief? What had he done that was so wrong? Or was she misinterpreting what he was saying?

"I don't want there to be any confusion between us. What I'm saying is that I love you. I want to be with you. All this—" He gestured around them. "—is me trying to commit to you. I don't have everything worked out, but I don't want to. All I want to know is that you feel the same way about me and we'll figure out the rest together."

"Don't you think this relationship is moving a little fast? We've only known each other for two weeks and you're suggesting..."

Could she twist the knife any deeper into him?

She hadn't said she loved him back. Hadn't even acknowledged that he was making a grand gesture.

"What? What am I suggesting that's so scary to you?" He hated the annoyance in his voice, but he was fast losing control over his emotions. She didn't love him back. She didn't even see a future with him.

"We've only known each other two weeks. I told you the reason I haven't started the camp at my family ranch is because I don't want to start something and then have it yanked away from these children. They have nothing permanent in their lives. You blew into town with the intention of starting something here and leaving. How do I know that doesn't include me, too?"

"Because I'm telling you right now."

She stepped close to him, her mouth set in a firm line. "Can you tell me you'll stay in Royal if I ask you to?"

"That's not really fair."

"Why not?"

"You're not even ready to commit to a business proposition, but you want me to change my entire life plan and move here?"

"That's the point, Dev. Your plan is to open a restaurant and leave, but my life is here in Royal."

"So you expect me to upend my entire life, let go of all of my plans and move here to Royal?" He immediately regretted the hostility in his voice. He hadn't meant for the conversation to go this way. Perhaps he had jumped the gun.

She sighed, and a tear streamed down her cheek. He brushed it away with his finger. She grabbed his hand and kissed it. "I can't do this, Dev. I'm sorry, I can't."

Eleven

"I don't understand, Caitlyn." Alice was sitting on the pool lounger staring at her. This time Caitlyn was the one who'd drunk most of the chardonnay that sat between them. It had been two days since she'd seen Dev. After she'd refused to talk anymore, he had dropped her at her house and left. Since then, he hadn't texted or called. He hadn't responded to the text she'd sent that night saying she was sorry.

Alice had come over unannounced when she'd heard the story from Russ. "You know he's planning to leave tomorrow."

Her heart lurched. The last couple of days had been a jumble of emotions for her. The conversations with Alexa and Alice, with Jax, and then with Dev had all crashed into one tightly knotted tangle that she couldn't separate no matter how hard she tried.

"Look, I know I was against you and Dev getting together, but I can't see you like this. Russ says Dev is a mess. He's never seen the poor guy like that." She moved from her pool lounger to Caitlyn's. It was a rare cloudy and cool day so they were both in their sundresses enjoying the weather. Alice put an arm around Caitlyn. "What happened, darlin'? Did things not go well in bed?"

Trust Alice not to mince words. "Not this time. We didn't even try." Though that was not completely true. That morning in the barn was imprinted on her. She hadn't forgotten how her body had responded to him.

Alice waited patiently. Caitlyn's throat was tight. "It's Jax. I saw him, and we talked."

Alice hugged her tighter. "Oh, darlin', why didn't you call me? What did that rascal say to you?"

"Nothing that wasn't true. He pointed out that I jumped right into the relationship without even getting to know the man he'd become. That I put so much pressure on the relationship that it was inevitable for it to fail." She filled Alice in on their entire conversation. "He didn't say anything about our last night together, but he didn't need to. He blames the pressure I put on him—that was clear."

Alice gasped. "That little turd. How dare he?" She turned toward Caitlyn and squeezed her shoulders. "You listen to me. When he came back to town, you're the first person he asked about. He was just as hot 'n' heavy into it as you were."

Caitlyn hiccupped as the tears rolled down her cheek. "He's right, though. As soon as he came back to town and we started dating, I was hearing wedding bells. I put my entire life on hold for Jax. And I'm doing the same thing with Dev, putting my plans for the camp on the back burner."

"That's not what you're doing. You put your plans on hold because of that claim on the Lattimore land, not because of Dev."

Caitlyn shook her head. "When Dev took me to that ranch, I realized that I should have been the one to have found it. He's right, it is the perfect place for my camp, but I was so focused on Dev that I didn't know the ideal ranch went up for sale. I missed it completely."

"Caitlyn." She picked up the bottle of wine and topped up both their drinks. Caitlyn gulped a big sip of her wine. She knew that determined look on Alice's face—she was about to get a lecture.

"You are the most loving person I know. You dedicate yourself to the people and the projects in your life. That's why you stuff snack packs in your free time and run yourself ragged doing all the Lattimore business your siblings don't want to take on. That's who you are. Jax wasn't just some guy you dated. You two had been best friends. It was hardly as if you were startin' at the gate. Jax wants to blame you because he doesn't want to take responsibility for himself."

"He said it was both our faults. If I put too much into the relationship, he didn't put enough." She could tell she'd taken the wind out of the rest of Alice's speech. "But that doesn't change the fact that I'm falling into the same trap with Dev."

"It's hardly the same. He wanted to buy that place for you because he's committed."

"How do I know that? How do I know that he'll stick around? That the first time his family calls, he won't go running?"

Even as she said the words, she remembered him telling her that he loved her. That he was setting up his own business so his family didn't have leverage over him, so he could marry who he wanted.

"Caitlyn, do you hear yourself? What are you so afraid of? What do you have to lose?"

Everything. She had everything to lose. One bad experience with Jax and she'd become a cold fish. What would happen if she let Dev burrow even deeper into her heart than he already had?

"What do Dev and I really have? We've been playing a childish game where he pretended to humor me with boyfriend lessons." She spat out the last words, feeling ridiculous saying them out loud. "I don't want to repeat the mistakes I made with Jax. If it was real with Dev, he would've called me. Instead, one thing goes wrong and he's acting the exact same way as Jax."

"That's not fair, Caitlyn. It's really not the same situation."

"I'm done talking about this." She was done thinking about it, too. For two days she'd sat around the Lattimore mansion, moping. She'd started on this ill-thought-out endeavor with Dev because she was worried that Jax had ruined her for all men. Dev seemed to have brought out the sexual desire she thought she didn't have. But was it Dev, or had she finally conquered her demons? There was only one way to test her theory.

"Listen, I could use a night out. Do you want to go to the Lone Star?"

"Are you sure that's the best place for you to be right now?"

Caitlyn nodded. "I need to be someplace where I don't have to be myself."

Twelve

"I'm not sure this was a good idea." Alice grabbed her arm. Caitlyn shook it off. Whatever curse Jax had put on her had been broken, and she was determined to enjoy it. She'd managed to talk to half a dozen guys tonight, flirted, even danced with a couple of men. All without feeling the familiar tightness of panic in her chest. Maybe that's one thing Dev had been good for—being a practice boyfriend. That's all she had asked of him, after all.

"I'm not drunk, Alice. I'm perfectly in my senses and doing what you've been telling me to do for ages—letting loose."

The Lone Star was packed. It was a Friday night, and the smells of beer, peanuts and sawdust filled the air. The place was decorated like an Old West saloon with cowboy hats and horseshoes on the wall, a big, polished wood bar and a square dance floor. There was even a mechanical bull in one corner that was getting good use.

"Can I buy you a drink?"

Caitlyn turned to see a tall, muscular man with dark hair and thick eyebrows. He looked vaguely familiar, but Caitlyn couldn't remember where she'd seen him before. Alice placed a hand on Caitlyn's arm. She sighed. Alice was right. Partying all night wasn't Caitlyn's thing. She'd come here to test a theory, and she'd proven it. There was nothing wrong with her, never had been.

"I'm sorry, but..." She stopped. She didn't know what compelled her to, but her eyes suddenly went to the door. Her heart stopped in her chest. *How could he possibly be more handsome than I remember?* Dev walked in behind Russ wearing jeans that showed off his long legs and an untucked T-shirt. Hadn't he said Russ wanted him to come here to pick up women? Two days since they'd last spoken and he was already cutting his losses and moving on?

She tugged on her ear, a signal to Alice that she was happy to talk with the guy. They had a system. A tug on the ear for *go away, I am interested in this guy*, and a touch on the nose if she needed Alice to rescue her.

She turned to the handsome stranger and put a hand on his arm. "I'd love a drink. Beer will do."

He nodded and gestured to the bartender. It took Caitlyn and Alice the better part of half an hour when they'd ordered their drinks, but this guy had no trouble getting the female bartender's attention.

When they had their beers, she took a sip, then turned to him. "I'm Caitlyn," she said.

"Heath." Her pulse quickened. It couldn't possibly be the same Heath, could it?

"Yes, I am that Heath Thurston," he said, as if reading her mind.

"By that I assume you know I'm a Lattimore."

"The door isn't that far away, if you'd like to run."

Actually, what I'd like to do is throw this drink in your face. She took a breath and lifted her beer. "It's nice to meet you."

He clinked his beer mug with hers. "Mighty nice of you not to throw that in my face."

She smiled. "I considered it, but then I figure it's better to get you drunk and pump you for information."

He threw his head back and laughed. She snuck a look at Dev, who was staring right at them. A pleasant zing went through her at the murderous look in his eyes. She forced herself to turn back to the conversation with Heath. Perhaps she could find out more about his plans.

"It's nice to meet you, Caitlyn. I know I can't be very popular with your family right now."

"Yeah, they don't take kindly to having our home threatened."

Heath leaned over. "Listen, it's not my intention to cause chaos in your lives. I just want to do right by my sister's memory."

She nodded. "I can understand that."

"Tell me, Caitlyn, what is a beautiful girl like you doing in a place like this?"

His eyes sparked. He was flirting with her. She glanced at Dev, whose eyes were still fixated on her. Were her feelings for Dev real or just a rebound from Jax? Could she have the same chemistry with another man? Heath was certainly attractive enough.

"You think I'm beautiful?"

He smiled and she leaned forward, putting her elbow on the bar so their faces were barely an inch from each other.

"I think you're stunning."

"Well, you're not that bad yourself."

She leaned in farther, and mentally scanned her body for the heat and lust she should be feeling. Heath was devastatingly handsome. She hoped that the morning at the ranch with Dev had also unlocked the mental block her therapist claimed was her problem. Surely sitting this close to someone as handsome as Heath should have her as hot as bothered as one look at Dev.

Alas, she felt nothing.

Russ slapped Dev on the back. "You stare at her any longer, bud, and your face will freeze like that."

Dev rolled his eyes. The Lone Star was the last place he wanted to be, but Russ had insisted, and Dev didn't have the will left in him to fight. He'd spent the last two days wallowing in self-pity, asking himself how he could have misread the situation with Caitlyn. The first woman he'd fallen for and he'd managed to screw it up royally.

He glanced toward her again and caught her eye for just a second. She looked stunning in skintight jeans, a strappy red sequined top and high heels that made her entirely too sexy for a place like this. Why was she sitting so close to that guy? Why was she leaning into him as if she was going to kiss him? He clenched his fists. *That man better not lay a hand on her.* How could she let another man touch her? What did that guy have that he didn't?

Then it happened. The man kissed her. The bubble of anger that had been growing inside Dev boiled over. He stood and made his way to them. He pushed the man away from Caitlyn, breaking their kiss.

"Whoa, man! What the hell?" the man muttered.

"Dev!" Caitlyn screamed.

"What are you doing, Caitlyn?" Dev demanded.

"That is none of your business." Caitlyn said.

He looked daggers at the man who had been kissing the woman he loved. "Beat it."

"Listen, I don't want trouble, but it seems to me you're the one that should leave."

Dev glared at the man. He moved toward him, but Caitlyn grabbed his shoulder. "Dev, don't!"

He looked at her. Did she want to be with this loser? Had she already moved on from him? Had he just been a practice boyfriend all along so he could prepare her for the likes of this guy? She met his gaze, then sighed. "Heath, it was nice meeting you, but I need to talk to Dev."

She opened her purse to pay for the beer, but he waved her away. "Don't worry about it. Least I can do…considering."

She nodded.

Considering what? He wanted to ask her, but there were more important things on his mind. Like what was bar guy offering Caitlyn that Dev couldn't. *Royal.* The answer slammed into him. The man was from Royal. He could offer her the one thing Dev couldn't.

"Come on, Dev, let's find a quiet spot to talk. Just give me a sec." She turned to Alice, who was a few stools down on the bar, talking to a man, and whispered something to her. Alice turned to look at him for a beat, then nodded.

Each corner of the bar was louder than the last, so they decided to take the side exit and step into the alley. It was dark, lit only by the light spilling from the apartment building windows on either side. It smelled of tobacco smoke and something sweeter.

"What were you doing in there?" Even in the shadows, he could see the anger in her eyes.

"Me? What were you doing kissing that guy?"

"Excuse me? What's it your business who I kiss?"

He stepped back, the anger that had consumed him just moments ago replaced with a cold ice that seeped into his veins. Who was he indeed? "You know what, you're right." He shook his head. "I'm the crazy one. What was I thinking? All you wanted was a practice boyfriend, somebody to warm you up so you could go out with guys like him." He waved toward the bar door, then turned away from her.

"I guess you're done practicing with me."

Thirteen

The last thing Dev wanted to do was leave Caitlyn standing in the alley, but he'd already made his play. It was her turn now.

She made a strangled sound, and he closed his eyes. "Dev, don't go."

He hadn't even realized he'd been holding his breath until she said those words. He breathed out. She came around so she was facing him. "I need to tell you something."

That was not what he was expecting her to say. Especially not with that look of pain etched on her face. Instinctively, he put his hand on her shoulders. "Hey, are you okay?"

She nodded. "Can we go someplace and talk?"

It was getting late, and most of the Royal cafés

and restaurants were closed, so he drove in silence to his hotel. He was curious as to what she wanted to say, trying not to hope that she'd changed her mind. He handed his car key to the valet and directed her toward the hotel lobby.

She shook her head. "I want to talk someplace private. Can we go to your room?"

He sucked in a breath. "Caitlyn, are you sure?"

"Just to talk," she reiterated.

He shook his head. "I can't promise you that. I'll stick by what I told you on our first date. It'll be up to you when you want to move on from practicing, but being together in a hotel room is more than I can handle."

A pinkish tinge rose from her neck to her cheeks, and he tamped down on the heat that rose deep in his belly. She led the way to the elevator, and they went up to his room. When he'd checked in, all the suites were already taken, so he was in a standard room that had one large bed, a small desk and a little round table with two chairs.

It was hard to ignore the bed that took up most of the space, but he walked resolutely to the small table. "Let me order drinks from room service. Do you want something to eat?"

She shook her head. "Just coffee."

He ordered a pot and sat across from her. She bit her lip. He waited patiently.

"My best friend in high school was a boy named Jax. We never dated in high school, but there was always something between us. What I didn't know until just before Jax went off to college was that my father had paid for his tuition so that I'd have a friend. It broke my heart."

His heart lurched for her. She looked up at him, gauging his reaction. He gave her a small smile. "When I was in high school, I was a bit of a pimply-faced, chubby little boy."

That brought a smile out of her. "I have a hard time picturing that."

"I'll show you my parents' Facebook account which has documented my teenage years in embarrassing detail. Anyway, I did not secure a date to the school dance. My dad didn't want me to stand around alone all night. So, he hired an escort to take me to the dance, thinking I'd be the cool kid. Except half the geeks in the exclusive New York private school had the same idea and the escorts knew each other, so they ended up spending the night hanging out with each other while I stood in the corner."

The smile on her face was much bigger and more genuine, and it pinged his heart. He'd fallen hard for her. Would she break his heart?

He softened his voice. "I don't think my dad would intentionally try to hurt me, just like yours wouldn't. They're convinced that they know what's best for us. What they don't realize is that in trying to protect us, they hurt us even worse."

She blinked, and a tear rolled down her cheek. She looked so innocent and full of pain, his heart squeezed painfully. He wanted to reach over and brush the tear away. Instead he tentatively placed his hand on hers. He didn't want to move any closer and scare her away. There was more to the story, he could tell by the deep breath she took, and he wanted to give her the space she needed to tell it her way.

"Jax went away for college, and we didn't keep in touch. I was mad at him for keeping my father paying his tuition a secret. Then he came back to Royal and by then I'd forgiven him. We reconnected. He admitted that he had loved me all through high school, but his mother had warned him to stay away from me because she worked for my family. He wanted to know if I'd felt the same way, and of course I did. Jax had been my best friend for years. He knew me—I could talk to him. We already had feelings for each other. It made sense to explore whether what we had was deeper."

He nodded—he understood perfectly. He'd never met another woman with whom he connected the way he had with Caitlyn. With other women, when he told the story about the high school dance escort, they were horrified and what followed was a discussion about how inappropriate his parents were. How could he tolerate their intrusiveness? He'd never met an American woman who could understand why he still lived in his family home at the age of twenty-eight when he was gainfully employed and, in their words, "not a loser." Caitlyn hadn't asked him to explain any of these things when he'd told her.

"Our relationship moved pretty fast. In hindsight, I didn't bother to go through the steps. I was just so excited to get my old friend and high school crush back." Her voice cracked, and he squeezed her hand even as his own stomach roiled.

"Jax was my first. I've been with a few men since him, but it's all ended in the same way."

He felt the tremor running through her body and he longed to take her in his arms, but he didn't want to lose this moment. He sensed that what she was about to tell him would explain her behavior. There was no way that he was the only one who had been feeling their connection.

"Jax and I planned a special night. It wasn't his first time, but he knew it was mine, and he wanted it to be a good experience for me." She visibly swallowed. "I don't even know how to tell you what happened. I'm not sure I understand fully. Jax tried so hard to pleasure me, but it just wasn't working…for the both of us…" Her voice cracked again. "We tried again a few times, but it just got worse. He started having problems, too. When we broke up, he told me that he'd never had a problem being with a woman, but I was a…a cold fish."

She hung her head. How could any man be with Caitlyn and think of her as anything but the passionate woman she was? He wasn't sure if there was more to the story, but he also didn't want to scare her away by getting too close.

"I've spent months in therapy trying to figure out what's wrong with me. My therapist encouraged me to date, and I did. But the same thing has happened each time I've gotten close to a man. My therapist calls it a fear of intimacy."

"Caitlyn…"

"No, Dev, don't say anything. Don't tell me that I'm wrong or how I'm beautiful or that I turn you on. I've heard that before. The problem is not with you, it's with me."

You're wrong, Caitlyn. Just thinking about that morning in the barn aroused him. How responsive she'd been, how wet and hot her body got with his touch. Dev had been with enough women to know that there were different levels of attraction he himself felt with each partner, but not once did he question the red-hot chemistry Caitlyn ignited in him.

"The last time you and I met…at the ranch… I had bumped into Jax that day. He lives in Royal too but we have been studiously avoiding each other. He finally decided he was ready to talk. He said that I had put too much pressure on our relationship. We moved so quickly, going from old friends to a serious relationship in one step. It was too much too fast."

"Oh, Caitlyn." He squeezed her hand, at the same time aching for her and relieved to find out why she'd reacted the way she had. He had moved too fast, pushed her to make a commitment when she wasn't ready. He was doing exactly what Jax had accused her of doing.

He pushed his chair close to hers, cupped her face and wiped away her tears with his thumbs. "I'm sorry I put pressure on you, that I rushed things."

"I don't want the same thing to happen to us that happened with Jax."

He nodded. "I understand that, Caitlyn…and…"

A knock on the door interrupted him, and he swore under his breath. He'd forgotten about room service. He let the man in to set up the coffee service on the little table, glad that he'd thought to also order some cookies. Caitlyn looked a little pale and he wondered if she'd had dinner. The room service attendant poured the coffee while Dev signed the check, and then the man left.

Caitlyn automatically added cream to his coffee and sugar and cream to hers. They'd had coffee so often together she knew exactly how he liked his. With a twinge he thought about how lovely it would be to spend breakfast with her. But if there was anything their conversation had taught him, it was that he would lose her if he pushed too hard. She was running scared.

They finished their coffee in a comfortable silence, then he poured her another cup. "Caitlyn, I don't ever want you to feel like I'm pressuring you. I've never had a serious relationship like you had with Jax. You're the first woman that I feel like I've ever connected with. You get me. You know me. You understand me."

He couldn't read the expression on her face, and the coffee burned down his throat. Caitlyn was the first woman he'd loved and hadn't been afraid to tell. What she'd just told him solidified his feelings for her even more. He hadn't imagined their attraction, hadn't overestimated their chemistry or their connection. She felt what he did. But he also knew that there was only one way to convince her of that.

"But if friendship is all that you can give me, I understand, and accept."

Fourteen

Caitlyn stared at Dev. So, it was also happening with him. She'd admitted her deepest, darkest secret. The one only her therapist and Google knew about. What had she really expected? That he would take her into his arms and insist on proving her wrong? *Yes!*

She hadn't planning on telling him so much. But once she'd looked into his eyes, she'd realized that he was the only man who had ever told her he loved her and meant it. Jax had said "love you" once in a while, but it was in the way she said it to her siblings. He'd never told her he was in love with her.

Her brain screamed at her to call an Uber and go home. To save herself the humiliation that was sure to come. But she was frozen in her chair. He was looking at her expectantly, waiting for a response to his offer of friendship.

With every ounce of courage that she had, she stood. Her legs felt unsteady. Dev stood, too. "Caitlyn…"

"I have more than enough friends. I don't need another."

He stepped back, but she closed the distance between them. "What I need, Dev, is a lover. A man who can turn me on, who can show me that I'm not the passionless woman I think I am." His eyes widened, and she gave him a small smile. She stepped closer until she was well into his personal space.

Her legs felt like rubber. She wasn't sure how much longer she could stand. That's when his arm went around her, pulled her close. His head came down, and his lips seared onto hers. She met his kiss with a fervor of her own. Her body was on fire, and he was definitely aroused. She stepped back and lifted his shirt. He helped her get it off. She ran her hands across his muscular chest. He inhaled sharply, which spurred her on. She kissed his chest, ran her fingers over his nipples.

"I showed you mine, now you show me yours," he said cheekily and took off her shirt. She unclasped her bra, eager to feel her body naked and raw against his. He cupped her breasts and ran his thumbs over her nipples. She moaned, enjoying the feel of his hands on her. He bent his head and kissed the spot between her neck and shoulder, and her body pulsed with desire. She placed her hand on his erection, and his hardness made her even wetter than she was.

He wanted her. There was no awkwardness; she was enjoying his touch, not dreading it. In fact, she wanted—no, needed more of him.

She unbuckled his pants and slid them down, then kicked off her high heels and discarded her jeans and panties.

"Do you have a condom?"

He nodded and opened a drawer to retrieve it. He went to open the packet, but she stopped him. "Not quite yet." She smiled then pressed herself against him. She wanted to feel the full length of his naked body against her bare skin. He cupped her butt and lifted her up. She wrapped her legs around him and moaned as she felt him hard between her legs. He rubbed against her wet core and let out a guttural moan. Then he put his mouth to hers.

They were rubbing against each other, she hot and wet, he hard and strong. His shaft pressed against her clit, sending waves of ecstasy through her body. She wanted him so badly, she began writhing against him, inviting him to plunge inside her.

He walked them over to the bed and set her down. He took a deep breath, and she looked at him, taking in the fierceness of his erection. "Dev, please I need you inside me."

He shook his head. "Not quite yet." She hated that he was using her words against her. He put his mouth between her legs, and she lost it. His tongue flicked across her clit, then went in and out of her. His arms were beside her, and she grabbed onto them for support, bracing herself for the explosion about to go off inside her. She dug her fingers into his skin as he licked and sucked her. "Hmm, you taste amazing." He pressed his thumb against her clit as he flicked and sucked with his mouth, and she lost her mind. The pleasure that rocked through her body was sensational. She screamed and lifted her hips, and he cupped his mouth over her sex and sucked.

When she came down from her orgasm, her core was still throbbing. She grabbed his shaft and rubbed him against her clit. He moaned. "Caitlyn, oh my God, I can't hold out much longer." That just spurred her on even more. She grabbed and stroked him and could feel him pulsing in her hand. He stopped her, then quickly placed the condom on himself. When he entered her, she was sure she was going to shatter into a million pieces. He felt amazing inside her. She was already wet, but now her body molded itself to him, gripping his hard shaft as another orgasm pounded through her. She had wanted to do it with him, to finish the second time with him, but she couldn't wait. With her nails digging into his back, she tightened around him, giving in to raw, beautiful pleasure.

When she finally stopped pulsing, she noticed he had gone soft inside her. For a second, fear gripped her. Had it happened again? Had she managed to turn him off?

He smiled at her. "I'm sorry, I wanted to go a little longer, but I just couldn't hold off."

"You finished?" she asked shyly.

He pulled out of her and removed the condom. "A

little too soon for my liking, but we have all night for me to make it up to you."

He grinned at her.

"We do have all night? Don't we? You're not going to up and leave me again, are you?"

Caitlyn shook her head. There was no place she wanted to be other than in Dev's bed. She crawled under the sheets, and he joined her. She turned around so he could spoon her. Impossibly, he was hard again, but she wanted a moment to feel his body against her. To take a breath and process what had just happened. She'd seduced Dev, had made him hot for her, and he in turn had lit a fire in her body.

As they snuggled in together, she finally understood what her therapist had been trying to tell her. There really was nothing wrong with her. She needed to connect emotionally with a man to feel comfortable with the physical part of their relationship. That's why the kiss with Heath hadn't roused her, the way Dev did just by looking at her. She had opened up to him, shared herself with him and felt connected to him. Maybe she'd even fallen in love with him. The thought filled her with warmth, and she pressed close to him.

"Hmm, you keep doing that and I'm not going to be satisfied with just holding you."

She turned around to face him. He kissed her on the nose. "I wish you'd told me earlier about what happened with your ex. I can't believe that any man would think of you as cold. You are passionate, kind, caring…any man would be lucky to have you."

Her heart pinched. That day at the horse ring, he'd told her he loved her. Had his feelings changed? Had she managed to drive him away from her like she always did?

"I'm sorry for the way I reacted the other day when you suggested a business partnership."

He ran his hand down up and down her back, and her body responded immediately, involuntarily curving into him.

"I was just overwhelmed with the suddenness of the idea."

"Was it that or something else?"

There he was again, refusing to let her get away with the words she'd crafted. "What do you think it was? These days you seem to know me better than I know myself."

He smiled. "I doubt that." He pulled himself closer to her so his lips were almost touching hers. "But what I think is that you didn't like the fact that I was proposing a business relationship and not a personal one."

She shook her head. "That's crazy. We've only known each other for a few weeks—I wasn't expecting anything. You just took me by surprise, and I guess I didn't understand why you'd want to tie us together permanently without knowing where our personal relationship was going."

He kissed her briefly. "Where do you want it to go?"

She didn't hesitate. "You are my happily-ever-after, Dev. That's what I want."

"And where shall we live happily ever after?"

"In that ranch you found. We can make it a home. I can see some cozy farmhouse-style furniture, maybe curtains instead of the wood blinds that are there. I can take in horses and run my camp. You can see about turning that old Stevens brewery into your restaurant. You know, the more I think about it, maybe some remodeling could really make that place work. The location is so perfect, and..."

"Caitlyn," he interrupted gently. "You know I can't live my life in Royal."

She blinked. "I know. It was just a thought." He kissed her nose. "I'm not saying we can't come back here often to see your family, but my family business is based in New York, and if my restaurants are successful, I'll have to travel around."

She extricated herself from his arms and sat up. She'd known this conversation was coming and had been avoiding it. She hadn't had the words before, but now she understood why his plans for the ranch had bothered her so much. "What do you expect me to do? Stay by your side as we hop from one place to another? Or stay here in Royal, waiting for you to come home when your schedule allows?"

"I hadn't thought about it. We only just got together. Give us a chance, and we'll figure something out. My family has a private jet. We live in the same country. I have friends that make things work with partners in India—we'll find a way."

She wasn't sure she believed him. She wouldn't ask him to stay in Royal with her. He wouldn't be happy here. But she wasn't sure she could be happy anyplace else.

He ran a finger slowly from her lips, down her neck, between her breasts and down her legs. She was already wet and throbbing for him and more than happy to forget about the looming decisions between them. She had Dev right now, and his mouth was doing that thing he was so good at. She wasn't going to ruin it by thinking about the future. Tomorrow would come soon enough to ruin things.

Fifteen

When he opened his eyes, Caitlyn was next to him, naked and bathed in morning light. They'd had quite the night, finally falling asleep when the sun came up. He stared at her face, wondering how he was ever going to let her go. He was glad they'd put off having the conversation about the future last night. He hadn't wanted to ruin their first night together, but even after she'd fallen asleep, he'd stayed up thinking about what she'd said.

He couldn't ask her to follow him around while he set up his business. Nor could he move to Royal. While it was a charming town, it didn't feel like home for him. He'd seen his siblings give up their dreams for their spouses. He wouldn't do that, nor would he expect Caitlyn to do that for him. But he was having a hard time finding a happy medium. Wasn't he jumping the gun anyway? Caitlyn hadn't even told him she loved him, and here he was trying to figure out how to make their lives work together.

Caitlyn murmured something unintelligible, and he kissed her forehead and left the bed. He checked his phone to see what he had on the schedule and cursed under his breath when he realized he had a video call scheduled with his mother in a few minutes. He had overslept.

"What's got you lookin' like you got bit by a box full of mosquitoes?"

He turned and smiled at her. She was sitting up in bed, holding the white sheet to her chin, and he loved her innocent smile and big eyes. This was the Caitlyn he wanted to wake up to every morning—rosy cheeked and looking at him like he was her whole world.

"I guess you can't take the girl out of Texas." *Literally*.

She smiled. "No, you can't." She lifted an eyebrow toward the phone he was holding.

"I have a video call with my mom in five minutes."

The look of blissful pleasure on her face was replaced with panic. She scrambled out of the bed and began looking for her clothes. "I need to get out of here."

He stepped toward her and pulled her into his arms. "No, you don't. I want you to meet my mom."

She shook her head. "Not looking like this, I can't.

And I need to prep, figure out what I'm going to say. I need to research some Hindi words and..."

He placed a finger on her lips. "No, you don't. You just need to be yourself, like you are with me. Don't put on the armor. It'll just be a quick hello."

"I still can't have her see me wearing your bed-sheet!"

He smirked. "Fine, put on clothes. It'll be nice to take them off again."

She gathered her clothes and raced into the bath-room just as his phone rang.

"Hi, Ma!"

"Dev, *beta*, how are you?"

They chatted for a few minutes. Dev tried to keep the video focused away from the bathroom door so he could properly introduce Caitlyn. His mother talked about the cuteness of his niece and then the latest drama of his siblings. Against his hopes, his brother had not really stepped up to help his father. His sister was handling things well, but things were falling apart at home for her. "It's time for you to come home, son. I don't want Maya's marriage to suffer because of the work she is doing for your fa-ther. I think he sees how capable she is and he'll give her more permanent responsibility."

Dev sighed. What his mother didn't know was that if Maya's marriage was suffering, it was because she was finally beginning to realize everything she'd given up for her husband. Her long-buried resent-ment was surfacing. He'd seen it since the day she quit her job. But now was not the time to discuss all that. He heard Caitlyn carefully opening the bathroom door and saw her peeking out. He waved her into the room. She'd pulled her hair back into a ponytail and washed her face. She looked incredible.

She gestured with her hands to leave but he shook his head.

"Why are you shaking your head?" his mother demanded. Caitlyn froze.

"Ma, you remember Caitlyn, whose picture I showed you? She's here, and I want her to say hello to you."

His mother immediately switched to Hindi, even though they'd been talking in English. "You know that is not how things are done. It is not proper to introduce me to a girl you are sleeping with."

"Ma, she's much more than that, and I think you know it. I wouldn't introduce you to someone unless I was serious about them."

His mother sucked in a breath. "Guess I have no choice but to meet her."

Caitlyn was already strapping on her heels. Before she could bolt, he gestured to her. "Ma, meet Caitlyn. Caitlyn, meet my mother."

Caitlyn glared at him quickly, then turned to face the camera and smiled.

"You are even prettier than the picture Dev showed me." His mother said.

He let out a breath. He didn't think his mother would be rude to Caitlyn, but she could be passive-aggressive.

Caitlyn smiled. "It is so nice to meet you, Mrs.

Mallik. I had hoped we would meet under better circumstances."

His mother smiled. "My son is known to be very inappropriate, but we shall cover for his inadequacies, shan't we."

Both Caitlyn and his mother smiled and continued to make small talk. His mother asked about her family, and, immediately at ease, Caitlyn told her all about them. They talked a little about the charities they were each involved in. His mother even took one of Caitlyn's suggestions for a children's charity.

He was glad to see Caitlyn at ease with his mother. He wanted them to get along, to know that Caitlyn could fit in with his family.

"Tell me, Caitlyn, do you identify as a Black woman or as a white woman?"

Dev sucked in a breath. At least his mother had asked diplomatically.

She smiled. "It's a great question. Until a couple of years ago, I would've said both. But the truth is, my family, the Lattimores, is Black, and whether I realized it or not, I've been treated like a Black woman most of my life."

"As a woman of color myself, I understand, my dear. So tell me, how will your children identify?"

"Excuse me?"

"It's something to think about, isn't it? Take my grand-daughter for example, beautiful child she is. My son married an Indian woman, but my grand-daughter calls herself Indian American. When she makes little pictures of her family, she colors herself a different shade than her parents, even though she looks exactly like them."

He knew where his mother was going, and he wasn't going to let his mother sow doubt in Caitlyn's heart. "Well, we should get some breakfast, Ma, so I'm going to steal my girlfriend back."

"No, wait. I'd like to respond to that." Caitlyn took a breath. "There's no answer. All my life, I've felt like I didn't know how to describe myself. I wasn't white or Black. Personally, I think it's sad that we still define people by the color of their skin. I hope my children won't have to deal with that at school. But if they do, I'll tell them what my mother told me. *It doesn't matter. All I want is for you to love who you are.*"

"Your mother sounds like a good woman." Dev knew that tone in his mother's voice, and he was glad Caitlyn wouldn't recognize it for the condescension it was.

"It's time for us to go, Ma."

His mother switched back to Hindi. "Dev, she's a nice enough girl, but it doesn't change the fact that she's not Indian. It's time for you to come home and stop wasting your time in that backward Southern town." She hung up, and he took a breath to compose his face.

"She hated me, didn't she?" Caitlyn said quietly.

He shook his head. "No, she didn't hate you. She hates the fact that you're not Indian. That's something I'll work on with her." He tucked his phone away and cupped her face. "You did great."

"She has a point, you know."

"What do you mean?"

"What you wouldn't let her finish saying. That our backgrounds are very different. You don't know what it's like being Black, and I don't know what it's like to be Indian."

"So what, Caitlyn? How does that matter now? We have a lifetime to get to know each other's cultures and traditions."

She sat on the edge of the bed. "Until a couple of years ago, it wouldn't have mattered much to me, either. But one thing Jax made me see is how blind I'd been to the fact that I am Black, and that it affects how I see the world and how people treat me. It affects the responsibilities I have to my community as a member of the privileged class." She paused and swallowed. "It will affect how your family treats me."

"Listen, I've dated my fair share of Indian women, and let me tell you that what I value as a person is the same things you do. That's what's really important."

She shook her head. "Just now, your mom wanted to tell you what she thought of me, so she switched into a different language. That's how it'll always be. Your siblings married within your culture. I'll be an outsider in your family."

He sat beside her and took her hand. "I won't let that happen."

"Then you'll be an outsider in your own family."

He couldn't deny that she was right. It would take a long time for his family to get used to speaking

English at the dinner table. They'd made a pact to only speak Hindi at home to make sure the next generation, his nieces and nephews, learned their language. But surely that was a small thing to overcome.

He leaned over and kissed her cheek. "I'll teach you the language. Don't worry too much about it."

"I don't think it'll be that easy."

He shifted so he could cup her face and make her look at him. "No, it's not going to be easy. But you know what's nearly impossible? Finding that one person who gets you and supports you and will be there for you. What we have is worth fighting for." He gazed at her. "I've been with my fair share of women, and the connection we have, it's nothing like I've had before. In my culture, we believe that there is one person who is made for us, our soul mate. You're mine, Caitlyn, and I'm willing to do whatever it takes to make it work."

Her eyes shone. "Are you sure, Dev? I know how much your family means to you. I don't want to be the one that comes between you and them."

He kissed her briefly on the lips. "You won't."

She turned her face and kissed his hand. "As long as you stand by my side, we'll face it together. My family won't be that easy, either."

"Is it because I don't speak with a Texas twang?"

She smiled. "Yes, and you're not a rancher, and you're not from Royal."

"That's a problem for you, too, isn't it? That I'm not from Royal."

She took his hands in hers. "I love you, Dev. I

think I've loved you since the moment I spit my wine in your face."

A feeling of warmth and relief flooded through him. "I love you, too, Caitlyn. I promise you, we will figure it out. Finding love, that's impossible. Figuring out where to live and how to make a business work, that's just logistics."

"You make it sound so easy."

She leaned over and kissed him, and he kissed her back. A slow, sweet kiss to let her know that he loved her and that he was willing to fight for them.

"How about we spend the rest of the day together, forget about our families and just enjoy the fact that we have each other?"

She nodded. "Can we start by ordering breakfast? I'm famished."

He bent his head and kissed the spot between her neck and shoulder that made her break out in goose bumps. "Can I feast on something else first before we start breakfast?"

She murmured her approval and took off his shirt. He happily obliged and took off his jeans as she shed her own clothes. He wanted to take his time, but she had other ideas. As soon as his clothes were off, she grabbed his erection. Her hands were soft but her touch firm, and he nearly lost it. How could it be that her merest touch set his body on fire? He was usually much more reserved, but found it hard to hold himself back with her.

"Caitlyn, one second..."

She shook her head. "I don't want to take it slow. I want you now."

The fire in her eyes matched the one burning through his body. He knew what this was about. The conversation with his mother had deflated the bubble they'd created around themselves last night, believing that a declaration of love was all they needed. They both needed an immediate and urgent reminder that it was real between them, and that it was worth it. Or perhaps he was the one who needed reminding. He couldn't admit it to her, but she was right about the fact that it wouldn't be easy with his family and he'd have to give up part of his own relationship with them to be with her. He needed to be strong. His family always had a way of pulling him back in, of sucking him into their fold and their needs. What he needed was Caitlyn.

She pulled his arm with one hand while the other stayed firmly on his impossibly hard shaft. She lay back on the bed and guided him inside her. She was slick and he tried to tell her to take it slow, but she wouldn't listen, arching her hips to take him deeper inside her. Somewhere a phone rang, but he ignored it. He kissed her and she moaned, moving her hips. He matched her movements, feeling her tighten around him. The sensation was too much for him, but he held on as long as he could, determined to make sure she finished before he did, though it was hard to hold on with her tight around him and moaning with pleasure. She lifted her hips as her orgasm took over, and he couldn't hold himself back as she vibrated and pulsed against him.

"What's that ringing?"

He registered the same phone ringing that he'd noted when they got started, but where was it coming from? It wasn't his cell.

"That's my cell phone," she exclaimed.

The ringing stopped and she relaxed against him, but a minute later, it rang again. He slid out of her, seeing the panic on her face.

"I better get it, make sure it's not an emergency."

She scrambled out of bed, and he smacked himself. He'd forgotten the condom. How could he have been so stupid and not protected her? He knew he was healthy and didn't doubt for a second that she was, too, but he should've been more responsible. He'd gotten caught up in the moment and lost his mind. He'd have to tell her, make sure she took whatever precautions she needed to. How would she react when he told her? If this had happened with any other woman, he would've been freaking out. Actually, this would never have happened with another woman. But if it had to happen, he was glad it was with Caitlyn.

She answered the phone. "Sorry, I wasn't near my phone." She was breathless. "I'm on my way. I'll be there in fifteen minutes."

She looked at him as she clicked End on her phone. He was already pulling on his clothes. "What's wrong?"

"The private investigator found something about the claim on our ranch. The Grandins are coming over—the whole family is gathered. I need to go."

Sixteen

"I'll drive you."

Caitlyn sighed. Was she ready to bring Dev into her family fold? The Grandins were like family. If she took Dev with her, he'd meet all of them. *What if they don't like him? What if they scare him off?*

She pulled on her jeans and checked her appearance in the mirror. She couldn't show up looking like she was doing the walk of shame. Even though she was.

"I don't have to meet them. I can just drop you off."

She looked at him as he was fixing his own appearance. He pulled on a fresh shirt and ran a comb through his hair. There was a five o'clock shadow on his face, but he managed to make it look like it belonged there.

"Caitlyn, I need to tell you something."

She turned to him, her stomach clenching at the hollowness of voice. *What's wrong now?*

He swallowed. "I'm so sorry, I forgot to put on the condom that last time."

She almost laughed. How could she have forgotten? She was so careful. Almost without thinking, she looked at her phone for the date. *Crap.* Of course it was the time of the month when she should be even more careful.

"I take full responsibility. I know we have to go now, but I want you to know that I will be there for you, that..."

She put a finger on his lips. "The responsibility was as much mine as it was yours. If something happens, we will figure it out together."

He gave her a quick kiss, and all she had to do was look in his eyes to know that he was all in with her. He'd introduced her to his mother. While he made it out to be no big deal, she knew it was. It was clear from the overly casual way his mother had asked her some pretty deep questions about her family. The very fact that his mother had known about her before she and Dev had even slept together meant his feelings were serious. If he could take a gamble on her, she needed to make the same commitment to him.

"I want you to meet my family. There's no time like the present." Plus, she knew her family would be better behaved in front of the Grandins.

He placed his hands on her shoulders, forcing her to look up at him. "You don't have to, Caitlyn. I want to meet your family when you're ready. I'm in no rush."

She smiled. "Let's do it."

When they arrived at the Lattimore mansion, her family was gathered in the living room. All eyes turned to them as they walked in. Her grandfather Augustus was sitting in the large wing-back chair that was his spot in the family room.

Every time she saw her grandfather, it was hard to believe that he wasn't the same person he used to be. While he was still the tall, physically imposing figure she remembered from her childhood, his mind was not what it used to be. Her grandmother Hazel sat with Caitlyn's father, Ben, and her mother, Barbara. There was an antique silver pot on the coffee table, which she knew held the special brew coffee that her grandparents liked. Royal Doulton teacups, the service set from her parents' wedding, were set out along with little sandwiches, scones and pastries. Caitlyn's stomach rumbled, and she remembered they hadn't eaten breakfast.

Jayden was sitting opposite her parents, but Jonathan was pacing behind the couch. Their living room held three grand sofas and several chairs.

She was holding Dev's hand, and he squeezed it as a silence fell over the room. Caitlyn straightened, trying to stand as tall as she could. "Hi, everyone. This is my...this is Dev." *Boyfriend* seemed like the wrong word for him. Jax had been her boyfriend. Dev was so much more.

Jonathan was the first to speak. He made his way toward them. "Welcome, Dev." He held out a hand, and Dev shook it.

Before anyone else had a chance to speak, the Grandins arrived. Victor Jr. was accompanied by his son Vic, and his daughters Chelsea and Layla. Their younger sister, Morgan, hadn't come. Layla's fiancé, Josh, was there, and for once Caitlyn didn't feel the ping of jealousy that she did when she saw them. They all greeted each other, and everyone gave Dev a not-too-subtle once-over.

Layla sidled up to Caitlyn when she was alone for a second. "Who is that handsome stranger with you?"

"Someone I care about," she answered honestly.

"Well, whoever he is, hold on to him." Layla winked at Caitlyn, then went to help herself to the refreshments.

Dev handed Caitlyn a cup of coffee with some pastries on the saucer. "Why don't you sit and have something to eat?"

"Could you hear my stomach grumbling?"

He smiled. "I have a feeling you're going to need your strength for this meeting."

She had no doubt. Usually when the Lattimores and Grandins got together, there was chatter and merriment, but today, everyone found a seat pretty efficiently, many forgoing food or coffee.

Jonathan placed a large speaker in the center of the coffee table. It looked like an octopus, with cables that connected to multiple mini speakers that he spread out. It was the conference room telephone. "I have the private investigator, Jonas Shaw, and Alexa on the line."

Caitlyn had never seen everyone so quiet. She and Dev had chosen to stand behind the couch where her parents were seated. Her hand trembled slightly, and she set her cup on a side table. Dev handed her a small scone from his own plate, but she shook her head. Her appetite had vanished. He took her hand and squeezed it.

Jonas Shaw's voice was deep and crackly over the speakerphone. "I know you folks are anxious to know what I found, so I'll get right to it."

The room stopped breathing, but all Caitlyn could think about was the secure feeling of Dev's hand on hers. What if she found out in two weeks that she was pregnant? How would she feel? *Why aren't I freaking out about it?* Was she crazy to believe that he was committed to her?

Jonas cleared his throat. "As y'all know, Ashley Thurston was born about nine months after Daniel Grandin had an affair with Cynthia Thurston. You guys hired me to investigate the legitimacy of the papers that Heath Thurston is using to claim the oil underneath both your lands. I found a lawyer that used to work here in Royal. He's long dead now, but his daughter had his old papers. I went through them and found a copy of the paper Heath Thurston has."

The room took a collective breath. Until now, their entire strategy had been to refute the authenticity of the papers Heath Thurston had produced with Victor Sr. and Augustus's signatures.

"What about Augustus's signature on those papers?" her father asked.

"I'm afraid that's more bad news. Among the lawyer's papers was a logbook. Each person who visited the office signed in. On the day the papers were signed, Augustus's name was in the log, along with his signature. The same signature that was on the papers."

Silence hung like dead weight in the room, then Alexa spoke up. "Did you check to see if Augustus could have been there for other business? Maybe he was using the lawyer for something else?"

Caitlyn hated that they talked about her grandfather like he wasn't in the room. She looked at Augustus. The scowl on his face suggested he didn't like it, either.

"I checked, but I couldn't find anything related to Augustus. I reviewed the logbook for the month before and after, and Augustus didn't go to the office on any of the other days. Looks like his signature is legit."

Alexa and Layla asked Shaw several more questions, trying to find a way to dispute the information he was giving them, but it was of no use. It was pretty clear that Heath Thurston's claim was real and both of their ranches were in danger. Once Jonas had hung up, her father turned to her grandfather.

"Daddy, do you remember Victor asking you to sign something?"

Augustus frowned at his son. "Why are you askin' me? And who was that on the phone besmirching my name? Why don't you ask Victor? Where is Victor anyway?"

Her grandmother stood and placed a hand on Augustus's shoulder. "Darlin, Victor can't be here right now."

"Then I'm not staying, either." Her grandfather rose from the chair, surprisingly agile for his age.

"I think I better take him back to bed," Hazel said.

When they'd left, everyone began talking at once.

"Augustus had no right to sign over our land to pay for Daniel's sins," Ben grumbled. Caitlyn had never seen her father so riled up.

"Excuse me, but how do we know that your father isn't the one that put my grandfather up to this?" Chelsea exclaimed, tucking her long, flowing hair behind her ear. As the eldest daughter of the Grandin clan, Chelsea was fearless, and not afraid of butting heads with anyone.

Jonathan spoke up, his tone sharp and cutting. "Augustus isn't the one who had an affair and a child out of wedlock."

Caitlyn noted the fear and anger on the faces around the room. Their families had been friends forever, and they were turning on each other.

Layla chimed in. "I don't for a second—"

"Everyone stop!" Caitlyn cut in, surprised at the strength in her voice. Since she rarely spoke, everyone turned in surprise.

She made eye contact with everyone. "Now is not

the time to turn on each other. Our only hope in getting through this is to work together. Both our properties are at risk here."

Alexa's voice crackled over the phone. "Only if there is oil. What if we can prove there isn't?"

Heads all around the room started nodding, obviously liking Alexa's line of thinking.

Victor Grandin Jr. spoke up. "I'll get Jonas working on that." He picked up his phone and left the room to make the call.

"It seems to me that what we need is a good lawyer," Caitlyn stated. "Our current ones don't have the personal investment we need to make sure this goes our way."

She didn't have to say more. All eyes turned to the phone.

"Alexa, we need you and your brilliant mind," Layla said softly.

"I know you weren't plannin' on coming home soon, honey, but this is too important," her mother said.

Alexa sighed. "I'll represent us on this. Caitlyn is right. We have to work together. Right now the most important thing is that no one from either of our families has any contact with Heath or Nolan Thurston. Is that understood?"

Caitlyn tensed and gave Dev a sideways glance. He didn't know that the man in the bar last night had been Heath Thurston.

"We don't know what the brothers' next steps are,

and what we don't want is to inadvertently give them information that helps their case," Alexa continued.

Everyone nodded solemnly even though Alexa couldn't see them. Barbara invited the Grandins to stay for brunch, but everyone seemed to have lost their appetite. The Grandins rose to leave.

"I think I should go," Dev whispered to Caitlyn as everyone said goodbye to each other.

She grabbed his hand. "Don't."

He shook his head. "I think you need to focus on your family right now. There will be plenty of time for them to get to know me. Right now, they need you to process the news they just got, and you need to be here for them."

She smiled at him, unwilling to let him go but loving him for being so considerate and understanding that her family needed her. "I'm sorry about our day together."

"There will be plenty more." He gave her a chaste kiss on the cheek, then slipped out quietly.

"Where'd your fella go?" her father said as he poured himself a cup of coffee from the fresh pot that one of the kitchen staff brought out.

"This wasn't the best time to bring him," Caitlyn said.

"There's never a good time," Jonathan said gruffly. Her brother was sporting his signature jeans, T-shirt and cowboy boots. "I kinda wanted to talk to the guy."

"What, so you could get his social security number?" Jayden piped up. He picked up a sandwich and tossed it in his mouth, much to his mother's chagrin. She handed him a plate, and he promptly set it down.

"Have you been researching him?" Caitlyn could see her brothers cyberstalking Dev. "Did Alexa tell you about him?"

"Relax, sis. He seems like a solid guy." Jayden said.

Jonathan cleared her throat. "I still have some questions I'd like to ask him."

Caitlyn shook her head. "This is why I didn't want him sticking around."

"Caitlyn, did you know that his siblings are both married to people from their culture?"

"Yes, Jonathan, I know that. I don't see what that has to do with me dating him."

"Oh, Caitlyn, darlin', I could see clear as day that you two are in love with each other. You'd never have brought him today if you weren't serious about him." Her mother patted the seat next to her, and Caitlyn went to her.

"Why do I feel like you're all ganging up on me?"

Her mother put an arm around her. "We just want to make sure you know what you're doing."

"I'm not a child, and for your information, he introduced me to his mother today."

"And how did that go?"

"It went fine."

"Has Dev talked to you about whether his family is willing to accept someone outside their culture?" Her father put a sandwich on a plate and handed it to her.

"Are you guys willing to accept him? He's not Black." She set the plate on a side table. Her stomach was churning, and she couldn't imagine eating.

"You know that doesn't matter to us," her mother said.

"There's no point in talking about this when we don't know anything about his family. We've barely known each other for three weeks. Aren't you all always on my case about getting out more and dating and getting over Jax? Well, how am I supposed to do that when the first man I bring home gets the Texas inquisition?"

Her siblings had the courtesy to look sheepish. Alexa called out and everyone suddenly remembered she was still on the phone. In her take charge voice, she asked everyone to sit down so they could discuss what their next steps should be. Only Alexa could command a room even when she wasn't in it. After a while, Caitlyn stood, grabbed the plate her father had given her, loaded it up with sandwiches and left. Talking to death about what lay ahead wouldn't change the situation. One thing hit her with certainty—she wouldn't be able to open her camp on the Lattimore property anytime soon. The legal machinations Alexa was talking about would take forever, and Caitlyn couldn't keep putting her camp on hold for that long.

Then another thought punched her in the gut. Dev was supposed to be leaving town today, and not once had he mentioned staying.

Seventeen

Caitlyn breathed a sigh of relief when Dev texted to ask if he could pick her up a few hours later. She had already washed her hair and blown it out. She went to one of her favorite boutiques in town and, much to the amusement of the shopkeeper, picked out a red dress that was unlike anything she owned. The neckline was scandalous, and that's exactly what she wanted. She wore it without a bra, as it was meant to be worn. The dress cupped her breasts and tied in the back, then came around the front of her body like a wrap and ended in a bow.

She shivered with excitement at the thought of Dev loosening that bow and unwrapping the dress from her. She wore it with a pair of strappy heels and a new silk thong. She closed her eyes and imagined

Dev's hand on that thong, and her core throbbed with anticipation. As she looked at herself in the mirror, she barely recognized the woman in front of her. Her cheeks were flushed, her skin glowed and the dress looked like it belonged on the cover of a fashion magazine.

She was ready just as Dev pulled to the front of the house, which was eerily quiet after the drama of the morning. Dev exited the car to open the door for her and looked at her quizzically. "Isn't it a little hot to be wearing a coat?"

She gave him a smile, then looked around to make sure there were no staff or siblings lurking nearby. She took off the raincoat she'd thrown on and twirled for him.

Dev whistled appreciatively.

"I can't be seen wearing something like this. I bought it just for you."

He touched her partially bare back and kissed her on the cheek. "You look sensational," he breathed into her ear, and her heart fluttered at the hungry look in his eyes. He looked back toward the front door of her house. "Any chance your family is gone? I don't think I can drive with you looking like that."

She shook her head, smiling. He sighed and got into the driver's seat. "I was going to take you out to dinner, but I'm not sure I can share you with anyone else tonight."

"There is no way I'm going out on the town looking like this. I have a reputation as a stuffy Lattimore to keep up. This dress is just for you."

The wolfish smile he gave her and the dark hunger in his eyes made the dress totally worthwhile.

"Why don't you drive to the corner of Main and Porterhouse? My favorite Italian restaurant is there, and we can get some takeout. I'll place the order now and it'll be ready by the time we get there."

Once they picked up the food, he turned down Porterhouse Street. "Wait, the hotel is on the other side."

He smiled. "We're not going to the hotel. Just wait and see."

He pulled up to one of the new condo buildings that had been built at the edge of town. He turned to her. "I rented a place here. Didn't feel right to keep taking you to a hotel room."

She refused to think about what that meant. He'd rented a place. That was a sign that he wasn't leaving anytime soon.

The condo he'd rented was on the top floor of the building with a great view of the neighboring ranches. The space was light and airy without being ostentatious. There was an open kitchen, living room, dining room and two bedrooms. It was sparsely furnished with basic but tastefully modern furniture.

"How did you get it set up so quickly?" It had only been a few hours since she'd last seen him.

"Well, I only had a suitcase to move. The place was already furnished and ready to rent."

He stepped behind her and circled his arms

around her. He kissed the back of her neck, and a shiver of anticipation zinged through her.

"It definitely needs some homey touches. Maybe you'd be willing to help?"

Setting up house with you? Sign me up!

"So you plan to stay in Royal?"

"For now."

There was that maddeningly unclear answer. *What does* for now *mean?* Before she had a chance to ask, he trailed kisses down her neck and to the bare spots on her back. He cupped her breasts and moved his thumbs over her nipples, and all thought left her mind as heat flooded her body.

"Now, how do I unwrap this dress and get to my present?"

She undid the bow in the front of the dress, her body electrified with the anticipation of what was coming.

Suddenly the doorbell rang. Dev cursed under his breath, and she looked at him quizzically. "Expecting someone?"

He adjusted his pants and yelled, "Coming." She began rewrapping the dress. "My mom said that she was sending a package, so I told the hotel to send the courier over here when it arrived. I assumed they would leave it by the front desk."

When her dress was rewrapped, Dev went to answer the door, and Caitlyn moved out of view. She didn't want anyone seeing her in that dress, even if it was just a courier.

"Dad, what are you doing here?"

Wait what? Who!

"Surprise!"

This was not happening to her. Pulse racing, Caitlyn looked for the raincoat and realized it was on the other side of the room. She couldn't get to it without crossing in front of the door and being seen. Would it be better to hide in the bedroom until Dev's father left? Hiding was not a good idea. With her luck, he would decide to stay the night and then it would look even worse for her to be caught in the bedroom.

The man who entered the apartment looked nothing like Dev. He was half a foot shorter and lean, with thinning hair and round glasses. Despite the heat, he was dressed in a business suit. Regardless of his small size, he had a booming voice, and Caitlyn could see Dev shrinking right in front of him.

"Your mother was worried about you. I came to take you back to New York with me. Our jet is at the airport. Things are..." He stopped when he caught sight of Caitlyn.

"Ah, I see you have company." He eyed Caitlyn, and she shrank back, wishing she had hidden in the bedroom. "Sorry, I should have called. I can come back."

"No, it's okay, Dad. I want to—"

"No, no, son. You paid for the night, you should enjoy yourself."

It was as if someone had seared her with a branding iron. She raced to the kitchen to collect her coat, threw it on and picked up her purse. She couldn't stay one more second. This was not the way to meet Dev's father. "I need to go," she mumbled.

"Caitlyn, wait, no, don't leave." Dev caught her hand as she tried to race past him and put an arm around her. "Dad, this is Caitlyn, my girlfriend."

Her father's eyebrows shot up. "I see why your mother is worried," he said.

"Dad! Don't be rude. Caitlyn is important to me."

"No, it's okay, this is not the right way for us to meet. I'm sorry." She pushed Dev aside, wanting nothing more than for the floor to open up and swallow her whole.

"Let me drive you home."

She met his gaze, her eyes pleading. She couldn't take any more embarrassment. She shook her head, "Dev, please, take care of your dad. I need to go. I'll take an Uber." She turned on her heels and left.

"Dad, you can't just show up like that."

"Why not? Because you're ashamed? And what is this about you moving from the hotel and leasing an apartment? I thought you were here to open a restaurant. Where is the restaurant? What have you been doing?"

Dev took a breath. He knew things looked bad from where his father stood. He was a traditional Indian man, and it was bad enough that his first introduction to Caitlyn had been in his apartment, but to have her dressed as she had been was a double whammy. He needed to calm the situation before things really got out of hand.

"Dad, let's start over. Why don't you come and sit? Let me get you a glass of water and then we can talk."

Temporarily mollified, his dad took a seat at the glass dining room table. Dev eyed Caitlyn's dinner favorites and sighed. He handed his father a glass of water, then plated the food for both of them. It was a practice in his father's business to serve tea and refreshments before every meeting. It irritated Dev, who considered it a waste of time and money, but his father had a saying that rhymed in their language. Translated, it meant that if stomachs are empty, words are, too. It's how business was done in India, and it went beyond hospitality. He hoped this time, it reduced his father's crankiness.

"*Beta*, I came to take you back."

"Dad, I told you when I left that I need to chart my own course."

"I understand that. I did the same thing when I was your age. Your grandfather was dead set against me coming to America. He even refused to pay for my ticket. Your mother and I came here with nothing. We stayed with relatives, and I used my savings and sold your mother's jewelry to buy my first business. From that I built up an entire empire. I understand your need to be your own man, and I want to support you."

There was a big *but* coming, Dev could feel it, and he braced himself.

"And I will support you, *beta*. But I need your support right now." His father sighed, took off his glasses and rubbed the bridge of his nose. All his life, his father had seemed larger than life. The great Vishvanath Mallik, the man who reduced competitors to tears after filling them full of tea and mini cucumber sandwiches. Right now, all Dev saw was how shrunken his father looked, and the bags under his eyes.

"I know you have pushed me to consider your sister and brother to run the business. What you don't know is that I have given your brother, Khushal, several chances. He likes the lifestyle but not the work. Your sister, Maya, is very capable, but this job comes at a cost. You know that her in-laws are old and live with them. The last three weeks that you've been gone, her marriage has suffered. Her husband has told her in no uncertain terms that she can't keep working the hours she's been working. Their household is falling apart. That's why I'm here. I had hoped to handle things without you, give you a chance to pursue your own dreams, but I'm getting to be an old man now. I can't handle it all. I need your help."

Dev's stomach knotted. "Dad, I've told you that we need to hire more executives. You have to trust people outside the immediate family."

"You haven't lived like I have, son. You don't know how vulnerable family enterprises like ours are. One mistake and the entire business can fall. I told you how your uncle inherited my father's factories in India. I was so busy running things in America that I trusted him to run the factories that were my inheritance. He ran them into the ground. Factories that your great-grandfather built under the British rule, when hardly any Indians were allowed to own property and have wealth. Those factories survived colonialism and crumbled because of some bad decisions. I can't trust someone else."

It was an argument that he and his father had been having since Dev had graduated from business school. He'd felt totally unprepared to be the CFO and COO of this father's company as a new graduate, but his father had never been convinced to hire someone for those roles.

"Dad, Maya is a grown woman. Don't you think she should make her own decisions? She loves working—she went to Harvard Business School. When I don't know how to handle something, I call her."

"Her husband came to me directly, and I promised him that I'd bring you back so Maya could return her attention to their marriage."

"Don't you think that's unfair of Neeraj? I've only been gone for three weeks, and he's already coming to you. He, and you, haven't even given Maya a chance."

"Dev, this is not up for debate. You know how your mother and I feel about marriage. We wouldn't have what we do if it weren't for your mother. Maya has the same responsibilities to her family."

"Aren't we her family, Dad?"

"Once married, a woman's priority is the family she marries into."

"Dad, the world has changed, and we aren't

in India anymore. You have to give up these old-fashioned beliefs."

"Does this have to do with that girl?"

Dev straightened. "No, Dad, this is much bigger than Caitlyn alone..."

"Because if it is, let me tell you that your mother and I are not going to let you throw your life away on a girl like that."

Dev dug his nails into his hands, trying to formulate his anger into a respectful sentence. "You don't know Caitlyn. What you walked into today was a private romantic moment."

"Look, Dev, I know you think me old-fashioned, but I'm not that traditional. Maya dated, and I don't expect your future wife to be pure and virginal, but I do expect her to have some decorum, family values and..."

"Caitlyn has all that and more in spades. Like I said, you caught her at a bad moment, but she comes from one of the most respectable families in Texas. She herself is on the board of the local hospital and several charities. She tirelessly supports her family every—"

"Your mother told me all about Caitlyn. The issue is not whether her family is respectable enough and if she herself has good values. It's whether she is willing to leave her family to come support you and your dreams. Your life is in New York. Will she leave her life in Royal to come be with you?"

Dev's mouth went dry. *No, she won't.*

Eighteen

Caitlyn turned off the phone so it would stop buzzing. It was Alice, who had heard from Russ, who had shown up to Dev's new digs to find his father there. Dev had not texted or called. She knew he needed time to talk to his dad and smooth things over, but it had been more than six hours since she'd left his place. Caitlyn couldn't shake the feeling that things were not going well with his dad.

Worse, she couldn't help wondering if his father had succeeded in doing what she feared most. Had he convinced Dev to go back to New York? To give up on Caitlyn?

It was late into the night and she was exhausted. She checked her phone again. No calls from Dev.

She turned off the phone and tucked herself into bed. There was nothing she could do tonight.

She slept fitfully. This time she dreamed that she was naked in bed with Dev and the Lattimores and Grandins all walked in on them and accused her of colluding with Heath Thurston. She woke up in a cold sweat and realized it was only 4:00 a.m. She checked her phone and cursed under her breath when she saw ten missed calls from Dev. He'd called right after she fell asleep.

Unable to return to sleep, she opened her laptop and pulled up the listing for the ranch Dev had wanted to buy with her. Her stomach clenched when she saw "under contract" on the listing. Someone had put an offer on the place. She slammed the laptop shut. It was a sign that she and Dev weren't meant to be. She'd planned to buy the place and surprise Dev with it, but clearly fate was also shitting on them.

It was too early to go riding. She didn't want to show up at the barns and screw up the morning chore schedule. She decided to go for a swim.

After a few laps, Caitlyn heard Alexa as she came up for a breath.

"You training for the Olympic team?"

Caitlyn propped herself on the edge of the pool where Alexa was standing. "Woke up early. It's too hot to run and too early to ride."

Alexa was in jeans, a loose t-shirt and carried a paper cup.

"You took the early morning plane from Miami?"

Alexa nodded. "I need to review all the family papers and whatever Jonas found."

"I know this whole legal business is horrible but the silver lining is that you'll be home more now."

Alexa tilted her head. "What's going on, Caitlyn? You only swim like that when you're upset. What's wrong?"

She bit her lip. The last thing she needed was Alexa's judgment. "Any more news after the bombshell yesterday?" Had that only been yesterday? She still couldn't believe how much had happened in one day. She'd gone from waking up to the promise of a new life with Dev to having the rug pulled from underneath her. In all that, she hadn't even stopped to think about what the call with Jonas Shaw meant for their family's future.

"No real new information, but what Jonas found is pretty damning for us. We need to figure out what Heath Thurston wants out of all of this, but we also need to be careful about how we approach him and Nolan."

"I know it was my idea, but are you really okay with taking this on?"

Alexa shrugged. "I have been thinking about this since it happened. This is too important to trust to an outsider. But I can't stay in Royal. My life is in Miami. I'm going to need your help." She took a breath. "Caitlyn, the family is going to need you in the coming months. This fight with the Thurstons is going to be tough. And Grandpa is getting worse. Dad tried talking to him alone yesterday, and he doesn't remember what he may or may not have signed."

Caitlyn took a breath. "What do you need help with?"

Alexa smiled. "We all know how much you do for the family, and we appreciate it. I'm counting on you to help me fight this claim. I can only stay for a short time. Can you help me with sorting through Grandpa's papers?"

Caitlyn smiled and nodded. Maybe it was a good thing that the little ranch had sold. Her place was right here with her family. They needed her. She exited the pool and got dressed, opting for the most conservative clothes she had, which was most of her closet. Despite the heat, she settled for a pantsuit with a white collared shirt. She added her pearls and drove into town to her favorite bakery. She'd called ahead for an order of coffee and pastries. When they'd come to Dev's rental condo the previous day, he'd put her name on the list with the front desk so she could get a spare key anytime. Dev tended to sleep a little later, so she picked up the key in case he didn't answer her knock. She hoped she was early enough to offer them breakfast. Though what had happened the day before was tough to overcome, she owed it to their relationship to talk to Dev face-to-face.

She knocked on the door, but there was no answer. She used the key to enter. The place looked exactly as it had yesterday, but something was amiss. She set breakfast on the counter and noticed both bedroom doors were open.

She walked to the first door, her legs rubbery. The bedroom was pristine. The bed looked like it hadn't been slept in. She peeked in the second bedroom, and it looked the same. Had Dev and his dad woken up really early? Something about the tight corners of the bedsheets bothered her. She doubted that Dev, who had grown up with household staff, could make the beds so well. She walked into the room and threw open the closet door. She raced into the other room and found the same thing. She looked in every corner of the condo.

Dev was gone.

Nineteen

Dev cursed at his phone when he woke. His wireless charger hadn't quite connected, so the phone hadn't charged and was now dead. He placed it on the charger again and went to get dressed. His parents owned a penthouse triplex on the east side of Central Park. His room was palatial by any standards but especially New York City standards—it held a king-size bed, his exercise equipment, a deluxe desk decked out with all the technology he could ever want and an en suite bathroom. Looking around the room he realized just how frat boyish it looked with his clothes from last night on the floor and the dark leather furniture. He made a mental note to ask his mother to call the decorator to redesign the room. He walked into the shower and let the ten body jets and rain shower wake him up. He hated waking up this early.

After arguing with his father for hours, he'd finally agreed to get on the family jet and come home for a few days. He'd called Caitlyn multiple times, but she hadn't answered. It was too complex to leave a voice mail. He'd just keep trying. He didn't want to leave things the way they were, but after talking with his father he'd realized that he had to come home and deal with whatever was going on with Maya. He was her older brother and had always protected her.

His phone was ringing when he exited the shower. It was his sister, Maya, calling to tell him that she was in the dining room downstairs. It was barely 7:00 a.m., but he shouldn't have been surprised that his sister had heard he was back and was ready for a fight. He sighed and threw on a collared shirt and dress pants.

"Maya," he greeted his sister as he walked into the dining room. His parents' penthouse suite spanned the better part of the top floor of the forty-story building, plus a portion of the two floors below. The dining room was on the topmost floor and had a floor-to-ceiling view of Central Park. The staff had set out coffee and pastries. His parents were late risers and typically didn't come down to breakfast until 8:00 a.m.

His sister was five-seven and dressed like the New York power broker she was in a smart white dress suit that looked like it should be on the cover of *Businessweek*. She gave him a warm hug and a kiss on the cheek. More so than his brother, Dev felt close to Maya; even when they were kids, he'd been both her best friend and protector. He'd vehemently disagreed with her choice of husband but had ultimately supported her because she'd asked him to. In fact, he couldn't think of a time when he hadn't done what she'd asked.

"I see Dad couldn't live without you."

She poured him a cup of coffee with the amount of cream he liked and selected his favorite chocolate croissant from the pastry basket that his parents' staff had set out for them.

He sighed. "Apparently your husband can't live without you."

She looked down, tears shining in her eyes. "That's why I came early. I wanted to talk to you before Ma and Dad wake up. I need your help, Dev. I don't want to put you in an awkward position, I know you're supposed to have this time to explore your dreams, but I really need my big brother right now."

His stomach turned. Maya was tough as nails. Whatever was going on was bad, and his sister needed him.

His phone rang. He looked down at the display. It was Caitlyn. He looked at Maya's teary face. He couldn't take the call. He silenced it.

"Hey, Maya, you know I'm here for you. Whatever you need."

Twenty

He wasn't answering her call. She hung up without leaving a message. A deep ache settled into her chest. Everything she'd been trying to ignore came rising to the surface and soured her mouth.

Yes, he'd called her last night, but to say what? That all it had taken was for his father to show up and he'd left without even saying goodbye?

She walked to the windows to stare out at the neighboring ranch. She watched the cattle grazing in the fields. What was Dev doing? Was he looking out at the Manhattan skyline wondering how foolish he'd been to think he could live in Texas?

Tears streamed down her face. Her phone rang and she looked down eagerly, only to find it was Alice. She answered, hoping Alice had some information about why Dev had left so suddenly, a small part of her hoping there was a family emergency that had compelled him.

Alice insisted Caitlyn come over to her house. When Caitlyn appeared at her door, Alice pulled her inside and gave her a long hug.

"Darlin', I'm so sorry."

Caitlyn hadn't realized just how much she'd been holding in, because suddenly her body was racked with sobs. Alice held on to her. When her tears finally subsided, Alice put her on the comfortable couch and went to make them coffee. Caitlyn remembered that the last time she'd been sitting on that couch, Dev had walked through the door. It was the first time she'd seen him, and she'd nearly spit out her wine. Was it just three weeks ago that her biggest problem was that she had trouble talking to men and needed boyfriend lessons?

Alice returned with a steaming cup of coffee and handed it to Caitlyn, then sat beside her. Caitlyn curled her legs underneath her and turned to face Alice.

"Dev called Russ last night when he couldn't get hold of you. He had to go back to New York with his dad."

Caitlyn nodded and took a sip of the coffee to see if she could loosen the lump in her throat.

"Russ said he was really broken up about it and was even debating showing up at your house, but Russ talked him out of it. He didn't want him getting shot prowling around your house in the middle of the night."

"What was so urgent?" Caitlyn managed to choke out.

Alice shrugged. "He didn't say, just that he had to leave but he would call you."

"You were right all along." She filled Alice in on the conversation she'd had with Dev's mother and the disastrous meeting with his father the day before.

"I think your boyfriend's father mistakin' you for a hooker beats me sleeping with a guy who took a call from his mama while we were having sex," Alice joked, and it brought a small smile to Caitlyn's face.

"I didn't even know you owned a dress like that."

Caitlyn smiled wistfully. "I didn't. I bought it just for him. I refused to even go out to dinner looking like that."

Alice rubbed her arm. "For what it's worth, Russ said he's never seen Dev like this with any other woman. I think his feelings are genuine."

"It doesn't change the fact that his responsibilities are to his family."

"And what about yours?" Alice asked gently.

"What do you mean?"

"If Dev had gotten hold of you last night and asked you to come with him to New York to sort out his family drama, would you have gone?"

The question slammed into Caitlyn like a freight train at full speed. She didn't even have to think about it. She filled Alice in on the meeting they'd had with the private investigator. "We can't keep hoping that claim isn't legal. I have to be there for my family. This is devastating them. Even Alexa flew in this morning."

They were silent for a while, then Alice finally spoke. "I'm your friend, and one hundred percent on your side. But don't you think it's hypocritical to expect Dev to drop his family obligations when you're not willing to do the same? He's the eldest son, and you're the baby of the family. Imagine the pressure he's feeling."

Alice had just voiced what Caitlyn had always known deep down inside. She was asking Dev to make a sacrifice that she herself wasn't willing to make.

Her phone buzzed, and she looked down to see that Dev had texted. Tried to reach you. Had to come back to New York. I'll call you soon. I promise.

Alice leaned over to read the text. "You need to talk to him."

Caitlyn shook her head. She wiped the tears that had fallen on her phone and typed, I can't talk about this. I understand why you had to leave. I love you and always will, but we were foolish to think we could make this work between us. Your life is in New York and mine in Royal.

Alice placed a hand on Caitlyn's. "You can't send that text. You have to talk to him."

Caitlyn shook her head. "What good will that do? I thought talking to Jax would help me come to terms with our relationship, but the only thing it did is sow more doubt about my bad relationship skills." She wiped the tears from her face. "What will Dev say? That he loves me but that his family comes first? And what will I say back to him? That my family is more important than his? That he needs to give up his family obligations when I'm not willing to do the same?"

Alice took both their coffee cups and set them on the table. She hugged Caitlyn, who cried into her friend's shoulder.

The only thing left to do was to was accept the fact that the love of her life was gone.

Dev looked at the text Caitlyn had sent and cursed under his breath.

"Did you see the biodata of Anjali Verma?" his mother asked from across the breakfast table. His father was sitting at the head of the table, his face hidden behind the *New York Times*. As far as Vishvanath Mallik was concerned, the matter of Caitlyn had closed when he'd gotten Dev to agree to come back to New York.

Dev set his fork down on the plate with unnecessary force, and it clanked loudly enough to get his father's attention. Maya had already left, and while Dev had agreed to help her, he couldn't deal with her problem until he addressed his own.

"Ma, you can send the biodata for every girl around the globe, I'm not going to look at them and I'm not going to marry any of them."

His father sighed. "Is it about that girl?"

"Caitlyn is the love of my life," Dev said, not bothering to hide his anger.

"Dev, you know that we are very modern-thinking parents, but the one request we have is that you marry someone Indian," his mother said quietly.

Dev took a breath. "Ma, you've always taught me that the most important part of our culture is our family values. That we take care of each other, and are always there for each other."

"And an American girl can't understand that. How many of your *gori* girlfriends understood why you were still living at home? How many of them would be comfortable with us living with you in our old age?"

"That's what I'm trying to tell you, Ma. Do you know that Caitlyn lives at home with her parents? That she works day and night to make her family's business successful?"

"It's not the same. Indian girls have a different level of respect for their elders that I've never known American girls to have."

"Actually, Ma, you're mistaken if you think that just because a woman is Indian, she's okay with the concept of a joint family. The last girl you set me up with—remember Priya, who I went out with for a few weeks?"

His mother nodded enthusiastically. Priya was one of the few women that Dev had agreed to meet from the endless biodatas his mother sent. She was an NYU law student, and Dev had thought she sounded interesting.

"I liked Priya. Her mother just called me last

month to say that she's still single," his mother said encouragingly.

"Well, I'm not surprised. She specifically told me that she had no interest in being with a man whose life revolves around his family and that she will never agree to live with my or her own parents. She thinks her grandparents ruined her childhood. Oh, and she also doesn't want any children, and she'd like a husband who is willing to fly around the world with her, because she's going into international law and expects to have clients all over the globe."

Even as he said the words out loud, a thought he'd buried deep in the recesses of his brain surfaced. Wasn't he hoping Caitlyn would do the same thing? Wasn't he planning to open a national chain of restaurants and go from city to city setting up his business?

His mother gasped. "*Hai*, what a liar Priya's mother is. She assured me that she raised her daughter with very strong family values. Don't worry, the biodata I sent today, that girl..."

"You're not hearing me, Ma!"

His mother gaped at him. His father cleared his throat then slapped a hand down on the table, making the cutlery rattle on the plates. "We are not going to argue endlessly." His voice dropped. "Let me put it this way, Dev. You have a choice to make. That girl or us. You decide who is more important to you."

Dev sank back into his chair. He hadn't thought his parents would go this far, but they had, and with it, they'd sealed his fate.

Twenty-One

Caitlyn sighed when she saw who was calling. For the last week since Dev had left, she'd spent most of the time either wallowing in self-pity or tediously going through her grandfather's papers, a task no one else seemed to want to do. It suited her just fine, she didn't want to be around people. She'd canceled several meetings and even postponed her volunteer shift at the children's services center. She didn't need another reminder of how spectacularly she'd failed. The only thing she'd accomplished this week was to help Alexa with sorting out the family papers in preparation for the battle that was coming with the Thurstons' claim.

She answered her phone. "Hi, Greg."

"Miss Caitlyn, I'm glad I got hold of you."

Caitlyn didn't even have the energy to correct him.

"You remember those two horses at the Frederick ranch you called me about?"

Caitlyn sat up. "Yes. Did you talk to the ranch hand about brushing them more often, and making sure that—"

Greg cut her off. "Yes…the new owner asked if you would possibly meet him at the ranch today round 7:00 p.m. to tell him what he needs to do with the horses. He's never owned horses before."

Caitlyn sighed. It was probably one of the city people from Houston or Dallas who showed up in Royal thinking they'd like a country house. She had seen too many of them who liked the idea of owning horses and then trusted ranch hands to take care of them. She'd rescued four horses who had been neglected like the ones at the Fredrick ranch.

She was inclined to say no but then thought of the horses. She didn't want them suffering because she was too busy mourning Dev to help them.

"I'll be there."

"Thank you, Miss Caitlyn."

She hung up and got herself out of bed just as someone knocked on her door. She opened it to find Alexa. Her sister was dressed in black pants and a light blue top—her lawyer clothes.

"Wake up, sleepyhead." She smiled. "I came to say goodbye. I'm going home."

"Aren't you already home?" Caitlyn said, rubbing her eyes.

"Cute. Anyhow, one of my clients has an emergency, and I need to go back."

"But what about the Thurston claim?"

"I don't have to be here physically to work on it. I'll come back when needed." She put her hands on Caitlyn's shoulders. "You know my life is in Miami, right? I've already been here too long. I need to go back."

Caitlyn nodded. She'd hoped her sister would come back for good, but she'd made her own life in Miami. Alexa had never let anything stand in the way of getting what she wanted.

"I'll be here to help with whatever you need." She hated how sad her voice sounded.

"Hey, Caitlyn." Alexa sat on the bed beside her and placed an arm around her. "Please don't stay here if you're not happy." She sighed. "I've always worried that we dump too much on you. Don't for one second give up your dreams because you're feeling stuck here." She pulled back and met Caitlyn's gaze. "Go out and do what you want. Open your horse camp. Go to New York and be with Dev. It's not all on you. Jonathan and Jayden are here."

After Alexa left, Caitlyn thought about her words as she showered. In the last week, she'd missed all her board meetings, and the world still went on. She'd managed to take care of things over email. Maybe the new ranch owner wanting to meet her was a blessing in disguise. Perhaps she could offer to buy the ranch from him, or rent the stables to open her horse camp. Then another idea struck her. She dressed for the day and got to work. She'd been working on the wrong goal this whole time.

She didn't need a boyfriend, and she was done mourning Dev. It was time for her to focus on what was really important.

She arrived at the ranch a few minutes early. A rental car was parked in the driveway. Her heart contracted painfully as she drove up to the house. She'd loved it since the moment she'd seen it. It would make someone a nice home. She couldn't bring herself to go inside. Since she was an invited guest, she decided to take a chance on it being okay for her to walk to the back. She strolled toward the horses. They were turned out in the ring. She spoke softly as she approached, and the appaloosa seemed to remember her. He came trotting over. She snatched some clover from the ground and held it out. He ate from her hand. The mustang came over, eager for his share.

"You two are looking a little better. I'm glad the new owner talked to your ranch hand." The troughs inside the ring were full of clean water. It was crazy that this was only her second meeting with these horses. She didn't even know their names, and yet she knew this wouldn't be her last visit with them.

"Their names are Smoke and Shadow."

She whirled. There was no way he was here.

Twenty-Two

Dev loved the look on her face when she turned around. The sun was still high in the sky, and it shone down on her like spun gold. Her hair was pulled back in a ponytail. She wore a V-neck T-shirt and jeans, and even though it had only been a week, it felt like he'd been away from her for a lifetime.

He hadn't responded to her last text, knowing that he owed her more than a text or a phone call. No matter how things turned out between them, he wasn't going to be a jerk like her ex. He was not going to let this all end without letting her know just how amazing she was and helping her make her horse camp come true.

She stared at him as he approached. Her face was

inscrutable, and his stomach clenched. She couldn't even spare a smile for him?

"What are you doing here? Why have you returned now?" She looked away from him but he kept walking towards her. When he was standing before her, she looked him in the eyes.

"Did you think I wouldn't be back? Do you think so little of me?" He moved closer but she took a step back.

"Let's not make this harder than it already is. You and I both know that it was never going to work between us. Your father's visit just hastened what would've happened anyway."

"Please let me explain why I had to go. I was never leaving for good."

"Not then, but eventually you will." She looked away from him and he wanted to reach out and touch her but wasn't sure how she'd react.

He rubbed the back of his neck. This conversation wasn't going the way he had planned at all. He hated the way she was looking at him, her eyes full of pain and mistrust.

"I bought this place for you," he blurted out.

Her head snapped up "What do you mean?"

"The night before I left. I bought this place. It's in your name. I bought it for you. No business partnership, no strings attached—it's for your horse camp. Or for you to do with as you want."

She stepped back another pace, her back now against the horse ring. Smoke, the appaloosa, trotted over and nuzzled against her neck. Her eyes were locked on Dev's. She didn't even notice the horse.

"So what is this? A goodbye present?"

Her tone was a punch to his gut. Was that what she thought he was doing? "No. I thought… It's…" He took a breath. "I bought this place for you so you'd know that you are under no obligation…"

"Why would I be obliged to you?"

Everything was coming out all wrong. He should just do what he came to do.

Stepping back, he dropped his knees.

Her eyes widened.

"Caitlyn, you are the love of my life. From the moment I saw you, I knew there was a connection between us. I've loved you from that first night at Alice's house, and since then my love has only grown and solidified. You are kind, you are caring, you are intelligent and being with you has given me the kind of strength I've never had on my own. I don't want to live without you."

He realized he didn't have the ring in his hand, and he pulled it out of his pocket. "This ring belonged to my *nani*, my maternal grandmother. She gave it to my mother to give to my future wife. I came here to ask if you'd marry me."

Caitlyn was staring at him, her eyes shining. Had she decided that she didn't want to be with him?

"How do we make it work between us? How do we split our lives? The first time your father showed up, you dropped everything and left." His heart stopped. Her voice seemed to be coming from far away even though she was only a foot away from him. Had he messed this all up? Had he taken too long to sort things out with his family?

"I'm sorry, Caitlyn. I didn't know how best to handle things. I needed to go, to put things to rest with my family so I could come back here to you. You have to forgive me."

"Where are we going to live? How are we going to make this work, Dev? Love doesn't conquer all. We can't keep ignoring these things."

He was still on his knees. Picturing this moment was what had kept him going through the last week. It was what had given him the strength to stand up to his family. But what he'd dreamed of was her screaming yes and flying into his arms. Had he miscalculated so badly? His knees were wet from the soft ground, and his joints were stiff as he stood. He didn't put the ring away.

He took a step toward her. She placed her hands behind her on the fence, and he retreated.

"I was hoping you might let me live here with you. I'm thinking this would make a really great house for us, and these barns would be great for your camp. I'll open my restaurant at that old Stevens brewery. I'll make it work. If you let me, Caitlyn, we will live right here in Royal, where you can be close to your family."

She shook her head. "I can't do that to you. I won't. I won't take you away from your family. It'll be fine at first, but then you'll resent me. You'll hate the fact that I stuck you in this town, that I took you away from your dreams."

It was time to give up hope that he was going to get his picture-perfect proposal. What he hadn't really thought about was what he would do if she said no. He put the ring back in his pocket.

"I've thought this through. This town will be my flagship restaurant. Then I'll open the chain I was planning. I'll have to travel a lot, and that's something you'll have to put up with. I promise when I come back, I'll make it up to you." He gave her a smile, and his heart skipped a little when she smiled back and took one small step toward him.

"It's not fair for you to give up everything. Your dreams, your family. Why do you want to do that?"

"My dreams have changed Caitlyn, there is nothing I want more than you. If this last week has taught me anything, it's that I can't live without you."

She took another step toward him and held out her arms, palms down. He took her hands, desperate with the need to touch her. Her eyes shone.

"I can't let you do that."

"I want to."

She shook her head. "That's not how it works in a relationship. My family can figure things out without me. My sister, Alexa, lives in Miami. She's here when the family needs her, but she has her own life. I can do the same."

"What about your horse camp?"

"That I'm not willing to give up. But I also don't

have to do everything by myself for it. I can steal a ranch hand or two from my father and delegate. The important thing is to have a place for the kids to go, I don't personally have to teach them to ride every day."

What is she saying? "You want to give up your family and your camp for me?"

She smiled. "It's not a matter of sacrificing or giving things up—it's making things work. If you reduce some of your family responsibilities, and I re-prioritize my time, we can make this work. In fact, I just resigned from several of my board seats today. There are any number of people who can fill those seats, but there is only one person who can make me happy."

His heart was pounding so wildly in his chest, he was sure it was about to burst. He pulled her close and she came willingly, lifting her chin so he could bend down and kiss her. He kissed her softly, savoring the feel of her lips. "I love you, Caitlyn. I'll do whatever it takes to make it work."

"I still haven't forgiven you for leaving me."

His heart lurched. "Tell me how I can make it up to you. Tell me what I need to do for you to forgive me."

She smiled and stepped back from him. "There is no forgiving you for what you put me through this last week. You're going to have to spend your whole life making it up to me."

Wait, what?

"Does this mean you'll—" He didn't get to finish his thought, because she stood on her tiptoes and pulled his head down, pressing her lips to his.

Twenty-Three

"I'm the only guy here not wearing a cowboy hat," Dev said. "You could've lent me one."

Caitlyn laughed. "Don't worry, I'm sure we'll find some here."

"So what is this place, exactly?"

"It's the Texas Cattleman's Club. Each year they throw this summer barbecue. Everyone who is anyone in Royal will be here, and you're going to have to meet them if you want that restaurant of yours to be a success."

The barbecue was set up on the sprawling lawns of the Texas Cattleman's Club. The day was hot, but a cool front had come in the night before, so there was a slight breeze. A giant white tent held cooling fans, but most everyone seemed to prefer it outside. The air smelled of smoked meat and whiskey.

"Caitlyn, tell me what I'm seeing on your finger is not an engagement ring!" Caitlyn turned to see Chelsea Grandin.

She smiled. "Meet my fiancé, Dev Mallik."

Chelsea smiled at him. "It's nice to see you again. Now let me see that ring." She tugged on Caitlyn's hand and inspected the ring. Chelsea was wearing a summer dress with cowboy boots, her long hair loose around her shoulders. "It's a really unusual stone. Is that a pink diamond?"

"Dev, you have to tell the story. When I first heard it, I started crying." It *was* an unusual ring, with a round-cut stone that had pink and orange hues depending on how the light hit it. The huge stone was set in a simple yellow gold band which just made it look even bigger. Her mother had fanned herself when she saw it, claiming it had to be around ten carats. She'd grilled Dev, who had no idea how many carats the ring was, and then proceeded to tell the story of how he'd gotten the ring.

"The stone is a padparadscha sapphire. They are rare sapphires that are mined in Sri Lanka. My *nani*—that's my mother's mother—was born in Sri Lanka. Her family emigrated to India to flee the famine in Sri Lanka. They had very few possessions, but the one thing they did have was this stone, which was originally set in a necklace that had been gifted to my great-grandfather by the mine owner in return for saving his life from a rockslide. My *nani* was the eldest child, and she wore it around her neck for safekeeping. She had two brothers and a sister, but they all died either during the travel or immediately afterward from disease. My *nani* is the only one who survived. She always held the belief that the stone protected her. Anyhow, she died last year, but before she did, she gave the necklace to my mother and asked her to reset it into a ring and save it for my future wife. Since she knew she wouldn't see me married, she wanted to give this stone as a way of giving our marriage her blessing."

Chelsea put a hand to her heart. "I will not lie, I am so jealous of you right now." They chatted for a few more minutes, then she gave Caitlyn a hug and left to socialize.

Dev steered her toward the tent. It was mostly empty, and the bar inside had no line. They each got a glass of wine. The last few days had been a blissful blur. After she'd accepted his marriage proposal, they'd gone back to her house to announce it to her family. Alexa had offered to fly home, but Caitlyn told her to stay put. She'd have to come home soon enough for whatever happened next with the Thurston claim. Caitlyn hadn't wanted her sister to run herself ragged flying back and forth.

She and Dev had picked out furniture for the Fredrick ranch, which they'd promptly decided to rename Smoke and Shadow, after the horses. Ol'Fred had helped Dev get a contractor, who was going to remodel the old Stevens brewery for his restaurant.

They found a quiet corner. "We've been so busy,

you haven't told me how you convinced your dad to make Maya the CEO of his business."

Dev smiled. "A combination of pleading, begging, threatening and cajoling." He took a sip of his wine. "Remember I told you that when I came to Royal, my sister had taken over dealing with the business. Well, the reason my dad came to get me is that Maya's husband had called him saying that his and Maya's marriage was on the verge of divorce because she was spending so much time in the office."

"But you were only gone for three weeks. That can't have been the sole reason."

He nodded. "It wasn't. Maya came to me the morning I arrived. Her marriage has been on the rocks for a while. She gave up everything she wanted to do with her career to help her husband deal with his family responsibilities. She hasn't been happy with her life for a while now, and getting back to work just reminded her of what she really wants out of life. She wants a divorce, and she needed my help to get it."

"Why did she need you?"

"Because she will be the first person in my family to ever get a divorce. It's not done in Indian families— at least not traditional ones like ours. Maya doesn't want to be estranged from my parents. I had to support her and convince them that Maya's happiness is what's most important to us."

"I'm so sorry. I wish you'd told me before you left. I would've understood."

"I know you would. But at that time, there was so

much to deal with in my family, I wasn't thinking straight. It took Maya and me some time to make my parents see that their stubbornness would've caused Maya lifelong grief. But in a way, getting them to see why Maya was unhappy helped my case."

Caitlyn smirked. "Did your mother mistake Maya's husband for a male escort?"

He laughed. "No, that honor will forever remain yours." She punched him playfully. "In all seriousness, they realized that their insistence on Maya marrying someone Indian had led her to choose the wrong the person. I told Maya about you, and she convinced my mother that she could be happy for us and have the opportunity to interfere in our lives, or hold on to her stubbornness and lose me. On the day I was scheduled to leave, she showed up with the ring and asked me to give it to you."

"Dad was really impressed that you asked him first."

Dev smiled. "That's how it's done in Indian culture. My mother would have never forgiven me. It was a bit of a challenge to come see your dad without you finding out."

"Wait, you came to my house?"

He nodded. "Around the time Alexa was leaving. She was dispatched to your room to keep you busy while I snuck in the house to go meet your dad."

"I can't believe Alexa didn't tell me. And she knew how miserable I was without you."

"Yeah, your dad did make me promise that I would make sure he never had to see that mopey look on your face. He also made me promise that I would propose that day, which was a bummer because I had this whole plan that I couldn't put into action."

"And what was that?"

He grinned. "Well, in Indian weddings, the groom rides in on a horse. So, I was going to get the ranch hand to saddle up Smoke for me, and I was going to ride him."

"Do you know how to ride a horse?"

He shook his head. "No, but I wasn't going for a race around the town. I figured I could just sit on him and have him walk a few steps."

Caitlyn sighed. "There is so much I'm going to have to teach you. Starting with the fact that you can't just get on a horse and ride him."

Dev leaned over and pressed his lips to hers. "I look forward to you teaching me all kinds of things." She couldn't resist kissing him back. Since he'd returned, she couldn't get enough of him.

"I see you two have kissed and made up."

Caitlyn turned to see Heath Thurston, and she tensed. Alexa had specifically told them not to speak to him.

Dev held out his hand. "Hey, man, I'm sorry about that night. I was out of line."

Heath took Dev's hand and shook it. "It's okay. I could tell just by looking at the two of you that there was something hot and heavy going on, and I wasn't going to get in the middle of that."

Caitlyn politely excused them and dragged Dev

outside. "What is going on with you and that guy?" Dev said.

"That's Heath Thurston, the guy who's making the claim against the ranch."

Dev raised his brows. "Well, then, it's a good thing I rescued you from him the other night."

Caitlyn rolled her eyes.

"Wait, if that guy was Heath, who's that guy talking to your friend?" Dev gestured toward a grassy knoll. The tent door where Heath had gone in was behind them.

Caitlyn turned to look where Dev had pointed, and the sip of wine she'd just taken came spurting out of her mouth. "Oh my God!"

She'd dribbled some on her dress. Dev dabbed at her dress with a napkin. "I guess we're going to have to take you home and get that dress off," he said with a sparkle in his eyes.

Normally she'd be embarrassed, but she was too distracted with what she was seeing. Chelsea Grandin seemed to be in a heavy conversation with a guy who looked exactly like Heath. But Heath was in the tent.

"That's Nolan Thurston, Heath's twin brother."

Caitlyn tried not to stare, but it was impossible. Chelsea was standing close to Nolan, and he was whispering in her ear.

"Those two look awfully chummy. Especially after Alexa told you guys not to talk to the Thurstons."

Caitlyn nodded. What was Chelsea up to? She

remembered her own encounter with Heath at the bar. She'd thought she could flirt with him and get information. Was Chelsea doing the same? Didn't she understand how dangerous the game was? After all, Dev was only supposed to have been giving her boyfriend lessons, and here she was engaged to him.

Then another thought struck her. "The Grandins have a lot more to lose than we do. If Ashley is Daniel's daughter, the Thurstons have a blood tie to the Grandins."

"Listen, I've seen this happen in a lot of families. I know your family is friends with the Grandins, but you need to watch out. When it comes to the family home, people will do anything to protect what's theirs."

She nodded. She would call Alexa. They needed to know what Chelsea and Nolan were up to.

"Now, it's nice to see that smile on your face." Ol'Fred interrupted her thoughts, and she grinned at him. "I assume this fella is the reason?" She nodded and held out her hand for Ol'Fred to inspect. "Well, that's a nice sapphire. A rare one, too."

Caitlyn laughed. "Trust you to know jewelry, too."

"So when's the big day? I hav'ta plan for all the fancy stuff you're gonna need."

Caitlyn looked at Dev, who looked back at her. The sooner the better, as far as she was concerned. They had both decided that they weren't going to wait for the wedding to begin their lives. She was flying to New York next week to meet with his parents—the right way. The permits for her horse camp had been filed. Smoke and Shadow were going to make great riding horses, and she'd put out the word in the community for old horses that would make for good trail riders.

"It'll be soon," Dev said. "I can't wait to make Caitlyn my wife."

After Ol'Fred had left, Caitlyn kissed him. "How about we leave this shindig and go practice being husband and wife?"

* * * * *

On Opposite Sides
Cat Schield

Cat Schield is an award-winning author of contemporary romances for Harlequin Desire. She likes her heroines spunky and her heroes swoonworthy. While her jet-setting characters live all over the globe, Cat makes her home in Minnesota with her daughter, two opinionated Burmese cats and a goofy Doberman. When she's not writing or walking dogs, she's searching for the perfect cocktail or travelling to visit friends and family. Contact her at www.catschield.com.

Books by Cat Schield

Harlequin Desire

Sweet Tea and Scandal

Upstairs Downstairs Baby
Substitute Seduction
Revenge with Benefits
Seductive Secrets
Seduction, Southern Style

Texas Cattleman's Club: Ranchers and Rivals

On Opposite Sides

Visit her Author Profile page at millsandboon.com.au, or catschield.com, for more titles!

You can also find Cat Schield on Facebook, along with other Harlequin Desire authors, at Facebook.com/harlequindesireauthors!

Dear Reader,

It's always a joy to visit Royal, Texas, and spend some time with the members of the Texas Cattleman's Club families who make these stories so much fun. This time around, I'm delighted to be contributing a story of star-crossed lovers who find themselves on opposite sides of a family feud. An enemies-to-lovers story is one of my favourite tropes both to read and write, especially when the stakes are high.

I love all the drama of the Texas Cattleman's Club books, and this Ranchers and Rivals series has it all. Yet it's the fantastic chemistry between the heroes and heroines that makes these stories so special. I hope you enjoy the romance between Chelsea and Nolan as this pair of opposites figures out what they're willing to risk for love.

Happy reading!

Cat Schield

DEDICATION

For my dad.

One

Chelsea Grandin was proud of the fact that she could outrope, outride and outlast half the men on her family's ranch. Unfortunately, none of her abilities had ever impressed any of the male members of her family. Eldest of her siblings, she had all the first-child traits. An ambitious, responsible know-it-all, she was always the first one out the door in the morning and the last one in the door at night.

Take today, for instance. She'd left the house at 4:00 a.m. so she could get all her work done in order to take off the afternoon for Royal's Fourth of July celebration. With the sun at its zenith, she'd already put in a full day with no sign of her brother, Vic.

"Oh, to be the only boy and presumptive heir," she muttered, wincing as she lost control of her seething resentment. No matter how hard she worked, her father made it clear he intended to turn control of the ranch over to his son. And because of this, Vic behaved like it was his due. "Entitled jerk."

The siblings had different management styles. Chelsea loved working side by side with the ranch hands, believing if she contributed significantly to the daily activity, she was more in tune with the pulse of the ranch. Plus, she took satisfaction in all the physical activity. Vic, in contrast, preferred to delegate. While she wasn't deluded into thinking she was the only person who knew what was going on, Chelsea was convinced she was far more informed than her brother. Not that this had ever given her a leg up when it came to impressing her father or her late grandfather.

Grief gave her heart an agonizing wrench. They'd buried Victor John Grandin Sr. two short months earlier, but Chelsea continued to miss the family's strong patriarch. He'd been such an enormous presence in her life, inspiring her to work ever harder to prove herself, even though the patriarchy was alive and well on the Grandin ranch.

Chelsea slipped out of her truck and approached the front porch, where her sibling sat with his feet up on the railing.

"So I guess you're taking today off," she said, slogging up the steps to the porch, feeling her early morning catching up to her.

"It's the Fourth of July," Vic said, arching one eyebrow at her.

"Your point?" Chelsea hated being constantly irritated with her brother.

Daily she grappled with the certainty that their father would bypass her and hand the reins to Vic. It was just so unfair that being born a girl meant she had no shot at being in charge of the ranch, no matter her qualifications or dedication.

Equally frustrating was the lack of recognition she craved. If she'd been born into another family, she'd be basking in her parents' approval. Instead, both her father and mother saw her contributions as something to keep her occupied until she got married and moved out. They didn't recognize how tied she was to the land her family had owned for generations.

"The point is," Vic began in the unruffled tone that always set her teeth on edge, "today's a holiday, and I'm not working."

As if that explained it all. And maybe it did. With her working so hard, did he really have to?

"No," Chelsea grumbled, "it's not like you're working."

Entering the massive house she shared with her entire family, Chelsea contemplated the moment when Vic took over. How she could possibly stay, knowing that every time they butted heads he would win? Yet the ranch was her everything. What would she do instead?

As Chelsea crossed the spacious living room, her gaze fell on a recent family portrait taken at Layla's engagement party. Her sister Layla was buying her own spread with her fiancé, Joshua Banks. Like them, Chelsea could strike out on her own.

Or she could start a business like her youngest sister. Morgan owned a successful fashion boutique in town called the Rancher's Daughter. Chelsea suspected that her sister had realized early on that with three older siblings managing the ranch, there wouldn't be room for her. The feisty redhead seemed perfectly happy doing her own thing. Could Chelsea find joy being anywhere but here?

She angled toward her bedroom, hoping a shower would clear her head and revive her flagging energy. She had a full day of celebrations ahead of her. The whole family was attending the town's annual Fourth of July parade and picnic. Later, they would head to the Texas Cattleman's Club. Every year the club hosted a barbecue and fireworks to celebrate the holiday.

As she reached the hallway that led to her bedroom, she spied her mother coming down the hall toward her.

"I was just looking for you." Bethany Grandin made no attempt to hide her disappointment as she surveyed her daughter's disheveled appearance. "Oh, you're not ready to go."

"I just got back from…" She trailed off, seeing her mother wasn't really listening. Bethany shared her husband's resistance to their daughters working the ranch. Chelsea had long ago learned to just do things and stop explaining herself.

Bethany glanced at the gold watch on her wrist.

Diamonds sparkled on the twenty-fifth wedding anniversary present from her husband. "The parade starts in an hour."

"I know. It won't take me long to shower and change." Chelsea eased past her mother. A garment bag lay on her bed. "What's that?"

"Just a little something from your sister's boutique that I thought would work for today." Bethany adored shopping and often bought things for her children to wear.

Clearly her mother believed that Chelsea was neglecting her appearance. And maybe Bethany was right. As much as Chelsea enjoyed dressing up, lately, when left to her own devices, she wore jeans, boots and whatever shirt came to hand.

"That's really nice of you."

Bethany seemed to relax at her daughter's response. No doubt she'd been expecting a battle. Chelsea sighed. Was she really that prickly and difficult to deal with? She didn't want to be. She just wanted to be appreciated for who she was, not ignored or changed into somebody else's vision of her.

"I saw it at Morgan's boutique, and I immediately thought of you." Her mother unzipped the garment bag and pulled out a red halter dress with a full skirt.

"Wow." The obligatory smile she'd pasted onto her lips turned into an oh of appreciation as Chelsea pictured how great the bold color would look against her dark hair and brown eyes.

"And there's lipstick to match." Bethany scooped up a gold tube from Chelsea's nightstand. "I looked all over until I found the perfect shade to go with the dress."

Chelsea took the lipstick and opened it. The bright red color triggered her anxiety. She was not the family beauty. Layla and Morgan were the ones who'd inherited their mother's delicate features and fair coloring, while Chelsea and Vic favored their father, with dark brown hair and eyes. But where Victor John's strong bone structure and eyebrows made her brother handsome, their boldness left Chelsea feeling far from dainty and feminine.

"I know it's not something you would've chosen," her mother said, fondling the soft material. "But you have the perfect figure for this dress, and I thought you might like it."

Translation: *it would be nice if you went back to dressing like a girl again.* Chelsea knew her mother was right. She just hated falling short when compared to her beautiful, stylish sisters.

"It's very nice." And she would definitely get noticed wearing the dress. Unfortunately, it wasn't the type of recognition she craved. Chelsea briefly wallowed in regret. She wanted to stand out for her achievements, not her appearance. "But is it a bit too much for a parade and TCC barbecue?"

"Too much?" Bethany's face fell, and Chelsea silently cursed.

"You have such wonderful taste." Seeing her mother was only partially mollified by the compliment, Chelsea cast about for a way to distract her further. "In fact, I was thinking that maybe you could help me with something else."

"Of course I'll help. What did you have in mind?"

Spying the outdated Paris-themed wallpaper and matching decor in her room, Chelsea latched on to an idea. Little had changed since she'd gone off to college seventeen years earlier. At the time she'd been obsessed with Paris and even considered spending a year studying overseas, but in the end, she'd decided to be more practical and selected an agriculture major that made sense for a future rancher.

Now the room was a vivid reminder of paths not taken. Perhaps it was time to erase this reminder of the possibilities she'd once embraced. Time to forget that her dreams had involved something besides running Grandin Ranch. She just needed to redouble her focus and convince her father to listen to all her ideas to improve the ranch.

If he heard her out, he'd see the value in instituting new pasture rotation techniques to maximize the quality of the grass their herd fed on and agree to incorporate new bloodlines to strengthen the quality of their stock. Already she'd implemented a number of technology-based applications that allowed her to monitor the health of the cattle.

"I was just thinking that maybe I should do something with my room. It could use a makeover." Seeing her mother's eyes begin to glow with excitement, Chelsea impulsively rushed on. "I honestly don't know what I would do in here. And you are so good at decorating."

"Oh, that's a wonderful idea. I've been dying to renovate this room for a while now." Bethany didn't add that Chelsea's room was the last one in the ranch house lacking her mother's creative flair. In fact, many rooms had been through two or even three renovations.

Chelsea winced at her mother's obvious enthusiasm. "I guess it's a little bit like a time capsule in here."

"A bit." Her mother gave a relieved laugh before enfolding her daughter in a spirited hug. "I'll leave you to get ready. Do you want us to wait for you?"

"I'll drive myself." If she took her time making herself presentable, Chelsea didn't want to hold any of them up.

Bethany looked worried. "You are planning to come?"

"Yes, I promise I'll be there." She pumped extra cheer into her tone to be convincing. "Wearing that." She indicated the dress and then held up the lipstick. "And this."

"You're going to look fantastic."

Her mother's prophecy turned out to be closer to fact than Chelsea expected, which was confirmed by her best friend as the two women rendezvoused on Main Street to watch the parade.

"Girl, you look amazing." This was quite a compliment coming from Natalie Hastings, who had a stylish wardrobe that would be the envy of the pickiest fashionistas. "Where has this Chelsea been hiding these last two years?"

Tall and curvy with long, dark hair and flawless tawny-brown skin, Natalie shared Chelsea's ambition when it came to her career, but she hadn't abandoned her personal life entirely. It was just that the younger woman had an unrequited crush on the elusive Jonathan Lattimore, Chelsea's neighbor. But if Natalie lacked confidence when it came to love, she was always on the prowl for her friend.

"Hey."

The parade had been underway for half an hour, and Chelsea had let her thoughts drift back to the ranch and what it would take to convince her father that she—and not Vic—should take over running things when he retired.

"Ouch." Chelsea hadn't responded to her best friend fast enough and received an elbow nudged into her ribs. Scowling, she shot Natalie a frown and found her friend's attention wasn't on the parade. "What?"

"Don't look now, but Nolan Thurston has been staring at you for the last ten minutes."

"Nolan Thurston?" Icy dismay raised goose bumps on her arm. "Are you sure?" Chelsea was glad her gaze was hidden behind designer sunglasses as she scanned the crowd across the street. "I don't see him."

"He's standing in front of Royal Gents."

A float interrupted her view, and Chelsea shook her head. "I'm sure it's nothing. Or maybe it's because of what's going on between our families."

Nolan had returned to Royal right around the time Chelsea's grandfather had died and had joined his brother, Heath, in making the Grandin family's lives hell. Nolan and Heath had produced documents claiming their mother, Cynthia Thurston, owned the oil rights beneath the ranches belonging to the Grandin family and their neighbors the Lattimores.

"I don't know. It was more like a sexy stare." Natalie's lips pursed. "Like he saw something he liked and wants to get it naked."

Natalie's assessment was a bottle rocket zipping straight at Chelsea's head. Adrenaline shot through her, prompting a shocked laugh.

"That's nuts."

Although she'd seen Nolan around town and at the Texas Cattleman's Club, they'd never once spoken. She'd gone out of her way to avoid both the Thurston brothers, not wanting to vent her wrath at whatever they were up to and get into a public argument.

"Is it?" Natalie sounded wistful.

"Layla is more his type." Once again Chelsea was searching through a gap in the parade for Nolan. "He hit on her when he first came to town."

"Because he wanted information about your family. Not because he was interested in her."

The mysterious granting of the oil rights by Chelsea's grandfather had shaken all parties. At first the Grandin family had suspected the whole thing had been a huge scam perpetrated by the Thurston twins, but soon it became apparent that Chelsea's uncle David had actually had an affair with Cynthia around the time she'd gotten pregnant with her daughter, Ashley. Mysteriously, the document hadn't come to light until after mother and daughter had died in an accident. Now Heath Thurston, in concert with his twin, was determined to grow their wealth at the expense of the Grandin and Lattimore ranches.

"Maybe since he struck out with Layla, he's coming for me next?" Chelsea proposed.

"You know, there's another possibility..."

"Such as?"

As she asked the question, her gaze found the dark-haired twins standing on the opposite side of the parade route. Even with the width of the downtown Royal street between them, she could tell that Nolan was indeed staring at her. Something dangerous and exciting lit up her nerve endings. Strangely short of breath, Chelsea barely registered Natalie's answer.

"It's possible he didn't recognize you all gussied up like this. We've been best friends forever, and I almost walked past you earlier."

Chelsea didn't think she'd deliberately downplayed her femininity because of her father's unfair prejudice against her gender, but for the last few years, she'd ignored her closet full of dresses in favor of strutting around town in jeans and cowboy boots. It was foolish to think by dressing like a guy that her father would see her as a capable rancher first and his eldest daughter second.

"Maybe he's just a gorgeous guy interested in a sexy gal." Natalie's gaze bounced from Nolan Thurston to Chelsea. "With his yummy dark eyes and those bold eyebrows, combined with your fantastic bone structure, you two would make beautiful babies."

Chelsea was a second too slow to stop the bark of

shocked laughter that burst from her. "Oh, jeez." She rolled her eyes dismissively while her stomach did a disconcerting somersault. "Whatever. I don't have time for anything having to do with Nolan Thurston and his luscious bedroom eyes."

"Not even if it meant getting a leg up on your brother?"

"I'm listening." Chelsea brought her full attention to bear on her best friend.

"What's the biggest crisis on the ranch right now?"

"The oil rights claim."

Natalie nodded sagely. "So Nolan offered to take Layla to lunch to 'talk things out.' But obviously Layla knew he just wanted to get information. What if you turn the tables on him and do the same thing to him? If you save the ranch by stopping the oil rights claim, your dad would have no choice but to put you in charge."

Most of the time she used straightforward tactics to try to beat out her brother for control of the ranch. She wanted to win through hard work and good judgment. But sexism cloaked in tradition was alive and well in her family. And thinking about it now, Chelsea reckoned if she didn't give it everything she had, maybe she didn't deserve to be in charge.

Resolve blazed inside Chelsea. "I like the way you think."

Whatever it took to beat Vic. That was what she'd promised herself.

Her gaze flicked toward the Thurston twins and skimmed over Nolan. A little weakness invaded her knees as she thought about what dating him might entail. One thing was for certain—spending time with such a handsome man would be equal parts pleasure and satisfaction.

And in the end, she'd save her ranch.

Maybe it was about time that being female became an asset.

Chelsea linked arms with her friend. "How do I go about casually bumping into Nolan Thurston?"

The heat that consumed Nolan Thurston had nothing to do with the ninety-four-degree temperature radiating from the pavement or the confining press of the parade crowd around him. No, the cause of the inferno was that the sizzling brunette in the sexy red dress had finally noticed him. Damn, the woman was striking. He liked his women tall, lithe, but with curves in all the right places, and she looked to be the perfect blend of all that. Her dark brown hair fell in sexy waves over her delicate shoulders, and he imagined himself twining the silky locks around his wrists as he pulled her in for a hot, deep kiss.

When was the last time he'd gazed at a woman and felt something hit him like a brick wall? A long, long time. A float interrupted his view of the woman who'd sparked his interest, and it was as if a cloud had passed in front of the sun. Suddenly Nolan was desperate—he had to get across the street before she vanished. He simply had to get up close and personal to see if she was as bewitching in person.

As Nolan began to edge his way forward, a hand caught his arm. "Hey! Where are you going?"

Nolan glanced over his shoulder at his brother. Being apart from Heath for fifteen years had made him forget what it was like to look at his twin and feel that crazy disorientation of seeing himself reflected in another's features. It was a little like looking in the mirror but not recognizing yourself.

Heath had always been the more serious and responsible brother. These days the somber stranger with the weight of the world on his shoulders bore no resemblance to the mischievous twin of old. The brothers might share the same features, but they each wore the years differently.

"There's a woman I'm dying to get to know." Nolan indicated the opposite side of the street, where the lady in red stood.

A grin transformed Heath's features, making him much more approachable. "Who?"

"That's what I'd like to find out."

Between the two of them, Nolan was the flirt, the one women flocked to because of his easy charm and daring ways. Heath's more serious demeanor didn't scare away the ladies—his handsome features and rugged physique always attracted attention—but he wasn't usually focused on romance.

"Which one is she?" Heath eyed the crowd opposite them as if he might be able to guess his brother's taste in women.

"The one in the red dress across the way." Even as he spoke, the trailing edge of the float moved by and revealed her once more. A bottled-up sigh slipped free. Absolutely stunning.

"Let's see. A red dress, you say... Whoa!" Heath gave his head a vigorous shake. "You definitely cannot go there."

"Why?" Nolan felt his insides clench at his brother's emphatic declaration. "Did you date her?"

"Did I date...?" Heath gaped at him. "Don't you know who that is?"

Nolan was utterly confused. "Should I?"

"That's Chelsea *Grandin*."

Hearing the emphasis his brother put on the last name, Nolan narrowed his eyes and inspected her once more. "Are you sure? That looks nothing like Chelsea." Where was the no-nonsense rancher's daughter in sensible denim and boots? This vision in red had wayward, touchable hair, big brown eyes and glorious, full red lips. "She's a knockout."

"I'm sure." Heath's statement sounded like the fall of a judge's gavel. The decision was final. Nolan could have nothing to do with anyone in the Grandin family.

Two months ago, he'd been stunned when Heath explained about the document he'd found among their mother's things granting her rights to the oil beneath the Grandin and Lattimore ranches. And when Heath had asked him to come to Royal, Texas, to help him make the claim, of course he'd said yes. The brothers had not been on the best terms even before Nolan left town at eighteen. Nolan was hoping to repair that.

While Heath had always felt connected to their

family's ranch and worked hard not just to keep it
going, but to make it thrive, Nolan had a completely
different passion. Unconcerned by money or the need
to hold tight to things, he'd packed up his limited
possessions, slung a backpack over his shoulder and
headed west. A few weeks later, he'd landed in Los
Angeles.

For many young hopefuls, Tinseltown was the end
of the journey, but for Nolan, it was only the beginning. Within a week, he'd connected with a guy looking for crew to help him deliver a yacht to Singapore.
With the experience he gained during that voyage,
Nolan then spent the next three years working a series of private yachts doing charters. It was during
one of these voyages in the Mediterranean that he'd
met wealthy studio executive Skip McGrath and em-
barked on a career in reality TV production. Scouting
filming locations gave him the opportunity to work
in any number of exotic areas. Seeing the world had
been his dream since he was a kid, and making a living while doing so was absolutely perfect.

The only dark spot in an otherwise idyllic life was
his estrangement with his twin. The only time in fifteen years that Nolan had returned to Royal was to
attend the double funeral of his mother and sister two
years earlier. He'd been worried how Heath would
react to seeing him again, but grief had provided a
bridge for the brothers to reconcile. Since then, their
relationship had improved somewhat. The shocking
loss had sparked their communication, and they'd
spoken more often, but they had a long way to go.

Which was part of what had spurred Nolan to return to Royal. He hoped that a shared goal would reignite the close bond they'd enjoyed as kids, but Heath's obsession with getting the full value of what was theirs left him prickly, and Nolan couldn't seem to gain his brother's trust.

That his mission was going to stir up the town and compel their friends and neighbors to pick sides didn't seem to worry Heath at all. Small-town living wasn't for everyone, and all the reasons Nolan had put Royal behind him came rushing back. Even though Royal was an affluent town with sprawling ranches, high-end shopping and luxury hotels, Nolan had felt confined by the community. Maybe it was how everyone knew what was going on with their neighbors, or the way his family was tied to the land they owned.

Nolan had been obsessed with getting beyond the city limits and seeing what the world had to offer. He'd been lucky that a series of opportunities had landed him in Skip's orbit and led to Nolan traveling to some amazing parts of the world—as well as some seriously sketchy locales and rough terrain. He'd loved every dangerous, uncomfortable, eye-opening moment of his years spent adventuring. But the cost of living his dream was losing the brother he loved.

"You really think she's attractive?" Heath's thoughtful murmur caught Nolan off guard.

"Yeah. Of course." He glanced toward the attractive brunette only to realize that she'd disappeared. His mood dipped. "Don't you?"

Heath shrugged. "I've never really thought about it."

"If I recall, you were always more attracted to blondes." Nolan thought about his own failed attempt to cozy up to Layla Grandin in an effort to gain some insight into why their mother, Cynthia, had had a document granting her rights to the oil beneath the Grandin ranch. "Maybe you're the one who should've taken a crack at Layla. She's pretty enough, but my heart wasn't really in it. I think that's why I asked Layla to bring Chelsea along, but I had no idea Chelsea could look like that."

As sexy as he found beautiful, confident women, when he'd seen Chelsea around town, she'd hidden her expression beneath the brim of a Stetson, and he realized that he'd seen more of her backside heading in the opposite direction.

Confronted by this new insight, Nolan frowned. Could she have been avoiding him? Given the conflict between their families, it would make sense that she might not wish to have anything to do with him. His senses tingled in anticipation of a chase.

"What if I get to know Chelsea a bit?" Nolan proposed, glancing toward his twin. "I might have better luck connecting with her than I did with her sister."

"This isn't a good idea." But Heath wasn't as emphatic as he'd been earlier.

"Look, I can do this. Half my job is negotiating."

"Just remember, don't give up more information than you get."

Since he had very little knowledge about his brother's strategy or motivation, that wasn't going to be a problem. And maybe if he found out something that would help their cause, Heath would start treating him like his twin again instead of keeping Nolan at arm's length.

"I've had dinner with billionaires in Istanbul, spent weeks living in the jungle while hunting for the perfect location in Indonesia and been confronted by crocodiles in Australia. I'm lucky, resourceful and persistent."

"Chelsea is smart and will see you coming from a mile away."

Nolan shrugged. Why waste time touting his skills when he could let his success speak for itself? "No harm in taking a swing."

"You'll strike out."

"It's a chance worth taking. And you never know—" Nolan shot his brother a cocky grin. "She might have a taste for adventure."

Heath snorted. "I doubt that."

"Challenge accepted," Nolan crowed, mentally rubbing his hands together.

Two

Nolan hadn't imagined a knockout in a red dress would all be that hard to spot, but he hadn't taken into account that most of the town would be wearing an assortment of red, white and blue clothing. Still, after coming up empty after half an hour of searching, Nolan was starting to worry that she'd already left. Disappointment hit. He hadn't realized how much he'd been looking forward to encountering Chelsea Grandin until his hopes had been dashed.

Hoping he'd have better luck at the barbecue, Nolan headed for the Texas Cattleman's Club. On the drive, he realized a lot of women had passed through his life, some more memorable than others. He wasn't accustomed to pursuing any of them with anywhere near the enthusiasm that drove him to search through the barbecue attendees. Nolan acknowledged that he had a mission. They needed information—or, better yet, an ally. He also recognized that he'd keyed into her before discovering that she was a Grandin.

Someone bumped into his back. The impact jarred him out of his thoughts. Given the crush of people milling about the gardens, he wasn't surprised by the contact.

"Oh, sorry," came a husky female voice.

Nolan caught a whiff of passion fruit and was transported to Brazil. He'd spent nearly a month in the southern end of the country, scouting a location near Iguazu Falls. The scent of wild passion fruit had hung heavy in the air as macaws had flown through the dense canopy above his head. He pivoted to face the woman who'd run into him.

Chelsea Grandin.

His heart did a crazy jig at his first glimpse of her large brown eyes, soft with apology. Although he'd been searching high and low for her, Nolan hadn't been prepared for the lightning that went through him at suddenly finding her within arm's reach. A smudge of sauce near her mouth drew his attention to her ruby-red lips. Shocked by the urge to bend down and lick the barbecue sauce from her skin, Nolan backed up half a step.

"It was all my fault," Nolan responded, a little short of breath. An irrepressible smile twitched at his lips as he noticed a dimple appearing in her cheek at his suave counter.

"Not true. You were standing still. It was entirely me. I think I stepped in a hole."

Nolan's gaze followed hers as she glanced down at the ground near her feet. Given the fancy dress she wore, he expected her to be in high-heeled sandals. Instead, she wore a sensible pair of cowboy boots in cognac leather, inset with white stars.

"I just lost my balance for a second." Her enormous eyes went impossibly wide. "Oh, I didn't get any barbecue sauce on you, I hope."

Before he could assure her he didn't care if she had, she slipped around him, her fingers trailing over his shirt as she checked for damage. Nolan stood frozen while a thousand nerve endings blazed beneath her light touch.

"Oh, good," she declared on a relieved sigh. "Looks like we dodged a bullet."

Had he?

His clothes might have been all right, but the hit to his equilibrium rocked him. Thunder rumbled through his muscles as she completed her inspection and returned to stand before him.

"I'm Nolan."

For some reason he'd left off his last name. Maybe given his immediate, intense physical reaction to her, he was reluctant to see her open expression slam closed when she realized he was a Thurston. Yet he and Heath were twins. He scoured her expression for some sign of recognition. When he glimpsed neither caution nor hostility, he grew suspicious. His brother had overset her entire family by pursuing a claim for the oil rights beneath her land. Why wasn't she treating him like the enemy?

"Chelsea." Her wide lips curved in a genuine smile, further confusing him.

After making sure her right hand was free of barbecue, she held it out to him. The rough calluses on the palm that connected with his affirmed that this wasn't a woman who sat back and let others do the work. His interest in her flared still brighter, making him regret the animosity between their families.

"I've seen you around town," he said, dipping his toe into the murky situation. "But never dressed like this." He let his appreciation shine as he flicked his gaze along her slim form. "You look like a firecracker ready to explode."

Her husky chuckle raised goose bumps on his arms. The bold interest lighting her eyes twisted up his insides. Lust at first sight wasn't an unfamiliar phenomenon to him, but few women presented the sort of intriguing danger Chelsea Grandin embodied.

Heath's warning filled his thoughts. Nolan wished he understood his brother's obsession, but Heath hadn't been all that forthcoming with explanations, and Nolan hadn't wanted to rock the boat by demanding answers. When Heath trusted him, Nolan would get clarity. Until then, he'd support his brother and hope that when he'd proved his loyalty, Heath would confide in him.

"It's hot enough that I just might." She sent him a

smoky look from beneath her lashes before indicating a nearby booth. "Feel like buying a girl a glass of lemonade?"

"Sure."

Without a backward glance to see if he was following, she headed off. Obviously, she was confident he wouldn't let her get away. Nolan hesitated a brief moment, just long enough to admire the way her hips flared out from the indent of her tiny waist. Loath to lose her in the crowded garden, he shot after her, neatly navigating between two converging groups to reach her side.

At the lemonade stand, he exchanged a bill for two paper cups adorned with lemons.

As they moved away, Chelsea scanned the nearby picnic tables. "Let's find a place to sit down?"

"How about there?" He indicated a narrow space that they could both just squeeze into.

She eyed his selection and then gave an approving nod. He waited for her to settle before joining her. Although he was firmly sandwiched between her and a beefy cowboy, Nolan only noticed the soft, feminine body pressed against his left side.

"Here," she said, nudging the plate his way. "Have some of these. It's way too much for me to eat all by myself."

He considered refusing, but as the scent of the fragrant barbecue reached his nose, his stomach picked that moment to growl. "I am a little hungry." A pause. "I could go get my own…"

Even as he offered, he hoped she'd repeat her invitation to share. He was afraid she'd disappear again if he left her even briefly. What if someone approached her while he was gone and filled her ear with warnings?

To his relief, Chelsea shook her head.

"Help me finish these first."

"Sure."

The meal that followed went into his memory as one of the most delicious, carnal events he'd experienced. Not only were the ribs tender and perfectly smoked, but watching Chelsea's even white teeth tear the meat off the bone made the July day even hotter.

"What do you think of Royal's Fourth of July celebration?" Chelsea asked when there was nothing left of the feast but a pile of bones. "Did you enjoy the parade?"

"To be honest, I wasn't paying attention."

"Too small-town?" she teased.

Nolan shook his head. "Too distracted."

"Oh?"

At one point during the parade, he'd been certain that she'd noticed his interest, but since she'd been so far away and wearing sunglasses, he couldn't say for sure. Equally mystifying was the way she was acting as if she had no idea who he was.

While the oil rights claim that had put their families into conflict loomed large in his thoughts, he hesitated to bring the matter up. If she didn't mention the elephant in the room, he wasn't going to. Maybe she, too, wanted to explore the attraction between them—or could it be that she was planning on pumping him for information?

"There was a certain woman across the way who caught my eye, and I couldn't seem to look away."

"Can you describe her? Maybe I know who she is."

Was this one big flirtation, or was she as ingenuous as she appeared? As a tactic, it was working. The uncertainty had thrown off his rhythm.

"Long brown hair. Scorching-hot red dress. Kissable red lips. She blew my mind."

"From thirty feet away?" Chelsea blinked in surprise. Color had bloomed in her cheeks at his description. "Wow! She must have made quite an impression."

He set his elbow on the table and dropped his chin into his palm. With his gaze resting on her, Nolan said, "She was a total knockout."

"So, if you found this woman, what would you want to do with her?"

She was testing him, trying to decide what sort of man he was. Nolan realized that, for all her banter, Chelsea Grandin was cautious, guarded and maybe even controlling. In many ways she reminded him of Heath. Although his twin wasn't firstborn—their sister, Ashley, had been five years older—but Heath had been the firstborn boy, and where Nolan had been outgoing and self-centered, Heath had shouldered responsibility without complaint."

"I'd like to get to know her better." A shiver stole down his spine as her red lips curved into a crooked smile.

"And if she's already spoken for?"

Her counter caught him off guard. Was Chelsea dating someone? Heath hadn't mentioned a boyfriend, but then, his brother's singular focus kept him from visualizing the big picture.

"Obviously if she's married, it's my loss. But any other relationship status I consider fair game."

"You're pretty sure of your appeal. What do you bring to the table that might interest her?"

Damn. This woman was making him work. Not that he was afraid of a challenge. He'd tackled the Bhutan Snowman Trek, a twenty-five-day journey over eleven passes of forty-five hundred meters in elevation that defined the border between Tibet and Bhutan. He'd trained for six months before attempting it.

"Adventure. Excitement. Romance."

With each word he spoke, eager curiosity grew in her soft brown eyes.

"Hmm," she murmured. "Sounds nice."

Convinced he was taking the right tack, Nolan stroked a strand of hair off her check and slid it behind her ear. "What do you say, Chelsea? Are you game?"

Chelsea found herself shockingly short of breath beneath Nolan's intense regard. Was she game? Hell, yes. Maybe too game? She'd need to watch herself with this one. Even without the troubles between their families, he was not the sort she'd usually choose to go out with.

The men she preferred to date were structured and

predictable. From the moment she'd met him, she'd decided Nolan Thurston was going to be anything but.

"What did you have in mind?"

"Dinner?" His eyebrows rose. "Unless you'd like to try something more adventurous."

Excitement ignited at his dare, sparking her uneasiness. Chelsea had never met anyone as intriguing as Nolan. Which probably explained why, since seeing him at the parade, she'd avoided thinking about the ranch and the problems filling up her bucket of woes. Now she reveled in his engaging grin and come-hither dark brown eyes. With his solid, muscular body pressed against hers in the narrow space, she had a hard time keeping her wits about her.

She took a second to remind herself that spending time with him was a means to an end. She'd approached him because of the oil rights claim against her family's land. Still, there was no reason she couldn't enjoy herself while convincing him that pursuing their claim wouldn't be worth their while. A successful outcome for her family would demonstrate once and for all that the Grandin Ranch should be hers to run.

Chelsea shook herself free of his spell. "Let's start with dinner and see how it goes."

"Wonderful. Are you free this week?"

"I'm available Tuesday or Thursday." She didn't want him to think that her social schedule was wide-open, and a weeknight was more casual for a first date than a weekend. Plus, to keep him wanting more, she could always cut the date short, claiming that she started her mornings early. Which she did.

"Tuesday, then. I don't want to wait any longer than I have to." His wolfish smile curled her toes.

Did he really not know she was a Grandin? Granted, they hadn't exchanged last names, but he'd been standing next to his brother at the parade, and Heath knew exactly who she was. The fact that neither one of them had acknowledged their connection or brought up the oil rights claim reminded her to be wary of trickery.

They exchanged phone numbers, but neither made any move to part. Instead, they stood smiling at each other like a couple of smitten teenagers while the sounds emanating from the crowded garden faded to white noise.

"This has been fun." Chelsea heard equal notes of pleasure and reluctance in her voice as she attempted to extricate herself from Nolan.

Sharing the plate of barbecue with him had proved as distracting as it had been delightful. What it hadn't been was productive. Neither one of them had acknowledged the connection between their families.

"A lot of fun," Nolan agreed, pinning her with a smoky gaze. "I can't recall a meal I enjoyed more."

Chelsea told her feet to move, but none of her mental goading convinced her muscles to function. She'd gotten him to bite, now she just needed to set the hook. That meant walking away. *Leave him wanting more.*

"We could get dessert," she suggested instead, cursing her craving for more time with him.

"It is a hot day." His gaze glanced off her lips, making her shiver. "Ice cream back in town?"

"Perfect." The drive should give her time to start thinking straight.

He dropped the remains of their shared barbecue into nearest trash receptacle. She gave him directions to her favorite ice-cream shop on Main Street and told him she'd meet him there.

In the shop's cool interior, Chelsea breathed in the vanilla scent of freshly made waffle cones mingling with the rich aroma of hot fudge. They each chose their favorite flavor—Nolan surprised her by choosing cookie dough.

With the sweet taste of chocolate melting on her tongue, Chelsea and Nolan meandered along the shady side of Main Street where the parade had passed several hours earlier and settled on a bench outside the bank. While Nolan half lounged with his long legs stretched out before him, one arm draped over the back of the bench behind her, Chelsea perched on the edge, knees primly locked together, and surreptitiously peeked at his magnificent physique.

Having no idea what to say, she couldn't believe it when she blurted out the first thing that came to mind. "What is your favorite color?" She quickly used her tongue to chase a drip running down the side of her cone to hide her embarrassment.

When Nolan didn't immediately reply to her question, she glanced over and caught him watching her with intense fascination. Something sexy and primal vibrated behind her belly button as she imagined gliding her tongue along his skin in a similar fashion.

"Red. I spotted you across the road and couldn't take my eyes off you." His voice dipped into husky undertones as if he truly meant what he said.

"Oh." Chelsea was at a loss. Despite knowing that he was trouble, he seemed so damned genuine, and she wanted to be swayed by his openness. In fact, several times over the last hour, she'd lost track of the real reason she'd approached him in the first place. "Are you always this direct?"

"Usually. When I see something and immediately know in my gut that it's right, I tend to be single-minded and straightforward."

Should she infer that she was that something right for him? It was flattering to think a glimpse of her from so far away could have caused such conviction in him, but maybe that's exactly what he intended for her to think. Hadn't their connection formed a little too smoothly? He had to know who she was. After all, he'd been in town for a couple months. Heath would've pointed out the entire Grandin clan to Nolan. This sudden burst of insight triggered Chelsea's guards. And just in time. She had been on the brink of believing all his romantic chitchat.

Recalled to the dangerous nature of her mission, Chelsea reviewed their conversation. What tidbit of information had she let slip that might've given Nolan something he could take back to his brother? Nothing came to mind. But she'd been pretty swept away by his charm.

He'd proven to be far more charming and interesting than she'd expected. Chelsea was no longer confident in her ability to manipulate Nolan.

The Texas heat prevented Chelsea from lingering over her ice-cream cone. The frozen treat was melting fast, and she had to gulp it down before the sticky mess dripped all over her. As she popped the last bit of sugary cone into her mouth, she decided it was a blessing in disguise. If she delayed her exit much longer, he might get the idea that she was smitten.

"This has been fun, but my family is probably wondering where I got off to," Chelsea said, getting to her feet. "I guess I'll see you on Tuesday."

"No guesswork needed." Nolan's slow smile made her vibrate with anticipation. "You definitely will."

Chelsea made no effort to hide her delight as she flashed him an answering grin. Playing games wasn't her forte. That being said, it was exactly what she'd committed to doing with Nolan. Still, if she hadn't found him attractive, she'd never have been able to flirt with him in a genuine way.

She'd walked a block before realizing that she'd headed in the opposite direction from where she'd parked her car. Cursing her addled brain, she traveled another half block to her sister's boutique and ducked into the Rancher's Daughter. The tinkling bell over the door notified the salesclerk that someone had entered the shop. Kerri looked up from the accessories she was unpacking and smiled when she caught sight of Chelsea.

"Is Morgan around today?" Chelsea indicated the dress she was wearing. "I just wanted to show her the dress Mom bought for me here."

"She's in the back." Kerri's attention returned to the necklaces she'd been pulling from their plastic wrapping.

Chelsea found the youngest Grandin sibling in her small office at the back of the store. Morgan was perusing an online catalog of dresses and jotting notes on a legal pad beside her keyboard.

"Working on a holiday?" Chelsea asked from the doorway.

With seven years and two siblings between them, Chelsea and Morgan had never formed the tight bond that Chelsea shared with Layla. It didn't help their relationship that Morgan sided with Vic all the time. Not only was he her older brother, but they were close in age, and as such the pair was thick as thieves. So it wasn't a surprise that when it came to the debate on who should be in charge of Grandin Ranch, Morgan thought her brother was the right choice.

"I've got a few things I wanted to check on before heading to the Texas Cattleman's Club for the fireworks." Morgan sized up her sister's ensemble and nodded in approval. "The boots are a surprising choice, but they work. You should really dress up more often."

Chelsea thought about her upcoming date with Nolan and decided she would buy something sexy and sophisticated to boost her confidence. "You're right. I'm going to take a look around and see if anything catches my eye."

When Morgan nodded absently and returned to work, Chelsea headed back into the shop. Buzzing with anticipation, she selected several dresses and went to try them on. Once again, she marveled at her sister's fashion sense as she narrowed her choices down to three. After much deliberating, she couldn't settle on which one to buy. It wasn't like her to dither when making decisions. Of course, lately all her decisions had been to benefit the ranch. There, she could weigh the pros and cons of various strategies and formulate the best solution.

This was different. She was trying to create an emotional reaction in someone she didn't know at all. What would appeal to Nolan? Did she hit him with something flirty and romantic or drop-dead sexy? Did she want to win his heart or scramble his brains with lust? The latter seemed far easier and less emotionally treacherous.

As the full impact of what she was doing struck her, Chelsea sat down in the dressing room. What had seemed like a perfectly sensible scheme when Natalie proposed it was quickly becoming complicated. Was she really considering hooking up with Nolan under false pretenses? She was both excited and horrified at her daring, but the potential to save the ranch and win her father's approval was hard to ignore.

She balled her fists in her lap and told her racing heart to chill. There was a lot at stake, both for her and the ranch. She'd never balked at high stakes before. Why start now? As long as she kept her own emotions under control and her eye on the prize, nothing would go wrong.

Three

After parting from Chelsea, Nolan headed to his rental. The thousand-square-foot converted loft in a former furniture store off First Avenue was similar to his place in downtown LA and more familiar than the ranch house he'd grown up in. He'd been worried that living with Heath would bring up too many uncomfortable memories. Sharing tight quarters with people for extended periods of time could be stressful—a little something he'd learned while crewing on a luxury yacht for nearly a year.

Unfortunately, he'd forgotten this lesson three years ago when he'd agreed to produce a documentary about a research vessel studying whale migration near the South Pole. Four months of flaring tempers and personality conflicts had reminded Nolan why he preferred to travel solo.

No doubt most people would find his lifestyle lonely and undesirable, but Nolan liked the freedom to do as he chose. He wasn't used to having his comings and goings tracked, and even though he wasn't living on Thurston Ranch, Heath was keeping close tabs on him. Maybe his brother was worried that Nolan would vanish into the night again. Whatever Heath's concerns, Nolan was finding that being back in Royal was proving to be more of an adjustment than he'd expected.

It brought up the same urge to hit the trail as when he was eighteen. Back then Royal had felt small and confining despite its proximity to Dallas. Looking back, however, Nolan thought his discomfort had been less about the town and more about everyone's expectations. Not that he'd felt pressure to take over the ranch. Heath had stepped into their father's shoes after he died, but having to decide about college and a career had made Nolan feel constrained. The last thing he'd wanted was to be tied down.

His phone chimed to indicate an incoming text as he shut and locked the front door behind him. As he dropped his keys onto the counter, Nolan wondered if he was heading back to LA. He was waiting to hear about several reality show projects that would soon need him to scout locations. If the studios were ready to head into development, Nolan would have to decide if he should turn down the lucrative work and stay in Royal to help Heath, or leave his brother to fend for himself.

Passing on the scouting jobs could mean the executive producers would be less likely to reach out to him later. He needed to figure out how long he expected to stay in Royal. He was on a month-to-month lease with this loft, so he could pick up and go at any time. Of course, it was also a risk to abandon his brother to battle the oil rights claim alone against the Lattimores and Grandins. This might set their relationship back to square one.

To Nolan's relief, Heath was the one reaching out. He wouldn't have to make a lose-lose decision today.

How'd it go with Chelsea Grandin?

Although the question was straightforward, Heath's tension came through loud and clear. Nolan's twin had been consumed by the oil rights for reasons he hadn't made clear. It wasn't that Heath needed the money. The ranch was doing well, even better than it had been when Nolan left. He wished his brother would confide what was really going on. Not that he blamed Heath for his reticence. It wasn't like the twins had communicated in the years since Nolan's precipitous exit from Royal at eighteen.

I have a date with her Tuesday night. Any idea where I should take her?

Below his text message, a trio of blinking dots indicated his brother was typing a message. Nolan watched it for several seconds, anticipating a reply. When none came and the seconds ticked by, he set the phone down and went to grab a beer from the refrigerator. By the time he picked up his phone once more, there were no dots and no message.

Nolan was about ready to give up and do his own research when his phone lit up with a call.

"Tell me everything she said," Heath demanded without preliminaries.

"I don't know that I remember everything," Nolan hedged, suspecting Heath wouldn't appreciate how much energy Nolan had expended flirting with Chelsea and that they'd not discussed the oil rights or even mentioned that their families were connected.

"Well, what do you remember?"

Nolan sighed. Sometimes Heath was too direct. Could he convince his brother that an investigation into her family history was going to take time and finesse? And maybe even a little seduction.

"We didn't talk about the document you found, and I didn't bring up our shared family history." Nolan paused for a second, hearing his brother's heavy exhalation. "Look, I need to gain her trust, and that's not going to happen over a plate of ribs."

"I get it." Heath sounded resigned—unsurprised. "Thanks for trying."

That his brother was already throwing in the towel made Nolan grind his teeth. It was just like Heath to dismiss Nolan's abilities. He was one of the most sought-after location scouts in the industry and a stellar negotiator, but Heath only saw his twin as his younger brother.

As a kid, Heath had never hesitated to voice his strong opinions and bully his twin if Nolan's ideas differed. Several times in the last couple months, Heath had offhandedly disparaged what Nolan did, not understanding how his twin could make a good living while getting to do something he loved.

"Oh, I'm not done," Nolan said, growing all the more determined. "I fully intend to figure out everything Chelsea knows. That way we can establish a strategy for winning the legal battles that are sure to be waged against your claim."

"*My* claim?" Heath sounded taken aback. "You're part of this family. This involves you just as much as it does me."

"Sure." A lump formed in Nolan's throat. His relationship with Heath was neither straightforward nor easy, but that didn't stop Nolan from wanting to improve it. "But I've been gone so long I didn't really think you considered me part of the family anymore."

A silence greeted his statement while both men processed the doubts that Nolan had dared to voice.

"I'm sorry you feel that way," Heath said at last. "I'll admit that it's been hard without you around all these years, but Mom often reminded me that you had your own path to follow. You always did have a restless nature, and there's not a lot of new ground to discover here in Royal."

An overwhelming surge of relief and sorrow washed over Nolan. For the first time since he'd returned home, Nolan felt as if Heath at least understood his need to leave Royal, even if he didn't like that his twin had gone.

"I'm sorry I took off and left you holding the bag."

Heath huffed. "I don't believe that for a second. You always had your eyes on the horizon. I can't imagine that you gave any thought to how I would take being left here without you."

Nolan winced at the shotgun blast of guilt his brother had unloaded on him. "Actually, I did think about it," he said, forcing down his resentment. "I almost didn't leave, but then I thought about how miserable I would be and how you had everything under control with the ranch. Also, I never expected to be gone so long. I thought I'd see some of the world and eventually come home. Turns out there was more world for me to see than I anticipated."

"Considering we're twins, you and I are completely different people," Heath said, sounding unusually thoughtful. "The ranch is where I belong. I have no interest in leaving Royal. Even with all the troubles we've had in the last few years, with the storms and droughts, and then losing Mom and Ashley, I never even thought about selling and doing something else."

"Of course not," Nolan agreed, unable to imagine Heath as anything but a rancher. "You were made to be a cattleman."

"So, Chelsea Grandin agreed to go on a date with you," Heath mused, bringing them back to the original topic. "Interesting."

"We hit it off."

"I wouldn't have guessed you'd have any luck with her."

"I'll be honest, I'm a little surprised myself." Despite their significant chemistry, Nolan presumed the trouble between their families would've been too great a barrier. "But she was definitely into me."

"She's a little too practical to be swept off her feet," Heath said, his voice dry. "Even by a charmer like you."

"So what are you saying?" Even as he asked, Nolan anticipated Heath's answer.

"That she might be using you the same way you're using her."

"That occurred to me." Nolan decided to play it cool. Heath had made it clear that he didn't trust any of the Grandin family. No need for Nolan to divulge his eagerness to get acquainted with Chelsea. "But she also might be looking to have a little fun."

"That doesn't sound like Chelsea," Heath said. "She's the most sensible of all her siblings. And she's devoted to the Grandin Ranch. She'll go to great lengths to keep it safe."

"Including dating me?" Nolan cursed the trace of disappointment audible in his voice. Although he recognized that his brother was right to be cautious, Nolan was convinced that the attraction between them was real.

Heath waited a beat before replying, "Just watch yourself."

"I'll be careful."

* * *

"Where are you off to?" Chelsea's mother looked up from the crossword puzzle she been working on. Her eyes widened as she took in her oldest daughter. "Dressed like that?"

For her first date with Nolan, Chelsea had decided on a body-hugging long-sleeved dress in midnight blue with a reverse V neckline. Viewed from the front, she looked sexy but covered up from collarbone to knee. The drama came when she turned away—a gold zipper ran from the low point of the back V to the hemline, just begging to be undone. She'd gotten a little thrill putting it on and imagining Nolan's reaction. Would he see it as an invitation or a challenge?

"I'm having dinner with somebody." Chelsea was proud of her nonchalant tone, even though her insides were churning with excitement and anxiety.

"She's having dinner with Nolan Thurston," Layla piped up. She'd come for dinner since her fiancé was working late.

"You're dating a Thurston? Why would you do that with everything that's going on?" Her mother looked scandalized.

Chelsea shot her sister a withering glance. She'd explained to Layla her plan to go out with Nolan in order to gather some inside information on his brother's strategy regarding the oil rights. Since Layla had been Nolan's first target a couple months earlier, Chelsea had been hoping to get some insight from her sister.

"You could have your pick of any bachelor in

town," her mother continued. "Why did you choose someone who is trying to ruin us?"

"It's for that exact reason that I'm going out with him." Chelsea hated feeling like a misguided teenager. Why couldn't her family ever see her as an intelligent, competent individual who knew exactly what she was doing? "Honestly, you can't seriously believe I'd be interested in dating him otherwise."

"Well." Bethany sniffed. "You don't have the best track record when it comes to picking men."

Chelsea didn't need to be reminded of her woeful dating blunders. She'd had more than her fair share of being ghosted by men she'd dated. It had happened often enough to make her reluctant to go out with anyone. But Nolan was different. She wasn't actually dating him.

"I'm hoping to get some insight into what he and Heath are planning."

Layla smirked. "If he's anything like his brother, he's not gonna tell you a thing."

"You don't know that," Chelsea fumed. "We had—" Damn. It sounded idiotic to say it, but what the hell. "—a connection."

"It's more likely that he's going to try and use you to get information the same way he tried when he asked Layla for a lunch date," her mother said, sending a speaking glance her daughter's way.

"Hey!" Layla exclaimed. "I knew exactly what he was up to, and I'm sure Chelsea does as well."

"I do," Chelsea agreed. "I don't need any of you worrying about me. Sometimes I think you all forget that I'm a capable thirty-five-year-old woman who knows how to take care of herself and this ranch."

"You should just let your father and Vic take care of this oil rights business," her mother said, returning to her puzzle.

Chelsea ground her teeth together, frustrated by her mother's persistent exclusion of Chelsea's participation in major decisions surrounding the ranch. It was bad enough that her father and grandfather had clung to the notion that a male heir should be in charge, but Bethany Grandin was just as old-fashioned.

Just because their mother's sole ambition in life was to marry a rich rancher and manage his personal life didn't mean that her daughters were cut from the same cloth. Not that she'd stood in the way of Morgan opening the Rancher's Daughter. It was just when it came to Chelsea's dream of running the ranch that her mother couldn't get on board.

It stung that none of her family valued her input or gave her any credit. Especially after the changes she'd made to the land and animal management had improved the quality of the stock they raised. How maddening that her father refused to acknowledge a more efficiently and productively run ranch if it meant that any of the daughters—and not the son—were responsible for the improvements. To Chelsea's mind, this was incredibly shortsighted. But what could she do when her parents' mindsets were firmly entrenched in traditional patriarchy?

"Besides," Chelsea continued, tabling her resentment for another time. "Haven't you heard the old saying 'keep your friends close and your enemies closer'?"

"Which category does Nolan fall into?" Layla asked, arching a skeptical brow.

"Do I really need to answer that?" Chelsea snapped, rising to her sister's bait.

"Just watch yourself," her mother said. "Those Thurston boys are out for blood."

Chelsea thought over her initial meeting with Nolan. While her mother had every reason to judge the brothers harshly, Chelsea couldn't help but wonder if they had the Thurston twins pegged accurately. Sure, their potential ownership of the oil rights threatened the ranch, and that of their neighbors and dear friends the Lattimores. But wasn't it possible that Nolan and Heath were couching the matter as a business venture rather than some sort of vendetta.

On the heels of that question came the realization that she was already giving Nolan the benefit of the doubt—and that was certain to play straight into his hands.

No, her family was right. Chelsea needed to keep her wits about her. She had too much to prove and their ranch to save.

"I didn't fall for Nolan Thurston's charm," Layla said, coming to her sister's aid at last. "And neither will Chelsea."

Although Chelsea could see their mother wasn't convinced by anything she had heard in her daughter's defense, she left the ranch filled with a greater sense of determination. All her life she'd been living with her family's lack of faith in her. She hadn't let it get her down before. It certainly wasn't going to affect her now.

Chelsea had agreed to meet Nolan at the bench in front of the bank where they'd eaten their ice cream. She arrived five minutes early and discovered Nolan was waiting for her. She'd parked a block down and made her way slowly along Main Street. It had been months since she'd put on a pair of heels, and she was unaccustomed to walking in the five-inch stilettos.

"Wow!" He studied her with open admiration as she drew near. "I didn't think you could get any more beautiful, but I was wrong. You look gorgeous."

She'd styled her hair in artful, beachy waves and swept the entire curtain over her left shoulder. With her large eyes, strong bone structure and overly wide mouth, Chelsea knew she was more striking than beautiful.

For a long time she'd resented her ugly duckling status and the praise her prettier sisters received. While she'd eventually made peace with her short-comings and learned to enhance her best features, being told she was beautiful by a handsome guy who also happened to be sexy and charismatic was going straight to her head.

"You look pretty great yourself." She took in his charcoal-gray suit and black button-down shirt. The dark shades combined with his swarthy complexion gave him an edgy look. With the top button of his shirt undone, it was a struggle to tear her gaze away from the exposed hollow of his throat. If his dimples hadn't been flashing, she would've reconsidered going anywhere alone with him. "I was a little worried that I might've overdressed."

Taking her hand in a familiar grip, he leaned forward and placed a warm kiss on her cheek. A searing zing snatched her breath away. Feeling as giddy and idiotic as a naive teenager on her first date, Chelsea wondered what had come over her. Was she really this susceptible to the man's over-the-top sex appeal?

"You're perfect." Another sizzling smile melted her bones as he gestured toward a rugged black Jeep that looked like it could tackle any terrain Texas decided to throw at it. "Shall we go?"

"Sure." Chelsea had nearly reached the passenger door before realizing that Nolan hadn't followed her. Wondering if she'd mistaken which car he'd meant, she turned and found him rooted to the sidewalk, his espresso eyes wide, his full lips pursed in a silent whistle. "Are you okay?"

"Am I okay?" He set his palm against his chest and staggered dramatically. "That dress is the sexiest thing I've seen all year. When you walked away, you nearly killed me."

"Did I?"

As Nolan strode her way, Chelsea caught herself grinning with feminine satisfaction. Okay, she'd achieved the exact effect she'd been after, but was it merely delight that her plan was working or was she testing her sexual power on a man she desired?

She might be in trouble if she was doing something

other than scoping out how much Nolan knew about his brother's intentions or discovering the truth of his mother's connection to her uncle Daniel. Better still if she could convince him to leave her family's ranch alone—or persuade him to encourage Heath to drop the claim. Her main purpose in dating him was to achieve any or all of these goals and to prove to her family once and for all that Grandin Ranch should be hers.

But as Nolan reached her side and skimmed his fingertips along her spine, to the top of the zipper, and gave the tab a little tug, she wasn't sure where ambition stopped and hunger began. Trembling with yearning, she bit her lip. The temptation to beg him to unfasten the zipper was both dangerous and all-consuming.

Nolan lowered his head and murmured, "Sexy as hell, Ms. Dreamy."

The endearment tickled her. "Isn't it a little early for nicknames?" she queried in a shaky rush as his breath puffed against her neck.

"I call 'em as I see 'em. And you are definitely as dreamy as they come."

Four

Damn the woman, Nolan thought with grudging admiration as he fingered the tab at the top of the zipper. He hadn't been exaggerating when he declared that she'd nearly killed him with this dress. As soon as he saw that gold zipper stretching from neckline to hem, all he could think about was snatching the tab and sliding it all the way down. She'd caught him off guard, and that rarely happened these days.

Maybe she needed a lesson in what happened when he was provoked.

He slid his finger along the vein in her neck, feeling as well as hearing her breath catch. Her eyes lifted to meet his, and her look was direct and unwavering. Not quite a challenge, but not exactly consent. But then she leaned just ever so slightly in his direction, and he saw an invitation in the subtle curve of her lips.

Now it was his breath's turn to hitch. Rationally, he knew they were playing a game, but she'd reeled him in. Before he could give in and taste her, Heath's warning blasted through his mind.

She might be using you the way you're using her.

Nolan pulled back before temptation led him into trouble. "You know, we never properly introduced ourselves."

She nodded, as if seeing where he was going. "Chelsea Grandin."

"Nolan Thurston." He watched her reaction to his name and saw no surprise. So, she had known who he was from the start. "Is this going to be a problem?"

"Probably." Her wry smile made his pulse race. "I'll just have to see if you're worth it."

Her reply stunned him into laughter. "I guess I'll have to be on my best behavior."

With that out of the way, he helped her into the passenger seat and circled to the driver's side. Nolan appreciated the brief respite to restore his equilibrium. Chelsea Grandin had taken a blowtorch to his cool control, and he had to figure out the best way to find his way back.

"Where are we off to?" she asked as he backed out of the parking space and headed for the highway leading out of town.

"I thought we'd have dinner at Cocott in downtown Dallas. I've heard the food is pretty good."

"Cocott?" Chelsea's frown was equal parts con-

fused and concerned. "You do realize that it's so popular it's impossible to get a reservation."

Nolan nodded. "I've heard that."

"So...do you have a reservation?"

"I do." Nolan shot her a smug grin. "I'll bet you're
dying to know my secret."

"I am curious."

"The owner is a friend of mine. I don't know if
you're familiar with the travel show *Fork and Backpack*? I worked on it with Camila Darvas. She and
I crisscrossed France for several months while she
filmed it." The series had featured the cuisine and
culture of small towns, and he'd had a blast learning
about the various regions in France. "She opened Cocott shortly after the show aired, and it sounds like
the restaurant is doing very well."

"What is it you do, exactly?"

"I scout international locations for television
shows. Reality TV mostly, but I've worked on a few
film projects as well."

"That's a very unusual career. And one that must
require a lot of travel."

"The amount changes every year and depends on
how busy I want to be. On average I'm on the road
thirty to forty weeks."

Chelsea's eyes went round. "I can't imagine being
away from home that long." Her gaze turned thoughtful. "Although I did go through a phase in high school
when I wanted to spend a year studying in Paris."

From her wistful expression, he could see she regretted not doing so.

"What happened?"

"I decided it didn't make sense if I intended on majoring in agriculture. Ranching is in my blood, and it's all I've ever wanted to do." She gave a half-hearted shrug. "How did you get started scouting locations for TV?"

"I was eighteen when I left Royal. I was a man without a plan. Maybe that helped me. I don't know. I was open to whatever opportunities came my way. All I knew is that I wanted to see more of the world."

Chelsea shuddered. "I don't know whether that's brave or insane, but I could never have taken a leap of faith like that."

"Don't forget I was just out of high school. And prone to rash behavior." Nolan thought back to those first few months living on his own and couldn't imagine too many people who'd embrace that sort of freedom. "I went to LA and took a job working on a private yacht as a deckhand. The captain took a liking to me, and when he got a boat in the Caribbean, he took me along. From there I got enough experience to bounce over to Europe, where I worked the summer in the Mediterranean. It was during a private charter off the Amalfi Coast that I met a studio head." Nolan smiled, remembering that fortuitous meeting. "Skip McGrath took a chance on me, and I never looked back."

"It must've taken a lot of courage for you to strike out on your own at such a young age. It was hard enough for me going off to college." She fiddled with her gold bracelet. "I have no idea how I would've survived the way you did."

"Everyone has their own path. Even though I got into several schools, college wasn't for me. My mom encouraged me to take a gap year to decide what I wanted to do with the rest of my life."

"I'll bet she never expected that you would go and never come back."

"Things might have ended up different if I hadn't stumbled into an industry that pays me very well to do what I love. Can't get much better than that."

"With that amount of traveling, how often do you get back to Royal?"

"I don't get back to Royal at all. My mother and sister's funeral two years ago was the first time I'd been back."

She gawked at him. "But why? Were you that busy or was it something else?"

Her question hit too close to home. He knew Chelsea was tight with her family. Hell, there were three generations of Grandins living together on that ranch. She probably could never imagine anything that would put them at odds.

"I felt like I let them down, given the way I left. And I wasn't sure I'd be welcome." Nolan wasn't sure what possessed him to confide such a painful truth, especially when he didn't know if he should trust her.

"What happened?"

"None of them knew about my plans to leave Royal until after I was gone." He nodded at her aghast expression. "It wasn't the best way to handle things, but I knew that it would be hard enough to go without them putting pressure on me to stay. And then the longer I stayed away, the harder it was for me to face coming home."

From Chelsea's stricken look, it was pretty clear that she perceived his absence as upsetting. No doubt someone who'd surrounded herself with family and never considered leaving Royal would find it hard to distance herself from home.

"Weren't you lonely?" She frowned. "I mean, what did you do for holidays?"

"I had friends who I spent time with. Also, a lot of times I was out of the country. I kinda got accustomed to it after a while. And I was always comfortable being alone."

"So you and Heath aren't close?"

Inwardly, Nolan flinched at her dismay. Her need for family and his need for individualism were at odds. It was just one of the many things they didn't have in common.

"I think people expect twins to be the same. Given the shared DNA and all. But Heath and I are quite different. I was held back a year before entering first grade."

"How come?"

"Heath and I were born on August 20, and my parents thought while Heath was ready for first grade, I wasn't." Although studies claimed that keeping a child back a year wouldn't affect him in the long run, the decision had caused a rift between the twins.

"That must've been an adjustment for you both."

"More so for me than Heath. We had different friend groups and were never studying the same subjects. I always felt as if I was behind him, even though we made similar grades all through school. It definitely meant we weren't as close as we had been."

"I guess that's why I didn't recall you growing up. I kinda remember Heath…"

No wonder. His brother had always been the more outgoing twin.

"I would've been a lowly freshman when you were a senior. Even if we'd gone to the same high school, I wouldn't have expected you to give me the time of day."

"I'm sorry." She sounded more confused than apologetic. "I feel like I should've noticed you. I mean, Royal isn't that big."

He was unsure if she was merely flirting with him or if he should trust the confusion underlying her remark. She genuinely seemed perplexed by her limited memory of him.

Nolan's own recollection was quite different. Chelsea had been a cheerleader and president of her school's student council, and pretty in a way that had started his teenage hormones buzzing. "A two-year age gap isn't anything now," he said, "but back then it was a lifetime. I'm not surprised at all that you don't remember me."

"I guess you're right. Huh."

Her pensive expression faded away, replaced by a dawning realization. She fixed her keen brown gaze on him and quirked an eyebrow. But whatever was turning over in her mind remained unspoken.

"What are you thinking?" he prompted, intrigued by the vibes rolling off her.

Her brow puckered. "I've never dated a younger man before."

The level of sexual tension between them ratcheted up a notch as she bit her lip and shot him a smoky glance. Nolan was having a hard time keeping track of his purpose in asking her out tonight. Heath had described Chelsea Grandin in a way that didn't jibe with the flesh-and-blood woman seated beside him.

"Seems like you might be interested in giving it a try." At least, he sure as hell hoped that was the case.

Her low hum filled the car as she gave the matter serious thought. "I think I just might."

Cocott definitely lived up to its stellar reputation. The decor was simple—dark gray walls adorned with enormous sepia images of Paris. Indirect lighting in the tray ceiling. Basic white tablecloths. A votive candle glowing on each table. The star of Cocott was the exquisite food.

The hostess led the way to a table in the back and left them with a warm smile. Nolan gallantly helped Chelsea settle into her seat before taking the chair opposite her.

"No menus?" She looked at Nolan in confusion.

He shrugged. "When I called Camila, she said she'd prepare something special for us."

"Mysterious," Chelsea murmured, a little thrill chasing across her skin.

She'd suspected that tonight's dinner would be one to remember, but she hadn't anticipated this level of intrigue. Then again, she'd never imagined Nolan would be well-connected enough to get a reservation at a place like Cocott, much less secure them a private tasting by a world-renowned chef. If the man was trying to impress her, he'd scored huge.

As she was mulling over her dinner companion, a waiter arrived with a bottle of wine.

"Good evening. I understand you are special guests of Cocott tonight." The man had salt-and-pepper hair and a lean smile. "My name is Richard, and I will be your waiter. Chef Darvas has prepared a special menu for you tonight. Starting off, I have a pinot gris from Alsace for you."

What followed was course after course of the most delicious food Chelsea had ever eaten. Seared Hudson Valley foie gras, a salad with kale and white truffle honey, and then salmon with leeks, dandelion and green apple.

While they ate, Nolan described his months of travel with Camila and all the fascinating places she'd taken him. The stories stirred young Chelsea's longing for a year spent studying abroad, and she wondered how her life would be different if she'd let her heart guide her instead of her head.

As the waiter was taking away their empty entrée plates, a beautiful woman in chef's whites approached their table. Given the success of her television show and this Dallas restaurant, Chelsea had expected a much older woman. Instead, Camila Darvas looked to be close to Chelsea's age, thirty-five. Since Nolan had his back to the kitchen, he didn't see the chef approach until Camila set her hand on his shoulder. Nolan sprang to his feet and exchanged a set of cheek kisses with her before throwing his arm wide to introduce Chelsea.

"Nice to meet you," Camila said in her accented English, her warm smile encompassing both Nolan and Chelsea.

"Your food was fantastic," Chelsea gushed, liking the Frenchwoman immediately. "I'll be honest, my sisters and I have been dying to come here, but getting a reservation is nearly impossible."

"I'm so glad you enjoyed it," Camila said. "I was a little surprised when Nolan called me to say he had someone he wanted to bring to my restaurant."

"Why is that?"

"When we traveled together, he didn't exactly appreciate my cooking."

"How is that possible?" Chelsea gaped at Nolan. "Her food is fantastic."

"I'm not a fan of all the sauces."

An affectionate look passed between Camila and Nolan that made Chelsea's heart clench. Had they been lovers? If the talented chef was Nolan's type, Chelsea questioned why he'd be interested in her. Wouldn't he be drawn to someone who shared his passion for travel and adventure? Did this confirm that he really wasn't attracted to her at all, but that he was only using her because of the oil rights?

Chelsea's chaotic thoughts were interrupted by the arrival of dessert. Her mouth watered as Camila described the final course, a bittersweet chocolate marquise with anise-scented cherries and crème fraîche ice cream.

"Nolan said you enjoyed chocolate," Camila said, her hand on the back of his chair. "I think you'll really enjoy this dessert."

"I'm sure I will," Chelsea assured the chef even as she told herself to not get too excited that Nolan had noticed her love of all things chocolate.

With a fond smile for Nolan, Camila took herself back to her kitchen. As much as Chelsea had liked the chef, she was glad the woman was gone. While meeting her had been enjoyable, it had also raised too many questions when it came to Nolan.

If he noticed that she was quieter on the way back to Royal, Nolan made no mention of it. Perhaps he assumed she was in a food coma, which wasn't far from the case. The delicious meal, combined with the different wine pairings with each course, had put Chelsea in a blissful physical state that lasted until they arrived in Royal.

"I'm parked over there." She indicated her truck, dreading the evening's end.

Despite the disquiet fluttering over Nolan's motivation for asking her out, she'd had a wonderful time. Far better than she'd expected. The type of man she usually dated had a stable profession, was pragmatic and tended to be a little dull. Nolan had fascinated her with stories of the exotic locations he'd visited, and his disarming charm had put her at ease. His adventurous spirit had sparked something restless inside her, and that, combined with her earlier worries about his reasons for asking her out, made her more than a little uncomfortable.

So, what was her next move?

Tonight, as if by mutual assent, they'd steered clear of all talk of the oil rights he and his brother were pursuing. If her whole purpose in dating him was to find out what they planned to do next, she'd abjectly failed. Instead, she'd flirted away as if she'd been on a regular date. She couldn't trust him. Planned on using him. And must avoid getting burned in the process. But damn if she didn't want a good-night kiss.

While she'd been locked in a fierce battle between her head and her hormones, Nolan had brought the Jeep to a stop behind her pickup and thrown the vehicle into Park. He turned his torso to face her. As they stared at each other in silence, Chelsea wondered if he, too, was struggling with how to end the date.

Nolan broke the silence. "Thank you for tonight."

His deep voice rumbled through her like an earthquake. She quivered in the aftermath.

"That's supposed to be my line," she responded, devouring his strong masculine features with her gaze, appreciating how his well-shaped lips softened into a small smile. Chelsea was pretty sure she could drown in his dreamy brown eyes. Had she ever dedicated so much energy to just appreciating the way a man looked? "Thank you for dinner. It was just perfect."

"I'm glad you enjoyed it."

"I really did."

Impulsively, she cupped his cheek in her palm. He drew in a sharp breath but didn't move a muscle. Her stomach clenched at the intense light in his gaze.

"I'd really like it if you would kiss me," she said, unsure when she'd decided to go off script.

"I can do that."

She stroked her thumb over his lower lip, tugging at it. "A slow kiss. One that tells me I am worth breaking the rules for."

She didn't explain what rules, but he had to recognize what they were doing was going to make their respective families unhappy. She was convinced this was why he'd decide to take her to Dallas for dinner rather than dine at one of Royal's excellent restaurants. The fewer people that saw them together, the easier it would be to deny they were dating.

If that's indeed what they were doing. Dating. Her breath hitched. Worry intruded. Maybe his mind was on something different. One way to find out...

She tilted her face and leaned ever so slightly toward him. To her relief, he dipped his head and stroked his lips against hers in the softest, most tender of kisses. The gentleness made her senses ignite. She wanted more. For his lips to own her. His hands to learn every inch of her skin. For his tongue to glide over all her sensitive areas.

Moaning as hunger flared between her thighs,

Chelsea sank her fingers into the soft texture of his hair and pressed hard into his mouth. He groaned low and deep, and suddenly he was with her in the kiss, sliding his tongue across her lower lip, taking the tender flesh between his teeth and then claiming her with a deeper contact that she could feel sizzling through every cell in her body. Feverish and wild, she longed for more, for him to slam her against a wall and run his hands all over her.

By the time he broke off the kiss, Chelsea had lost track of time and place. Groggily, she opened her eyes and caught sight of her surroundings. Whoa. She and Nolan had been making out like horny teenagers in full view of anyone wandering Main Street at nine o'clock at night.

She cursed.

"You okay?" he asked, holding her face with the tips of his fingers.

It took a huge amount of willpower to pull away. "Perfectly fine. It's just this is pretty public..."

"And Royal is a small town." He nodded in understanding. "It's still early. Do you want to go back to my place?"

Chelsea immediately perked up at his offer. She'd enjoyed spending time with Nolan and really didn't want to head home so early. "I'd like that."

Whoops. Did agreeing to go back to his place after that passionate kiss give him the idea that she intended to sleep with him on the first date? She'd better correct that assumption fast. Still, she hesitated. All too often she was criticized for speaking her mind. Would being blunt turn him off? Or maybe she didn't need to worry with Nolan. He seemed the sort of guy who could handle a little straightforward communication.

"Uh-oh," Nolan said, peering at her with a slight pucker between his eyebrows. "What's wrong?"

Chelsea blinked. "Wrong?"

"You got really serious all of a sudden."

"Oh."

She focused on his handsome face, and the concern reflected in his gaze made her want to start kissing him all over again. Damn the man for seeming too good to be true.

"I don't want you to get the wrong idea." Despite her best intentions, heat rose up her throat and burned in her face. Still, she managed to keep her tone casual. "I'm not agreeing to sleep with you."

To her relief, his teeth flashed in a broad smile. "Ever?" he teased.

The warmth in her cheeks lanced straight to her belly and coiled there like a purring cat. The vibration hit all the right spots, turning her on like crazy.

"Not tonight."

When his dimples flashed, she realized what she'd given away. Her mouth popped open, but it was too late to take it back. A second later she decided she didn't want to. Her body longed for Nolan Thurston. Good or bad, she was not strong enough to withstand the attraction between them. She just hoped when she gave in, she'd be able to survive the coming storm.

Five

"I'm surprised you're not staying at your family's ranch," Chelsea said, glancing around the loft's open floor plan. Her gaze ricocheted off the king-size bed at the far end before returning her attention to him.

They sat sideways on his couch, facing each other, their knees a whisper apart. The energy between them crackled and popped. Nolan drank in the bold drama of her features and traced the length of her slender neck to the delicate hollow of her throat. He recalled the graceful flare of her shoulder blades and the gentle wave of her spinal column as it disappeared behind that tantalizing gold zipper.

"I thought it might be a lot to expect that I would stay there after being gone for fifteen years."

Nolan hoped he'd imagined the fleeting speculation in her eyes at his remark. He wanted to believe that she was here without an agenda.

"So, how come you're still single?" he asked, deciding to distract her with personal questions. "Is every man in Royal blind?"

A startled laugh burst from her. "Thanks for the compliment, but once you get to know me better, I'm sure you'll realize that I'm no one's idea of a catch."

"Not from where I'm sitting." Nolan cocked his head and tried to suss her out. "If you're single, it's because that's the way you want it."

"Let's just say I'm so focused on the ranch that my personal life suffers." She smoothed her palm along her skirt.

He leaned his upper body forward and spoke softly. "Maybe you just haven't found the right guy."

The way her lashes fluttered and gaze zipped away, Nolan sensed he'd struck at a sore spot. Given her strong will and confident nature, he couldn't imagine any guy getting away with breaking her heart or bruising her spirit. Could he be wrong?

"Sure..." After grappling with something, she released a huge sigh. "Or I'm the problem."

Her admission startled him. Obviously, she had a story to tell. Still to be determined was whether she wanted to share it with him.

"Why would you say that?"

"The men I date have a tendency to disappear."

"Maybe you have a secret admirer who's taking them out." He made an exaggerated martial arts move with his hands and drew a faint smile from her.

"It's more like they dump me for someone less complicated and demanding to date."

"Or they're not man enough to handle an intelligent, accomplished woman."

"And it's really not that things don't work out," Chelsea said, her lips tightening with remembered annoyance. "It's more that instead of having a conversation and breaking up like civilized people, they ghost me. A couple of enjoyable dates where it feels like something might be developing, and then nothing."

"That's a crappy thing to do," Nolan said even as he wondered if he'd been guilty of that in his past. He'd assumed the women he'd gone out with had understood the nature of his business, but it was possible he'd vanished from their lives in a similarly abrupt way. "How many times has it happened?"

"Four. But the worst was Brandon. We'd dated several months before he disappeared. And I think I'm making it worse because I expect it now. I have a really hard time trusting anyone, and that gives men the impression that I'm an iceberg."

"But you're not." Half statement, half assurance. Nolan felt her relax and knew he'd struck the right note. "Trust me. That kiss earlier was dynamite, and the chemistry I feel with you tells me that you're a smoldering volcano."

"You are great for my ego," she told him with a wry smile that didn't quite mask her relief. "And a breath of fresh air."

"Maybe what you need is to date someone different from your usual type. What sort of guys do you usually go for?"

"I gravitate toward serious types who are focused on business. Men like my dad, I guess." She looked slightly dazed by her sudden insight. "As much as it drives me crazy that he's so traditional, I keep dating men that don't appreciate women who are serious about their careers."

"And that's not you."

"Far from it. I'm always trying to do things better. Most of the time I forget that every second of my day and every thought in my head doesn't have to revolve around cattle."

Nolan reached out and took her hand in his. Turning it palm up, he drew circles on her skin. "Sounds like you haven't met anybody who could take your mind off your problems."

"It's not an easy thing to do." Her lashes fluttered at his caress, and rosy color stole into her cheeks. "I'm always working twice as hard as my brother to get noticed." She made a face and looked uncomfortable with the admission.

"Why are you competing with your brother?" Nolan smiled as his light touch lured her into revealing more about her family dynamic. "It seems to make sense that as the oldest you'd be in charge."

"It's my dad. I described him as traditional." She bit her lower lip as he slid his fingers between hers. The contact was disrupting her wariness and loosening her tongue. "He believes the only person who deserves to be in charge of the ranch is a man. That means my brother."

"That seems very shortsighted of him. There are four of you, right?"

Chelsea studied their entwined hands. "Three girls and one boy. My youngest sister, Morgan, has no interest in running the ranch. She owns a boutique on Main Street. The Rancher's Daughter." With her free hand, Chelsea indicated what she was wearing. "This dress is from there."

"I think you already know my opinion of it," Nolan murmured.

"I don't dress up very often anymore." Chelsea made a face. "After Brandon ghosted me two years ago, my parents started pushing eligible men at me. I think they hoped I'd find a husband." The disgust in her voice came through loud and clear. Clearly this was not her goal.

"You don't want to get married?"

"I don't have anything against it." Chelsea shrugged. "But I don't like my parents' assumption that it's what I was born to do."

Obviously, she was a modern woman whose contemporary ideas were in conflict with her family's perception of what their daughter ought to do.

Chelsea grimaced. "Maybe that's why I've put my personal life on hold. The last thing I want to do is prove my parents right. At least not until I've achieved my goal of taking charge of the ranch. Even though it's an uphill battle, I'm convinced that I'd be com-

pletely out of the running if I started dating someone
my family found acceptable."

Although Nolan doubted she meant to point out
that her family would never approve of him, she had
to be thinking about it. As the brother of the man who
was trying to interfere with the smooth running of
her ranch, she was courting trouble by not keeping
her distance.

Of course, this left him wondering if, for all her
casual air, she had an ulterior motive for being here
with him. His chest constricted as disappointment
trickled through him. He had no reason to feel this
way. Hadn't he approached her with the idea of getting into her good graces and finding her family's
weaknesses?

"I'm not sure why I told you that," she murmured,
tunneling her fingers into her hair and giving the dark
locks a sharp tug.

"You're not what I expected," he said spontaneously.

"No?" She tensed. A frown appeared to mar her
smooth forehead.

He immediately saw that his offhand remark had
made her wary and recalled what she'd revealed of
her insecurity. "You have a reputation around town
for being all business. I thought I'd have a hard time
getting to know you."

She let loose a rusty laugh. "I guess that's a fair
assessment. My focus has always been my family's
ranch. I went to college to study ranch and animal
management with the intention that I would be in

charge someday." A dark cloud passed across her features.

He thought of his own ambitions and how Heath had stepped up when their dad died. "It was never a question between Heath and me. He was always going to run our ranch."

"So he's older?"

"By about fifteen minutes."

"You two never considered sharing responsibility?"

Nolan shook his head. "Never. I wasn't keen on ranching, and Heath likes to do things his own way." He paused and shot her a wry smile. She was a lot like his brother. Another thing that might cause trouble between them in the future. "It worked out for both of us," Nolan continued. "Heath got the ranch, and I was free to let my wanderlust run wild."

Chelsea sighed. "I wish my brother, Vic, felt the way you do."

"You mean you wish he would give you the ranch and go do something else?"

"Frankly, yes. I'm the one with the passion for ranching." She practically growled the last word.

Obviously, Nolan could tell this was a sore subject, but one that provided much-needed insight into the Grandin family dynamic. "Does he want to be in charge?"

"I'm not sure he wants it the way I do. He's just always assumed the ranch would come to him. It's frustrating. Between all my siblings, I have the best vision for where the ranch should go. Yet my father

can't imagine handing over the reins to me. I don't
know if he assumes I'll one day get married and move
out." Resentment poured off her in waves, an abrupt
shift from the mellow mood she'd been in all evening.
"It's what Layla has done. She and Joshua are getting
a ranch of their own. What my dad doesn't understand
is that he left her no other choice."

As if concluding that she'd shared enough about
her family, Chelsea turned the conversation to things
Nolan enjoyed doing when not traveling. She seemed
unsurprised that his favorite activities involved adventure and often took him off the beaten path. Several
times he glimpsed a wistful flicker in her eyes as he
shared his pastimes. It was almost as if she regretted
the lack of excitement in her life. This didn't seem to
jibe with the no-nonsense businesswoman Heath had
described. Nolan was quickly discovering that Chelsea
Grandin was beautiful, intelligent and complicated.

"I should probably get going," Chelsea said, indicating the large, decorative wall clock. She slipped
her feet from beneath her and settled them into her
high heels. "I can't believe it's two in the morning."

Although he was loath to end the evening, he stood
and held his hand out to assist her. "It's pretty late.
Why don't I walk you down to your car?"

Up until the offer spilled from his lips, he'd planned
to escort her as far as his front door and say goodbye
with a lingering kiss that would leave her craving another date with him. But as he opened the condo door
and gestured her through, Nolan could already feel
himself missing her. The ache unsettled him.

Chelsea glanced up at him as she passed. "I'm sure I'll be okay."

"I insist."

"That's very gentlemanly of you."

There was laughter in her voice and speculation in her gaze. Nolan hadn't figured out yet if Chelsea was wary because of her dating failures in the past or of him in particular. Maybe both.

"You'd be the first woman who'd think so."

"I don't believe that. I saw the way Camila looked at you tonight. She was very happy to see you."

"We never hooked up," Nolan confessed, sensing it was important to reassure Chelsea of this. As they strolled side by side along Main Street in the direction of her car, Nolan peered at her expression. "She's great fun to travel with, but I don't cross professional lines."

"What about after the show was done? Did you have any interest in seeing her?"

Nolan shook his head. "We are great friends, but that's it for me."

"Are you sure?" Chelsea stared at him as if she didn't believe he could be so clueless. "She's beautiful and talented. Or is it because she's here in Texas and you're based out of LA?"

"She's too serious for something casual, and I wasn't interested enough to want more."

"Huh." Chelsea looked as if his answer had thrown her.

"What?"

"Just huh."

His travels had given him plenty of opportunity to meet and romance women of all kinds. Not that he was a player. Far from it. He truly enjoyed the company of women and didn't put scoring as his top priority for spending time with any of them. It just seemed as if he drew women who enjoyed sex without strings. Uncomplicated fun. Which had been great in his twenties, but since turning thirty, he'd begun to feel a different sort of restlessness.

Sitting still for the last few months had given Nolan time to mull his future. He'd caught up with some of his high school friends—many married and starting families—and gained a different perspective on his love life. He'd never imagined himself going down that road. Settling down had never been his plan, but he couldn't deny that his old classmates really seemed to enjoy having someone to come home to.

Yet Nolan recognized that domestic bliss wasn't for him. He had a globe-trotting career that kept him on the go. Sustaining a relationship under those circumstances would take a special woman. One Nolan had yet to meet.

All of a sudden, Chelsea stopped walking, jolting Nolan out of his thoughts. Looking around, he realized they'd arrived at her car. She was seconds away from escaping. He couldn't let her go without something to dream about. Catching her arm, he drew her toward him. He set his forefinger beneath her chin to tilt her head up and dropped a light kiss on her full lips. A sigh puffed out of her as he dusted a second kiss across her cheek.

"Do you want to go out again?" she murmured, sounding drowsy and content. She'd rested her palms on his waist right above his belt, and her touch seared straight through his fine cotton shirt.

He kissed her earlobe and felt her shiver. "I was going to ask you the same thing."

"Great minds…"

"Tomorrow?"

She gusted out a chuckle. "It's already tomorrow. How about Friday?"

"You're going to make me wait three whole days?"

"I'm sure you'll manage." And then she was pulling free and turning toward her car.

Nolan received another gut-kicking glimpse of that damned gold zipper running down the length of her dress before she unlocked her truck and climbed in. There was something so damned sexy about a well-dressed woman in a pickup, he thought with a grin. He might have been out of Texas nearly half his life, but some things remained the same.

"Text me when you get home," he called to her before the driver's door shut.

Chelsea leaned out to frown at him. "I'll be fine."

"You're already better than fine," he insisted, a trace of steel entering his tone. "Text me."

"It'll take me half an hour. You might be asleep by then."

"I won't be able to sleep unless I know you're home safe." Seeing that his request had spurred some sort of conflict inside her, Nolan stepped up to her car door. "I know you are capable of taking care of yourself, but I always insist my staff check in at night when we're on location. Humor me."

Her eyes softened. "I'll text."

With a satisfied nod, Nolan stepped back and watched until she'd driven off. Then he headed back to his loft to ponder what he was going to do with the dreamy Chelsea Grandin.

Despite the late hour, Chelsea was wide-awake as she drove back to Grandin Ranch. Her senses buzzed in the aftermath of Nolan's kiss, a dangerous intoxicant for a levelheaded woman like her. What if she grew addicted to the high and lost her way? Maybe she was more tired than she realized. A couple kisses weren't going to turn her head. She was dating Nolan as a way of finding out more about the Thurston brothers and their strategy for going after the oil beneath her family's land. Yet it bothered her that she found him so attractive.

She'd learned a lot from Nolan, more than she'd expected. The most important item had been that the relationship between the brothers wasn't as tight as her family believed. Chelsea felt a rush of optimism. Maybe there was an opportunity to win Nolan to her side.

But how?

The obvious answer lay in the chemistry percolating between them. Unfortunately, tonight had demonstrated that she was woefully out of practice at flirting. Look how she'd confessed that she refused to fall in love until her father accepted her as an independent woman capable of running the ranch. She'd also shared how much she hated the way her parents had tried for years to set her up with every eligible man in the county.

Overcome with remembered humiliation, Chelsea clenched the steering wheel. Why couldn't her father open his eyes and see her as his equal instead of a commodity he could use to cement relationships in the community?

To her dismay, lights still burned in the living room when she got home. Wondering if her mother had left the light on as a courtesy or if someone was actually waiting up for her, she parked her truck and braced herself as she entered the house.

Vic sat in their father's favorite chair, acting like he was already head of the family. Irritation bloomed at the sight, but it was his scowl and the fact that he was obviously waiting up for her that caused heat to steal into her cheeks. Honestly, she'd done nothing wrong, yet here she was blushing like a wayward teenager.

"What are you doing dating Nolan Thurston?"

"Not that it's any of your business," she declared coolly over her shoulder, keeping her voice low, "but I'm not dating him. I'm looking out for our family's best interest."

"How? By getting into bed with the enemy?"

Chelsea counted to ten even as she kept walking toward her bedroom. She didn't owe Vic an explanation. Still, she should've expected that with her family on edge about the Thurston brothers, they would've discussed what she was up to.

Despite all she'd learned from Nolan, Chelsea wished she'd come straight home after dinner. Or anytime in the five hours that followed. No doubt rolling in after two in the morning looked suspiciously like she'd slept with Nolan. Hell, she couldn't even deny that's what she'd wanted to do. Chelsea couldn't remember the last time a man intrigued her the way Nolan did. He wasn't like any of the men around town. All the things he'd seen on his travels had inspired her imagination and made her question the way she'd let her ambition monopolize her life.

"I didn't get into bed with anyone," Chelsea said, cursing as she paused to defend herself rather than head straight to her bedroom.

"What do you call spending all night with Nolan Thurston?"

It hadn't been all night. Vic was just trying to push her buttons. And as usual, it was working.

"Reconnaissance." She forced her lips into a smirk while her stomach roiled at the picture she was painting of herself. Coming off strong and ruthless was a defense mechanism. Their father ran Grandin Ranch like his father before him, with an iron hand. If she expected to be taken seriously, she must appear tough and determined. "I think he's the key to getting through to Heath about dropping the claim."

Vic was looking less sure of himself. "Or it's just an excuse because you're into him."

Chelsea rolled her eyes. "Give me some credit." The phrasing of the comment made her wince. She shouldn't be asking Vic to give her the benefit of the doubt. She didn't need to convince him of anything.

"Everybody thinks you should stay away from him."

"Then everybody is wrong." Chelsea was used to fighting for recognition in her family, but this path she was walking with Nolan left her feeling more alone than ever. "Anyway, what does it matter? It's not like I'm going to ever stop fighting their claim. The destruction that would happen to our ranch if they lease those oil rights to a drilling company would ruin our land forever. *I'm* not gonna let that happen."

"Maybe, but what if you fall for him? Maybe he's planning to seduce you in the hopes that he can change your mind."

For a split second, Chelsea considered arguing further. But why bother wasting her breath when the power belonged to her father? "You know that everything is going to be in the hands of the lawyers."

"Still, it looks bad, you hanging out with the enemy and all."

"Then I guess I'll just have to be more careful about being seen in public with him." She meant the remark to be sarcastic, but Vic took her seriously.

"It'd be better if you didn't see him at all, but if you can get some intel, then I guess it might be worth doing whatever."

Doing whatever? Chelsea felt a little bit ill. Had she gone too hard at the do-whatever-it-takes-to-win attitude?

"I don't think you and I should discuss the topic of my spending time with Nolan Thurston anymore."

"Why not?" Vic smirked. "Afraid to admit I'm right?"

Her brother was a little too cocky when it came to throwing his weight around. Maybe if he worked harder than she did on the ranch she might feel differently, but he was assuming their father would put him in charge, and that left him resting on his laurels.

Mired in his sense of entitlement, Vic didn't push himself, and his unwillingness or inability to take the initiative, think things through and make decisions drove her crazy. She'd respect him more if he behaved as her equal instead of just insisting he was.

"Because I don't answer to you," she replied. "Which means it's none of your business."

Her phone chimed. Reflexively, she glanced at the incoming text and caught her breath. It was from Nolan. Her heart fluttered as she read his message.

Home yet, Ms. Dreamy?

Cursing the nickname and her breathless state, Chelsea fired off a response.

Just arrived.

I had a great time tonight.

Me too.

Sweet dreams!

You too.

The text exchange made her forget all about the argument with Vic.

"Is that Thurston?"

She tore her attention away from the phone, her irritation returning in a rush. "It's late, and I have to be up in three hours. Unless you want to oversee the feeding this morning? Believe me, I'd be happy to sleep in for a change."

"I've got my own work," Vic grumbled.

"Of course you do. So, I'll see you around ten?" And then before her brother could reply, she stepped into her room and closed the door in his face.

With adrenaline surging in the aftermath of her fight with Vic, she wondered how long it would take for her to get to the sweet dreams Nolan had wished for her. She smiled again as she recalled the brief exchange.

Was it worth using someone to achieve her goals? Of course, there was always the possibility that Nolan was using her in turn. If they were both playing an elaborate game of cat and mouse, she might be the one in danger of getting hurt. Was she brave enough to continue?

Once upon a time, she'd let her heart lead her down a treacherous romantic path. Given the strong chemistry between her and Nolan, it would be easy for her emotions to lead her astray once again. Dating him would be a lot less complicated if she kept in the front of her mind the myriad reasons they could never work out. That way she wouldn't give her heart a chance to betray her.

And yet, did any of that matter if she succeeded in preventing the Thurstons from acting on the oil rights? Her father couldn't help but notice if she saved the ranch. Then he would have no choice but to put her in charge.

Wasn't a little heartache worth achieving everything she'd been working for all along?

Six

Nolan glanced at the woman occupying his passenger seat. Today, Chelsea wore a buttery-yellow sundress with thin straps that showed off her toned arms. She had a body built by hard work. All lean muscle beneath smooth, tan skin. He loved her athleticism and suspected she was one of the few women he knew who could match him for endurance.

"Where are we off to today?" she asked as Royal disappeared behind them.

While it wasn't unusual for him to plan fun adventures—ferreting out once-in-a-lifetime experiences was what he did for a living—he wanted every date with Chelsea to be memorable. Still, as he'd helped her into the car, a glimpse of her long, sleek thighs had set his pulse to dancing. Every instinct shouted for Nolan to bail on his plans for the evening and head straight to his place.

"I have a special surprise for us."

He'd found a company that specialized in gondola rides in Irving, Texas. It wasn't Venice, but he hoped the Italian meal, served while cruising the city's Mandalay Canal and Lake Carolyn, would appeal to her. Normally the cruise lasted two hours, but he'd paid extra to double their time. He had no intention of rushing anything with Chelsea.

"Sounds quite mysterious," she replied, delight shimmering in her wide brown eyes. "Do I get a hint?"

"Nope. I want you to be surprised."

Nolan reached across the space between them and captured her hand. Her fingers meshed easily with his, as if they'd done this a hundred times, and he brushed a kiss across her knuckles. A slight tremor went through her at his romantic gesture, and he felt a spasm of guilt. She'd been hurt several times by men she'd thought she could trust, and he was doing his damnedest to tear down her walls.

Dating Chelsea was like walking a tightrope without a net. With their families soon to be engaged in some pretty hostile conflict over the oil rights Heath intended to claim, she had to wonder if Nolan had ulterior motives for taking her out. Her intelligence was one of her strongest features. Yet the chemistry between them was real, and she seemed to be going with it. Something like that was incredibly hard to fake, but he had to consider that she might be playing him in turn. Nolan hoped the latter wasn't true.

Even as the thought popped into his mind, he knew he was in trouble. When Heath no longer needed him, Nolan planned to go back to his regular life. And with Chelsea completely bound to her ranch—and her family—it was unlikely that she would give up either one to follow him around the world. Which meant he'd better not get any more attached to Chelsea Grandin.

This realization should've made it easier for Nolan to temper his interest in her. Yet the sexual energy between them was hungry and strong. And he wasn't all that good at resisting adventures. When something called to him, he had no choice but to answer. And what he sensed about Chelsea's hidden depths called to him. He wanted to explore everything about her and, once seized by determination, no challenge was too much.

Nolan just had to keep his fascination with her on the down low. No need for Heath to know that his brother had strayed from their original mission. As long as Heath thought Nolan was simply using Chelsea to get intel on the Grandin family, the fledgling relationship between the two brothers would remain untested. At least where Chelsea was concerned.

Heath's obsession with the oil rights was a different matter.

It wasn't that Nolan didn't want to pursue the claim. He just didn't understand why their mother had owned the rights for years and never once mentioned them or tried to do anything about them. Surely, the millions a contract like that would be worth could've helped in the days when the Thurston ranch had gone through hard times.

In Nolan's opinion, too many questions remained about the situation. He wished he understood what drove his brother's obsession. He sensed more to it than the potential of adding to his wealth. Yet every time Nolan tried to raise this point with his brother, Heath refused to discuss the matter. Not wanting to upset their tenuous rapport, Nolan squashed his curiosity. Heath wasn't responsible for their falling-out. Nolan's absence from Royal had put distance between them. That made repairing the rift Nolan's responsibility, and he wasn't going to fix anything by arguing with his brother.

"Ever been here?" Nolan asked an hour later as they strolled hand in hand toward the dock where the gondolas waited.

Her voice was husky with awe as she murmured, "I had no idea this existed."

A man dressed as a traditional gondolier smiled as they approached. "Good evening," the man intoned in a passable Italian accent and extended a single red rose to Chelsea. She accepted the token with a bemused expression and turned to glance over her shoulder at Nolan.

"We're going in that?" She nodded toward the long, narrow boat. Since it was evening, he'd opted to go with the traditional open gondola rather than one of the covered varieties.

"Since a trip to Venice was a little much for a second date, I thought this would do."

He shot her a sideways glance, eager for her approval. His heart clenched when she gave his fingers a brief, fierce squeeze.

"I absolutely love it."

"I'm glad."

The gondolier handed Chelsea into the boat, and as she settled in a comfortable seat at the middle, Nolan stepped in. While the waitstaff placed plates loaded with their three-course meal on the intimate table before them, Nolan scrutinized her expression and decided he'd chosen well. For someone who didn't stray far from home, he sensed that Chelsea was actually enjoying getting outside her comfort zone.

"To your first gondola ride," Nolan murmured as the boat glided away from the dock. He touched his champagne flute to hers, enjoying her delight.

"I could get used to this," Chelsea said, humming in appreciation as she eyed the delicious plates of food. "Although I'm not sure how we're supposed to get through so much."

"I ordered a variety of dishes, unsure which you'd prefer."

"I'm not sure, either. I think I'd like to taste everything."

With the sun dipping toward the horizon, the July heat eased as they skimmed across the lake surface. A light breeze ruffled the hair framing Chelsea's face, and he used the excuse to slide a sable strand behind her ear. With a long sigh, her soft body relaxed into his side.

"Earlier, when I said I could get used to this," Chelsea said, gazing at him from beneath her lashes, "I wasn't just talking about the food or the boat ride. I meant you."

Should he take her declaration at face value? This was only the second time they'd gone out, and while he was feeling the strong vibe between them, she might be deliberately trying to give him a false sense of security by pushing the impression that she was more into him than she was.

Before he could decide how to respond, she added, "I'm just not sure that's a good idea."

Nolan registered a silent curse. Just when he had her figured out, she switched things up. Was she truly conflicted, or was this just a bit of gamesmanship?

"It's sensible of you to feel that way."

"That's the trouble. I struggle to feel sensible when I'm with you." She spun the stem of her champagne flute with her fingers. "We haven't talked about what's going on between our families."

"We don't have to get involved," Nolan stated, ignoring the fact that he had already agreed to help Heath by gleaning her family's strategy for opposing the claim. "You've already said you don't have control when it comes to the ranch and the decisions being made."

"That's true." She tensed as he probed this sore spot. "But the same can't be said for you."

"Heath is the one who wants to claim the oil rights."

"Are you trying to tell me you'd walk away from millions of dollars?"

He heard her skepticism and for a second wondered if their pleasant evening was over before it began.

"Yes." That wasn't a lie. If the decision was left up to Nolan, he would drop the matter. "I've made enough money with my scouting company to live comfortably for many lifetimes. But my brother is determined to fight to the bitter end."

Chelsea let out a long, exaggerated sigh and shook her head. "I wish I understood why my grandfather and Augustus Lattimore turned over the oil rights to your mother. It makes no sense."

"Maybe it was for child support. She was pregnant with your uncle's child."

"Was she?" Chelsea stared out across the water. "Other than the right timing, there's no real proof that your half sister was Daniel's daughter. And he claims he didn't know Cynthia was pregnant."

"Or maybe he knew and fled to France all those years ago to avoid the responsibility." It wouldn't surprise him. Nolan was no stranger to running away from obligation, implied or not. "How come he didn't stick around to help your father run the ranch?"

"I could ask the same of you," Chelsea countered.

"Even if I'd wanted to stick around, I don't know how much Heath would've let me help."

The instant the words escaped his mouth, Nolan regretted it.

"You know, I've been wondering why you never came back to Royal all these years." Her eyes gleamed with curiosity. "Something happened between you and Heath, didn't it?"

"Not really between us. I don't honestly think he had a clue…"

Nolan didn't talk about his family with anyone. When asked, he usually gave a pat answer about how his family owned a ranch in Texas and that ranching wasn't his thing. He should've known that Chelsea could inspire him to spill more than he usually shared.

"Heath was Dad's right hand and spent every spare second following him around the ranch, learning how to run it. When Dad died, even though we were only in elementary school, Heath stepped up and helped Mom a lot, eventually taking over running of most things by high school." Nolan thought about the ranch journal his father had kept and how he'd specified that it should go to Heath.

"I know firsthand what it's like to compete with a sibling. Even though my father loved Heath and me equally, there was no question that they were more in sync."

Chelsea leaned into his understanding, and her head settled against his shoulder, as if to take comfort from being close.

"At the time, our mom couldn't afford to hire a manager, and besides, Heath was convinced that everything would fall apart without him overseeing the operations." Nolan recalled how he'd sometimes felt like an outsider when he and Heath did things with their father. Dad and elder son had so much in common and so much to say to each other that a lot of the time Nolan just retreated into his own imagination. "I was jealous."

"Jealous? Why?"

"He was always closer to my dad. They had so much in common, and I always felt like a third wheel. It caused me to pull away from them. Even my mom and sister." This fact hadn't occurred to him at the time, but looking back on it, especially after losing his mom and Ashley, he acknowledged that his resentment had caused him to build walls.

"I get that," Chelsea said. "I've never been close with my dad, either. While he showers my brother with his time and attention, I had to learn about ranching from the foreman and at college." She toyed with the silverware as she continued, "But what really kills me is when Vic gets the credit for things that I've done. I still remember the shock I felt when I realized that being the oldest gave me no extra edge. I committed to doing whatever it took to prove myself. The problem is, no matter how hard I work, my father is blind to my achievements."

"I'm sorry your dad is like that. Even though I wasn't interested in ranching, when it came to fishing or running around on ATVs, the three of us had a blast. There just wasn't always time for fun. In the end, it all worked out. I got to see the world, and Heath gets to run the ranch he loves."

"I guess we are just destined to find our way based on what we want out of life. You are interested in seeing the world, and I'm interested in running it." Her lips curved into a wry grin. "Or at least my corner of it."

It bummed Nolan out a little that they were both

so different in this way. Eventually, he would have to leave Texas. He couldn't ignore his business forever. Many of the projects in the works would begin to ramp up, and he would start to scout locations. He thought about traveling with her, sharing many of the places that he'd loved. But she was so tied to her ranch. And with her locked in competition with her brother, he couldn't imagine convincing her to leave it, even for a few weeks. Was it crazy that this was only their second date and he was already uncomfortable at the thought of leaving her behind?

"Have you ever considered doing anything else?" Nolan posed the question as much to himself as to her and was unprepared for the stark anxiety that streaked across her face.

"Lately, I've been spending a lot of time wondering what I'm going to do if my father hands the reins over to my brother."

Her admission took him by surprise. Nolan reached out and took her hand. "That won't happen. He's going to come around."

But even as he reassured her, part of Nolan was hoping that one day Chelsea might lose the ranch and be forced to look for something new. He'd recognized that his stories had ignited her sense of adventure, and he wondered if a future existed where he could convince her to leave Texas and venture into the big, wide world. With him.

Chelsea stood on the back porch of the ranch house and stared across the side yard in the direction of the twenty acres her grandfather had gifted her on her twenty-first birthday. She'd planned to build a house there and demonstrate to her family that she was dug in. Although she enjoyed her close connection with her family, having three generations living in fifteen thousand square feet made for little personal space or privacy. Liking the idea of owning a home where she could be separate, yet remain close to her family, she'd hired an architect to draw up plans, interviewed contractors and had even gone so far as to pick out finishes. Yet she'd never pulled the trigger. In part because these last few years she'd focused so exclusively on the ranch that there was neither time nor energy for anything else. Plus, with her grandparents aging, she knew her time with them was limited.

Now, however, since starting to date Nolan, she wished she'd gone forward with the house. Every time she left for or came in from one of their dates, she ran into someone with an opinion about her activities.

"Chelsea!"

At the sound of her name, she wrenched herself out of her thoughts. Turning her head, she spied Layla standing beside her. "Sorry?"

The entire Grandin family had gathered for Sunday dinner to talk about the Thurston brothers and the oil rights claim. Anticipating the dread moment when the conversation would turn to her decision to date Nolan, she'd almost given in to his dinner invitation and bailed on her family. Instead, for the last hour, over predinner cocktails, she'd been defending her actions and reiterating her motivation while each one of her family members—with the exception of her grandmother Miriam, who at eighty-eight was having health issues—had dumped a truckload of censure upon her.

Simmering with frustration, she'd escaped to the back deck to cool off before dinner.

Her sister frowned. "I've been talking to you for ten minutes."

"Sorry."

"What is up with you? You've been so distracted lately." Layla gave her an odd look. "Ever since you met Nolan Thurston. It's like you're into the guy."

With her stomach in knots, Chelsea shrugged dismissively. "If I'm fooling you, then he's not going to catch on to what I'm doing."

"Are you sure it's him you're fooling?"

Chelsea sucked in a sharp breath. "What is that supposed to mean?"

"It's just that he's really different from all the guys you've dated before. It wouldn't surprise me if you fell for all his smoldering sexiness and masculine arrogance."

"I mean, he's sexy, sure." Her sister's description of Nolan made Chelsea frown. "But I don't see him as arrogant."

In fact, being with him left her awash in comfort. He seemed to understand her better than her family did. Having someone on her side was amazing. So much so that it only felt the littlest bit scary to let her guard down and allow herself be taken care of for a change.

Layla rolled her eyes. "Are you kidding? When he approached me a couple months ago, he was all, 'You and I should go out to lunch and discuss the oil rights claim. And bring your sister.'"

The commanding baritone Layla adopted sounded nothing like the Nolan Chelsea had been dating. Goose bumps rose on her arm. Was it possible that she wasn't seeing his true self? It wasn't unimaginable that he was playing her. In fact, the thought had crossed her mind often. After all, she was playing him.

As much as she wanted to reject her sister's insight, Chelsea would be unwise to ignore this reminder to be careful. If only it wasn't so easy to forget everything except her growing desire when she was with him. Simple things like the way he slipped his hand around her waist to guide her or his fondness for tucking strands of her hair behind her ear. The fleeting touches combined with the intensity of his gaze sometimes caught her off guard. He made her feel attractive and desirable, and she thrilled to the sizzle of their chemistry. He treated her as a woman he wanted to possess while reassuring her that he appreciated her intelligence and opinions.

"I thought the whole point of you dating him was so you could get in with the enemy."

"He never wants to discuss the oil rights," Chelsea told her sister. "I think we both recognize that we are on opposite sides of a fraught issue."

Her sister had driven a stake straight into the heart of Chelsea's dilemma. She had originally decided to go out with Nolan with the idea that she would dig for information. Instead, she'd avoided asking any questions that might disturb the positive energy flowing between them. Which meant she was doing exactly what her sister accused her of—she was dating the enemy and loving every second of it.

"Oh, for heaven's sake," Chelsea said, tossing her hands up in exasperation while her heart pounded erratically against her ribs. "It's been like a week and a half, and we've only gone out a few times." The actual number of official dates was six, but Chelsea kept that to herself. "It's going to take time to gain his trust."

"Time is of the essence," Layla reminded her.

"I know." Chelsea pinched the bridge of her nose to combat a growing headache. "I don't want them to ruin our ranch, but nothing is going to happen in the next few days."

Layla gave her a searching look. "This isn't like you."

"What isn't like me? I've never been one to rush into anything. I think everything through and then put a plan into place."

"Sure." Her sister sounded worried. "But you usually have a plan. I have not seen any sign of one. You are simply going out with that man and…" Layla cocked her head and studied Chelsea. "Enjoying him."

Chelsea made a strangled noise. "Don't be ridiculous."

"Deny it all you want, but I think you like him."

The only sound Chelsea could manage was some unimpressive sputtering. It was one thing to lie to her parents and Vic, but convincing Layla that she had everything under control was way harder.

"I do like him," Chelsea admitted and sighed. "He's been everywhere and has these amazing stories about all the things he's seen. Plus, he's easy on the eyes, and we've got great chemistry..."

"I knew it." With each syllable Chelsea had uttered, Layla's expression had grown more worried. "I just knew it. You are falling for him."

"*Falling* is a little extreme."

"You are falling for the guy. Why would you do that when you know the Thurstons can't be trusted?"

"I know they can't be trusted." Chelsea groaned softly. "Listen, I have everything under control. Honestly, when have you known me to do something rash?"

"You have always been the most sensible of any of us, and I know you're far more guarded since what happened with Brandon." Layla grew pensive. "But when it comes to love, none of us can see it coming."

Two months earlier, Layla had found love with Joshua, but a misguided ruse involving a twin switch nearly ruined their romance before it truly began.

"Whoa, no. Who said anything about love?" Chelsea waved her hands, desperate to ward off her sister's misguided assumptions. "There's no way I'm going there. I think he's hot as sin, and sure, I'm not going to deny that I wouldn't mind sleeping with him. But he's only in Royal temporarily. Eventually, he will have to get back to his globe-trotting ways. And my life is here. I'm not getting emotionally involved."

"I guess." Layla didn't seem all that convinced. "But I've seen you date other guys, and this is different. You're relaxed and seem really...secure."

Her sister's description made Chelsea flinch. Despite knowing their fling had an expiration date, she did feel secure with Nolan. Maybe because she had no possibility of a future with him, she could date him without expectations.

"I'm worried about you," Layla finished.

"You don't have to be. I just have a lot on my mind. Now that Grandpa is gone, Dad's timetable for choosing which of us will get control of the ranch has moved up. He's going to want to make sure his successor is thoroughly trained before he retires. Which means I have even less time to convince Dad that Vic doesn't deserve to be in charge. That's the only thing on my mind. Well, that and what might happen to the ranch if Heath succeeds in laying claim to the oil rights."

"Heath...? What about Nolan?" Layla never got her question answered, because Chelsea's phone began to ring.

When she glanced down and saw the caller was Nolan, her pulse jumped in anticipation of his whiskey-smooth voice in her ear.

"I have to take this." Chelsea stabbed her finger against the green button. Not until she spied her sister's astonished expression did she consider what her actions had revealed about her feelings for him.

"This is exactly what I'm talking about," Layla

protested, adding an exaggerated eye roll to further punctuate her disgust.

"Hey." Chelsea shot daggers at her sister before turning her back and striding the width of the house away from Layla. "What's up?"

"I just wanted to finalize our meeting time tomorrow."

She liked that he never left her hanging regarding plans. She'd dated guys in the past who left things until the last minute or never bothered to call when they were running late. To her mind, that was the height of rudeness. She knew that some men didn't communicate well, but what was the big deal about letting a girl know that you couldn't make a date? And then there was Brandon. She'd thought they were serious until one day he'd neglected to show up and then didn't respond to her texts or calls asking him what was going on.

"I'll be by your place around two o'clock."

"Can you give me a hint what we're doing?" he asked.

"Nope. It's your turn to be surprised."

"I guess I'll just have to be patient. And speaking of that, are you sure you can't come by tonight?"

A surge of heat coiled in her midsection. His voice had taken on a smoky tone that drove her mad with longing.

Chelsea glanced toward her sister and sighed with regret. "No. The whole family has gathered for Sunday night dinner, and there's no way I can sneak away."

Layla was gesturing toward the French doors that

led from the deck to the great room. Chelsea waved at her to go ahead. Instead, her sister stood beside the doors with her arms crossed, looking like she planned to scowl at Chelsea until she ended the call and came inside.

"Then I'll just have to wait and see you tomorrow."

"It'll be worth the wait, I promise."

"I'm counting on it. G'night, Ms. Dreamy. Sweet dreams." His warm goodbye sent pleasure spiraling through her.

"You, too."

It seemed hard to believe they'd only gone out a handful of times, and each time was more amazing than the last. Not that they'd all been as noteworthy as the gondola ride or dinner at Cocott, but Nolan was fun to be around and made even the most mundane activities a lot of fun.

If only she'd been able to find this sense of camaraderie in someone who wasn't trying to mess with her family's ranch. The unfairness of it all felt like being clocked in the jaw. For a brief second, her chest grew uncomfortably tight.

All too aware that her sister continued to radiate disapproval, Chelsea composed her face into bland disinterest and headed for the house. After one final look over and an *uh-huh* of disgust, Layla—and her opinions about Chelsea's feelings for Nolan—preceded her sister into the house.

To Chelsea's relief, Layla made no attempt to bring her concerns up to the family over dinner. This didn't mean that the conversation wasn't at the forefront of

Chelsea's mind. Was she too wrapped up in Nolan? Well, obviously, she found him handsome, charming and intriguing, but while every inch of him appealed to her, he was in league with his brother to ruin her family's ranch. That should bother her so much that she found Nolan detestable. Only she didn't.

The man had a body to die for and the engaging personality to match it. He made her laugh at a time when she was too stressed to even smile. She in turn made excuses for what he and Heath intended to do to her and to her family.

Why was she doing this to herself? Even without the feud between their families, it was never going to work between them. And yet she couldn't bring herself to stop seeing him. Despite knowing he would eventually run off in search of adventure. In spite of the worry that he could be using her to further his family's claim to what lay beneath her family's land.

Layla was right. Chelsea was becoming emotionally invested in Nolan. The game she was playing was a perilous one, because the person most in danger of getting fooled was her.

Seven

When Chelsea showed up at his door in tight jeans and a red crop top that bared her chiseled abdomen, Nolan had no idea how he was going to get them both out of the loft before he lost his battle with lust. The top was held together by a line of tiny strawberry buttons, and Nolan imagined he could hear them pinging off his walls as he tore it open. Did she have any idea how much he adored her in red? Before meeting her, his favorite color had been blue. Now he was obsessed with shades from crimson to scarlet, as long as they encased Chelsea's lean curves.

"I hope you're ready for anything," she said, her eyes glowing with excitement.

They'd been out to dinner several times when she could get away from the demands of the ranch for a few hours. Today, they had a longer date planned, an outing Chelsea insisted on keeping a surprise. Her saucy grin broadcast how much she liked being in control. In fact, Nolan enjoyed it as well.

Nolan raised an eyebrow as he gestured her inside. "I'm game if you are."

"I'm so game."

Not only was she a treat for the eyes, she smelled good enough to eat. Her shoulder brushed his chest as she passed by, and he caught a whiff of her berry-scented lotion. Suddenly besieged by the need to nibble his way up and down her fragrant skin, Nolan took in her playful updo and red lip as she sashayed into his living room. Her cowboy boots gave her hips a gentle rolling motion that seized his attention and wouldn't let go.

"You look great," he rasped, losing control of his voice.

"So do you." Her gaze held smoky approval as she took in his worn jeans and snug V-neck T-shirt. She reached out and picked up the medallion he wore around his neck, the light brush of her fingers singeing him through the thin fabric. "This is cool. Something you picked up on your travels?"

"Tibet. It's a Kalachakra, a powerful mantra for peace. It reduces suffering by calming negativity and conflict." He covered her hand with his so that they held the necklace together. "These represent the moon, the sun and the flame. It's a symbol of good fortune and protection for the wearer."

"All that sounds like something I could use." A

wistful sigh puffed from her lips. "Next time you're there, pick me up one, will you?"

"How about you just take the one I'm wearing?" He lifted the chain off his neck and dropped it over her head. The pendant settled amid the column of strawberry buttons between her breasts, and Nolan gave himself several seconds to admire the way the silver chain looked against her tan skin.

"Are you sure? It came all the way from Tibet. Are you sure you can part with it?" She turned her big brown eyes on him, and Nolan knew he'd give her this and more to make her happy.

"It looks like it was made for you."

"Thank you." Sending her fingers tunneling through his hair, she drew him down for a grateful kiss. She nipped at his lower lip before opening her mouth to the thrust of his tongue. Eager to take things further, he groaned as she eased away, whispering, "I'm going to treasure it."

With his hormones dancing in appreciation of her soft breasts grazing his chest, Nolan smiled down at her. Her lips remained softly parted, and Nolan knew if he kept staring at them, he'd claim her mouth all over again. He was close to surrendering to the urge to scoop her into his arms, carry her to bed and rip off every one of those strawberry buttons with his teeth. His fingers twitched as he imagined himself giving the top one a fierce twist. One by one, they would fall to the floor, exposing her beautiful breasts. He was mentally sliding his lips over one lush curve when the fingers gliding down his cheek fell away. The sudden loss knocked him out of his trance.

"Should we get going?" From her bright tone, Nolan suspected she had no sense of the fierce hunger raging inside him.

With the imprint of her final caress lingering on his skin, Nolan scrubbed his hand across his jaw and somehow summoned the strength to croak, "Sure."

If he didn't get them out of the condo, he would never know what surprises she'd organized for him. And from the gleeful anticipation sparkling in her gaze, she was looking forward to whatever she had planned.

Nolan watched her charming butt as she descended the stairs ahead of him. Damn. It was going to be a long afternoon.

Since Chelsea knew where they were going, she drove. Whatever she'd planned must've been a doozy, because she was bubbling with excitement. Nolan liked this take-charge side of her, mostly because reveling in her power made her that much more attractive. Her brown eyes glowed with satisfaction while a mysterious smile teased her lips. Her high spirits were infectious, and Nolan found his nerves humming as they traveled a series of two-lane roads.

"Almost there," she assured him, casting a teasing look his way. "You are going to be so surprised."

She turned off the highway onto a road that ran parallel to a well-maintained landing strip.

Mystified, he searched the small airfield. "Are we flying somewhere?"

"You might say that."

They flashed past a sign. "Skydiving?" The one-word question burst from him on a laugh. "This is what you want to do?"

"You're certified, and I called and confirmed that with your credentials we can jump tandem."

Nolan's entire body flushed with anticipation. She'd been intrigued when he talked about his experiences, but he'd never imagined she'd be interested in jumping herself.

"Are you sure about this?"

"Aren't you?"

"Of course. I've made nearly a hundred jumps..." He trailed off as she parked. "You trust me to keep you safe?"

It wasn't just the jump he was asking about.

Flashing her even, white teeth, Chelsea shut off the engine and turned to face him. "There's no one I'd rather jump out of a plane strapped to."

Nolan slid his fingers into her thick hair and tugged to draw her closer. "You, Ms. Dreamy, continue to bewitch and amaze me."

"I'm glad." Her lashes fanned her cheeks as his head dipped and their lips grew steadily closer. "With everything you've seen and done, I wasn't sure I could find something adventurous enough for you."

He dusted soft kisses across her lips, mingling their breath. "If you're doing this for me, it's not necessary. Being with you is adventure enough for me."

"That's sweet." While her fingertips traced a line of fire down his neck, she nipped his jawline and then lightly raked his earlobe with her teeth. "But being with you has inspired me to be a little reckless, and I want to test the mettle of my bravery."

Nolan shuddered as his nerves went incandescent in response to her tantalizing touch. "I've been trying like hell not to ravish you these last few days, but I can't promise to be good after jumping out of an airplane with you strapped to my body."

"The anticipation has been killing me, too," she whispered, her eyes blazing with hunger. She took his hand and placed his palm over her breast, then moaned as his fingers kneaded gently.

For the last week, he'd been reminding himself that anticipation could heighten pleasure. When he at last slept with Chelsea, he intended the moment be absolutely memorable. For both of them. But he was near the end of his rope, and skydiving with her was sure to push him beyond the limits of his control.

"We could just go park somewhere deserted and take the edge off." His fingers roamed over her abs and teased the waistband of her jeans. She rotated her hips in his direction and slid her foot over his leg. The console between them was a problem.

"I think about you at night," she whispered, her voice fierce and urgent as her tongue flicked against his neck. "I imagine you doing all kinds of things to me."

The sexy words made him desperate for her. "Do you come when you think of what I'm doing?"

He dipped his hand between her legs. She gasped as he stroked her sensitive flesh, the heat of her no less tantalizing for it being muffled by the fabric of her jeans. They both panted as she rocked against his palm. Nolan sent his lips roaming down the delicate column of her neck. When he reached the spot where her shoulder started, he eased the edges of his teeth into her skin, gently but with enough pressure to leave the tiniest of marks.

"Yes," she moaned on the thinnest whisper of air, and even more softly she added, "Again."

As he gave her what she wanted, Nolan found himself spiraling into another reality, a sensual, intoxicating realm that existed for just the two of them.

Nolan dimly noticed the sound of a car door slamming, and a second later he was jerked back into awareness of their surroundings by the staccato blast of a horn as someone locked their vehicle. He set his forehead against hers, all too conscious of his ragged breathing and unsteady pulse. They sat that way for a long time while their bodies calmed. But even as his heart rate steadied, his need for her continued to smolder.

"Being with you is all the rush I need," he told her, wondering how she'd feel about him after jumping out of a plane at ten thousand feet.

"That's music to my ears." She dropped a brief kiss on his lips. "Now, let's go skydiving."

Chelsea barely felt the impact as she and Nolan landed in the empty field that had been designated as the landing site. Her entire body was lit up with adrenaline and desire. The jump had been spectacular, a breath-stealing plunge through the heavens, followed by a leisurely drift along the thermals after the chute had bloomed above them. For someone who normally kept her feet firmly planted on the ground, the experience had electrified her. And left her pondering all she'd given up by choosing to focus her energy on the ranch.

"That was crazy," she yelled as Nolan released her harness from his. "Amazing."

Robbed of his strong, reassuring presence behind her, Chelsea stumbled and would've fallen, except he caught her and spun her into his arms. Her heart fluttered wildly at the intensity of his expression as his arm wrapped around her, squeezing her against him once more. Before she had a chance to say a word, his lips crashed down on hers. Wild, intoxicating emotion exploded through her, and she pushed into the kiss, wrapping her arms around his neck and feasting on his mouth.

He lifted her off the ground, and she wrapped her thighs around his waist. Her arms encircled his shoulders as the press of his erection against the most sensitive parts sent her body into spasms of joy. She wiggled her hips, driving her heated core against him. Nolan dropped to his knees and, with his arm binding Chelsea to his chest, lowered her to the cushion of grass in the big, empty field.

His lips coasted down her throat. She cupped his head and arched her back, offering him more of her skin to nibble on. The heat of the July afternoon was unbearable, but it was nothing compared to the inferno raging inside her. Chelsea squirmed in an effort to free herself from the binding harness, and sensing her distress, Nolan rolled them until he lay beneath her.

With a triumphant gasp, Chelsea sat up, popped the catch in the middle of her chest and ripped the straps off her shoulders. Panting, she attacked Nolan's clasp. His fingers curved over her bare waist between the crop top and her jeans, thumbs riding the ripple of her ribs, making her hands shake as she struggled to get her hands on his skin in turn. Seconds later, she let out a satisfied sigh as she successfully tunneled her fingers beneath the hem of his shirt and rode his six-pack to his impressive pecs. As he groaned in pleasure, she curved her fingers and lightly raked her nails across his nipples. She grinned as a sharp expletive escaped his parted lips.

"I want you, right here, right now," she told him, leaning down to seize his lower lip between her teeth.

"You're killing me, you know that, right?"

"I'm glad." She didn't mean to come off all cocky and was glad to see he didn't take her words at face value. His crooked smile gave her a second to gather her wits. "What I mean is every time you touch me, I go wild, and I'm really glad I can do the same for you."

"Trust me, you do."

Nolan lifted his hips and drove his erection against her tender flesh. She met his thrust with a little twist of her own that made them both moan with frustration and pleasure.

"As hot as it would be to do this here and now," he said, "we really are not gonna have time to do it right before we're picked up." Yet even as he said this, he sank his long fingers into her hair and pulled her close for a sizzling kiss. After a long time, he released her lips and murmured, "And I want all the time in the world to make love to you."

Chelsea shuddered at his declaration and recognized that he was right. As hungry as she was for him, a frantic coupling in a field was not how she wanted their first time together to happen.

"So, back to your place right now, or dinner first?" She'd planned for the latter, but with desire raging through her veins, she wasn't sure she could eat anything. Not while she was starved for the six feet of sizzling male who'd slid his fingers beneath her crop top and cupped her lace-covered breasts.

"Definitely dinner," he teased, whisking his thumbs over her nipples. "I want the anticipation to build."

"You don't think it's been building?" she asked, finishing with a little gasp as he nibbled on her ear.

"It has for me from the moment I set eyes on you across Main Street."

His admission sent a familiar thrill up her spine. She wasn't used to having a man seduce her with words. She'd always been so practical with those she chose to date in the past.

"Please, can we just go back to your place?" She made the request in a small, breathless voice, unaccustomed to begging for what she wanted. "I can't wait any longer to be with you."

"I'd like that more than anything."

As more kisses followed, each one hotter and deeper, Chelsea wondered if he had any idea that she'd shared more with him than with any man she'd ever known.

She'd confided how her father's lack of faith in her abilities saddened her. Voiced the question if Vic became the sibling in charge, what that meant for her future. Most days she got up and applied a tough persona along with her mascara and lipstick. None of her family knew about Chelsea's deep anxiety, but she'd drawn back the curtain and put her fragile confidence on display for Nolan.

It should terrify her that she'd revealed her insecurity. Yet maintaining her defenses with Nolan hadn't seemed necessary. He'd given her a safe space to explore her fears because he'd been willing to share his concerns about his relationship with his brother, the pain of losing his mother and sister and his regret that staying away these last fifteen years had robbed him of precious time with them.

They were oblivious to the vehicle that rolled up on them until the light tap of a horn roused them from their sex-fogged delirium. Chelsea and Nolan jerked apart, laughing as they resettled their clothes and got to their feet. Another time, a different man, and Chelsea would've been mortified to be caught making out in public, but being with Nolan was so easy and fun that she didn't mind the knowing looks cast her way by the driver and his passengers.

Hand in hand, she and Nolan headed to the van.

They settled into the back and grinned at each other in delight, but the intense gleam in his eyes made Chelsea uncomfortably aware of the throbbing heat between her thighs. How was she supposed to survive the hour-long drive back to Royal? Anticipation, hell. She was in serious distress.

"Let's get out of here," Nolan whispered in her ear once they were back at the skydiving base. He slid his hand into the back pocket of her jeans and gave a little squeeze. "I need to be inside you before I lose my mind."

His sexy words made her breath hitch. "I want that, too." She handed him her keys. "Feel like driving? I don't feel all that steady at the moment."

Taking the keys, he planted a quick, hard kiss on her lips before nudging her toward the passenger side of the truck. If the drive back to Royal seemed to take forever, at least she was lost in a blissful daze. She distantly heard herself asking Nolan about his other skydiving adventures and tried to pay attention to his answers, but with her blood pounding hot and fierce through her veins, she struggled to concentrate on anything but what would happen when they returned to his loft.

They barely made it through the door before Chelsea launched herself at him. She dived her fingers into his lush, wavy hair and reached up on tiptoe to press her mouth to his. The kiss started hot and hungry but quickly slowed down as Nolan gently caressed her burning cheek and ran his tongue along her bottom lip. A breath eased out of her tight chest as he played with her lips, pressing and nibbling kisses that were both tender and hungry.

Instead of moving them to his waiting bed, Nolan picked her up and set her on the nearby kitchen counter.

"Here?" she squeaked, losing control of her voice as he stepped between her parted thighs and ground his erection into her.

"For a start."

Eyes glowing with wicked intent, he gripped her boot and slid it off her foot. She barely heard the bang as it hit the wood floor above the pounding of her heart. While he loosened the second boot, she shimmied out of the crop top, letting it fall. His eyes lit with approval as he scanned her pale breasts encased in red lace.

"Damn," he murmured. "I do love you in red."

She reached behind her for the clasp. "How do you feel about me out of it?" In seconds the bra had come undone, and his gaze found hers as he peeled the straps down her arm, exposing her.

"You are perfection," he murmured, his lips easing onto the delicate skin behind her ear, making her quiver.

His palm pressed hard between her thighs, inviting her to rub her tender parts against him. In a rising frenzy of desire, she realized how close she was to coming.

"Nolan," she panted. "This is… You are… I'm…" She fumbled with the zipper on her jeans, needing his fingers inside her. Before she'd done more than popped the button, an orgasm broke over her like a wave, shattering her into pieces. "Damn." Part relief, part protest, the curse made him chuckle.

"Most women enjoy coming," he muttered before his mouth clamped down over hers. He drove his tongue forward to tangle with hers, and she half sobbed as aftershocks pummeled her.

Her release was only partially satisfying. What she truly craved was his possession. To be filled by him and made whole. And Nolan seemed to understand, because he finished stripping off her jeans and underwear, hooked his fingers in the waistband and tugged the denim off her hips and down her legs.

A startled laugh escaped as her naked butt connected with the cool stone countertop, but then his hand found the heat between her legs and she went up in flames.

"You're so wet," he said, sliding his fingers across her.

A greedy moan poured from her lips. "That feels so good. I've been waiting so long..." She captured his face in hers and kissed him hard. "You know what would feel better, though? If you got naked, too, and we went over to that big bed of yours. I need your skin against mine." Their hearts beating together.

That last bit was too romantic to say out loud. As much as she might enjoy talking dirty in bed, she was terrified to send him running by divulging that her need for him was more than physical.

Nolan bracketed her hips in his strong fingers and lowered his forehead to hers. "I want that, too."

She reached between them to unfasten his jeans and worked feverishly until she had them off his hips. Hissing in appreciation at the impressive tent his erection made in his boxer briefs, she carefully released it from the confining fabric. He set his head against her shoulder and shuddered as her hand closed around him.

A curse slipped from his lips as she explored his hard length, learning its velvety surface and the shape beneath. All too soon he covered her hand with his and pulled it away from him.

"No more." He lifted her palm to his lips, nibbling on the sensitive mound near her thumb. "There's only so much willpower available when I'm with you."

"I don't want you to hold back."

He snorted. "Ms. Dreamy, I'm just trying to hold on."

And then he was stepping out of his jeans, ripping his T-shirt over his head. She barely got a chance to appreciate the impressive cut of his biceps, the rolling muscles of his shoulders or the toned beauty of his abs before he slid his hands beneath her butt cheeks and lifted her. With a surprised murmur, she wrapped her arms and legs around him as he carried her—at long last—to his bed.

Eight

Nolan set Chelsea down on her feet beside his bed and took a step back, astonished at his rapid heart rate and the irregular cadence of his breathing. "Let me look at you," he said, his eyes roving over her naked perfection, seeing the effort it cost her to hold still beneath his scrutiny. "You are gorgeous."

"You're not so bad yourself."

"I can't wait to get to know every inch of you."

"I want that." She blew out a ragged breath. "Can we get started?"

"You're in a hurry?"

"I'm suddenly really nervous."

This was his moment to reassure her, so Nolan stepped closer and cupped her cheek in one palm. "You don't need to be nervous. I'll take care of you."

He threaded her long hair through his fingers and gave a gentle tug.

"I know you will," she responded, edging closer until the heat of their skin leaped across the narrow distance between them and burned away her hesitation. She smoothed her hand over his chest, fingers dancing over his pecs. "In fact, I'm counting on it."

Nolan drew in a deep breath and sighed as she raked her nails down his abs, letting her nerves settle as she explored his hard planes, the structure of bones beneath his overheated skin. At last he could take no more and took her by the shoulders, pivoting her toward the bed. As the backs of her knees encountered the mattress, she flopped backward, spreading her arms wide as she landed. Nolan stared hungrily at her firm breasts, watching her nipples harden beneath his regard. Shooting him an enticing grin, she wiggled her way toward the middle of the bed.

Reaching into the nightstand, he pulled out a condom and slid it on. Her eyes flashed, feral and wild, as she watched his every movement.

"Nolan." Greedy and impatient, his name was a growl torn from her lips. She arched her back and drew her fingertips from her navel to the cleft between her breasts. "Touch me, please."

He smiled wolfishly. Setting his knee on the bed beside her, he caressed along her thigh and into the indent of her waist, riding her ribs to the soft curve of her breast. She sucked in a breath as he cupped her gently and then squeezed before feathering fingertips across her tight nipples.

"This is where I've wanted you from the first moment I saw you," he murmured, his voice hot and hungry. Nolan captured one rosy bud between his lips and flicked his tongue over it. "Naked, in my bed."

"I want you," she whispered, her thighs falling open as she rocked her hips. "Make me yours."

Her plea lanced through him like lightning. It felt so good to have her hands roaming over his body, but he'd waited so long to have her, and holding back much longer might have catastrophic consequences. He shifted between her thighs, settling his hand on the back of her leg, opening her wide, making room for himself. She obliged with a soft purr of delight, raking her fingers through his hair.

He took his erection in one hand and teased her with the head, coating himself in her wet heat. She gasped as he sank into her, and he stilled.

"Does it hurt?"

She shook her head. "You feel amazing. More. I want all of you."

"I can give you more." He circled her thigh with his fingers and hitched it over his hip, opening her up so he could go deeper.

"Yes." She gave a breathless nod and sank her fingers into his forearm as he pulled back and stroked forward once again. "Like that."

This time, as he lay fully embedded in her, he brought his hand to her face and dragged his thumb over her soft lips. He'd never felt this closeness with anyone before and knew she'd gifted him with a glimpse into the tender emotions she kept hidden.

"You're incredible."

Her lashes fluttered. "You make me feel that way."

And then desire took over and Nolan had to move. He kept his strokes smooth and rhythmic, watching her reaction to each thrust. A delectable smile curved her soft lips, and she lost herself in their lovemaking. Watching her, Nolan found his own grin forming. What was it about her?

"Harder," she commanded.

With a reverent groan, he obliged, pumping faster, harder, aware that she was dissolving beneath him, her cries growing more reckless and abandoned. Panting as he surged toward the threshold of ecstasy, Nolan had just enough presence of mind to make sure Chelsea came with him.

"Come for me," he coaxed, each second carrying him nearer his climax. He loved how the world had fallen away and there was only Chelsea.

She wrapped her legs around him tighter, signaling she was close to the edge as well. Nolan watched her, waiting for the telltale signs, feeling her body quickening as his own screamed at him to let go. And then she was there, her body bucking with the power of it, her inner muscles contracting on him, drawing him deep and hard into her as an orgasm tore through her like a tornado. Nolan took it all in for several heartbeats, watched her shatter and then let himself be pulled apart in her arms.

In the aftermath, Nolan's lips drifted along her damp skin, smiling at the salty taste of her, breathing in the sexy musk of her arousal. He wanted to know all her scents and sounds and flavors. To hear her snore softly in her sleep and press her round backside against his morning erection. So much to learn. Yet he couldn't help but hear a ticking clock in the background. A warning that stolen moments like these wouldn't last forever.

"You know, I could get used to this," she murmured, nuzzling into his throat, her teeth nipping suggestively. She'd draped her arms over his shoulders, and despite her boneless lassitude, he could tell her thoughts were spinning. "Let's stay in bed like this forever."

As Nolan processed her statement, a wave of goose bumps rushed over his skin. Little by little she was shedding all the protective layers she wore to keep herself safe. Originally, he'd thought he could romance her, get the information Heath needed and move on. Assuming what was between them was strictly physical, he'd stupidly believed that afterward, he could walk away. But each hour in her company had brought him to a new level of understanding, of appreciation.

"I wouldn't mind that." His palms glided over her silken curves, noting the hard muscle beneath.

Her body was the exact opposite of her personality. She presented the world with this fierce toughness, while inside she was tender and vulnerable. No doubt most people believed she was hard as nails. It's probably why she got hurt over and over. This was how she'd allowed herself to be misunderstood in the past. She'd fallen for men who never saw or couldn't appreciate the fragility hidden beneath her thick skin.

"But of course, that's truly unrealistic," she went on as if he hadn't spoken. Her breath puffed against his skin as she sighed. "I mean, I can't let myself get used to this, because I don't know how long you're going to be around."

Nolan's gut clenched as he heard the resignation in her voice at their inevitable separation. "I haven't really decided what I'm gonna do," he said, which was the first time he'd voiced his inner turmoil out loud.

"You don't expect me to believe that you'd consider staying in Royal. Not after being gone for fifteen years. Your business involves location scouting around the world."

He'd known she was too shrewd to believe such a glib response. "Being back here has been nice." Claiming he'd had a change of heart and intended to stick around might've worked on another woman, but not Chelsea. Still, that didn't stop him from trying. "I've enjoyed reconnecting with my brother, and meeting you has given me food for thought."

She set her chin on his chest and hit him with a solemn gaze. "I don't believe you."

Her declaration really did give him food for thought. She'd been burned so often that winning her trust might be nearly impossible. And he wanted her to believe him. Not to help with his brother's plan regarding the oil rights, but because each glimpse past her shields had touched his heart. It made him want to enclose her in Bubble Wrap and take care of her, even as she claimed she needed no one's help. He'd never put another person's welfare before his own, and the change in his perspective rattled him.

"You don't believe people can change their minds about things?" he asked.

"I'd be every kind of fool to be that pessimistic when I am doing everything in my power to change my dad's mind about letting me be in charge of the ranch." She rolled her head to the side so that her ear rested over his steadily beating heart. "Yet there's a big part of me that doubts I'll be successful."

Her expression grew so pensive that Nolan decided she was unaccustomed to coming clean about her own inner demons. His gut tightened. That she'd trusted him with something so private warned him to tread carefully.

"I've learned that getting what you want often involves making compromises. Sometimes when I find a perfect place to shoot, convincing the owners to let us disrupt their property for several months means we have to find some way to make it worth their while. Maybe it's as simple as writing a big check. Sometimes they want to be a part of the action."

"Are you saying I'm wrong for wanting it all?"

"Never. I'm just saying that sometimes what you think you want isn't what you need. Like, our budget was super tight on one shoot and we found the perfect spot, but the property owner asked five grand for two weeks. He was an aspiring songwriter, so instead of paying him the money he wanted, we arranged for him to write one of the songs on the soundtrack."

"What I want is to run the ranch." She paused, and her eyebrow quirked in challenge. "What do you think I need?"

"Me."

"Hello, stranger," Natalie teased, but her tone wasn't at all lighthearted as she slid into the booth opposite Chelsea.

The women had decided to meet for lunch at the Royal Diner, a popular eatery in downtown that was decorated like an old-fashioned 1950s diner with red faux-leather booths and black-and-white-checkered floors, where owner Amanda Battle served classic diner meals.

"What do you mean, stranger?" Chelsea protested, her enthusiasm for this lunch with her best friend dimming. "I saw you just the other day. We went shopping, remember?"

"For an outfit you could wear on your next date with Nolan."

"I thought we had fun trying stuff on. I didn't realize… I mean, does it bother you that I'm dating him? You were the one who suggested he was interested in me in the first place."

"I know." Natalie made a face. "I thought you'd have some fun with him and loosen up a bit. All you've done for months is obsess about your dad picking Vic to run the ranch. But it just seems like you've traded one obsession for another."

Chelsea's mood dipped still further. She was tired of everybody harassing her about Nolan. Why couldn't her family and friends just accept that she knew what she was doing?

"Don't you realize that the two things are connected? If I can convince Nolan that he and Heath shouldn't pursue the oil rights, then I will have saved the ranch and my dad will have to put me in charge."

"I know." Natalie frowned. "It's just that ever since you and Nolan started getting serious—"

"Serious?" Chelsea interrupted, panic stirring as she contemplated Natalie's take on what was happening between her and Nolan. "We aren't serious. I mean, we've only been going out for a couple of weeks."

"A couple of weeks where I've never seen you so preoccupied. Not even after Brandon ghosted you right before you were supposed to meet his parents." Natalie paused and frowned at her. "You've changed a bunch since you've started seeing him."

Chelsea considered the way Nolan brought out her adventurous side. "Maybe I needed to change a little. I mean, for years people have been telling me to lighten up and have some fun. Why is it the minute I start taking that advice, you all get on my case for it?"

"I don't think anybody begrudges you some fun." Natalie looked uncomfortable. "I just wonder if you should be having fun with Nolan Thurston. You are moving really fast."

"Fast?"

She thought about her friends from college who jumped into bed with a guy on the first date. At least she'd waited until the seventh date to sleep with

Nolan. Okay, so it was fast for her. She'd dated her last boyfriend for three months before taking things into the bedroom. And look how that one had turned out. Brandon had been the perfect guy on paper. Well educated. A great job. Sophisticated. They'd gone to the best restaurants. Attended concerts and the theater. Things had been going great until they slept together. And then, after arranging for them to have dinner with his parents, he'd just vanished.

"Yes, fast."

"Well, maybe it is." Chelsea reflected on the last two weeks. "The fact is, I like him, and he makes me feel things I've never known before."

She'd never connected with anyone this fast or with this level of confidence. Natalie might think Chelsea had fallen hard for Brandon, but in fact, she'd turned a blind eye to many warning signs. Nolan aroused no such misgivings. Well, except for his part in claiming the oil rights beneath the Grandin ranch.

"And that's my point," Natalie continued, oblivious to her friend's turmoil. "You usually start dating a guy armed with a checklist and a clear idea of the sort of future you could have with him. Have you considered just how complicated any sort of relationship with Nolan would be? He and his brother are coming after the oil beneath your land."

"And I'm hoping that I can change his mind about that."

"Have you considered that maybe he's hoping to get you on his side?" Natalie's look of utter pity shoved Chelsea hard against the back of the booth.

"He's not." But her claim lacked conviction.

"You don't know that. You don't know anything about him." Natalie sighed in exasperation. "It's crazy that you are throwing yourself into a relationship with him when you have no idea what tricks he has up his sleeve."

Was she misreading Nolan's signals?

"First of all, we're not in a relationship. You don't think I realize that he's not going to settle down in Royal?" Chelsea's throat tightened. She had grown accustomed to Nolan and hated contemplating the day when he'd have to go. But she wasn't unrealistic about it. For the moment, she just wanted to enjoy their time together. And having everyone throwing their suspicions in her face was making that damned hard. "Maybe he is using me. Maybe I'm using him. It's not like I'm clueless. Maybe I'm not being my normal sensible self, but I'm sick of playing it safe. It hasn't gotten me anywhere, and I like the way Nolan makes me feel."

Natalie shook her head. "I just think you're asking for trouble."

"A little trouble is what I need at the moment." Before Nolan came along, she'd been making herself miserable fighting an upward battle against her family's patriarchal leanings. What if after all her hard work, Vic ended up in charge and she'd never taken the time to ride on a gondola or jump out of an airplane? "What's so great about playing it safe?"

"You don't get hurt." Natalie's voice had taken on a hollow tone.

"But you don't have any fun, either." Chelsea leaned her arms on the table and pinned Natalie with her gaze. "Maybe you need to take a risk. Why not jump-start your own social life with somebody interesting?"

"Interesting like who?"

"Jonathan Lattimore comes to mind," Chelsea said, paying close attention to her friend's reaction. "You've had a crush on him for a long time. Why don't you make the first move?"

The Lattimore family owned the ranch next door to the Grandins. Victor Sr. and Augustus Lattimore had been best friends. Like Chelsea, Jonathan was the oldest child of their generation. The families had a warm relationship—so much so that both sides had hoped Jonathan would marry either Chelsea or Layla, but the trio had never been anything but good friends.

Although Natalie hid it well, Chelsea knew her friend well enough to recognize that she had a crush on the eldest Lattimore son. It had often surprised Chelsea that her confident, beautiful friend had never let Jonathan know she was interested in him. Maybe she hadn't had the courage to do so before Jonathan got married, but now that he was divorced, Natalie still hadn't made her feelings known.

"I don't want to talk about Jonathan," Natalie grumbled. She picked up her menu and deliberately stopped talking.

"Oh, so you can badger me about Nolan, but I make one comment about you asking Jonathan out and that's the end of the conversation?"

"Jonathan isn't interested in me." Natalie was

sounding as annoyed as Chelsea had felt moments earlier. "Nothing could ever happen between us."

In Chelsea's opinion, Jonathan had been so devastated by his failed marriage that he'd closed himself off. "Maybe he'd be interested in you if he had some inkling you had a crush on him."

Natalie looked aghast. "I can't let him know I'm attracted to him. What if he's not interested and it gets awkward between us?"

"You don't think it's awkward between you now? Well, maybe not on his part, because he has no clue how you feel." Chelsea wished her stunning, talented best friend had half the confidence when it came to romance that she demonstrated in her career. "But I've seen you when he comes into the room—you get completely tongue-tied."

"I know what you're doing. You're trying to distract me from warning you about Nolan."

Chelsea sighed. "Not at all. I am simply trying to point out that taking a risk with your heart might be better for you than you think."

"You are falling for Nolan Thurston, aren't you?"

"I don't know if I'd say I am falling for him," Chelsea demurred. "I know that we don't have a future. He will eventually return to his international travels, and I will remain in Royal and hopefully be running Grandin Ranch. No matter what happens, I will always cherish this time with him."

Chelsea was proud of herself. She sounded so practical and matter-of-fact, just the way she approached everything in her life. But thinking about the day when Nolan would leave tore her up inside. The old Chelsea would've stopped herself from becoming invested long before her heart had gotten engaged. But getting to know Nolan had changed her, opened her to joy and optimism. Her spirit soared in his company. His passion for adventure had awakened something exhilarating and irrepressible inside her.

There were moments she could actually imagine herself traveling with him to all the exotic places he visited in search of film locations. Of course, she would never want to experience the rough conditions he had told her about, but she could imagine herself on safari in South Africa or riding an elephant in Indonesia or camels in the Moroccan desert.

"Maybe that's the secret," Natalie murmured.

"The secret to what?"

"You're happy dating Nolan because there's no pressure from expectations. You recognize that eventually you'll both go your own ways, not because of some dramatic breakup, but because your lifestyles are incompatible."

Chelsea was glad she hadn't confessed to Natalie about the tiny seedling that had taken root in her subconscious. If her dad put Vic in charge, Chelsea might not end things with Nolan. She'd be in for even more lecturing if anyone got wind of that.

"I think the secret," Chelsea continued, "is to recognize what makes you happy and go after it."

Nine

Nolan was alone in the living room of the house he'd grown up in, talking on the phone to Chelsea. He'd agreed to have dinner with Heath but planned on joining Chelsea at his place later for dessert. They'd been together every night this week, but tonight was different—she was staying over for the first time. Since it was Friday night, she had the weekend free and was planning to spend her time off with him. The sleepover marked another stage in their relationship, and Nolan was surprised how smoothly things were progressing between them.

"Looking forward to seeing you later," he murmured into his phone, unable to resist a smile as he added in sultry tones, "And, of course, I mean *all* of you."

"The feeling is mutual," Chelsea replied in the throaty purr that drove him wild. "Eight o'clock. Don't be late."

She often said things like that, a holdover from other men she'd dated, who'd disappointed her by either being late all the time or not showing up at all. Nolan recognized it as a defense mechanism turned habit and promised he'd never give her a reason to doubt him.

"I won't."

The more time he spent in Chelsea's company, the harder it was to imagine any man standing her up. When they were apart, his thoughts were filled with her. No woman had ever appealed to him more. Her combination of intelligence, practicality and directness kept him on his toes, and their sexual chemistry was off the charts, leaving no doubt in his mind that she was as into him as he was into her.

In fact, the only negative thing about dating her had to do with her family and his being on opposite sides of the oil rights claim.

"You're seeing Chelsea again?" Heath asked, carrying two beers into the room and extending one to Nolan. He'd been in the middle of his own phone call when Nolan had arrived a few minutes earlier, a quick update from the lawyer, from what he'd overheard.

"Later tonight."

"Are you making any headway?" Heath's closed body language and the way he asked the question suggested he already knew Nolan was no longer on task.

He wasn't wrong.

As much as Nolan wanted to be on Heath's side, he could also sympathize with how afraid Chelsea was of what might happen to her family's ranch if Heath granted the rights to an oil company. That company would then be able to use the surface above the oil deposit as "reasonably necessary," and it was legally murky what that meant. After yesterday, when Chelsea had shown him a photo of her horse on her phone and told him all the things she loved about the ranch, he'd done some research and discovered that an oil company that leased the mineral rights could enter the property, build roads, use caliche found on the leased property, install pipelines to transport products from the lease, store equipment and inject salt water in disposal wells. Further, unless provisions were spelled out in the contract, an oil company could select the locations of wells and pipelines to be placed on the property without input from the surface owner.

The amount of destruction that could happen if Heath leased the rights to an oil company could devastate the Grandin and neighboring Lattimore ranches.

"I don't know if I'm making the sort of progress you'd be interested in." Picturing Chelsea as she'd looked the night before in his bed, Nolan sighed.

"You're sleeping with her." A declaration rather than a question, and one wrapped up in concern. "I suppose she's trying to win you over to her side."

"She's told me a few things about the ranch, and we've talked about the repercussions of having an oil company drilling on the land."

"I should've talked you out of getting to know her when you first spotted her on July Fourth." Heath looked grim as he studied his brother's face. "I was wrong to think you and I were on the same page."

The last thing Nolan wanted to do was disappoint his brother, but after Chelsea had explained the potential devastation to her ranch, he was no longer as committed to his brother's plan. Nor could he imagine a choice that would make them both happy.

This was the sort of conflict he usually avoided in his private life. Was it any wonder that he rarely stayed still long enough for trouble of a personal nature to manifest?

With his profession running him all over the world, he rarely formed attachments with women. He could keep up with his friends via text and video calls, but romantic relationships required him to be present in a way his business didn't permit.

Chelsea was different. With each day that passed, he was more consumed with wanting to be with her. To make love to her every day and sleep with her in his arms every night. Being away from her brought him physical pain and emotional distress. She was on his mind nonstop. He constantly caught himself wanting to send her links to interesting stories or ridiculous memes that he hoped would make her laugh.

"From the research I've done, it's bound to disrupt their operations and do permanent damage to their land," Nolan argued. "It just seems like there's enough destruction in the world." In the fifteen years he'd roamed the globe, Nolan had witnessed the slow-moving devastation that mankind was doing to the planet in the name of progress and capitalism.

"I really thought you were on my side."

"I am on your side," Nolan insisted, starting to realize that as long as he was involved with Chelsea, Heath would never believe him. "It's just that I have concerns."

Tension invaded Heath's body with each word Nolan uttered. The last thing Nolan wanted to do was worsen his relationship with his brother, but he couldn't turn his back on what was best for Chelsea and her family, either. Trapped as he was between a rock and a hard place, Nolan suspected if his feelings for Chelsea continued to grow, he would be forced to make a devastating choice.

"Have you wondered why Mom didn't assert her claim all these years?" Nolan asked. Was she too proud to take anything from Victor Grandin? Had Ladd Thurston known about the oil claim? Or had the couple decided that exercising the rights would've been more hassle than it was worth? "I mean, there were some lean years when the money would've been helpful."

"We'll never know why Mom stuffed the document in a drawer and never did anything about it." Heath's brown eyes hardened into smoky quartz. "Maybe she was bullied and afraid to take action."

Given the way the families were fighting against Heath, Nolan could see where the scenario played into his brother's narrative about why they should treat the Grandins and Lattimores as their enemies. Which didn't help Nolan's quandary. The thought of having to battle with Chelsea's family made Nolan's stomach twist. He didn't want to be stuck in the middle of a bitter fight.

"Or she didn't want to take anything from the Grandins," Nolan pointed out, hoping his brother might see the logic of this.

"I know there's no hard proof that Daniel Grandin was Ashley's father," Heath said, restating the premise that motivated his action. "But Mom's papers, and the fact that Victor Grandin gave her the oil rights, point to it."

On that they both agreed. Yet the circumstances that had led to the creation of the legal document were less clear.

"While all that's true, both Mom and Ashley are gone…"

Nolan couldn't imagine how awful the loss of their mother and sister had been for Heath. Even though Nolan hadn't been home for years, their loss had hit him hard. But Heath's grief had taken him to a very dark place. In the grip of strong emotions, when it came to the oil rights, there was no reasoning with him. Yet Nolan was determined to try.

"And I, for one, don't need the money." Nolan braced himself for the next part. "I'm loath to do harm just so we can become wealthier."

"I'm not doing this for us." Heath looked disappointed by Nolan's assumption.

"You're not?"

"No. All this is for Ashley. She started a foundation but died before getting it off the ground. The money will fund her legacy."

"Oh, wow!" The knot in Nolan's chest began to ease as Heath went on to explain Ashley's vision for the foundation.

Heath's explanation shone a whole new light on his obsession. Two years ago, after burying their mother and sister, the brothers had talked long into the night about their mutual loss. Sadly, their shared grief hadn't been enough to bridge the chasm between them created by misunderstanding, resentment and distance. Now Nolan wondered if he'd done even more damage by misreading Heath's motivation.

Yet he couldn't be sure if that's all there was to his brother's crusade. If all Heath wanted was to ensure Ashley's foundation lived on, then why hadn't he come out and said this earlier? Nolan wondered if Heath knew perfectly well the destruction an oil company could do and wanted to hurt the Grandins. It worried Nolan that Heath might have lost his way.

"I want to do right by our sister," Nolan said. "And I know it's important to you that she live on through the foundation, but is it worth destroying someone else's dream in the process?"

"You mean Chelsea's dream?"

The accusation hit home, but Nolan pictured her beautiful face and worried brown eyes, his resolve hardening. "She's just trying to save her family's ranch."

"You realize that both sides can't win." Heath looked unconcerned by his brother's dilemma.

"Yeah, I guess I do."

Chelsea lay on her stomach, legs bent, feet in the air while she flipped through the Sunday paper. Beside her on the king-size bed, Nolan drank coffee and read the sports section. He wore only a pair of boxers, and Chelsea had a hard time focusing on the headlines.

"You know," she said, giving up trying to read and ogling Nolan from beneath her lashes. She adored all his rippling muscles and bronze skin. Nibbling on her lower lip, she pondered how wonderful it had been to wake up snuggled against him that morning and savor his fingertips roving over her curves. "Of all the things we've done these last few weeks, I think this is my favorite."

"Personally, I liked the cowgirl museum." Nolan looked absolutely serious. "It gave me a much greater appreciation of all the contributions the women of Texas have made."

If another man had said this, Chelsea might take it as sarcasm, but Nolan had shown such a genuine interest in all the exhibits. In fact, the entire time she'd known him, every reaction he displayed rang true. It was refreshing to date someone and not have to speculate where his head was. If she wanted to know his opinion, all she had to do was ask. He would give her insight into what was on his mind.

"That was nice, but I'm happiest when we're hanging out. Like this." She gestured with her hand to indicate the bed. "I hope we get a lot more weekends like this." She noted his fleeting frown, and doubt crept in. "I suppose that's not likely to happen. You are probably going to be contacted about a project anytime now." He'd mentioned that several of the production studios he'd worked with in the past were in the development stage for new and returning shows.

"I'm not sure I'm ready to leave Royal," he said, inflating her hopes once more. "But I've been thinking how much I'd like to take you to all the places I've loved the most, and then I remember you don't want to be away from the ranch."

His comment zipped through her like an electric shock. It was exciting to hear that she wasn't the only one pondering their future. The connection between them seemed to grow stronger every day.

"I've been thinking about that, too," she admitted. "Ever since meeting you, I've realized I need to expand my horizons beyond Texas. Maybe after things are settled with..." She trailed off in horror.

By mutual consent, neither of them had mentioned the oil rights issue during their time together. Chelsea recognized that eventually being on opposite sides of the issue was going to blow up in their faces, but she'd been enjoying Nolan's company far too much to make waves.

Nolan put aside the paper and rolled onto his side, facing her. He took her hand in his and brought her palm to his lips. "I think we both know that the situation between our families is going to get worse.

Heath told me he's doing this for Ashley. She started a foundation before she died, and Heath wants to use the money from the oil rights to fund the charity. He wants her name to be remembered."

"That's a wonderful gesture." Chelsea snuggled against Nolan, buried her face in his neck and breathed in his warm, masculine scent. Just being near him brought her comfort. "Enough talk about families. Let's live in this moment and forget everything else."

"I'm down for that," Nolan said, capturing her lips for a long, lingering kiss. "What do you wanna do today?"

Breathless and giddy, Chelsea grinned. "You."

"I'm down for that, too."

Chelsea quivered as his fingertips drifted along her bare thigh. Immediately desire awakened, and a hot hum of longing throbbed between her thighs. She sighed as he stroked the hair off her neck and nuzzled the sensitive skin below her ear. No matter where the man touched, her body came alive. He took her hand, and she thrilled to the physical connection that sent her emotions spiraling. She loved the way he toyed with her hair. This lightest of touches caused goose bumps to break out on her body.

His hands roamed down her chest, long fingers circling her breasts. Pleasure shot through her as he gently captured her nipples through the thin T-shirt she wore and tweaked with enough pressure to make her gasp. The pain awakened her desire, and Chelsea dug her nails into his sides as he skimmed the shirt off her body and closed his mouth over one tight bud.

She parted her legs and rocked her silk-clad core against the steely length of him. He moaned as wildfire streaked through her veins, setting her on fire. Her breath hitched as he sent his fingers diving beneath the waistband of her panties. He caressed the seam between her thigh and body, tantalizingly far from where she needed him most. Anticipation of his touch made her vibrate. Every fiber of her screamed for him to stroke into her wetness and fill her up. As he continued to deny her, Chelsea squirmed in an effort to show him how badly she needed him.

"Look at me."

Her lashes felt as if they were dipped in concrete as she struggled to obey his command. The heat in his eyes made her feel unique and desirable, as if she was the only woman he'd ever wanted like this. It changed her, turned her on, took her to a place of reckless bliss she never wanted to leave.

"Now say my name," he demanded in a rough voice.

"Nolan."

His smile broke her into pieces and then made her whole again. It was an expression of satisfaction and wicked eagerness. He slipped her panties down her thighs, the silky fabric grazing across her feverish skin, making her burn even hotter.

"You are gorgeous," he murmured. "The most amazing woman I've ever met. And I'm dying to taste you." He shifted downward, sliding along her body. "Spread your legs for me."

Chelsea did as he asked, biting her lip as he set his

hands on her thighs and moved his shoulders between them. She was spiraling up to heaven, and he hadn't even gone anywhere near her. Her breath caught as he bent down and sent his tongue lapping through her wetness. Momentarily blinded by a lightning strike of pure pleasure, Chelsea forgot how to breathe as her entire world narrowed to Nolan and the sensation of his hands, lips and tongue driving her mad.

She sank her fingers into his thick, dark hair, anchoring herself to him as he drove her burning need hotter and hotter still. Nothing had ever felt as true or as real as Nolan making love to her. He transported her to places she'd never dreamed existed. Her hips bucked as he flicked his tongue against her clit and then sucked. Incoherent babble broke from her throat as he slid two fingers into her. She bucked against him, her head falling back as she lost herself in the scrape of his stubble, the softness of his lips and the driving hardness of his fingers.

His name poured from her lips and careened around the walls of the loft. She'd never been so glad that the building was built so well as her climax built and her frantic ramblings grew louder. Then she was coming on his mouth, driven by his tongue into a wild, moaning frenzy as she begged for more, rocking against him, tugging on his hair, writhing harder, faster, panting erratically as she fell off the edge and soared.

She was shaking in the aftermath as he kissed his way up her body and nuzzled into her neck. Belatedly, Chelsea realized she'd never released her death grip on his hair and was shocked at the effort it took to unclench her fingers and send her palms gliding over his bare shoulder.

Despite the rigid length of him pressed against her hip that proclaimed he was ready for round two, Nolan seemed content to let his hands and lips drift over her skin.

"That was amazing," she murmured as his tongue drew lazy circles along her collarbone. "You are incredibly gifted."

His breath puffed against her skin as he chuckled. "Glad you think so."

Being with Nolan made her more deliriously happy than she'd ever imagined possible. This was the relationship she'd longed for all her life. The one that had always seemed so elusive. They connected so perfectly that she was convinced they were soul mates.

Chelsea snatched the thought to her chest, imagining how such a declaration would be ridiculed by everyone she loved. Until meeting Nolan, she hadn't realized how narrow her focus had become. By contrast, Nolan's outside-the-norm experiences fascinated her. He meditated unusual deals, acquired amulets to protect the wearer from harm, spoke three languages and had done things most people only read about.

With the amount of time they were spending together, they both realized their need for companionship had been growing. They'd discussed how their contrasting perspectives about family had led to regrets. He'd admitted that although he'd spent half his life avoiding Royal, he felt guilty about the time he'd lost with his mother and sister, adding that he wanted to mend his relationship with Heath. In response, she'd shared that her competitive nature had put her at odds with her siblings. And she'd begun to realize that by focusing all her energy on the ranch, her work-life balance was skewed.

Chelsea found him a great listener. She shared her passion for her family's long history on the land. She knew he wouldn't truly be able to appreciate what it meant to have deep roots and multiple generations growing up on the same acreage. Although he had grown up on a ranch, unlike his brother, Nolan had no attachment to the land. His values weren't in acquiring and maintaining property but in discovering new places and enjoying experiences. Still, she had hoped that her enthusiasm for growing her family's ranching legacy would persuade him to her side.

Although Chelsea hadn't gone so far as to ask him if he'd be willing to convince his brother to drop the claim, she was certain that he'd been sympathetic when she discussed her fears about how her family's land would be damaged by oil companies drilling on the property. He'd seen the devastation wrought by the deforestation of the rain forests in Brazil.

Yet even as she thought she'd won him to her side, Chelsea wasn't sure his help would matter in the end. According to Nolan, Heath was bulldozing ahead with the claim, and although Nolan contended that his brother wasn't solely motivated by wealth, he hadn't explained what was driving Heath.

Oh, why had her grandfather given the oil rights to Cynthia?

"You're tensing up," Nolan commented, his lips gliding into the hollow between her breasts. "What are you thinking about?"

Although she'd spoken freely about so many of her secret desires and the insecurities she kept hidden, the one thing Chelsea couldn't share with Nolan was her anger with Heath over the situation he'd inflicted on her family. The last thing she wanted to do was create conflict between herself and Nolan over something that wasn't his fault. The fact that both of them would eventually have to pick sides was a dark cloud hanging over them.

So she projected an image that she was fine. Pretended to be strong and confident while, inside, her emotions were a Gordian knot of dread.

And instead of confessing what was at the top of her mind, she tackled something that had been brewing for several days. "Do you think we should come out of the closet, so to speak?"

Nolan lifted his head and arched one dark eyebrow at her. "What do you have in mind?"

"Maybe drinks at the Texas Cattleman's Club." Chelsea let out her breath on the suggestion, relieved that he hadn't balked.

"Followed by dinner?"

"We could…" She trembled as his fingers trailed over her abdomen. Reaching up, she stroked her palm over his shoulder, appreciating the solid muscle beneath his warm skin. "It might kick up a whole lot of dust, but I'm so happy that we're dating, and I want everyone to know it."

Plus, if her family saw how good things were between them, how great they were together, surely they'd come around. Her parents were always telling her they only wanted her to be happy. This would be a quick way to see if that was true.

When several seconds had passed and Nolan hadn't responded, uneasiness stirred. Had she misread their relationship? Maybe Heath didn't know Nolan was dating her and he wanted to keep it that way to avoid conflict.

"Unless you don't want to go public," she said, offering him a way out.

"You have to live here. It's more of an issue for you."

Chelsea wasn't sure how to take his response. He wasn't wrong that she had stronger ties to the community than he did, but should she infer that he didn't care about other people's opinions because they weren't important to him—or because he wasn't planning on being in Royal much longer?

Instead of mulling over the issue, Chelsea decided not to spend any more of her Sunday worrying about what might happen in the future. She was in bed with a sexy, half-naked man who deserved her full attention. Making love with Nolan was a much better use of her energy. Chelsea reached between them and took his erection in her hand, loving the way he sucked in a sharp breath as she circled her fingers over the velvety head. She could deal with the rest of the world later.

With a smile, she bent down and flicked her tongue over the bead of moisture on the tip.

Much later.

Ten

Nolan's phone rang as he slid his Jeep into an empty space in the Texas Cattleman's Club parking lot. He glanced at the display as he shut off the engine and grimaced as he recognized the caller. Lyle Short, a producer for GoForth Studios, had warned him a week ago that the studio was close to green-lighting the latest season of their unscripted series *Love in Paradise*. When Nolan had left LA a couple months earlier, he'd left behind several projects in the development stage that would eventually need his attention. Before heading to Royal, he'd submitted preliminary reports on the reconnaissance he'd accomplished, but none of the studio heads had settled on any locations.

"Hey, Lyle," Nolan said. "What news do you have for me?"

"We reviewed your reports and have decided to locate next season in Bora Bora. Can you meet with us at one o'clock tomorrow? We just forwarded all the specs to your assistant, so you will know what we are looking for."

"About that..." The pressure to immediately jump on a plane and head to the South Pacific constricted his chest like a hungry python. "I'm still in Royal. Things here are a little out of sorts at the moment. How much time do I have before you need the location finalized?"

"By the end of the month." Lyle chuckled. "I guess that's the end of next week. You'll see our notes in what we sent to you. We've made some changes to this season's scenario, so there will be a few more arrangements for you to make."

Nolan cursed silently. "That quick?"

He hadn't been prepared to exit Royal so abruptly. It wouldn't sit well with Heath, who was counting on his support in dealing with the Lattimore and Grandin families. Of course, Nolan wasn't handling his dealings with Chelsea to his brother's satisfaction. Which brought up the other reason he was reluctant to leave Royal at this moment—his connection to Chelsea was growing each day. It was too soon to decide if it made sense to take their relationship to the next level, but if he left now, based on how her relationships had ended in the past, Nolan suspected she'd be resistant to a long-distance relationship.

"What's going on, Nolan? It isn't like you to hesitate."

"I know I've always been the first one on a plane, but my brother asked me to come home to help him out with some things, and I really need more time."

"How much time?" Lyle's frown came through loud and clear.

"A couple months."

"I'm not sure that's going to work for us. What's the soonest you could be available?"

"I'd like to give my brother a heads-up. Can I let you know tomorrow?"

Although Nolan used his brother as an excuse for stalling, he recognized that his reluctance centered on Chelsea. The feelings she aroused in him were too new and too scary for him to speak them out loud.

"Sure. But, Nolan, you've already put in a lot of work on this project," Lyle reminded him. "If you can't meet the deadline, we may be forced to turn the job over to someone else."

"I get it." Nolan didn't feel threatened at all by Lyle's ultimatum. It was the nature of the business that production studios were hog-tied by impossible timelines, tight budgets and the constant pressure to produce the next hot thing. "I promise I'll let you know tomorrow if I'm going to do the job or pass."

"Because I know you and how you work, we can wait until tomorrow morning for your answer." Lyle sounded regretful, as if he sensed that Nolan was going to turn down the project.

"Thanks. I owe you one."

He'd come to a crossroad. He either needed to leave Royal and return to his old life or attempt some sort of hybrid situation so he could stay in town part-time while scaling back his traveling and relying on his staff more. Nolan's gut was telling him he was going to pass on this one. He just wasn't ready to leave Royal. Staying away for so long had done too much damage to his relationship with Heath.

Although he'd made inroads with Heath, the brothers had a long way to go before they could be considered close again. If he left now, he risked alienating his brother again. One thing Nolan had decided in the last few weeks was that he didn't want to keep isolating himself from those he cared about the most.

And then there was Chelsea. He'd never been so preoccupied with a woman before. He wanted to be with her all the time, and when they were apart, he struggled to keep his attention focused on matters at hand. If he left now, he might never find out if they could work. Yet was he being a fool to risk his business for a woman he'd only known a couple weeks?

With uncertainty jangling his nerves, Nolan headed toward the entrance to the Texas Cattleman's Club clubhouse, where he was meeting Chelsea for drinks. Choosing to meet at this particular location meant they were publicly stating that they were seeing each other. Up until now, they'd kept a pretty low profile by going outside the city limits of Royal for their dates. While Nolan was ready to let everyone know he was into Chelsea, he recognized that the decision didn't carry a lot of risk for him. He was a relative stranger in town, and with the exception of his brother, Heath, no one really cared whom he was dating.

Chelsea, on the other hand, had family and friends to answer to. No doubt letting everyone know they were a couple was a greater risk for her. Which was why it had surprised Nolan when she'd suggested they be seen together at the Texas Cattleman's Club. Yet despite his surprise, he was also deeply moved that she didn't want to keep the relationship hidden anymore. That had to mean she was serious about him. Which was why he was so conflicted about the project in Bora Bora.

Riddled with clashing emotions, Nolan crossed the threshold and entered the cool dimness of the lobby. After the brightness outside, he was momentarily blind and paused to let his eyes adjust. A shape blocked his path before he'd fully transitioned, and Nolan stepped aside to let the other pass. To his surprise, instead of walking past, the man stopped and greeted him.

"Here to meet my sister, Thurston?"

Nolan might not have recognized the unfriendly voice, but the question made his identity clear. Vic Grandin, Chelsea's brother. Was this the first of many confrontations with a member of Chelsea's family?

"I am," Nolan replied, maintaining a neutral tone as his instincts warned him to be cautious.

"You know that Chelsea is only dating you to find out what you and your brother are up to about the oil rights."

Vic's words went through Nolan like lightning.

He flushed hot and then cold as the disquiet he'd suppressed these last few weeks awakened with a roar. At a loss for what tack to take as a response, Nolan arched an eyebrow and struggled to keep the hit from showing on his face. If Vic was telling the truth, Nolan had been an idiot to open his heart to Chelsea. Yet their time together had been so perfect. Too perfect?

"Don't tell me you're worried about my welfare." Nolan could see his sarcastic rebuke hadn't shut down the other man. Vic was too determined to make a point.

"I just hate to see a guy get played."

"What makes you think that's what's happening?" Nolan was proud that his voice didn't reflect how Vic's insinuation had twisted him up inside. The gut punch of this exchange with Chelsea's brother had shattered the romantic bubble Nolan had been existing in. "It could be your sister and I are merely enjoying each other's company."

"Maybe you're into her, but Chelsea is all about the ranch. She has no personal life. Doesn't give any men in town the time of day. And then you come along, and suddenly she's taking time off and neglecting her responsibilities." Vic sounded put out by this last part. "Don't get me wrong, it's been great to see her screw up. She's always so organized and efficient. But she always puts the ranch first."

Nolan slid his hands into his pockets and regarded the other man in silence.

"Chelsea always thinks she knows best." As Vic

continued his rant, his bitterness came through loud and clear. "She thinks she should be the one in charge of Grandin Ranch."

"She's right," Nolan replied calmly, seeing his matter-of-fact reply struck home.

"She believes if she's the one who saves the ranch from you and you brother, our dad will be convinced that she should run things."

Taking Vic's words at face value was tricky, but the explanation was too plausible for Nolan to ignore. Given what Chelsea had shared with him about her struggles with her brother over control of the ranch, it made sense that she would do whatever it took to win. Even use Nolan.

"Do you know this for a fact or are you guessing?" Nolan had entertained the same conclusion in the beginning.

"It's a fact. She told my whole family that's what she's doing."

"Maybe she told you that to keep you all off her back about being with me."

"Well, well, well." Vic's hearty chuckle was riddled with mockery. "Looks like she has you good and fooled."

Incensed that by defending his relationship with Chelsea, he'd played into Vic's hands, Nolan ground his teeth. "If that's true, and I'm not saying it is, seems to me that by giving me a heads-up about this, you're making trouble for your sister. You must be nervous that she's going to win."

"The ranch is mine."

This glimpse into the other man's motivation didn't ease Nolan's disquiet. Nor did it make his own regret any less potent.

"Maybe if you spent less time sabotaging your sister and more time working as hard as she does, then you wouldn't have anything to worry about." Nolan saw his retaliatory strike hit home. Not surprisingly, this didn't ease the ache in his own chest. "Now, if you'll excuse me."

Nolan brushed past the younger man and headed toward the bar, but as he walked along the wide hallway, he couldn't help but replay his conversation with Vic. Perhaps both he and Chelsea had started out misleading each other, but somewhere along the line, his emotions had engaged.

He was no longer merely interested in her as a way to help his brother. He'd actually begun to consider what sort of relationship she would want when determining his future plans. Given what was going on between their families, he'd known their relationship would be buffeted by negative outside opinions. Nolan had believed that they could weather the storm together. That their ever-strengthening connection would be the bedrock they could build a foundation on. Now it appeared as if the whole thing had been nothing more than a fantasy.

His steps slowed.

So, if he was being played, like Vic claimed, the question of whether he should stay in Royal or take the job in Bora Bora might have just been answered. It might be smart to get away for a while and clear his head. Suddenly, Nolan found himself veering away from the bar.

Heath would not be happy, but Nolan could make him understand. He would just assure his brother that after the location scout, he would return to Royal. He'd only be gone a few weeks. Surely that would be enough time to sort out his feelings for Chelsea and lead with his head and not his heart.

Convinced he was making the right decision, Nolan retraced his steps through the clubhouse and shoved open the door to the outside. He hit the redial button on his phone. The call rolled into voice mail.

"Lyle, hey, it's Nolan. Things have changed here, so I'm available to head to Bora Bora as soon as I can assemble my team. I'm headed back to LA tonight, and I'll see you at the 1:00 p.m. meeting tomorrow."

Chelsea had dressed with care for her rendezvous with Nolan at the Texas Cattleman's Club. She'd borrowed from Natalie a ruched, off-the-shoulder dress in black that hugged her curves, and paired it with black-and-white sandals. Although Nolan loved when she wore her hair down, he also loved plucking the pins free and sending it cascading around her shoulders. Tonight, she'd fastened the mass of chocolate waves into a free-spirited bun with face-framing tendrils. Big gold hoops swung from her ears, and a gold tennis bracelet sparkled on her wrist.

When Chelsea had suggested she and Nolan meet for drinks and dinner at the social hub for her family, friends and neighbors, she'd been on an emotional high after spending the weekend with him. They'd had an amazing time together, and Chelsea's confidence in their strengthening relationship had led her to feel invincible. As long as they faced all opposition together, she was convinced they could overcome everyone's negative opinions.

Unfortunately, two days later, Chelsea was seeing the situation from a more pragmatic point of view, and the excuse she'd been using with her family—that she was seeing Nolan as a way of spying on him and his brother—was going to fall apart when they saw the fondness Chelsea couldn't hide. So she'd convinced Natalie to join her and Nolan for drinks, hoping that having a third person along would prevent anyone from making a public scene.

She'd thought she was prepared for anything, but Nolan neglecting to show blindsided her.

Natalie's gaze flicked to her watch. "You're sure he knew you were meeting at six?"

"He confirmed this afternoon." Her voice sounded as if it was fraying around the edges. "He always texts me to verify we're on. Even before I told him about how Brandon ghosted me, he was great at touching base. He knows it's a sensitive issue for me."

"It's a little after seven," Natalie said cautiously.

Chelsea was well aware what time it was. She felt the tick of each second like the poke of a needle against her skin. For the last forty-five minutes, her emotions had run the gamut between panic, annoyance and deep hurt. Logically, she knew it was ridiculous to let herself be bothered by his lateness, but Nolan was either on time or early, and if he was running late, he would've let her know. Since he'd confirmed that they were meeting at the Texas Cattleman's Club today, all she could think was that he'd gotten cold feet at the last second. This was a big move for them. Today they were broadcasting to all of Royal that they were seeing each other.

"I'm sure he's just running late," Chelsea said, refusing to entertain that it was anything other than an unavoidable delay.

She was convinced that if he'd been able to, Nolan would've let her know what time he'd arrive. Maybe he was having car trouble and was stranded in a zone with no cell service. There were numerous places around Royal like that. Or he could've been in an accident or damaged his phone. She told herself to be patient. Just because he hadn't yet arrived, and hadn't called to let her know he was on his way or that he couldn't make it, didn't mean anything dire had happened.

"It's weird that he hasn't called or texted," Natalie said, her musing scraping Chelsea's raw nerves. "You said he's really good about staying in touch."

"He really is." Chelsea picked up her phone, hoping she'd just missed the notification of his text. Nothing. "It's possible he lost track of time."

"Sure." Pity flickered in Natalie's brown gaze. "That must be it."

Or should she surmise from his delay that he really didn't care about her? Had his innate charm led her to read too much into all his romantic gestures and the amazing sex? What if she wasn't special to him? No doubt she was the most recent in a string of women he'd hooked up with and moved on from. Since he probably didn't linger in a single place for more than a few days, she wouldn't be surprised if she was his longest relationship ever. Rather than flattered, Chelsea felt ashamed of herself for ignoring all the signs.

"You're really bugging out right now, aren't you?" Natalie was peering at her in concern.

"No. Of course not." Chelsea huffed out a pathetic chuckle. "I mean, he's just running late. No big deal."

"For many people, it's probably not a big deal, but you hate tardiness, and I'm sure you're feeling panicky right about now."

"A little panicky. He's never done anything like this before." But then, she'd only been dating him a few weeks. Shouldn't she have suspected that dating a man who was constantly on the move made for an unreliable relationship? "I'm worried something has happened to him."

"Do you want to message him again?"

"I already sent him a text, but he hasn't responded." Chelsea ground her teeth, fighting her worst instincts. "I'm sure he will when he gets the chance."

"And while we wait for him to reply, why don't we have another drink?"

They'd been sipping red wine, but when Chelsea got the bartender's attention, she ordered a shot of whiskey. Ignoring Natalie's worried frown, she tossed back the entire drink. Her eyes teared up as the strong liquor scorched her throat. She gave an inadvertent cough and blinked rapidly.

"Smooth," she muttered, hitting the bartender with a determined stare and gesturing for another shot.

After the second whiskey, a comforting warmth spread through her body, transforming her agitation into reckless disregard. Damn the man. She'd actually let herself trust him. So much so that she'd opened up her heart. She'd ignored everyone's warnings to be cautious. Instead, she'd plowed straight into danger, confident in her judgment. Which, in hindsight, had been completely idiotic. When had she ever done the right thing when it came to her love life? As shrewd as she could be when making decisions for the ranch, the instant she turned over control to her heart, she stopped perceiving reality and created a fantasy based on what she craved.

"Okay," Natalie said, waving the bartender away when Chelsea tried to order her fourth shot. "I think you've had enough."

With her head buzzing, Chelsea was consumed by a sudden urge to emote. "I really love you. You know that, right?" Although she was feeling fairly foggy around the edges, she maintained enough of her faculties to rationalize that keeping her emotions bottled up had led to the explosive pressure that resulted in her making bad decisions regarding Nolan. Maybe if she'd opened herself up more all along, she wouldn't have been so needy when he entered her life.

"I love you, too," Natalie said, laughter edging her

voice. She put her hand atop Chelsea's and squeezed gently. "I'm really sorry Nolan did this to you."

It just couldn't be happening. He'd seemed unruffled by her suggestion that they take their relationship public. Had she misread him? Worse, had she pressured him? Was that what had caused Nolan's abrupt change in behavior? The logical part of her tried to shut down her overly emotional response to Nolan's absence and his lack of communication. But she'd been here before, geared up for a relationship-changing event, only to be left hanging. Was it any wonder she couldn't slow the torrent of insecurity and doubt that washed away every joyful moment she'd spent in Nolan's company?

"You know, it's fine," Chelsea ground out, resentment racing through her.

The dark emotion exploded outward from her aching heart and speared straight into her insecurities. Ghosted again. And by Nolan. What made it worse was that he knew how sensitive she was to being dropped. She'd trusted him and spilled all her fears and self-doubt.

"I mean, it's not like he and I make any sense whatsoever," she went on, grief making her swing wildly. "He's never going to settle down in Royal, and I'm never going to leave here. Everybody got on my case about why I was seeing him and telling me I was so foolish to get involved. Except I'm not foolish." She jabbed her finger into her chest, bruising her breastbone in the process. "I'm Chelsea freaking Grandin. I was using him to find out what he and his brother were planning about the oil rights. That makes me the smartest woman around."

"Ah, Chelsea." Natalie's gaze had gone past her friend, coffee-brown eyes opening wide in concern.

"I'm never going to get played by any man," Chelsea continued, her rant barreling forward unchecked. Damn the man for messing with her heart. He'd actually made her believe he cared. Bastard. "If anyone's doing the playing, it's me."

"That's good to know," came a hard voice.

As the deep timbre of Nolan's tone cut through the fog of Chelsea's misery, regret blazed through her, dispelling much of her self-pity. Enough remained, however, that she wore a scowl as she turned on her bar stool to face Nolan.

The hard planes of his face had never looked more chiseled as he stood like a statue before her. Only his eyes glittered with reproach, making her heart cower. But instead of apologizing for anything she said, Chelsea tilted her chin and went on the offensive.

"So, you decided to finally show up."

He nodded tersely. "I didn't want to leave town without seeing you in person one last time."

"You're leaving?" She heard herself sounding like a small, disappointed child and cursed. "When?"

"Tonight. I'm flying back to LA. There's a project waiting for me, and I have to meet with the producers to get all the specs before I head out to Bora Bora."

The moment she'd been dreading. He was leaving Royal. Leaving her.

"I guess I shouldn't be surprised. You were bound to go at some point."

"Yeah." A muscle jumped in his cheek as he stared down at her. "Too bad you didn't get what you needed before I left."

For a second, she had no idea what he was talking about, and then she realized that he'd heard her whole speech about how she'd only dated him to find out what he and Heath were up to. She froze in horror. She'd stopped pursuing that angle almost immediately. His company had been too enjoyable for her to jeopardize by scheming.

In the weeks since they'd started dating, she'd recognized that her desire to run the ranch had become so important because it was a substitute for the love she wasn't finding in her personal life. She couldn't control her romantic victories, but she could work damned hard to convince her father to give her Grandin Ranch.

"So, you're done with Royal? You're not coming back at all?"

"I don't know." His gaze raked over her. "I still have some unfinished business here."

Chelsea trembled as a familiar heat burned her up. She loved this man. She'd gone and done the one thing she shouldn't—she'd fallen hard. And now she was going to lose him unless she was brave enough to explain that his not showing up had triggered all her insecurities.

"What sort of unfinished business?" She held her breath and waited for the answer she craved.

"I came back to Royal to help out my brother—"

"Of course. It's all about the claim. All along, I figured that's why you hit on me in the first place. Was it your idea or your brother's?" Chelsea couldn't stop her stupid fear from continuing to push him away. "Did Heath tell you about my terrible track record with men? You probably assumed I'd be easy to charm. And I guess you were right."

Nolan scowled at her. "That's not it at all."

"No?" Chelsea couldn't bring herself to confront him directly. Staring into his gorgeous brown eyes always made her melt inside. She couldn't afford to be weak now. "Seems to me after you struck out with my sister, you decided I'd be easier pickings. And I guess I was."

"I never once saw you as easy pickings. And I never hit on your sister. I approached her with the idea that we should talk about the claim, not because I wanted to date her."

"So you're saying you wanted to date me?" She gave a rough laugh. The ache in her chest grew with every syllable he uttered. "Or maybe getting me into bed was just a side benefit to your scheme."

Beside her, Natalie gasped. Tears sprang to Chelsea's eyes, but she blinked them back. She was saying all the wrong things. They both were. In the deepest levels of her heart, she didn't for one second believe that Nolan had been manipulating her. They were both attacking because they were afraid and hurt. And neither of them was brave enough to stop.

"You're accusing me of scheming after admitting

that the only reason you started seeing me was to use me to get my brother to drop the claim?" His lips twisted into a sneer. "That's really rich."

"So you're telling me that you never once considered I could be useful where your family's claim was concerned?"

"Maybe in the beginning—"

"Ha!" she interrupted, crowing in satisfaction even as his confirmation made her cringe inside.

"I said *in the beginning*," he reiterated. "Once I got to know you, and you explained the potential damage to your ranch, I really didn't want to pursue the claim. I tried to talk to my brother—"

"Stop. Please just stop. None of that matters. You're leaving, and that's all there is to it."

"Chelsea," he began, a deep throb in his voice that touched off a wildfire of sorrow inside her.

"Please don't. Whatever it is you want to say, just don't." Even now, after he'd admitted his true motivation for asking her out, he was still trying to charm her. But it was all lies. "No matter what motivated us to get together, we had fun. Let's just leave it at that. We took a swing and missed. No harm, no foul."

As she spouted platitudes, Nolan's expression grew ever more grim. "I guess we're both a couple of players. We used each other, and neither one of us came out the winner." He held out his hand like some sort of sports competitor.

Chelsea didn't want to touch him. To do so, to feel the warm, strong clasp of his hand around hers, would remind her of every time he'd ever touched her. Of the passion that burned so hot between them. Of how she'd loved waking up in his arms. Of the way she'd started dreaming of a future for them.

"It's a draw." She gripped his hand, squeezing hard as she focused on pretending he was nothing more than a business associate in a busted deal. "Good luck in Bora Bora."

She didn't realize until she was halfway to the exit that she'd left her friend behind. Chelsea was so close to losing it that there was no way she could hesitate or stop. Her heart was slowly shattering with each step she took. As the distance between her and Nolan increased, she was terrified that if she looked back, she wouldn't be able to prevent herself from breaking down. As it was, she barely made it to the ladies' room. Her stomach began to turn as she pushed through the door and scrambled for a stall.

The three whiskey shots came up, acid burning her throat in the aftermath of her encounter with Nolan. Tears stung her eyes while ice raced through her veins, making her shake uncontrollably. Her entire world had just ripped apart. Losing the ranch to Vic wouldn't have hurt a fraction of what she was going through as her relationship with Nolan ended. Chelsea stuffed her fist into her mouth and bit down on her knuckles to stop herself from surrendering to the sobs that threatened.

"Chelsea, are you okay?" Natalie had entered the bathroom without Chelsea hearing the door open.

"Of course I'm fine. Why wouldn't I be?" Her overly perky tone failed to mask the bitterness beneath. She'd spent too much of her adult life being strong and never showing weakness. When it came to the ranch or her personal life, she couldn't bear to let anyone think she was anything other than one hundred percent in control.

This outward show of strength, however, didn't work on Natalie. The two women had shared all the ups and downs of both career and personal lives. Natalie was probably the only person on earth who knew all Chelsea's demons.

"Because for the first time ever, you didn't play it safe?" Natalie suggested, her tone gentle and sympathetic. "You let Nolan all the way in."

And in the process, she'd let herself be blindsided.

"I am such an idiot," Chelsea moaned, resting her head against the cool metal of the stall wall. "Why didn't I listen when everybody told me not to get involved with Nolan?"

"Because you two are the real deal."

"Did you not listen to what he just said?" Chelsea unlocked the stall door and stepped out. She avoided Natalie's gaze and stared at her own reflection. Pale face. Enormous, haunted brown eyes. She looked dazed, as if she'd been kicked in the head by a horse. "It was all just a big game to him. And I made such a fool of myself, thinking we had a future. I'll bet he and Heath had a great time laughing at how needy I was."

Natalie let out a weary sigh. "He didn't much look like a man who'd come to gloat. In fact, while you were talking, before you knew he was there, he looked like he's been hit upside the head with a two-by-four."

"No doubt he was surprised that he'd been played in turn."

"I don't think so. He didn't look angry or chagrined. He really looked devastated."

"Well, he's a good actor. He had me completely bamboozled."

"What if the same thing happened to him that happened to you?" Natalie asked. "What if he started out dating you to see what he could find out about the oil rights and ended up falling for you?"

"I'd be more inclined to believe that if he hadn't declared that's why he'd been dating me."

But her words were sheer bravado. Chelsea wanted to believe that at some point he'd begun to care for her. Surely, after all her dating failures, she wouldn't have slept with him if she hadn't sensed genuine emotion.

"Maybe he was just reacting to what you said to save face," Natalie argued. "The way you did. I mean, it's not like after you went on and on about how you were playing him that he would come clean and admit that he had real feelings for you."

Deep inside she hoped Natalie was right. But as she recalled what he'd said, her confidence shrank.

"No. It's not like that." Chelsea shook her head, locked in the grip of her past romantic disasters. "And it doesn't matter, anyway. He's leaving. I'm staying. It was never going to work."

"That's a load of crap and you know it," Natalie declared. "That man makes you happy."

"So what if he does?"

"If you let him leave without telling him how you really feel, then you are not as strong and brave as I thought." Natalie fixed her with a challenging glare. "So, what's it going to be?"

Eleven

Nolan cursed the impulse that had prompted him to return to the Texas Cattleman's Club in time to hear Chelsea confirm her brother's accusations. After his confrontation with Vic, Nolan had been consumed by the need to get as far away from her as possible, so he'd headed back to his loft and made arrangements for a late-night flight to LA. But as he began to pack, it became pretty obvious that much of what he owned was tangled with a number of items Chelsea had left behind.

His instinct had been to toss everything. In fact, he'd been in the process of stuffing a pair of her jeans into a trash bag when he'd come across the T-shirt he'd bought for Chelsea at the cowgirl museum. Emblazoned on the red fabric was the slogan

Well-Behaved Cowgirls Rarely Make History, and Nolan recalled how she'd sauntered around the loft in the shirt, silk panties and her boots. That memory of her was only one of a hundred that had been burned into his brain like a brand. Her brand. He belonged to her in a way that was permanent and irreversible.

The initial shock following his conversation with Vic had worn off by then. He'd rationalized that Chelsea's brother had been making mischief. What better way to mess with his sister than to interfere with her love life? Especially when she was already extraordinarily vulnerable from being treated badly by the previous men she'd dated.

It was then that he'd decided he couldn't leave Royal without seeing her. In retrospect, he should've texted or called her as he was on his way to the airport. He might've saved himself the pain of hearing her brother's accusation confirmed. She had been using him from the start in an effort to save her family's ranch. As much as Nolan had wished it otherwise, Vic Grandin had not been wrong. His sister had played him and nearly won.

Nolan decided to call Heath to let him know he was heading back to LA. While he waited for his brother to answer, Nolan let himself back into the loft to finish packing. Being on the road as much as he was, he was accustomed to packing light. When he'd arrived in town two months earlier, he'd brought little more than his clothes, his electronic devices and a few personal items. He'd signed a month-to-month lease on the fully furnished loft, which meant there was only a week to go. Even though the project in Bora Bora was a quick turnaround, Nolan wasn't sure when he'd be back in Royal. Or if he intended to return at all.

"Hey," Nolan said when Heath answered. "Just wanted to let you know that I'm on my way to LA to take a meeting with some producers. They want me to head to Bora Bora to scout a location for their upcoming show."

The abruptness of Nolan's decision must've caught his brother off guard, because it took him several seconds to respond.

"How long are you gonna be gone?"

A brusque intensity had entered Heath's tone. Was Nolan's brother recalling the first time the brothers had parted? A time when Nolan had disappeared, not to return until their mom and sister's funeral. He couldn't help but feel a familiar urgent need to escape Royal and clear his head.

Nolan wasn't sure what to say to his brother. Given what had happened with Chelsea, Nolan couldn't promise Heath he was coming back. Avoiding entanglements had kept Nolan from slowing down. He liked adventure and experiencing different cultures, but there was also a part of him of him that knew if he kept moving, it was nearly impossible to make the deep connections that lead to expectations, disappointments and heartache. Look at what he was feeling now. If he hadn't let down his guard and gone all in with Chelsea, he wouldn't feel like his insides were being shredded.

"I'm not sure." Feeling the way he was at the moment, Nolan didn't want to come back to Royal at all, but he also didn't want to disrupt the healing relationship between him and Heath. "It depends on the scope of the project."

"I see." From Heath's stiff response, Nolan could tell that his brother wasn't happy.

"I'll know more after the meeting tomorrow." Nolan hated that he felt guilty about disappointing his brother. Strong emotions like this were the exact thing he usually avoided. Yet he couldn't deny that reconnecting with his brother these last few months had made him happier than he'd been in quite some time. Maybe he could learn to take the bad with the good. Surely it would all balance itself out, and in the end, he would have a stronger relationship with his brother. "Look, I know it probably seems like I'm running out on you, but I really do need to get back to work."

"I thought maybe you'd stay in Royal and join me on the ranch."

For a second, Nolan couldn't breathe. He'd never imagined that Heath would offer up such an invitation. Heath had been managing the Thurston ranch since their father died. He'd never needed or wanted Nolan's help before. Why would he include him now?

"I don't think I'd be any help," Nolan said, unsure what to make of the offer. "I've forgotten more than I ever knew about ranching."

"That may be true, but it's been good having you

around." Heath's admission was another blow Nolan hadn't seen coming.

"It's been good being back here with you," Nolan echoed, his chest tight as emotion swept through him. "Makes me wish I hadn't stayed away as long as I did." Swallowing past the lump in his throat, Nolan fought down anxiety. Ever since his mom and sister had died, he'd been buffeted by an emotional storm. Coming home had stirred it further. Reconnecting with Heath was both a blessing and a curse. He liked feeling as if he belonged somewhere, yet at the same time the old tension between the brothers couldn't be resolved without talking through why Nolan had left in the first place.

"I get that work is taking you away. Don't worry about anything here. I just hope you know that you can come back anytime."

"Thanks. I appreciate your understanding. I'll be in touch."

Nolan ended the call and tossed his cell phone on the bed. The conversation with Heath had briefly taken Nolan's mind off his encounter with Chelsea, but as he emptied the closet and dresser drawer, his mind replayed the statements she'd made.

If asked, he never would've pegged her as someone who played games. She'd always struck him as straightforward, someone who believed in hard work and dealt with people honestly. To hear Vic's insinuations confirmed by her had absolutely blown him away. Maybe if he hadn't trusted her and given her the benefit of the doubt, he wouldn't feel like she'd carved out his heart.

A knock sounded on his door. Since the only person who ever visited him was the one person he didn't want to talk to at the moment, Nolan considered pretending he wasn't home, but no doubt she'd already seen that his car was parked in his reserved spot. So, he opened his door and found Chelsea standing in the hall.

"What are you doing here?" he asked, not bothering to moderate his unhappiness.

"I didn't like the way we left things and wanted to clear the air before you left."

He narrowed his gaze and took her in, recognizing her unsteadiness and trouble focusing. "You've been drinking."

"I was drinking before you showed up," she explained. "It's why I said what I did." Her gaze avoided his. "I didn't mean what you heard."

"So you didn't start dating me because of the oil rights claim?"

"Okay, that part was true. But once I got to know you, I stopped thinking of you as a means to an end."

Nolan heaved a sigh. "Why did you come here?"

"I didn't want you to leave Royal with us on bad terms."

She looked absolutely wretched, and Nolan remembered all the times when she'd let herself be vulnerable with him. When she'd shared the most humiliating, heartbreaking moments she'd been through. Had that all been an act to garner his sympathy? To make him want to cherish and protect her? Nolan no longer trusted her or his own reactions to her.

"What does it matter? I'm leaving and we're over."

She made no effort to hide her wince. "Is that what you want? For us to be over?"

What was she playing at? Nolan scrutinized her expression, seeing frustration and hopelessness. For someone who was usually so forthright, Chelsea was certainly dancing around whatever was on her mind.

"I don't know. After talking to your brother—"

"You talked to Vic?" Her eyebrows crashed together. "What did he say to you?"

Nolan was a little taken aback by her vehemence, until he realized this was a symptom of her fierce struggle for control of the ranch. "Exactly what you told Natalie in the bar. He said you've been playing me all along."

"When did you talk to my brother?"

"I was on my way into the Texas Cattleman's Club to meet you when I ran into Vic. He was pretty convincing." Nolan crossed his arms over his chest and stared down at her. "So much so that I decided to head to LA without saying goodbye."

Chelsea glowered while her hands clenched into fists. "He had no right to say anything to you."

"It took me a little while to realize that he might've been actively trying to cause trouble between us. But imagine how I felt after deciding to give you the benefit of the doubt, to show up and hear you echoing exactly what your brother had told me."

"I was upset. You didn't show up when you said

you would, and you weren't answering my texts. It brought up all the times that Brandon did the same thing before ghosting me entirely. I thought the same thing was happening all over, and I went a bit crazy. I had too much to drink and started spouting stupid stuff."

Nolan braced himself against the misery in her eyes even as his heart lurched. Her acute distress was causing his resolve to waver. He'd been ready to give her a chance to explain, even though logic told him her brother had been completely right.

"All great excuses, but the fact remains that you did date me in order to get information on what Heath planned to do about the oil rights."

"Are you trying to tell me that never crossed your mind when we were together?" Chelsea gave him a skeptical look. "Or that your brother put no pressure on you to spy on me in return?"

"So we're both a couple of opportunists." Nolan refused to feel guilty for his part in the scheme. He'd come back to Royal to support his brother, and he'd done a terrible job so far. Both he and Chelsea had known that one day they would have to pick a side, and today he was choosing Heath's.

Chelsea's warm brown eyes dominated her face, unshed tears making them appear larger than ever. "Does that mean everything you said to me was a lie?"

"No." She was amazing. Beautiful. Brilliant. As the tightness in his throat bottled up the words, Nolan's heart ached for what he was pushing away. "It's just that we landed on opposite sides of a bad situation, and even if we wanted to be together, too many things stand in the way."

"That was true in the beginning, and it's no different now," she agreed. "But we could make it work. I really want to give us a shot. Would you be willing to try?"

Would he? His life was a lot less complicated without her in it. The entreaty in her eyes almost sold him, but the turmoil in his chest was a discomfort he couldn't ignore. Was it possible that a mere hour ago he'd been heading to the Texas Cattleman's Club to declare to the public that he and Chelsea were a couple? He'd been happy at this big step in their relationship. Now, all he wanted to do was get away from her and ease the chaotic emotions roiling in him.

"I have this job in Bora Bora to do." It wasn't any kind of an answer, and from the way her shoulders sagged, it wasn't what she hoped to hear. "I don't know how long I'll be gone. If some of the other jobs come through while I'm there, it could be a long time."

"You sound like you're not coming back." She looked stricken. "Is this the end for us?"

Although Nolan had already accepted that they were finished, he reeled at the finality in her question. Before, he'd been so angry with her that he hadn't considered what being parted from her would truly mean. Now, with his outrage fading, he was at the mercy of all his memories of their time together. No woman had ever burrowed so deep into his heart, and the thought of leaving her behind was a knife twisting in his gut. He'd been ready to change his lifestyle for this woman, to make compromises and plan a future with her. But if he'd learned anything in the last hour, it was that the forces at work to keep them apart were stronger than their desire to be together.

"I guess we're lucky we didn't let ourselves get carried away," Nolan said, doing his best to keep his voice light. "At least this way we can part as friends."

"That's not what I want," she said, frowning as she realized how her statement came across. "I mean, I don't want to be parted from you."

Nolan hardened his heart against her entreaty. "So, you're willing to leave everything behind and come with me?"

Her expression said it all.

"I didn't think so." All of a sudden, he had to get away. From her. From Royal. From the longing that made him feel so empty inside. "I have to get to the airport. My flight leaves in a couple hours." He couldn't control the impulse that compelled him to bend down and place his lips against her forehead. "Take care of yourself, Chelsea."

And then he was walking out the door and out of her life for good.

Twelve

Nolan had never thoroughly scouted a location so fast in his life. Nor could he have managed to do even half of what he accomplished without his stellar staff. They worked tirelessly and seemed unfazed that their boss was being an unusually demanding asshole. Perhaps that was because after filling in his assistant about his legal and personal problems in Royal, he'd made sure his employees understood that his distraction and bad mood had nothing to do with the project or them.

It also helped that he'd bought several rounds in the resort bar where they were staying by way of apology.

Every one of the seven days after arriving in Bora Bora, he'd been beating himself up for how he'd left things with Chelsea. She'd pleaded with him to find a way to compromise so they could be together, and he'd been too afraid of his strong emotions to meet her halfway. Telling himself it would never work and that he was better off ending things before he was in too deep was idiotic. He'd never been so miserable. Usually getting on a plane to an exotic location was a cure for whatever ailed him. For the first time in his life, he couldn't wait to get home. And that *home* meant Royal, Texas, instead of Los Angeles was yet another hit to his belief system.

Yet what he longed for wasn't a place, but a person. Chelsea. She was the home his heart craved. The safe haven for his restless soul. Except he'd gone and blown it with her. The one thing he'd promised himself he'd never do, he'd done. He'd made her doubt him. Worse, he'd made her feel less than thoroughly desirable. Even if he returned and somehow convinced her to take him back, that breach of her trust would always be between them.

All that and more should've convinced him to get over her and move on, but with each hour they were apart, he was consumed by the need to run back to her. He hadn't achieved closure by leaving her behind in Royal. Her refusal to give up her life there and follow him around the world hadn't settled his mind about their lack of a future. He kept wondering what would've happened if he'd given in.

Which was why, after most of the details had been handled to his satisfaction, he'd turned the project over to his capable assistant and hopped on a plane back to Texas.

After landing in Dallas, he picked up a rental car and headed for Royal. Conscious that he couldn't speak his heart to Chelsea without first clearing the air with Heath, Nolan headed to the Thurston ranch. He found his brother in the barn, chatting with his foreman.

Heath looked surprised to see him. "You're back? From the way you talked, I thought you'd be gone for quite a while."

"I was running away again," Nolan admitted. "It seems that after fifteen years, it's something I still do."

"At least it didn't take you fifteen years to come back this time."

"Nope. This time I realized that what's most important to me is right here. I love you." Nolan wished he'd declared himself sooner. "I'm sorry I went away for so long. I want us to be close again." He paused to read Heath's expression, and although his brother was nodding in agreement, he seemed to be waiting for the rest of Nolan's intentions. "But this fight you're in with the Grandins is not for me."

"This is about Chelsea, isn't it?"

"I love her." He'd been tossing those three words over and over in his mind for the last few days, but it was the first time he'd said them out loud to anyone. To his surprise, he felt empowered by the announcement. "Being away from her even for a day has been eating me up. I can't go back to living my life the way it was. I want to be with her."

"How does she feel about that?"

"I don't know. I came to you first. I want to clear the air with us."

"This fight with the Grandins is only going to get uglier," Heath warned. "What if she chooses her family over you?"

Nolan was ready with his answer. He'd thought long and hard about his divided loyalties and planned to go with his heart. "Then I'll have to prove that I'm on her side. I'm always going to choose her."

The silence that followed ate into Nolan's soul like acid. Two months earlier, he'd come back to Royal to fix his relationship with his brother, and here he was shattering their alliance into pieces. This wasn't how he'd wanted things to go. But who could've predicted that he would fall in love with Chelsea Grandin?

"I see."

"I know you need to do this thing for our mom and Ashley, but is it worth doing if it tears apart everything that you have built? The Grandin and Lattimore families combined have so many resources to fight with. Is there some way we could just let it go?"

"I can't. Ashley was ignored and denied her birthright." The pain in Heath's voice rang through loud and clear. "She was a Grandin, and they ignored that."

Seeing the bright light of determination burning in his brother's eyes, Nolan decided it was the years he'd spent away that kept him from picking up the same torch that Heath raised. Both their mother and Ashley were dead. They would not benefit from the money. But Nolan understood that his brother's grief needed an outlet, and funding her foundation with the idea that their sister would be remembered was what Heath needed to heal.

"You're right," Nolan said, "but Mom never did anything about the claim."

"She didn't have the strength to take them on," Heath countered. "But I do."

Heath's fervor was getting through to him. Nolan understood more and more what drove his brother, and yet he couldn't believe that Heath would be happy to destroy the Grandin and Lattimore ranches in order to achieve his goal.

Nolan reminded his brother, "I don't think she'd be happy if we end up hurting someone."

"Someone like Chelsea Grandin?" Heath asked. He didn't seem particularly angry at Nolan's attempts to talk him out of pursuing the oil claim rights. More like disappointed.

"Chelsea. Me. You."

"Nothing's gonna happen to me or you." A muscle jumped in Heath's cheek. "I can't say anything about the Grandins or Lattimores, however."

With his brother's ominous words ringing in his ears, Nolan got back into his vehicle and headed to the Grandin ranch. He didn't spend any energy contemplating what sort of reception awaited him there. Deep in his heart, he knew that he would do everything in his power to convince Chelsea to give their relationship a shot. She deserved nothing less that his all. He'd failed her once. Nolan was determined never to do so again.

* * *

Chelsea sat on her bed, her knees drawn up to her chest, her gaze on her laptop screen, where an image of Bora Bora glowed in all its white-sand, turquoise-blue-water glory.

Nolan had been gone for over a week, and she'd never known such misery. It made every breakup she'd ever gone through pale by comparison. In fact, this was worse than every one of them rolled into a single enormous heartache.

Worse, she couldn't even bring herself to be mad at him for ending things. Even if she'd not succumbed to her insecurities and tried to sound all tough and confident, successfully chasing him away in the process, when Nolan had invited her to come away with him, she'd been too afraid to go.

That moment had tormented her for ten days and nights. She couldn't focus on work or even summon the energy to care that in the midst of her battle for the ranch, she'd stopped fighting. The victory she'd labored long and hard to achieve no longer held any luster. What the weeks of dating Nolan had revealed was that she'd been miserable before he came along. And now that he was gone, her life was an endless, desolate landscape once again.

She'd even considered booking a ticket to Bora Bora to surprise him, but fear of his rejection kept her from acting. The whiff of distrust continued to linger. What if he'd been playing her all along? Unable to shake the anxiety that was driven by her past romantic failures, Chelsea continued to grapple with doubt. Nolan wasn't like the other men. He'd had a good reason for ghosting her at the club. Her fingers dug into the coverlet beneath her. Vic had driven him away with his sly meddling.

Still, she'd been the one who'd overreacted and failed to agree to Nolan's offer when he'd extended it to her. If she'd been brave, they could be happily ensconced in paradise together. Blissful with Nolan sounded better than heartbroken alone. Chelsea's resolve swelled. She pulled her computer onto her lap and opened a new browser window.

As she was evaluating which of the twenty-plus-hour flights would work best, she heard a soft knock on her door frame. Glancing up, she spied her dad standing in the hall and closed the laptop.

"Your mother and I are on our way to the cookout at the TCC," he said, frowning as he took in her mood. "Just checking to see if you want to ride with us."

She'd forgotten all about the party at the Texas Cattleman's Club. The all-day affair included a pool party for the kids, a barbecue and a live band. The idea of having to pretend that everything was fine made her stomach roil.

"I'm not really in the mood to be around people right now," Chelsea said.

"You okay?"

She exhaled slowly, emptying her lungs. "Fine."

Chelsea was surprised when her father didn't accept her answer at face value and retreat. Victor Grandin was a straightforward man with old-fashioned ideas about women. The one he'd married, while not a pushover, embodied the traditional role of wife and mother. In contrast, Layla, Chelsea and Morgan had shown a strong preference for having successful careers and Chelsea was sure their father struggled to understand what drove them.

"I haven't seen you much around the ranch these last few weeks." Victor stepped inside the room and leaned against her dresser. With his arms crossed over his chest, he regarded his daughter with a solemn expression. "Some things have been slipping through the cracks."

On a normal day, this criticism would have sparked her irritation. But with Nolan gone, she couldn't summon the energy to point out just how much she did around the ranch. As long as her father was determined to give Vic control, Chelsea was more like a hired hand. Let him see what happened she stopped making decisions that benefited the ranch. Or maybe he would never appreciate how many of her changes had ended up improving things.

Chelsea shrugged, feeling no guilt for acting like a moody teenager for once in her life. "I guess I've been a bit distracted."

"That Thurston boy?"

"Among other things." Chelsea resisted the urge to throw a pillow. "Mostly I'm tired."

Tired of struggling to gain stature in her father's eyes. Tired of fighting a losing battle for a birthright that should've gone to the one who worked the hardest instead of the one who happened to be born male. Tired of telling herself that there was something wrong with the men she chose to date when she suspected that her stubbornness and ambition were the reasons they abandoned her.

"It occurred to me lately that I haven't taken any time off this year," she continued. "I thought I might go visit a friend of mine in Houston. She and her husband are having a baby, and their shower is next weekend."

"I guess you're due for some time off. You work hard around here."

Chelsea's eyebrows shot up. "I didn't realize you noticed." A month ago this admission would've been the confirmation of her worthiness that she'd craved. Today, all she felt was annoyance.

"I pay attention to everything that goes on around here."

"That's interesting," Chelsea said, in no mood to pull her punches. "Because you haven't been noticing that your son has let Layla and me handle the bulk of the problems that come up around here." Seeing her father's surprise, Chelsea warmed to her topic. "You've basically told him he will be in charge, and he thinks that gives him a free pass when it comes to doing things."

"I haven't noticed."

"You don't want to notice." The frustration she'd used to fuel her campaign suddenly had a new target. "You never want to see that your daughters are better at ranching than your son. Because we want the ranch to thrive, and we are willing to work damned hard to make sure it does."

When her father seemed at a loss for words, Chelsea kept going.

"I was willing to do whatever it took to prove to you that I deserved to be the one you should put in charge. Thinking I could save our ranch, I even went so far as to scheme to convince Nolan to talk his brother out of pursuing the oil rights claim." Chelsea's throat locked up at this reminder that her single-minded drive to win at all costs had cost her a future with the man she loved.

"I take it you couldn't."

Chelsea stared at her father in disbelief. Was that the message he'd taken away from her rant?

"More like I didn't want to in the end. Nolan and Heath don't intend to keep the money for themselves. Heath wants to use it to fund his sister's foundation. To do something wonderful in her name. We shouldn't stand in their way."

She could see her father's disapproval grow as she spoke. Chelsea wasn't surprised that he rejected her declaration of support. Her father had very strong opinions. She's been fighting against them all her life. No doubt, he viewed her as a traitor because she wasn't putting the family interest first. It was difficult to choose between two things she loved so much.

With their families on opposite sides of such a fraught issue, and neither party willing to give, they would never be able to please everyone. A relationship between her and Nolan had been doomed from the start.

His decision to leave Royal and take up his old life had probably saved both of them from even greater heartache. Which probably was a good thing, because Chelsea didn't think she could've survived a pain worse than what she was feeling at the moment.

"I'm sure you're disappointed in me," Chelsea said into the silence that had invaded her room. She struggled against the heavy emotions weighing her down. Her father's opinion had always meant so much to her, and going against his wishes added another layer of sadness to her burden of misery.

"I'm not disappointed in you," her father said, crossing to the bed and sitting beside her. He reached for her hand and clasped it in his warm palm. "Maybe I haven't appreciated your contributions the way I should. It's become pretty apparent these last few weeks just how much you do around here. A lot of things have been neglected. Your brother has had a hard time keeping up with everything on his own. Seems to me that you're an asset I've taken for granted."

Chelsea gave her father a watery smile. "I've been waiting a long time for you to recognize everything I contribute to the ranch."

"Maybe you and I should spend some more time together, and you can give me a better sense of all the things you do."

"I'd like that. Running this ranch is all I've ever wanted to do. But I've sacrificed a lot to win your approval. I think I need to find a better balance." As satisfying as it was to hear her father realize that his son wasn't the perfect choice to run the ranch, dating Nolan had awakened her to the need for fun as well as work in her life.

"Does that mean I'm gonna have to get used to seeing Nolan Thurston around here?"

"No." Chelsea dug her nails into her palms to keep from succumbing to tears. "We're over. He left Royal."

"I'm sorry." And to Chelsea's surprise, her father actually looked like he meant it. "I didn't realize what was between you was serious."

"I don't know that it was for him, but I liked him a lot." Way more than a lot. She'd fallen in love with him.

Her father seized her chin and turned her head until she met his gaze. "He's a fool if he doesn't see what a treasure you are."

"Thanks, Dad." Since Chelsea sensed that she'd made inroads where her father was concerned, she decided she could make an effort. After all, he'd come looking for her and had made the effort to get to the bottom of what was bothering her. "I think I've changed my mind about the cookout. Give me ten minutes to change and I'll meet you outside."

After donning a white lace sundress and her favorite boots, Chelsea tied up her hair in a messy topknot and applied mascara, liner and lipstick. She might be miserable inside, but at least she looked good.

As she neared the living room, she heard the low

rumble of conversation and paused to collect herself before entering the room. She expected to find her parents and maybe her brother—but stopped short at the sight of the man who stood in the foyer.

Thirteen

Nolan hadn't known what to expect when Chelsea entered the room, but he didn't expect the flare of joy mixed with despair that erupted as their eyes locked. She looked sad and tragic, but so beautiful in a white lace dress and cowboy boots. Given that he'd thrown down an impossible ultimatum before he'd walked away, he'd half expected she would immediately show him the door. Instead, she stopped dead, as if she'd seen a ghost. Her shoulders collapsed as she reached her left hand across her body and grasped her right forearm.

"Nolan?" She said his name as if she couldn't comprehend that he was standing in the same room as her. "You're here?"

All too conscious of her parents watching the exchange, Nolan nodded. He couldn't seem to make his facial muscles work. Where he wanted to smile and welcome, all he could do was stare at her like a man possessed.

"I'm sorry I didn't call before showing up, but I was afraid you'd tell me not to come. And I needed to talk to you." Nolan shot a glance at her parents, hoping they would get the hint and make themselves scarce. When they showed no signs of moving, he ground his teeth. "Feel like taking a walk?"

"We are on our way to the TCC cookout."

"I could drive you."

Chelsea seemed to have forgotten her parents were in the room. Her gaze stabbed into him as if she could tear him open and get to the heart of why he'd returned. She looked unsure of the situation, which struck him as odd, because he'd never seen her as anything but completely confident.

"Why are you back?" Chelsea asked, showing no sign of going anywhere with him. "I thought you were supposed to be going to Bora Bora."

"I did." Nolan wanted so badly to cross the room and pull Chelsea into his arms, but he'd messed up with her. "My team is still there. I couldn't concentrate with you so far away. So I came back."

"Oh, I see." But from the subdued tone in her voice, Nolan guessed she didn't see it all. "But if there are still things to do, you must be going back."

"The scope of the project requires me to take several trips over the next few months," he said. "And

I realized I couldn't stand being away from you that long."

"Away from me?" she echoed, frowning. "I don't understand. You gave me the impression we were done."

"I didn't want us to be done," he admitted, taking several slow steps in her direction.

She stared at his chest, refusing to meet his gaze, but didn't back away from his advance. He took that as a positive.

"That's not the impression you gave me. You were pretty clear that you weren't coming back. And if you did, you wouldn't be coming back for me."

"I was confused and angry. Your brother said all those things..." Nolan grimaced, all too aware of their audience. "But I should've trusted you."

He glanced toward Chelsea's parents, who were watching the exchange with avid interest, and willed them to go. He wanted this moment with Chelsea to be for just them. So much needed sorting out.

At last, Victor Grandin seemed to get the hint. He captured his wife's elbow in his hand and steered her toward the front door. "We'll wait in the car." As he passed Nolan, Victor gave the younger man a stern glare and muttered, "You be good to my daughter or I will track you down wherever you may run and make you pay."

Nolan wasn't sure if he was more shocked by the man's threat or the backhanded approval of him as his daughter's suitor. Either way, Nolan knew that regardless of the hurt feelings between them, he had to do whatever it took to win her heart.

In the seconds after he found himself alone with Chelsea, Nolan took stock of the tension in her body language. She seemed equally relieved and unhappy to see him.

"The hour I spent waiting for you in the bar was the worst. You'd never given me any doubts before that moment, and when you didn't call or respond to my texts, I didn't know what to think. I was frantic that something had happened to you. And then my insecurity kicked in, and I convinced myself that I'd pushed you into doing something you didn't want and that you'd left me like everyone else."

"I'm so sorry I did that. It was a dick move on my part. I knew perfectly well how you've been treated in the past, and I never should've disappeared on you."

"No," she agreed, her spine stiffening. "You knew how it would devastate me."

"I'm more sorry than you'll ever know," Nolan declared, reaching for her hand. To his relief, she didn't resist as his fingers curved around hers. She seemed to be fighting herself as much as him. "Leaving you was the biggest mistake I've ever made."

"I think we've both made mistakes."

"Can you forgive me?"

"I think I would do anything to have things back the way they were," Chelsea admitted. "And that terrifies me."

"I don't want you to be afraid to be with me."

"I'm not."

"Does this have to do with the oil rights claim you and your brother are making? If it does, then you should know I've already told my dad that we shouldn't stand in your way. I just hope that we can find a way to make it so that our land isn't completely ruined."

"You did?" Nolan couldn't believe what he was hearing. "Why the change of heart?"

"I got to thinking that it wasn't fair for us to fight you when my grandfather gave your mother those rights fair and square. He must've had a reason, and knowing him the way I do, I'm sure it was a good one."

Despite what should be his success in winning her over, her explanation left him ice-cold. She obviously persisted in believing he was committed to the claim, when in truth the only thing he was committed to was making her happy.

"I really don't care about any of that." He grabbed her by the shoulders and gave her a little shake. "I came back for you. Nothing else. I don't care about the oil rights or some job waiting for me in Bora Bora. All I want is you."

"Me?"

The way she said it ripped into his heart. Here stood a woman who understood her worth, yet she questioned whether anyone else saw her value. She worked so hard to prove she was strong and competent, yet her accomplishments hadn't received anywhere near the recognition they were due.

"You." He took her hands in his and brought them

to his lips. "From the minute I laid eyes on you across that Fourth of July parade, I was smitten. My feelings for you only grew stronger the more time we spent together. You are more fascinating than any exotic location could ever be."

"That's not possible. All I've done is focus on this ranch. It's my all-day, every-day fixation." She paused and bit her lip, glancing up at him from beneath her long lashes. "Or it was until you came along. Now, I realize I'd give up running the ranch to be with you. If that means spending the rest of my life on the road, as long as you were there, I could be happy."

Her willingness to sacrifice her passion made his heart clench painfully. The long flights to and from the South Pacific had given him a lot of time to think. Before leaving Royal, she'd pleaded with him to keep their relationship going, and in a moment of cowardice he'd tossed out a ruthless ultimatum, knowing she'd never agree to leave her world behind to be with him. Yet here she was, being braver than any person he'd ever known. And he adored her for it.

"You wouldn't be happy if you couldn't be here, where you belong, making Grandin Ranch the best in the county. Hell, in the whole state of Texas." Nolan put his whole heart and soul into the next two sentences. "And I'd like to be by your side, helping you with that. If you'll have me."

Her eyes went wide with shock. She dug her fingers into his. "But you left Royal because you didn't want to be stuck here ranching."

"I was eighteen when I ran off to see the world. I

couldn't see a place for myself here. But now, after everywhere I've been, recognizing that there are exciting and magical destinations still to visit, I know that what's here in Royal is all I'll ever want. And that's you."

Chelsea stared at Nolan across the inches that separated them. He was telling her that not only did he intend to give up his claim on the oil rights, but he also planned to side with her and her family. Doing so would put his relationship with his brother at risk. He genuinely seemed ready to do that. For her. For them. Did she need more proof that he loved her?

"I love you," she said, willing to take a risk of her own. "It scares me how much I need you. That's why I was so stupid that day at the Texas Cattleman's Club. I fell into my old patterns of self-doubt when you didn't show up, and I went a little crazy."

"I never should have left you there alone. I knew how much it would bother you, and I was so afraid of how you made me feel that I did what I always do and ran. But it didn't take long before I realized that running didn't make me feel better. In fact, I've never been more miserable in my whole life."

"I think we might find a way to overcome our worst fears if we do it together."

Nolan nodded. "It won't be easy."

"I'm not afraid of a little work, and I don't think you are, either." As Chelsea's resolve grew, her fear and anxiety eased. She trusted the bond between her and Nolan. That her confidence in him had developed despite the trouble between their families meant their connection was real and strong. "As long as I have you by my side, nothing else can hurt me."

"Not even if your father decides to let your brother run the ranch?"

A month earlier Nolan's question would've sparked hot emotion. Now, she saw her obsession with running the ranch as a distraction from loneliness and disappointment. She'd longed for someone to share her dreams with, not understanding that she'd lost sight of what made her happy.

"Once you and I began dating, I started to realize that I've sacrificed far too much to my ambition. I can't imagine ever not being a part of running the ranch, but I've focused too hard on changing my father's mind. It led me to think it would somehow be all right to manipulate you into turning on Heath. I'm ashamed that I went there. It's not the way I want to be."

As she bared her soul to Nolan, Chelsea felt stronger than she'd ever been in her whole life. He was a beacon of joy and delight. Together they would be a family and, hopefully one day, welcome children.

Yet, even as these thoughts popped into her mind, Chelsea wondered if she was jumping the gun.

Nolan must've seen her concern, because he cupped her cheek in one hand. "What?"

"I realized that once again I'm throwing myself into the future before I've bothered to find out what you see for us. You love to travel. I'd never ask you to give that up. I want us to explore the world, but I want to make babies with you and see them grow up here." She trailed off, unsure if he wanted to have kids. "Wow, that's a lot." She chuckled self-consciously.

"I've been running around the world for a long time, searching for a missing piece to make me feel whole and never finding it." Nolan's thumb grazed her skin, soothing her worries. "Imagine how surprised I was when I came home to the place I'd fled long ago to discover what I wanted was here all along."

When his hand dived into his pocket and produced a small black box, Chelsea's throat locked up. In that instant, she realized she no longer gave a damn about running Grandin Ranch. This man, the love glinting in his dark brown eyes, filled her with a sense of belonging she'd never known.

"I hope I'm being clear enough," Nolan said. "If not, let me state quite simply that I want you. In fact, I'm really glad that you're imagining a future with me, because otherwise this would've been really awkward." As he finished speaking, Nolan dropped to one knee and popped open the box. A sparkling ring featuring a large oval diamond sat nestled on a cushion of black velvet. "Chelsea Grandin, I love you."

Chelsea threw her hands over her mouth, reeling at his words and unable to believe what she was seeing and hearing. "I love you, too," she repeated, the fierce declaration reduced to a hoarse whisper as emotions overwhelmed her.

"I want to spend the rest of my life with you." The hand holding the ring box shook as fierce emotion burned in his gaze. "Will you marry me?"

Chelsea reached down and clasped his hand between hers, feeling her own body trembling in the acute rush of her joy. "Yes. I want us to be together forever."

Nolan plucked the ring from the box and slid it onto her finger. Chelsea could barely see the diamond through the tears gathering in her eyes. And then he was springing to his feet and wrapping her in his arms. He kissed her with blinding passion, his lips moving over hers with possessive hunger. Chelsea tunneled her fingers through his hair and held on tight as they feasted on each other's lips.

At long last they broke apart, chests heaving as they grinned at each other in giddy, stunned joy. They were so lost in each other and the momentous transformation of the relationship that they didn't realize they were no longer alone until someone cleared their throat.

"Looks like everything's okay in here," Chelsea's father said, sounding somewhat bemused.

Chelsea turned toward her father and spied her mother standing just behind him, looking anxious. Her expression cleared as she gazed from her daughter's face to the man who had wrapped his arm around her and held her possessively at his side.

"Better than okay," Chelsea said. She held out her left hand, where the diamond winked on her ring finger, and braced herself for her parents' reaction. "We're getting married."

"Oh, that's wonderful." Bethany Grandin rushed to embrace her daughter, shocking Chelsea to no end.

"All I ever wanted was for you to be happy," she whispered in her daughter's ear.

She was still absurdly perplexed by her parents' easy acceptance of the "enemy" into their midst as her dad hugged her tight. While Chelsea's mother gave her soon-to-be son-in-law a warm hug, Nolan met her gaze. His warm brown eyes and steady smile filled her with a sense of belonging.

As her father hugged her, Nolan seemed utterly at ease as he basked in the glow of her parents' positive reaction to the news. Yet even as she recognized his solidarity with her family, she worried what would be the cost in his ongoing campaign to repair his relationship with his brother. The conflict drew a line in the sand. In order to be together, they would have to choose a side.

While she recognized that Nolan was willing to make that sacrifice for her without hesitation, if the tables were turned and she'd chosen to support Heath and his claim, the loss of her family would've been devastating.

She needed to make sure Nolan was completely at peace before moving forward. Twisting the ring on her finger, Chelsea prepared to take it off at the slightest indication that he would regret his decision to take her side against his brother.

"Are you sure you're okay with becoming part of my family? I know how much you wanted to repair your relationship with your brother."

"Heath is coping with his grief the best way he can, and while I appreciate that he wants to fund Ashley's foundation and create something in her memory, I can't get past the fact that our mother had the oil rights for years and never did anything about them. It seems to me that she wouldn't agree with what he is doing. If my mom wanted us to take something from you, she would've told us the oil rights existed."

While Nolan's explanation made sense, she couldn't help but argue the same thing from her family's point of view.

"Does that mean you'll talk to your brother on our behalf?" Victor asked before Chelsea could speak her mind.

"Absolutely not," Chelsea answered for him. She wrapped her arm around Nolan's waist and faced her parents. "Grandpa and Augustus granted Cynthia those oil rights. None of us understand why, but the fact is they did. The Thurstons are legally entitled to do whatever they want with them. Neither Nolan nor I will have anything more to say about the rights. You and the Lattimores can fight it, but from now on, we remain neutral."

"This is your ranch we're talking about," Nolan reminded her. "Your family's legacy."

"This is our life," she countered. They were a team now. It was no longer a situation where they sided with his family or her family. From now on, they would prioritize each other and the family they would one day make together. "As far as I'm concerned, we are what's important. Whatever it takes to keep us strong. That's what I intend to do."

Fourteen

Instead of heading to the Texas Cattleman's Club as planned, Nolan and Chelsea took a little detour to his loft. When Nolan had called from Bora Bora, the landlord told him no one had rented it yet, so the loft was Nolan's as long as he wanted it. After a ten-day separation, they were ravenous for each other and didn't get farther than the closed front door before Nolan had Chelsea up against the wall in a hot, desperate kiss.

In minutes, Chelsea had shimmied out of her panties while Nolan freed his erection, and then he was lifting her up and spearing into her. They drove wildly toward a fast orgasm, each thrust a hungry, frantic attempt to get closer and closer still. He loved how she didn't hold back, how she told him exactly how badly she wanted him. With her hands knotted almost painfully in his hair, her breath coming in short, urgent pants against his face, she proclaimed in words and actions just how much she loved him. Nolan lost himself in her desire, and as she came apart in his arms, he was right there with her.

Afterward, they stripped bare and ran to his bed to start all over again. This time the build was slower and hotter as he relearned every inch of her body with his hands and tongue before sliding home. As she closed around him, tight and wet and warm, she gave out a giant, ragged sigh that lanced straight through his heart.

"Are you okay?" he asked, stopping all movement so he could dust kisses across her eyelids and down her nose.

"Better than okay," she murmured, cupping his face between her palms. "I'm absolutely perfect. Being with you is all I could think about these last ten days, and believing that you were gone forever was..." She shuddered. "I can never go through that again."

"Trust me when I tell you that I'm never going to leave you. You're mine and I'm yours. We belong together, and nothing will ever change that."

That seemed to be everything she needed to hear, because her arms and legs tightened around him and she began moving in a way that made every cell in his body come to life. She was perfect and glorious and Nolan knew he would never tire of making her come.

As much as he would've loved to spend the rest of

the day and night in bed with her, Chelsea received several texts from her family demanding to know where she was and reminding her that she had an obligation to join them at the charity event. After grabbing a quick shower together, they managed to get themselves redressed and out the door.

Before he started his rented SUV, Nolan reached into the back seat and pulled out a long, thin jewelry box. Chelsea's eyes widened as he extended it to her.

"What's this?"

"I'm afraid this is going to be anticlimactic after this." He scooped her left hand into his and kissed the spot where her engagement ring rested. "But I thought you might enjoy wearing it to the party."

She popped open the box and gasped at the bracelet of golden Tahitian pearls that lay upon the black velvet. "This is gorgeous." She lifted the strand and placed them on her wrist. The warm gold color looked fantastic against her tan skin. "Can you help me with the clasp?"

Once the bracelet was fastened, Chelsea gave him an enthusiastic thank-you kiss that very nearly sent them scrambling back to his loft for round three. Instead, she wiped her lipstick from his lips, fixed her makeup and shot him a saucy grin.

"Shall we go face the music?"

Nolan pulled a face and started the engine. "It's not going to be that bad."

"Here's hoping you're right."

The last time he'd gone to the Texas Cattleman's Club, he'd intended to meet Chelsea and proclaim their relationship to one and all. To say things had not gone well was an understatement.

This time, as he strode hand in hand with Chelsea through the members who had gathered to eat barbecue, socialize and enjoy the music, Nolan knew a new confidence and contentment. For the first time since returning to Royal two months earlier, he felt as if he belonged in the community. If this was what the love of a wonderful woman did to a man, Nolan knew he would never mess it up.

"Mom and Dad just told me you two are engaged." Layla had appeared in their path with Joshua in tow. While the men nodded in greeting, Layla's blue eyes bounced from Chelsea to Nolan before landing on their clasped hands. Her mouth dropped open as she spotted the large oval diamond. She pointed at it. "It's true. Wow!"

"We are," Chelsea confirmed. Her broad smile was half smug pride and half amusement as her sister enveloped her in an enthusiastic hug. "Do Morgan and Vic know?"

"They do."

"How'd they take it?"

"Morgan's delighted for you, of course, but Vic…"

Layla glanced over her shoulder to where their brother stood talking with his best friend, Jayden Lattimore. The pair cast speculative glances toward the two couples. After the conversation he'd had with Chelsea's brother, Nolan wondered how Vic would react to the engagement.

"It's the whole oil rights thing," Layla continued,

shooting Nolan a glance from beneath her lashes. "His family. Our family."

Chelsea stepped closer to Nolan and pressed her body against his in a show of solidarity. Her chin rose ever so slightly in defiance. "Nolan and I aren't taking sides," she said. "Eventually he's going to become part of our family. Just like I'll be part of his."

Layla looked stunned. "But the ranch—you know that if an oil company gets the right to drill on our land, it will be ruined."

"I know." Chelsea winced. "But Grandpa knew that as well, and both he and Augustus are the ones who signed over the rights to Cynthia."

Nolan squeezed her hand, offering both sympathy and support. "Heath has his reasons for what he's doing and grief is playing a big role in motivating him, but I don't want to see your family's ranch damaged."

"That's good to hear." Morgan had appeared beside Layla. She scrutinized Nolan a long moment before adding, "Welcome to the family."

Beside him, Chelsea relaxed visibly. Despite her brave words earlier, Nolan knew it was important that her parents and sisters supported her decision to marry him. It was also occurring to him how much of a change the Grandin family would make in his life. Since leaving Royal, he'd not been a part of any family, much less one as large as this. The acceptance from Chelsea's sisters delighted him more than he'd expected.

"I love you," he murmured into her hair.

She tipped her head up, and the smile on her face made his heart soar. "I love you," she murmured back. Lifting on tiptoe to kiss his cheek, she added, "Now, let's get out of here and go do some more celebrating back at your loft."

"You do make the best suggestions," he replied with a grin.

Unfortunately, it took them nearly an hour to extricate themselves from the cookout as word of their engagement spread and more people stepped up to congratulate them.

Now, however, they were finally alone. A flush of color high on her cheekbones matched the hungry fire licking his nerve endings. Nolan kicked the front door shut behind them and took both of her hands in his, slowly backing toward his bed. Halfway there he paused, seeing she had something on her mind.

"You're thinking hard about something," he said.

She pulled his arms around her and rested her cheek on his shoulder. "Are you going to be happy here? I mean, you are used to being on the go all the time."

"Wherever you are is where I want to be. Of course, I'll have to travel for my business, but I have an excellent staff who can do most of the day-to-day operations, and LA is a plane ride away."

She leaned back and gazed up at him. "So, you're really okay with being back in Royal."

"This is your home." The ranch was important to her. Her happiness was important to him. "I want to make it mine as well."

"And I want you to know that I'm going to come with you when you travel." Her eyes glowed with fervent joy. "The ranch can survive without me better than I can survive without you."

"That's also how I feel." He framed her face with his hands and kissed her gently. "When it comes to you, I'm—always and forever—all in."

"We're going to have such an amazing life."

"I can't wait to get started."

* * * * *

Keep reading for an excerpt of a new title
from the Western series,
A TEMPORARY TEXAS ARRANGEMENT
by Cathy Gillen Thacker

CHAPTER ONE

"YOU'RE REALLY GOING to go in there. Alone. Just before dark?" The low, masculine voice came from somewhere behind her.

With the brisk January wind cutting through her clothes, Tess Gardner paused, house key in hand, and turned toward the Laramie, Texas, street. Senses tingling, she watched as the man stepped out of a charcoal-gray Expedition, now parked at the curb. He wasn't the shearling coat-wearing cowboy she had expected to see in this rural southwestern town she was about to call home. Rather, he appeared to be an executive type, in business-casual wool slacks, dress shirt and loosened tie. An expensive down jacket covered his broad shoulders and hung open, revealing taut, muscular abs. Shiny dress boots covered his feet.

Had it been any other day, any other time in her recently upended life, she might have responded favorably to this tall, commanding man striding casually up the sidewalk in the dwindling daylight. But after the long drive from Denver, all she wanted was to get a first look at the home she had inherited from her late uncle. Then crash.

The interloper, however, had other plans. He strode closer, all indomitable male.

Tess drew a bolstering breath. She let her gaze drift over his short, dark hair and ruggedly chiseled features before returning to his midnight blue eyes. Damn, he was handsome.

Trying not to shiver in the cold, damp air, she regarded him cautiously. Drawing on the careful wariness she had learned from growing up in the city, she countered, "And who are you exactly?"

His smile was even more compelling than his voice. "Noah Lockhart." He reached into his shirt pocket for a business card.

Disappointment swept through her. She sighed. "Let me guess. Another Realtor." A half dozen had already contacted her, eager to know if she wanted to sell.

He shook his head. "No." He came halfway up the cement porch steps of the century-old Craftsman bungalow and handed over his card, inundating her with the brisk, woodsy fragrance of his cologne. Their fingers touched briefly and another tingle of awareness shot through her. "I own a software company," he said.

Now she really didn't understand why he had stopped by, offering unsolicited advice. Was he flirting with her? His cordial attitude said *yes*, but the warning in his low voice when he had first approached her, and had seen that she was about to enter the house, said *no*.

He sobered, his gaze lasering into hers. "I've been trying to get ahold of you through the Laramie Veterinary Clinic," he added.

So he was *what*? Tess wondered, feeling all the more confused. A pet owner in need of veterinary care? A potential business associate? Certainly not one of the county's many successful, eligible men who, she had been teasingly informed by Sara, her new coworker/boss, would be lining up to date her as soon as she arrived.

Curious, she scanned his card.

In bold print on the first line, it said:

Noah Lockhart, CEO and Founder

Okay, she thought, so his name was vaguely familiar. Below that, it said:

Lockhart Solutions. "An app for every need."

The company logo of intertwining diamonds was beside that.

Recognition turned swiftly to admiration. She was pretty sure the weather app she used had been designed by Lockhart Solutions. The restaurant finder, too. And the CEO of the company, who looked to be in his mid-thirties, was standing right in front of her. In Laramie, Texas, of all places.

"But even though I've left half a dozen messages, I haven't gotten any calls back," he continued in frustration.

Tess imagined that wasn't typical for someone of his importance. That was just too darn bad.

Struggling not to feel the full impact of his disarming, masculine presence, Tess returned his frown with a deliberate one of her own. She didn't know if she was relieved or disappointed he wasn't there to ask her out. She did know she hated being pressured into anything. Especially when the coercion came from a place of entitlement. She propped her hands on her hips, the mixture of fatigue and temper warming her from the inside out. "First of all, I haven't even started working there yet."

His expression remained determined. "I know."

"There are four other veterinarians working at the animal clinic."

"None with your expertise," he stated.

Somehow, Tess doubted that. If her new boss and managing partner, Sara Anderson McCabe, had thought that Tess was the only one qualified to handle Noah's problem—whatever it was—she would have called Tess to discuss the situation, and then asked Tess to consult on the case. Sara hadn't done that. Which led Tess to believe this wasn't the vital issue or 'emergency' Noah deemed it to be.

More likely, someone as successful as Noah Lockhart was simply not accustomed to waiting on anyone or anything. That wasn't her problem. Setting professional boundaries was. She shifted the bag higher on her shoulder, then said firmly, "You can make an appointment for next week."

After she had taken the weekend to get settled.

Judging by the downward curve of his sensual lips, her suggestion did not please, nor would, in any way, deter him. His gaze sifted over her face, and he sent another deeply persuasive look her way. "I was hoping I could talk you into making a house call, before that." He followed his statement with a hopeful smile. The kind he apparently did not expect would be denied.

Tess let out a breath. *Great.* Sara had been wrong about him. Noah Lockhart was just another rich, entitled person. Just like the ridiculously demanding clients she had been trying to escape when she left her position in Denver. Not to mention the memories of the ex-fiancé who had broken her heart...

Determined not to make the same mistakes twice, however, she said coolly, "You're still going to have to go through the clinic."

He shoved a hand through his hair and exhaled. Unhappiness simmered between them. Broad shoulders flexing, he said, "Normally, I'd be happy to do that—"

And here they went. "Let me guess," she scoffed. "You don't have time for that?"

Another grimace. "Actually, no, I—we—likely don't."

"Well, that makes two of us," Tess huffed, figuring this conversation had come to an end. "Now, if you will excuse me..." Hoping he'd finally get the hint, she turned back to the front door of the Craftsman bungalow, slid the key into the lock, turned it and heard it open with a satisfying click.

Aware that Noah Lockhart was still standing behind her, despite the fact he had been summarily dismissed, she pushed the door open. Head held high, she marched across the threshold. And strode face-first into the biggest, stickiest spiderweb she had ever encountered in her life!

At the same time, she felt something gross and scary drop onto the top of her head. "Aggghhh!" she screamed, dropping her bag and backing up, frantically batting away whatever it was crawling through her thick, curly hair...

This, Noah thought ruefully, was exactly what Tess Gardner's new boss had feared. Sara Anderson McCabe had worried if Tess had seen the interior of the house she had inherited from her late uncle, before she toured the clinic and met the staff she was going to be working with, she might change her mind and head right back to Denver and the fancy veterinary practice she had come from.

Not that anyone had expected her to crash headfirst into a spiderweb worthy of a horror movie.

He covered the distance between them in two swift steps, reaching her just as she backed perilously toward the edge of the porch, still screaming and batting at her hair. With good reason. The large, gray spider was still moving across her scalp, crawling from her crown toward her face.

Noah grabbed Tess protectively by the shoulders with one hand, and used his other to flick the pest away.

It landed on the porch and scurried into the bushes while Tess continued to shudder violently.

"You're okay," he told her soothingly, able to feel her shaking through the thick layer of her winter jacket. She smelled good, too, her perfume a mix of citrus and patchouli. "I got it off of you."

She sagged in relief. And reluctantly, he let her go, watching as she brushed at the soft cashmere sweater clinging to her midriff, then slid her hand down her jean-clad legs, grimacing every time she encountered more of the sticky web.

Damn, she was beautiful, with long, wildly curly blond hair and long-lashed, sage-green eyes. Around five foot eight, to his own six foot three inches, she was the perfect weight for her slender frame, with curves in all the right places, and she had the face of an angel.

Not that she seemed to realize just how incredibly beguiling she was. It was a fact that probably drove all the guys, including him, crazy.

Oblivious to the ardent nature of his thoughts, she shot him a sidelong glance. Took another deep breath. Straightened. "Was it a spider?"

Noah had never been one to push his way into anyone else's business, but glad he had been there to help her out, he said, "Yes."

Her pretty eyes narrowed. "A brown recluse or black widow?"

He shook his head. "A wolf spider."

"Pregnant with about a million babies?"

He chuckled. "Aren't they always?"

She muttered something beneath her breath that he was pretty sure wasn't in the least bit ladylike. Then, pointing at the ceiling several feet beyond the still open front door, where much of the web was still dangling precariously, she turned back to regard him suspiciously. "Did you know it was there? Is that why you told me not to go in alone?"

He held her gaze intently. He hadn't been this aware of a woman since he'd lost his wife, but there was something about Tess that captured—and held—his attention. A latent vulnerability, maybe. "It never would have occurred to me that was what you would have encountered when you opened the door."

Squinting, she propped her hands on her hips. "Then why the warning about not going in alone?"

Good question. Since he had never been known to chase after damsels in distress. Or offer help indiscriminately. He had always figured if someone wanted his aid, that person would let him know, and then he would render it in a very trustworthy fashion. Otherwise, he stayed out of it. Tonight, though, he hadn't. Which was…interesting… given how many problems of his own he had to manage.

She was still waiting for his answer.

He shrugged, focusing on the facts. "Waylon hadn't been here for at least a year, before he passed four months ago, and he was never known for his domestic skills." So he honestly hadn't known what she would be walking into.

She scanned the neat front yard. Although it was only a little past five o'clock in the afternoon, the sun was already setting in the wintry gray sky. "But the lawn and the exterior of the house are perfectly maintained!"

"The neighbors do that as a courtesy for him."

"But not the interior?" she persisted.

"Waylon didn't want to trouble folks, so he never gave anyone a key."

Tess turned her gaze to the shadowy interior. All the window blinds were closed. Because it was turning dusk, the inside of the home was getting darker by the minute. And the mangled cobweb was still dangling in the doorway.

Noah knew it was none of his business. That she was an adult, free to do as she chose. Yet, he had to offer the kind of help he knew he would want anyone in his family to receive, in a similar situation.

"Sure you want to stay here alone?" Noah asked.

ACTUALLY, NOW THAT she knew what she was facing, Tess most definitely did *not* want to stay here tonight. "I don't have a choice," she admitted with grim resignation. "I don't have a hotel room. Everything in the vicinity is booked. I guess I waited too long to make a reservation."

He nodded, seemingly not surprised.

"The Lake Laramie Lodge and the Laramie Inn are always booked well in advance. During the week, it's business conferences and company retreats."

"And the weekends?" she queried.

"On Saturdays and Sundays it tends to be filled with guests in town for a wedding or family reunion, or hobby aficionados of some sort. This weekend I think there's a ham-radio conference... Next week, scrapbooking, maybe? You can look it up online or just read the signs posted around town, if you want to learn more."

"Good to know. Anyway..." Tess pulled her cell phone from her pocket and punched the flashlight button. Bright light poured out. "I'm sure I can handle it. Especially if we turn on the lights..."

She reached for the switches just inside the door. To her surprise, neither brought any illumination.

Noah glanced at the fixture on the ceiling inside the house, then the porch light. "Maybe the bulbs are just burned out," he said.

Stepping past the dangling web, he went on inside, to a table lamp. She watched as he tried it. Nothing.

Still wary of being attacked by another spider, she lingered just inside the portal, her hands shoved inside the pockets of her winter jacket. The air coming out of the interior of the house seemed even colder than the below-freezing temperature outside. Which meant the furnace wasn't on, either. Although that could be fixed.

Noah went to another lamp. Again, nothing happened when he turned the switch. "You think all the bulbs could be burned out?" Tess asked hopefully, knowing that at least that would be an easy fix.

"Or…" He strode through the main room to the kitchen, which was located at the rear of the two-story brick home. She followed him, careful to avoid plowing through another web, then watched as he pushed down the lever on the toaster. Peering inside the small appliance, he frowned.

Anxiety swirled through Tess, as she wondered what she had gotten herself into. "Not working, either?"

"No." Noah moved purposefully over to the sink and tried the faucet. When no water came out, he hunkered down and looked inside the cabinet below. Tried something else, but to no avail. As he straightened, three small mice scampered out, running past him, then disappeared behind the pantry door. Tess managed not to shriek while he grimaced, and concluded, "Both the electricity and water are turned off."

Which meant the mice and the spiders weren't the worst of her problems. "You're *kidding*!" After rushing to join him at the sink, she tried the ancient faucet herself. Again…nothing.

Noah reached for the cords next to the window above the sink and opened the dark wooden blinds. They were covered with a thick film of dust. As was, Tess noted in discouragement, everything else in sight.

Plus, the spiders had had a field day.

There were big cobwebs in every corner, stretched across the ceiling and the tops of the window blinds, and strewn over the beat-up furniture. Worse, when she looked closely, she could see mice droppings trailing across much of the floor. Which could mean she had more than the three rodent guests she had already encountered. *Ugh*.

"Seen enough for right now?" Noah asked.

Tess shook her head in dismay. She'd had such dreams for this place. Hoped it would give her the kind of permanent home and sense of belonging she had always yearned for. But while she was certainly taken aback by what they had discovered here tonight, she wasn't going to let it scare her off. Besides, in addition to the property, her late uncle had left her the proceeds of his life-insurance policy, with the expectation she would use the funds to fix up the house. "Maybe the upstairs will be better…"

Unfortunately, it wasn't. The single bathroom looked as if it hadn't had a good scrubbing in years. Two of the bedrooms were filled with piles of fishing and camping equipment. The third held a sagging bed, and heaps of clothes suitable for an oil roughneck who spent most of his time on ocean rigs.

On a whim, she checked out the light switch, and the sink in the bathroom, too. Neither worked.

Noah was gazing at her from a short distance away. "Well, that settles it, you can't stay here," he said.

Tess had already come to the same conclusion.

Although, after two very long days in her SUV, she wasn't looking forward to the two-hour drive to San Antonio for an available hotel room.

He met her gaze equably. "You can come home with me."

NEW SERIES COMING!

RELEASING JANUARY

Special EDITION

Believe in love.

Overcome obstacles.

Find happiness.

For fans of Virgin River, Sweet Magnolias or Grace & Frankie you'll love this new series line. Stories with strong romantic tropes and hooks told in a modern and complex way.

In-store and online 17 January 2024.

NEW NEXT MONTH!

There's much more than land at stake for two rival Montana ranching families in this exciting new book in the Powder River series from *New York Times* bestselling author B.J. Daniels.

RIVER STRONG

In-store and online January 2024.

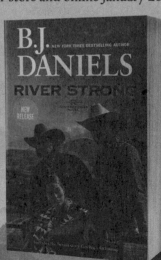

BONUS STORY INCLUDED

MILLS & BOON

millsandboon.com.au

MILLS & BOON

Want to know more about your favourite series or discover a new one?

Experience the variety of romance that Mills & Boon has to offer at our website:

millsandboon.com.au

Shop all of our categories and discover the one that's right for you.

MODERN

DESIRE

MEDICAL

INTRIGUE

ROMANTIC SUSPENSE

WESTERN

HISTORICAL

FOREVER
EBOOK ONLY

HEART
EBOOK ONLY

f @millsandboonaustralia 🐦 📷 @millsandboonaus

Subscribe and fall in love with a Mills & Boon series today!

You'll be among the first to read stories delivered to your door monthly and enjoy great savings.

WE SIMPLY LOVE ROMANCE

MILLS & BOON SUBSCRIPTIONS

HOW TO JOIN

1

Visit our website
millsandboon.
com.au/pages/
print-subscriptions

2

Select your favourite series
Choose how many books. We offer monthly as well as pre-paid payment options.

3

Sit back and relax
Your books will be delivered directly to your door.